Edward Robins

Benjamin Franklin

printer, statesman, philosopher and practical citizen, 1706-1790

Edward Robins

Benjamin Franklin
printer, statesman, philosopher and practical citizen, 1706-1790

ISBN/EAN: 9783337238605

Printed in Europe, USA, Canada, Australia, Japan

Cover: Foto ©Andreas Hilbeck / pixelio.de

More available books at **www.hansebooks.com**

Οὐ τείχη οὐδὲ ᾠδεῖα οὐδὲ στοαι οὐδὲ ὁ τῶν
ἀψύχων κόσμος αἱ πόλεις εἰσιν, ἀλλ' ἄνδρες
αὐτοῖς εἰδότες θαρρεῖν.

AILIOS ARISTEIDES (1. 9–189 A.D.).

NEITHER WALLS, THEATRES, PORCHES, NOR SENSE-
LESS EQUIPAGE, MAKE STATES, BUT MEN WHO ARE ABLE
TO RELY UPON THEMSELVES.

TRANS. BY ARTHUR WILLIAMS AUSTIN.

BENJAMIN FRANKLIN

FRANKLIN IN 1777.

AFTER THE PRINT REPRODUCED FROM THE DRAWING OF COCHIN.

Benjamin Franklin

PRINTER, STATESMAN
PHILOSOPHER AND PRACTICAL
CITIZEN

1706–1790

BY

EDWARD ROBINS
Author of "Echoes of the Playhouse," etc.

———

G. P. PUTNAM'S SONS
NEW YORK & LONDON
The Knickerbocker Press
1898

The Knickerbocker Press, New York

PREFACE

HE writer who puts forth a life of Benjamin Franklin may feel tempted to apologise for his seeming audacity. The literature devoted to the career of this great American is voluminous, and the works of Sparks, Bigelow, Parton, McMaster, and Morse form in themselves a noble tribute to his many-sided genius. Yet the years of this typical American were so full of action and variety, so rich in interesting detail, and so important in their general results, that the presentation of a record of them considered from a new point of view, is a congenial occupation which calls for no excuse. It would indeed be difficult to lay too much stress upon the story of one whose practical devotion to the common good should excite the liveliest admiration, particularly at a time when we hear loud complaints about '' political corruption,'' '' civic demoralisation,'' and the like. Franklin was the embodiment of public spirit. His curious combination of lofty patriotism and worldly sense offers a perennial object-lesson to the average statesman or average citizen of to-day, while his readiness to

serve his country, his province, or America at large, might be recalled with profit by those inconsistent voters who, although they refuse to share in the burden of government, cry out lustily for administrative reforms.

I need not, therefore, offer any plea of extenuation for thus adding to the formidable mass of Frankliniana, beyond acquitting myself of any vain desire to compete with, or to imitate, the biographies of the past. My purpose has been to give, as it were, a composite picture of the man, to show his character and activities, and to touch briefly upon the national conditions which brought the latter into play. That the narrative has been chosen as the forerunner of a series of biographical studies on American subjects, is an honour of which I am fully appreciative. I desire also to express my acknowledgments for the valuable counsel received during the preparation of my work at the rooms of the Historical Society of Pennsylvania, and my special indebtedness to Messrs. John W. Jordan and Thomas Allen Glenn.

PHILADELPHIA, February 1, 1898.

CONTENTS.

Contents

ILLUSTRATIONS

Illustrations

BENJAMIN FRANKLIN

CHAPTER I

THE "FATHER OF THE MAN"

1706–1727

OME of us have heard and laughed at the legend of the schoolboy who, being asked to prepare a composition with Benjamin Franklin as the subject, finally wrote the following exhaustive essay: " Benjamin Franklin was a wonderful man. He invented the Franklin stove." To this ingenuous student the " modern Socrates " was nothing more than a manufacturer of heaters, and the treatise bore amusing testimony to the danger of regarding greatness from only one point of view. Yet not a few better-informed persons, who are quick to smile at this piece of childish literature, have a fashion of falling into a similar error. They do not, to be sure, look upon the stove as the bright particular triumph of Franklin's existence, but they are

prone to see the man in one light, and in one light alone. It matters not whether that depicts him in the guise either of statesman, philosopher, printer, or mere utilitarian; the fact remains that to examine this heroic and yet essentially human figure without considering it as a whole is to lose all sense of its true proportion.

If, however, we take warning by the case of the boy and the stove, and give to Franklin the right perspective, we are impressed at once by the picturesque features of his career, and by the dramatic elements with which it was frequently tinged. Perhaps the terms, " picturesque " and " dramatic," seem startling to those who are apt to think of Franklin rather as a sage than as a man of action, yet the two adjectives are worthy of emphasis, and of more emphasis, indeed, than they usually receive. For, while this hero of an infant nation had nothing of the romantic in his spiritual or bodily equipment, his life was full of colour and stirring incident, with here and there a contrast almost theatrical in its nature. And of these contrasts none is more vivid than the one furnished by comparing the radically different surroundings which marked the earthly entrance and exit of Benjamin Franklin. He who was to chat with kings (albeit poor specimens of the craft) and enjoy the incense of admiration as it came from many parts of the civilised world, and who was to die in the odour of an international reputation, began to work out his existence amid the not over-inspiring atmosphere of a soap-boiling and tallow-chandlering shop.

Contrasts like this have since been reproduced in
American history, and are often used to point a
moral or adorn a biography, although there are instances of persons who, being thrown into the fierce
light of celebrity, become anxious to conceal or to
forget as much as possible the humbleness of their
early years. There was none of this affectation
about Franklin, and the story of his boyhood,
which he tells in so entertaining and dispassionate a
manner in the famous *Autobiography*,* is peculiarly
refreshing at a time when there is a tendency in
certain quarters of American life to attach vast importance to ancient lineage, and to linger a little too
long and lovingly over the pedigrees of useless but
aristocratic ancestors. Franklin was vain, after a
frank, pardonable fashion, but there was in his composition not an iota of false pride. He rather
revelled in the fact of his being what is now styled
a " self-made man." In the very first paragraph of
the *Autobiography* he explains as one of his reasons
for writing the memoir that " having emerged from
the poverty and obscurity in which I was born and
bred, to a state of affluence and some degree of
reputation in the world, and having gone so far
through life with a considerable share of felicity, the
conducing means I made use of, which with the
blessing of God so well succeeded, my posterity may

* The vicissitudes which befell the original copy of Franklin's
Autobiography form in themselves an interesting episode, and are
duly set forth by Mr. Bigelow in the first volume of the *Complete
Works of Benjamin Franklin.* G. P. Putnam's Sons. New York,
1887.

like to know, as they may find some of them suitable to their own situations, and therefore fit to be imitated."

And yet, even the self-successful author of the above lines owed something to his own ancestors, for they bequeathed to him that virility of character and clearness of mind which, like the presence of two guardian angels, influenced his whole life.

The Franklins from whom he took his name had kept a village smithy in Northamptonshire, England, for three centuries or more, and a rugged, honest, healthy lot of progenitors they seem to have been. Thomas Franklin, one of Benjamin's uncles, was a " chief mover of all public-spirited undertakings for the county or town of Northampton, and his own village," being endowed with much of the civic pride that was to shine, later on, in the nephew ; Benjamin, another uncle, who naturally took a laudable interest in his namesake, had a sprightly mind, with an ingenuity not unworthy of the greater Ben, and a talent, like the latter, for writing indifferent verse ; while Josiah Franklin, the father of our hero, was the happy possessor of a " mechanical genius," a " sound understanding, and solid judgment in prudential matters, both in private and publick affairs." In short, it is only necessary to read the earlier portion of the *Autobiography* to be convinced, apart from other and more scientific proofs, that the law of heredity at times wields a mighty force.

Josiah Franklin, this sturdy Englishman with the sound understanding, became a Nonconformist, and thereupon left the old country in 1682 to seek the

more congenial air of New England, bringing with
him his wife and three children, and settling down
peacefully in Boston.   Here he discarded his trade
of dyer to enter into the more remunerative business
of soap-boiling and tallow-chandlering; here the first
Mistress Franklin had four more children and then
died; and here, too, Josiah subsequently married
Abiah Folger, an estimable woman whose memory
would long since have sunk into oblivion had she
not become in January, 1706 (January 6th, old style;
January 17th, new style), the mother of Benjamin.
Were it not, likewise, for this natal incident, the
good lady's father, Peter Folger, would hardly be
known to fame in a hurried age, for the book in
which he is mentioned, Cotton Mather's dust-
covered *Magnalia Christi Americana*, is not to be
found in those distributing centres of fame, the cir-
culating libraries.   But, as it happens, we listen
with eagerness to what is written of old Peter in the
Autobiography, and when we are told that he was a
great advocate of liberty of conscience, the imagination is quick to trace a likeness between grandfather
and grandson.

The arrival of young Benjamin made Josiah
Franklin the proud father of fifteen children, and,
no doubt, incited the paterfamilias to renewed exer-
tion in the manufacture of soap and candles, for the
family had to be fed, and incomes, at the best, were
not very large in primitive Boston.   Those were
frugal days, when every penny counted, and the boy
was brought up in an economical yet kindly household.   Love of kindred and the husbanding of scant

resources must have been the prevailing virtues in this Puritan home, and both influences had their share in moulding the character of the youth who in after life was to be distinguished by an affectionate regard for his relations, and a financial wisdom which on occasion degenerated into parsimony. Furthermore, Josiah aimed to introduce at his table topics of conversation by no means confined to a discussion of what was spread thereon, and it was to this species of intellectual repast, wherein " little or no notice was ever taken of what related to the victuals," that Franklin owed his ability to maintain, when he so desired, an absurdly simple diet. He could, and sometimes did, enjoy the flesh-pots of Egypt in more senses than one, but there was always behind the grosser phase of his nature the power of abstinence, and even of self-sacrifice. If he knew how to gratify his tastes he also knew how to subdue them, and thereby displayed strength of mind, if not consistency.

Up to a certain point the youthful years of the boy offer nothing very striking or significant, excepting the fact that among the lads of his own age Ben was always the leader. Then, as later, he had the singular faculty of getting into prominence more through strength of character than from any apparent effort on his part. Then, as always, he might have been ambitious, but his fertility of resource kept pace with his ambition, and the one helped the other toward success. After two years of school life, during which he failed dismally in arithmetic, strange to say, but learned to write a good hand, he

was placed at the age of ten in his father's shop,
where the cutting of candle-wicks, filling of moulds,
and running of errands, gave the youngster plenty
of employment. This proved conclusively that
Josiah had abandoned his original intention of de-
voting his youngest son to the service of the Church
—a change of plan which may be considered as of
ultimate benefit both to Ben and to the Church.
And so everything indicated that he would develop
into a soap-boiler and chandler of the approved
type, succeed his father in due time, grow prosperous, marry, die, and be buried in oblivion.

Although in after life Franklin pointed out that
cleanliness was next to godliness, he had no great
affinity for soap so far as the making of it was concerned. He soon betrayed a vague restlessness, a
longing for greater things, which perhaps had its
most notable illustration in his passion for reading
with avidity all the books he could place his hands
on, theological pamphlets, the works of Bunyan,
Plutarch's *Lives* (the latter as delightful now as
then), Defoe's once famous *Essay on Projects*, and
Cotton Mather's *Essays to do Good.* Mather advocated the burning of witches, like other well-meaning
men of his ascetic cult, but for all that, he knew how
to write Christian sentiments, and many years later,
Franklin told the son of the pious Cotton that these
essays had exerted a great influence upon him. So
did the philanthropic *Essay on Projects*, wherein
Defoe was so far in advance of his time as to suggest
the establishment of colleges for girls—a heretical,
not to say dangerous opinion for an age when a

woman of education was looked upon with suspicion, as something weird and unpleasant.

In the meantime Ben had evinced such an open aversion to his greasy surroundings that Josiah, after much fatherly consideration of his youngest son's prospects, apprenticed him to James Franklin, an older son, who was tempting fate in Boston as a printer. There had been some idea of making the boy learn the cutler's trade, but fortunately for posterity his cousin Samuel, to whom he was to be bound, wanted a substantial fee for the transaction (he had the true Franklin attribute of looking out for the pennies), and so the scheme came to naught. Thus the Church and cutlery had each in turn lost a quick-witted apprentice, and the world, which may have been deprived thereby of some poor sermons and sharp knives, would come out the gainer in the end. And yet the boy was not enthusiastic over his new trade. It was, of course, far more congenial to him than the soap-making business, but there was deep down in his childish breast that peculiar longing known as " wishing to go to sea." He got over the malady soon enough, and probably often laughed at it in years to come, when he had to cross the Atlantic in uncomfortable, uncleanly sailing packets, the unworthy predecessors of our " ocean greyhounds."

It can be easily imagined that the apprentice's love of reading found stimulation in the printing-office of James Franklin. Books were easier to borrow, and friends to lend them proved more plentiful. And a little later, when the lad was fourteen or

fifteen, he tried dipping into poetry, or rather doggerel, but to no result other than that of finding how
utterly unsuited he was to this field of composition.
The versifying was soon abandoned, but the reading
continued, and there was a well-defined ambition to
excel in prose writing.   An odd volume of the
Spectator was triumphantly secured, the essays were
read and then rewritten from memory, after which
came the comparison with the original.   That these
comparisons were not always odious may be inferred
from Franklin's admission that he " sometimes had
the pleasure of fancying that in certain particulars
of small import," he " had been lucky enough to
improve the method of the language."   Even the
Spectator was not above improvement.

When he was about sixteen years old the young
printer read a book advocating a vegetable diet.
He accordingly followed out for a time the precepts
of the bucolic author, saved money thereby, and
devoted the surplus pence to the acquisition of new
volumes—a circumstance suggesting the rather cyni-
cal question as to whether or not many boys of the
present year, 1898, would half starve themselves in
order to buy literature with the coin thus accruing.
Then we find the vegetarian delving into Locke,
Shaftesbury, and Collins, getting very unsettled in
his religious views, and indulging much in arguments
on the subject with persons whom he always undertook to vanquish, according to the insidious Socratic
method of disputation.   They must have looked
upon him as a bit of a bore.   It was the case of the
youth filled to overflowing with the importance of

his newly acquired learning, and we all know that at
this stage he is generally a safe young gentleman to
avoid.

But these were boyish weaknesses.   The real business and struggles of Franklin's life were about to
begin in earnest, and he was first to try his hand at
what we now term "journalism."   The journalism
of the past and the journalism of the present have,
however, few points of likeness, and this is the more
readily to be understood when we contrast one of
the imposing newspapers of to-day, with its blanket-
sheet editions, its throng of editors, printers, and
miscellaneous employés, its enterprise and its prodigal expenditure of money in the search of news,
with the petty pamphlet which modestly appeared
in Boston during the latter part of September, 1690,
and thus established a claim to being the "first
American newspaper."   The number had four pages
(the last page was blank), with two columns on a
page, and the size of each page was seven by eleven
inches!   *Publick Occurrences Foreign and Domestic* was the title of the sheet; it was, according to
the prospectus, to be published once a month, or
oftener, "if any glut of occurrences happen," and
was to have an account of "such considerable things
as have arrived unto our Notice."   The aims of the
Occurrences were laudable, even ideal, and it is
interesting in this era of libel suits and "yellow
journalism" to mark that the publisher promised,
"toward the Curing, or at least the Charming of
the Spirit of Lying," that when "there appears
any material mistake in anything that is collected,

it shall be corrected in the next." This advocate
of truth — this really worthy forerunner of the
" Fourth Estate " in America — began its career
without advertisements, that feature so essential to
the life of the modern paper, and without editorials.
There are some cynics of to-day, by the way, who
think that advertisement plays entirely too prominent a part in the management of the average newspaper, and who could even dispense with editorials.

The career of *Publick Occurrences* was brief,
despite the praiseworthy intentions of its founder.
In four days the paper was suppressed, possibly because the editor (or printer, as he was then termed)
showed a tendency to discuss too freely the actions
of those in authority. He had yielded to the temptation of writing editorials, and that doomed him.
Fourteen years later John Campbell, the postmaster
of Boston, started the *News Letter*, a stupid venture
which finally attained the enormous circulation of
three hundred copies, and was wont to print European news anywhere from five to thirteen months
late. Then, in December, 1719, came the *Boston
Gazette*, founded by the new postmaster, William
Brocker, and in the printing of this James Franklin
was engaged. The postmaster lost his place; his
successor bought the *Gazette*, and James, who was
no longer employed to issue the sheet, began
(August, 1721) the publication of an enterprise of
his own, the *New England Courant*. It was a lively
affair, and what we should now characterise as essentially up to date; public matters were touched upon
with independence and humour. The *Gazette* by

comparison seemed duller than ever, as did the
News Letter. The three papers were soon engaged
in a triangular warfare that would have done justice
to the bickering spirit of three Arizona editors
obliged by an unkind fate to live in the same town.

The young but rapidly expanding Benjamin
jumped into this fray with nimbleness and ready
wit. Not content with assisting in printing the
paper, and then carrying it around the town to
subscribers, he must needs try his hand at contributing to it. James Franklin, he tells us, "had
some ingenious men among his friends, who amused
themselves by writing little pieces for this paper,
which gained it credit and made it more in demand,
and these gentlemen often visited us. Hearing
their conversations and their accounts of the approbation their papers were received with, I was excited
to try my hand among them; but, being still a boy,
and suspecting that my brother would object to
printing anything of mine in his paper if he knew it
to be mine, I contrived to disguise my hand, and,
writing an anonymous paper, I put it in at night,
under the door of the printing-house. It was found
in the morning, and communicated to his writing
friends when they called in as usual. They read it,
commented on it in my hearing, and I had the exquisite pleasure of finding it met with their approbation, and that, in their different guesses at the
author, none were named but men of some character among us for learning and ingenuity."

A familiar story, to be sure, but like some pretty
fairy-tale it bears repetition. And how one can

read between the lines the shrewdness which always
ran through Franklin's character, like a wee bit of
the fox lurking in the composition of some majestic
lion! Ben suspected, no doubt, that too much
ability on his part would bring down upon him the
jealousy of a less brilliant brother, and so he chose
to introduce his literary wares with secrecy. Those
wares were, it is believed, the " Do Good Papers,"
a series of articles more or less after the Addisonian
manner. One of them, representing a dream, was a
fling at that young scholastic institution, Harvard
College. The graduates of the college, typified in
the dream as the Temple of Learning, did not all
fare very well according to the imprudent young
critic, for many of them " lived as poor as church-
mice, being unable to dig, and ashamed to beg, and
to live by their wits it was impossible." And yet,
in time, Harvard would reward the writer with a
degree.

The office of the *Courant* must have witnessed
many an interesting incident, many an exciting debate, but none of them more interesting or more
exciting, perhaps, than those which marked the small-
pox controversy. This dread disease had made
itself felt in Boston after the wholesale manner in
which it was accustomed to stalk about, grim and re-
morseless, during the early portion of the eighteenth
century. The Mathers, more liberal in the art of
medicine than in the treatment of witches, strongly
advocated the new experiment of inoculation; the
Courant as resolutely opposed the innovation, and
as a consequence there was hard feeling, and a war

of very bad words. Increase Mather did what later readers have done when the opinions of their papers were not to their liking. He stopped his subscription to the *Courant*, abused James Franklin in terms of the choicest vituperation, lamented the degeneracy of New England, and pointedly hinted at the expediency of suppressing the articles of the offender. In the meantime, the controversy (which waxed so high that some miscreant threw a firegrenade into the Mather house) had the effect of increasing the circulation of the paper, and an observant reader may be pardoned for suspecting that the publisher had, through all the din and unpleasantness of battle, a keen idea of the value of advertising.

But greater troubles than inoculation disagreements were in store for the infant journal, and through these Benjamin was to make his *début* as a publisher and editor. The *Courant* had criticised with asperity the ways and measures of the Boston authorities, who, biding their hour, finally had James Franklin brought before them for printing a supposed news paragraph poking fun at their slowness of action. The Council interrogated the printer. He declined to name the writer of the paragraph. Ben also sturdily refused an answer to the same question—an independence of spirit for which he was excused on the ground, presumably, that an apprentice should not be called upon to testify against the interests of his master. James, less fortunate than his brother, spent a month in prison. During that time Ben directed the fortunes of the rapidly

growing if somewhat adventurous *Courant*. Six
months later James printed a bitter article reflecting
so savagely upon the governing powers that he was
forbidden thereafter to publish the *Courant* or any
other paper, unless under the supervision of the
Secretary of the province.

" There was a consultation held in our printing-house among his
friends [says Franklin, in writing of his brother's predicament], what
he should do in this case. Some proposed to evade the order by
changing the name of the paper ; but my brother, seeing inconveniences in that, it was finally concluded on as a better way, to let it be
printed for the future under the name of Benjamin Franklin ; and to
avoid the censure of the Assembly, that might fall on him as still
printing it by his apprentice, the contrivance was that my old indent-
ure should be returned to me, with a full discharge on the back of it,
to be shown on occasion, but to secure to him the benefit of my service, I was to sign new indentures for the remainder of the term,
which were to be kept private."

As Franklin adds, a " very flimsy scheme it was,"
but it was put into effect, and Benjamin became the
ostensible printer of the *Courant*. The elder brother
was in reality the controlling spirit, but the ex-
apprentice wrote for the paper, and often turned the
dart of his wit upon the austerity and what he chose
to consider the hypocrisy of certain professors of the
accepted religion. In short, the *Courant* seems to
have been anything but a conservative sheet, and its
articles sometimes amused, and sometimes scandal-
ised the Puritans who read it, ignorant as many of
them were that an important contributor to that fun
and scandal was the sprightly Ben himself. The
wonder of it is that the *Courant* was allowed to exist
at all, for the press was in its infancy, and there were

no theories as to liberty of public opinion, so far as the aforesaid liberty might concern a printer. In the eyes of the Boston magistrates a paper was something to be tolerated or suppressed according to their own august will.

As it happened, the *Courant* was soon to lose the services of its ostensible publisher. The two brothers had not been on the best of terms of late; Ben was saucy and provoking and puffed up, no doubt, with a boyish sense of his own talents and importance, while James, on his side, had become jealous of the youngster. To the impertinences of the lad the elder responded with blows, and it may be imagined that this state of affairs was not to last very long. As a result of some fresh altercation Ben made up his mind to leave the printing-office, shrewdly surmising that, his old indentures having been cancelled, and his brother being afraid to produce the new ones (for fear of exposing his little conspiracy against the Council), it would be very easy to depart unmolested by the law, which bound an apprentice to fill out his term. Not a strictly honourable episode in Franklin's history, and he afterward was quick to admit that he took an unfair advantage of his brother—" one of the first *errata* of my life," he terms it. But that point of honour had no consideration at the moment, so the inevitable break came. Nor was James more magnanimous, for he asked the other printers of Boston to refuse employment to his brother.

This fraternal move decided the apprentice to shake the dust of the Hub from his feet, and none

the less was he impelled thereto upon reflecting that
he had become, by his *Courant* diatribes, a *persona
non grata* to not a few of his fellow-townsmen.
There were many things in his native place which
he would have reformed, and he had already learned
that to be a reformer is not, necessarily, to be popular. Furthermore, Josiah Franklin sympathised with
James, and no encouragement under the paternal
roof-tree was rebellious Ben to expect. Accordingly, with the aid of John Collins, a " bookish lad "
with whom he used to discuss and settle to his own
satisfaction the affairs of the universe, he ran off,
or rather sailed off, to New York in a sloop commanded by a friendly captain. He soon found
himself in that city (October, 1723), at the age of
seventeen, without recommendation to any of its
inhabitants, and with no more money in his pocket
than the little he had raised by the sale of his
precious books. This was the youthful Benjamin
Franklin, as revealed to us in the *Autobiography*,
and there is no reason to doubt the truth of the
picture—a rugged, sturdy fellow, full of confidence
in himself, canny, clear of head, with undefined
ambitions, and if not always as disinterested as one
might wish, at least, full of that indomitable spirit
which was to waft him, slowly but steadily, toward
a noble success.

It has been said that a printer who understands
his trade need never starve. Probably, Ben was impressed with the force of this axiom, for upon arriving in New York he at once sought out William
Bradford, the pioneer typesetter of Pennsylvania,

2

now a practical exile from the Quaker province. The story of the young man's experience during this journey is familiar enough. How he was advised by Bradford to go to Philadelphia (where lived his son, Andrew Bradford), how he took the veteran's advice, crossed over to Amboy by boat, after several exciting adventures, including his rescue of a drunken Dutchman from drowning, and how he trudged on foot through New Jersey to quiet Burlington—these bits of itinerary have been described again and again, as, no doubt, they will be redescribed for many a year to come. A good story is always in order, and thus even the jaded historian finds something fresh and entertaining in the early wandering of the man whose son was, in after years, to become Governor of the very State through which the father wended his humble, uncomfortable way. Contrasts of this kind never lose their interest.

At Burlington Franklin lodged with an old woman of limited purse, but unlimited heart; there he managed to board a boat destined for Philadelphia, and reached his future home on a Sunday morning. It was a curious entry into Quaker life, when viewed in the light of subsequent events, and the hero of it never ceased to revel, pardonably enough, in the memory of it.

" I was in my working dress, my best clothes being to come round by sea. I was dirty from my journey; my pockets were stuffed out with shirts and stockings, and I knew no soul, nor where to look for lodging. I was fatigued with travelling, rowing, and want of rest; I was very hungry; and my whole stock of cash consisted of a Dutch dollar, and about a shilling in copper. The latter I gave the people of the boat for my passage."

He bought three puffy rolls at a baker's—Philadelphia bakers still sell puffy rolls—and putting a roll
under each arm, and eating the third, walked up
Market Street, passing a house where stood young
Miss Read, his future wife, who was much struck
with the ridiculous appearance of the boy.   That is
the incident as Franklin has recorded it, and while
skeptical persons have ventured to hint that the
philosopher chose to paint the scene in colours a trifle
too vivid for actual fact, there is no necessity to
agree with them.   Perhaps, if it were less familiar,
less hackneyed, no one would dream of smiling.

The wanderer spent his first night in Philadelphia
at a tavern on Water Street, and repaired the next
morning to the printing-office of Andrew Bradford.
There, to his surprise, he found Andrew's father,
who had travelled on from New York on horseback,
a mode of conveyance which the Bostonians had not
been able to afford.   There was no opening for the
boy with Bradford ; possibly Keimer, another printer
lately established in town, might aid him.   So to
Keimer Benjamin went, accompanied by old Bradford.   After a conversation in which Keimer made
the apprentice show his proficiency as a typesetter,
and in which he incidentally exposed his aims and
business secrets to Bradford (whom he did not
recognise), it was agreed that the newcomer should
be given work in a short time.   Then Bradford departed, and Keimer was disagreeably surprised upon
learning that he had been unbosoming himself to
the father of his rival.   As for Franklin, he had
already discovered that Bradford was a " crafty old

sophister," who had willingly drawn out the confiding Keimer, and that the latter was a " mere
novice." Wise Ben! You understood human nature even then.

Keimer has been characterised by Franklin as a
good deal of a knave, yet withal something of a
scholar, and very ignorant of the world. He was an
indifferent versifier, who " set up " his own doggerel
as it came into his head, and thus saved anyone else
the affliction of a compulsory perusal of his poems.
With him the stranger soon got employment, lodging, however, with Andrew Bradford, and finally
moving from the latter's home to the house of Mr.
Read, father of the before-mentioned young lady,
who was later to become Mrs. Franklin. By this
time his chest of clothes had arrived from Boston,
and the youth, who was not impervious in those
salad days or a little later to the charms of femininity, flattered himself that he made a more becoming
appearance in the eyes of Miss Read than he had
done when he startled her with his array of puffy
rolls. Thus life ran on placidly for several months,
as Franklin laboured for the poetic Keimer, spent
pleasant evenings with young Quakers of literary
tastes, and saved his money. He tried to forget
Boston, and the old times there, but, likely enough,
did not altogether succeed. Still he took comfort
in the thought that no one in New England, barring
his friend, the argumentative Collins, knew whither
he had gone. Yet one of his family, a brother-in-
law, the master of a sloop trading between Boston
and the Delaware, heard of the runaway, wrote to

him from New Castle, spoke of the grief of Ben's family over his departure, and begged him to return. To all of which Master Franklin wrote a polite reply, declined to play the Prodigal Son, and convinced the sailor, we are told, that he was not so much in the wrong as the latter had believed.

This letter, strangely enough, brought the printer to the admiring attention of Sir William Keith, then Governor of the province of Pennsylvania. It was an attention which Franklin would live to wish that he had never excited. The beginning of the affair seemed, however, full of promise. Keith was in New Castle when the reply to the brother-in-law arrived, saw it, and was greatly impressed that it should have been written by so young a fellow. When he returned to Philadelphia the Governor determined to seek out the truant who could so ably defend himself, and one day when Keimer and his apprentice were hard at work the two were startled to see his Excellency and Colonel French, of New Castle, standing in front of the house. Keimer, thinking the visit intended for him, hurried downstairs, only to find that it was the employé, not the master, whom the distinguished gentlemen wanted. Keith overwhelmed Franklin with cheap professions of friendliness, hurried him off with the Colonel to a neighbouring inn, and there, over a few glasses of Madeira, the Governor actually proposed that his *protégé* of an hour should set up in business for himself, to which end he promised to exert all his influence. Keith would not take *no* for an answer; he would write a letter to Franklin's father, asking

Josiah's assistance, and everything should work to a charm. Finally, after dining several times with the Governor, and being naturally much tickled with the fuss made over him, Ben took a voyage to Boston in the spring of 1724,—a short voyage, lasting a fortnight.

Josiah was glad to see his boy, but, like the sensible man he was, he thought that Ben was entirely too young to start a printing plant of his own. What sort of a man was Keith, to propose so foolish an undertaking? That was the question he very naturally asked, and if anyone had told him that the Governor was an emotional, insincere man, loud in promises, but not so loud in their fulfilment, no injustice would have been done. The upshot of the matter was that the father negatived the scheme, and all that the son obtained was the paternal blessings, a few small gifts, and a deal of good advice, including a caution to steer clear, in the printing business, of lampoons and libels.

Thus thwarted, Ben determined to return to Philadelphia, which he accordingly did, but not before he visited Brother James. Brother James was in a bad humour, Brother Ben behaved with gross want of tact, and the meeting proved a failure. On his journey back the sloop which was carrying the youngster touched at Newport. This gave him an opportunity to visit another brother, John, who had married and settled there, and to receive from him, unluckily enough, an order to collect in Pennsylvania a sum of thirty-five pounds currency due a Mr. Vernon, one of John's friends. From Newport

Ben sailed for New York. He was disposed to be a trifle wild on board the sloop, got in return a good moral lecture from a Quaker passenger, and finally reached the island of Manhattan, to find awaiting him his companion of former days, John Collins, who had left Boston intending to make Philadelphia his home. While lingering for Franklin in New York, Collins spent his time in riotous living, so that the remainder of his journey had to be paid for by his friend. This circumstance finally tempted Ben, before reaching Philadelphia, to appropriate for their necessities some of the money now collected for the confiding Vernon—" one of the first great *errata* of my life." It was an *erratum* that cost him many a bad quarter of an hour, and shows us that the young man had not yet acquired the moral firmness for which he was afterward distinguished. In time, Vernon was repaid, but Franklin never quite forgave himself for the weakness.

Had it not been for the wildness of Collins, who suddenly degenerated from a sober, clever Puritan into a drunken Bohemian, the short stay in New York would have been a very agreeable one for Franklin, if for no other reason than that he again attracted the attention of a governor. This one was Governor Burnet (son of the famous Bishop), and the two discussed books with avidity. The other traveller was not in a state to visit his Excellency, and it was fortunate that the young fellow soon dropped out of Franklin's life forever. On reaching Philadelphia he continued to be a drag upon his companion, borrowing from the Vernon money, and getting day by day more sottish and repellent. Finally Franklin rebelled, and the intimacy ended. Collins soon went away to the Barbadoes to become a tutor (poor pupils!), and nothing more was heard of him or the money he owed.

Sir William Keith had, in the interval, welcomed Franklin back with open arms, and now he himself proposed to furnish the money to set the printer up in business. Everything was nicely arranged ; Franklin, in the course of several months, should sail for England, there to choose the stock required to fit out the proposed printing-house. In the meanwhile, he was to work with Keimer, being careful, however, to say nothing of Sir William's project. Accordingly, the unsuspecting compositor continued to labour with the unsuspecting master, the two of them arguing abstruse points à la Socrates, discussing the feasibility of forming a new religious sect, trying a vegetarian diet, and indiscriminately indulging in the most congenial " isms " and peculiarities. Ben, although so practical in many ways, might have become the most hopeless of theorists, not to say a charlatan, had not the hard knocks of the world rubbed off the crotchets of his nature and dispelled his curious castles in the air. In addition to these occupations, he made love to Miss Read (whom it was understood he should marry on his return from London), and took many a delightful stroll along the banks of the Schuylkill with four companions of congenial taste. Among them was James Ralph, a poet in embryo, who was to be honoured by the great Mr. Pope with a savage sling in the *Dunciad*.

During all this time, Keith kept up his show of
cordiality toward Franklin, talked enthusiastically
about the letters of introduction and credit that he
intended to give him, and never for one moment
hinted that there would or could be the slightest
hitch in the arrangements.   When the ship for
which he waited was about to sail, the *protégé*
sought out his benefactor for the promised documents.   The Governor's Secretary explained that Sir
William was just then very busy, but would arrive at
New Castle before the vessel touched there upon her
way down the Delaware.   This seemed plausible
enough, and Franklin, accompanied by Ralph, who
had vague yearnings for London poetic triumphs,
confidingly boarded the packet.   Upon reaching
New Castle, he found that the Governor was there,
but again the Secretary made excuses.   His master
was " engaged in business of the utmost importance," but would send the letters to the ship, hoped
his friend would have a good voyage, make a speedy
return, and expressed the customary polite *et
cæteras*.   All this was very comforting, but the
letters were never delivered.   The Governor, who
loved to be popular with everybody, had the crime
of insincerity, which so often accompanies such a
disposition.   While he had taken pains to win the
affections and confidence of the printer, he went no
further.   His promises were broken; he had played
the poltroon; with deceit in his heart and lies upon
his lips he had sent his victim across the ocean on
an errand worse than fruitless.

There were six or seven letters in the ship's mail-

bag which Franklin thought might be the desired
ones. One of them was directed to Basket, the
King's Printer, and another to a stationer. It was
Christmas eve (1724), when Franklin reached London, and he repaired at once to the stationer, to
whom he presented what he supposed to be a note
from Sir William Keith. " I don't know such a
person," said the tradesman ; but, opening the letter,
he exclaimed : " Oh! this is from Riddlesden.* I
have lately found him to be a complete rascal, and
I will have nothing to do with him, nor receive any
letters from him." With that, Mr. Stationer turns
on his heel, and Franklin's castle in the air—a castle
made up of an elegant press, fine type, and what not
—falls to the ground. None of the letters were intended for him. A joyous Christmas eve for the
young colonist! " What shall we think," wrote
the victim many years later, when the bitterness of
the awakening was still fresh in his memory, " of a
governor's playing such pitiful tricks, and imposing
so grossly on a poor, ignorant boy! It was a habit
he had acquired. He wished to please everybody ;
and, having little to give, he gave expectations."

To work!—that was the only thing to be done;
the stranger's purse was scant, and the ambitious
Ralph was actually penniless. So the two secured
lodgings in Little Britain for the princely rate of
three shillings and sixpence a week, and while the
poet first tried to go on the stage and then to start

* Riddlesden was a Philadelphia attorney who is characterised in
the *Autobiography* as " a very knave." He was a friend of Keith's,
a fact which did not prejudice Franklin in his favour.

a paper " like the *Spectator*," the more practical
Benjamin obtained a place in Palmer's printing-
house. In the evenings, the two companions went
to the play, where they doubtless admired the dashing impersonations of Wilkes, the eccentricities of
Cibber, and the charms of the sprightly Oldfield.
From this enjoyment Franklin acquired his pronounced taste for the drama. Later in his varied
career, the humble theatre-goer would go to the
play in more pomp than that vouchsafed by a seat
among the apprentices, and would be honoured by
the acquaintance of Garrick, now, in this winter of
1725, an unknown boy of nine.

As for Ralph, he proceeded to forget the wife and
child he had left in America. Ben, hardly more
constant, gradually grew cold in his affection for the
absent Deborah Read, to whom, let it be said in
shame, he wrote one letter telling her he was " not
likely soon to return." Another of " the great
errata " of his life, albeit one for which he subsequently sought to atone. In fine, his first London
visit must have awakened in him a curious jumble
of good and bad instincts—industry, frugality, and
a desire for mental improvement on the one hand,
and occasional exhibitions of meanness, forgetfulness of his *fiancée*, and one disagreeable piece of
dishonourable conduct on the other hand. The dishonourable conduct need not be dwelt upon here;
everyone who reads the *Autobiography*, where the
author frankly puts it down as another *erratum*, re-
members it, and the vision it furnishes is not alluring. Suffice it to say, that as it was a species of

unfaithfulness toward Ralph (who did not, however, deserve any sympathy in the matter), the friendship between the two came to an abrupt end.

At Palmer's, Franklin was employed in setting type for the second edition of Wollaston's *Religion of Nature*, and, not agreeing with some of the author's conclusions, he wrote and printed a controversial pamphlet on the subject, styling it, ponderously, *A Dissertation on Liberty and Necessity, Pleasure and Pain*. An audacious proceeding, to be sure, but one that brought the lucky pamphleteer to the attention of several learned men and thus helped to make his stay in London the more congenial. Then he went to work at Watts's, a printing-house more important than Palmer's, and was much impressed with the amount of beer drunk by his companions. He persuaded many of the latter to give up that beverage, substituting therefor a porringer of hot-water gruel, seasoned with pepper, bread and butter—a pretty temperance lesson, were it not that he stood credit for the beer of less provident printers and closely watched the pay-table on Saturday nights, to collect the money due him. A strange mixture of philanthropy and—what shall we call it ?—usury. Possibly, he charged no commission for this service to the thirsty, although, even then, the idea of his preaching against beer and, at the same time, helping men to get it, is paradoxical to the verge of absurdity. That Franklin was careful about his pennies during this season is, at least, fully apparent, and it need hardly be added that he was not always in a position to be otherwise, partic-

ularly as he had lent twenty-seven pounds, in all, to
Ralph before his break with the latter.   When he
changed his lodgings from Little Britain to Duke
Street, he bargained with his new hostess, a widow
of genteel bearing, to take him for the same money,
three shillings and sixpence a week.   This she
agreed to do, but when the new boarder heard that
he could get cheaper rates elsewhere, he thought of
changing his quarters, agreeable as they were.   The
landlady capitulated at once.

> " She was lame in her knees with the gout, and, therefore, seldom
> stirred out of her room, so sometimes wanted company ; and hers
> was so highly amusing to me, that I was sure to spend an evening
> with her whenever she desired it.   Our supper was only half an
> anchovy each, on a very little strip of bread and butter, and half a
> pint of ale between us ; but the entertainment was in her conversa-
> tion.   My always keeping good hours, and giving little trouble in the
> family, made her unwilling to part with me."

If we read further into the first London visit of
the young American, we find that an aquatic feat of
which he was the hero came near changing, in all
probability, the whole tenor of his life.   He swam
from near Chelsea to Black Friars, a stretch of four
miles, performing on the way many wondrous evo-
lutions, upon and under the water, much to the
delight of several admiring friends.   One of these
grew so attached to the swimmer, partly as a result of this prowess, that he proposed to travel
all over Europe with Franklin, working at the
printer's trade along the route.   Had Ben acted
upon this suggestion, as he was tempted to do,
he might have ended, Fate only knows where—

perhaps as Grand Vizier for an Eastern potentate,
or anything else, ranging from an autocrat to a ped-
dler. It was a crucial period with the youth, a
period of transition, and his future seemed as inscrutable as a Chinese puzzle. However, he did not
foot it through the Continent, owing to the advice
of Mr. Denham, a Philadelphia merchant then in
London (the two had come over in the same ship),
who offered him a clerical position in a store which
he was to open upon his return home. Franklin
decided to accept the situation and go back to his
good friends the Quakers. He regretted a little
later that he could not stay in England to open a
swimming school—think of him as proprietor of a
natatorium!—and finally set sail with honest Mr.
Denham in the July of 1726. As it was not until
near the middle of October that the vessel reached
Philadelphia, the trip was a wearisome one, and
Franklin wisely helped to pass the time by keeping
a diary and drawing up a plan for the guidance of
his future conduct. For the matter of that, the
hours could never hang heavily upon him; he was
a man of infinite resources and possessed in a high
degree the art of interesting himself in many things
and under all circumstances. Unlike a certain unfortunate type of nineteenth-century humanity, he
was never " bored." His mind was an active,
healthy one, ever observing, ever working, and he
could see more in a day than do many persons in
the course of years. As a result he enjoyed nearly
every moment of his life; even sorrow could not
deprive him for any great length of time of his zest

for existence.   Thus it is that we find him extract-
ing pleasure from a trip which to the globe-trotting
men and women of to-day would appear unutterably
dreary, and securing plenty of material for thought
and record.

It may be imagined that when Franklin got back
to Philadelphia, he kept his eyes open, as usual, nor
did he attempt to close them when he passed on the
street the shamefaced Keith, now no longer governor.   Perhaps he opened them even wider than ever
upon learning that, as the result of his own defection,
Deborah Read had married a worthless potter, from
whom she soon separated for the very good reason
that he was accused of bigamy.   Having seen these
things and perceived that his friend Keimer was apparently on the high road to prosperity, Ben set
himself hard to work in the store which Mr. Denham now opened in Water Street.   To become a
thrifty merchant was the palpable destiny of the
clerk.   But there were to be many surprises in his
career, many changes of plan, and one of them now
occurred.   Denham and Franklin were both taken
ill, the former dying and the latter slowly recover-
ing, somewhat to his own disappointment, if we are
to believe him.   " I suffered a good deal [he had
pleurisy], gave up the point in my own mind, and
was rather disappointed when I found myself re-
covering, regretting, in some degree, that I might
now, some time or other, have all that disagreeable
work to do over again."   One fact stared coldly
into his bright, serene face.   The taking away of
Denham left his assistant, like *Othello*, with occupa-

tion gone, and with all those prospects of future
wealth vanished into air.   What should he do?
There was hardly time to ask the question, for
Keimer came forward with a proposition that the
management of his new printing-shop should be
taken by his former employé.   Call it a piece of rare
luck, if you will, but reflect that the offer was made
to one who by his business sense and his skill as a
printer well deserved it.

Here we have Franklin at twenty-one.   He has
travelled not a little, thought much, read much,
written much, worked incessantly, sinned too, and
so stands forth a puzzling figure.   Mixed in with
shining gold is a vein of baser metal.   Is the gold
to triumph?   There is hope that it may, for deep
in the printer's soul are energy of character and
strength of purpose.   These are virtues which he
has in common with so many natives of distant New
England, and they must have an important influence
upon him.   The Puritan spirit of self-reliance must
make itself felt in him, just as in years to come it
will put so deep an impress upon the patriotism of
the Revolution.

CHAPTER II

AN EDITOR OF THE OLD SCHOOL

1728-1740

THOSE cordial relations which some times exist between master and man, even outside of Utopia, had no place in the connection now established between the half-knavish Keimer and the observant Franklin. Keimer wished to have his crude printers whipped into shape, as it were, by the new foreman, whom he then intended to dismiss, and the latter was shrewd enough to fathom the whole plot. The days wore on, Franklin working philosophically and efficiently, and the little drama began to develop just as was expected. Keimer hinted that a reduction of Franklin's wages would be in order, " grew by degrees less civil, put on more of the master, frequently found fault, was captious, and seemed ready for an outbreaking." The crisis came soon enough.

There was a great noise in the street one day, and Franklin put his head out of a window of the printing-office to find out the cause of the outcry, when,

presto! Keimer called up to him, in angry tones, to
" mind his business." This may have been entertaining for the listening neighbours, but it proved
exasperating to the rebuked printer, particularly as
Keimer came up into the room, and continued the
quarrel.

> " High words passed on both sides ; he gave me the quarter's
> warning we had stipulated, expressing a wish that he had not been
> obliged to so long a warning. I told him his wish was unnecessary,
> for I would leave him that instant ; and so, taking my hat, walked
> out of doors, desiring Meredith, whom I saw below, to take care of
> some things I left, and bring them to my lodgings."

It was a row with a capital R, and we can picture
the stupid apprentices looking on open-mouthed
while Ben bounced out of the place with disgust on
his face and anger in his usually placid heart. Our
sympathies irresistibly go with him. Yet this was
the man who would come to have such a fine control
over his temper that he could stand unmoved while
an English enemy loaded him with insults.

The Meredith spoken of was one of Keimer's
journeymen, between whom and his foreman a considerable intimacy existed. He was a nice, honest
fellow, but trifled too much with the flowing bowl.
On the evening succeeding the " outbreaking " he
went to see his friend at the latter's lodgings, and
it was well he did. By this time the indignant
Franklin had made up his mind to return to Boston, where, for aught we know, he might have
degenerated into a commonplace soap-boiler, and
so, practically, buried himself. Meredith suggested
that when the spring (of 1728) came, and his own

time with Keimer had expired, he would form a
partnership with Franklin, into which the New
Englander was to bring the skill, and Meredith's
father the money needed for presses and types.
The offer was accepted ; the elder Meredith approved of the scheme, hoping above all things
that his son would be kept too busy to think of his
cups.   It was agreed that Franklin should try to
continue in other employment until the release of
his partner.   That employment, strange to tell, was
obtained with Keimer, who was anxious to have the
assistance of his former manager in the printing of
an issue of paper money for the province of New
Jersey.   Forthwith, Franklin journeyed to Burlington, where he contrived a copper-plate press for the
execution of the bills.   He was made much of by
some of the townspeople, who liked his conversation, and he was not grieved, possibly, because
Keimer met with a less cordial reception.   " In
truth," he writes complacently, " he was an odd
fish, ignorant of common life, fond of rudely opposing received opinions, slovenly to extreme dirtiness,
enthusiastic in some points of religion, and a little
knavish withal."   The Keimer type is not yet extinguished.

When the spring arrived, the firm of Franklin and
Meredith began life, not in an elegantly appointed
structure such as we would look for to-day, but in a
little house on Market Street, in which, to lessen
the rental of twenty-four pounds a year, a glazier
named Thomas Godfrey and his family were given
room.   It was a risky experiment, this starting of a

printing-house when there were two rivals in the field (Keimer and Bradford). The wise merchants who used to assemble at the " Every Night Club " predicted its failure. All of them did, at least, excepting a canny Scotchman who spoke up one evening in defence of the new firm. " For the industry of that Franklin," said he, " is superior to anything I ever saw of the kind; I see him still at work when I go home from club, and he is at work again before his neighbours are out of bed."

Soon there was business for the firm, despite the croaking. Meredith worked in a miserable, half-sober way (the *Autobiography* deals neither so gently or charitably as we could wish with his imperfections), and Franklin naturally proved the better partner. A hard life he must have led, but he always loved work, and by way of recreation, he could look forward to those intellectual Friday evenings devoted to the " Junto." This Junto was the most cherished offspring of Ben's mental activity, and may be considered as the forerunner of the American Philosophical Society. It was a debating club wherein morals, politics, and natural philosophy were discussed with the earnestness and dignity that one might have expected from the Senators of ancient Rome. To join this imposing club the would-be member had to answer, with his hand upon his breast, the following formidable questions:

" Have you any particular disrespect to any present member? *Answer :* I have not.

" Do you sincerely declare that you love mankind in general, of what profession or religion soever? *Answer :* I do.

" Do you think any person ought to be harmed in his body, name, or goods, for mere speculative opinions, or his external way of worship? *Answer:* No.

" Do you love truth for truth's sake, and will you endeavour impartially to find and receive it yourself, and communicate it to others ? *Answer:* Yes."

The man who could answer such questions in such a way, and do it without an atom of perjury, must have been a paragon of liberal-mindedness.   Yet there was a quiet toleration among Philadelphians that made the carrying out of this gentle creed less impossible than it might at first seem.   It was an indirect illustration of the Quaker spirit of non-resistance.   Franklin, while neither a Friend nor a follower of the non-combative theory, sympathised with the Quaker's policy, " to live and let live." He had no love for inquisitorial delving into the spiritual beliefs of his neighbours.   His own belief, be it noted, has now changed from a species of atheism to a reverence for a Supreme Being.   He was a Deist with a liturgy of his own making.

At this time, although Franklin was amusing himself with the abstract discussions of the Junto, he was also revolving in his mind a journalistic scheme. Pennsylvania had but one newspaper, a stupid sheet published in Philadelphia by the rival Bradford. Why should not the firm of Franklin and Meredith start one of their own ?   The idea was a good one, and Ben was foolish enough to mention it to a friend, who in turn immediately spoke of it to Keimer.   The latter thought so well of the plan that he appropriated it, and soon issued (December,

1728) the first number of the pompously titled *Universal Instructor in all Arts and Sciences and Pennsylvania Gazette*. Exacting critics who occasionally complain that the modern newspaper has too much current comment and too little solid information, might find the type of literature they desire in the *Instructor*, as published during Keimer's *régime*, for this wide-awake sheet contained, as a sort of alphabetical series, instalments of a standard " Dictionary of the Arts and Sciences." The learning was doled out in mechanical fashion, but there it was, nevertheless.

Franklin waxed wroth on the appearance of the *Instructor*, but did not lose his levelness of head. How was he to conduct a warfare against the paper ? By bolstering up its wearisome rival, Bradford's *Mercury*. So for this purpose he wrote for the latter a series of sprightly essays—" The Busybody," they were dubbed—wherein a few faults and vanities of the time were touched upon in a vein not unworthy of Addison. What more pleasantly suggestive of the satiric humour of the *Spectator* than the announcement of the first essay, wherein the " Busybody " predicts that he may displease a great number of the readers, " who will not very well like to pay ten shillings a year for being told of their faults." . . . But, he goes on to say, " as most people delight in censure when they themselves are not the object of it, if any are offended at my publicly exposing their private vices, I promise they shall have the satisfaction, in a very little time, of seeing their good friends and neighbours in the same circumstances."

The " Busybody " made what would now be graphically styled a sensation. It contributed to the local reputation of the writer and involved him in a controversy with Keimer. Keimer lost his temper; the rival remained tranquil. Next Franklin handed over the writing of the " Busybody " to a friend, and plunged into the somewhat different field of work provided by the money question, then playing an important part in Pennsylvania. Coin was scarce in the province, there was among the poorer classes a cry for a new issue of paper currency, and yet the English Government was resolved to nega- tive any acts which might be passed by the Pennsyl- vania Assembly to supply the want. Just when the controversy was at its height (the proposed issue being opposed as fiercely in some quarters as it was favoured in others), Franklin jumped into the breach by writing a pamphlet entitled *A Modest Enquiry into the Nature and Necessity of a Paper Currency.* It was a strenuous plea for paper; it contained argu- ments which read to-day like wild financial heresies; it carried victory into the camp of the inflationists. Despite the warnings of the English Lords of Trade, thirty thousand pounds worth of new paper money was issued. The writer of the *Modest Enquiry* got the contract for printing it! To the victor belonged the spoils. Possibly in this instance the victor made a better showing as a printer than as a political economist.

Now began Franklin's editorial career. Keimer was financially ruined, as his former employé had foreseen, by his poorness of character and want of business capacity. He was very glad to sell his *Instructor*, with its ninety subscribers, to the hated house of Franklin and Meredith. This he did in the autumn of 1729. Then he was compelled to go off to Barbadoes, after having had the misfortune, as he expressed it, " to be three times ruined as a master printer, to be nine times in prison " (once was six years together), " and often reduced to the most wretched circumstances," besides being " hunted as a partridge upon the mountains." He was, however, a partridge who had plucked himself. No sooner did he dispose of the paper than Franklin dropped its awkward title, using the simple name of *Pennsylvania Gazette*, and dropping, too, the ridiculous extracts from the dictionary on arts and sciences. He made many welcome changes in the literary and typographical features.* He issued, with his initial number, a lengthy announcement or prospectus, in which, among other things, he sought timely contributions from the readers. " We ask assistance," he writes, " because we are fully sensible, that to publish a good newspaper is not so easy an undertaking as many people imagine it to be." He practically confesses that he is not the ideal editor, for he points out (perhaps humourously) that " the author of a gazette (in the opinion of the learned) ought to be qualified with an extensive acquaintance with languages, a great easiness and command of writing and relating things clearly and intelligibly, and in few words; he should be able to speak of

* The first number of the *Gazette*, under the ownership of Franklin and Meredith, appeared October 2, 1729.

M. T. CICERO's

CATO MAJOR,

OR HIS

DISCOURSE

OF

OLD-AGE:

With Explanatory NOTES.

PHILADELPHIA:

Printed and Sold by B. FRANKLIN,

MDCCXLIV.

war, both by land and sea; be well acquainted with
geography, with the history of the time, with the
several interests of princes and States, the secrets of
Courts, and the manners and customs of all nations."
He admits gravely that "men thus accomplished
are very rare in this remote part of the world."

To glance over the yellow, clearly printed leaves
of the *Gazette*, as carefully preserved in the Gilpin
Library of the Historical Society of Pennsylvania, is
to find an occupation as delightful to the layman as
to the antiquarian. Franklin's first number (No.
40) is in itself a mine of interest, from the prospectus on the first to the advertisements on the fourth
page. The "Foreign Affairs," on the second page,
also arrest amused attention from the fact that some
of the news is dated as far back as April (1729),
although the number was published in October of
the same year. Pass on to the later issues of the
Gazette, and it is seen that the advertisements (the
editor was keenly aware of their commercial value)
gain in importance and quaintness. Here, for instance, we have:

"A servant man's Time to be disposed of for Three Years and
Four months; he is by trade a Currier, and a perfect master of all
the Branches of that Business. Enquire at the new Printing office
near the Market."

Or classics like these:

"French is Taught at Mr. Cunningham's, a Barber, next Door to
Mrs. Rogers in Market Street, by Daniel Duborn."

"A Likely Negro Woman to be sold; She can Wash and Iron
very well, and do House-work."

" There is now in the Press, and will speedily be Published, *The Lady Errant Inchanted: A Poem Dedicated to Her most Serene Highness the Princess Magallia,*

". . . Gorgons hiss, and Dragons glare,
And ten horn'd Fiends and Giants rush to War ;
Hell rises, Heaven descends, and dance on Earth,
Gods, Imps and Masters, Musick, Rage and Mirth ;
A Fire, a Jig, a Battle and a Ball."

As we read on, Franklin himself, who has started a little shop to swell the profits of his establishment, looms up as an advertiser.

"Good Writing Parchment sold by the Printer hereof, very reasonable,"

is one of his announcements, and there are advertisements of ink, quills, and other commodities, such as

" Good Live Geese Feathers, sold at the Printer's hereof."

It might be supposed that the mechanical cares connected with the paper, and the publication of books, pamphlets, etc., joined to the carrying on of his store, would leave the editor little time for much original contribution. Yet such was his mental activity that he was able to pen many an article, both serious and light of vein, wherewith to hold the interest of the town and gain new subscribers. One of his favourite methods of enlivening the columns was to publish letters from imaginary correspondents, whose remarks were far better, as a rule, than anything which could have been supplied by his readers. If the public would not accept the epistolary invitation held out in the prospectus he would himself

meet the deficiency.   The ground which he covered
in this way had a wide scope, and ranged from the
discussion of abstruse questions of ethics to merry
quips and—on one occasion—a very adroit dig at
the slowness of his rival, the *Mercury*, in securing
news.   Certainly, if the *Mercury* was slower than
the *Gazette* in that respect, the circumstance demanded satirical mention.   Franklin, however, was
too polite to ridicule Bradford's paper as if with
intention.   No ; he wrote a letter to himself and
published it as follows : *

" *To the Printer of the Gazette :*
   " As you sometimes take upon you to correct the Publick [Frank-
lin knew how to play the Public Censor to good purpose], you ought
in your Turn patiently to receive publick Correction.   My Quarrel
against you is your Practice of publishing under the Notion of News,
old Transactions which I suppose you hope we have forgot.   For instance, in your Numb. 669 you tell us from London of July 20.
That the Losses of our Merchants are laid before the Congress of
Soissons, by Mr. Stanhope &c. and that Admiral Hopson died the
8th of May last.   Whereas 't is certain there has been no Congress at
Soissons nor anywhere else these three Years at least, nor could Admiral Hopson possibly die in May last, unless he has made a Resur-
rection since his death in 1728.   And in your Numb. 670 among
other articles of equal Antiquity you tell us a long story of a Murder
and Robbery perpetrated on the Person of Mr. Nath. Bostock, which
I have read word for word not less than four years since in your own
Paper.   Are these your freshest Advices foreign and domestick?   I
insist that you insert this in your next, and let us see how you justify
yourself.   " MEMORY."

It seemed from the above plaint that the *Gazette*,
rather than the *Mercury*, was at fault.   Read the

---

* The *Pennsylvania Gazette*, No. 206, dated November 2 to 9,
1732.

answer of the editor, printed directly under the communication :

"I need not say more in Vindication of myself against this Charge, than that the Letter is evidently wrong directed, and should have been To the Publisher of the *Mercury :* Inasmuch as the Number of my Paper is not yet amounted to 669, nor are those old Articles anywhere to be found in the *Gazette,* but in the *Mercury* of the two last weeks.   I may however say something in his Excuse, viz. : That 't is not to be always expected there should happen just a full Sheet of New Occurrences for each week ; and that the oftener you are told a good thing the more likely you will be to remember it.   I confess I once lately offended in this kind myself, but it was thro' Ignorance ; and that may possibly be the case with others."

Whereat, no doubt, Mr. Bradford winced.   The fling at his shortcomings, taken, as it was, in this quietly humorous way, was far more telling than would have been a whole page of invective.

If the *Gazette* was destined to make its weight felt in Philadelphia and throughout the province, even greater was the influence to be wielded by the almanac which Franklin began publishing about the time that he inserted " Memory's " communication. *Poor Richard*, with its proverbs, its verse, and the observations of *Mr. Richard Saunders*—otherwise Franklin—leaped at once into popularity, and was thereafter bought, quoted, and admired for many years.   It was in *Poor Richard*, indeed, that we see Franklin in his most striking light as a philosopher of the people—a hard-headed, practical thinker, an epigrammatic moralist, and an exploiter or adapter of adages, almost any one of which might have made him famous.   For *Mr. Saunders* had a terse way of telling plain truths, and while his sayings were not, for the most part, exactly original, nearly every one of them, even when a more modern setting to an ancient saw, bore the hall-mark of Franklin's genius for apt expression. Though the gifted *Saunders* has long since gone the way of all flesh, one still recalls such proverbs as:

" Necessity never made a good bargain."

" Diligence is the mother of good luck."

" An old young man will be a young old man."

" God heals, the doctor takes the fee."

" To bear other people's afflictions everyone has courage enough and to spare."

" Happy that nation, fortunate that age whose history is not diverting."

" Wealth is not his that has it, but his that enjoys it."

" Fish and visitors smell in three days."

" Forewarned, forearmed."

" Here comes the orator with his flood of words and his drop of reason."

" Keep thy shop and thy shop will keep thee."

" Deny self for self's sake."

" Three may keep a secret, if two of them are dead."

" There is no little enemy."

" Love well, whip well."

" Good wives and good plantations are made by good husbands."

" There are three faithful friends, an old wife, an old dog, and ready money."

" He that would have a short Lent, let him borrow money to be repaid at Easter."

" Keep your eyes wide open before marriage, half shut afterward."

" Let thy discontents be thy secrets."

" Let no pleasure tempt thee, no profit allure thee, no ambition corrupt thee, no example sway thee, no persuasion move thee to do anything which thou knowest to be evil; so shalt thou always live jollily, for a good conscience is a continual Christmas."

These and many other proverbs became household property, and the fame of *Poor Richard*, which grew

with the years, was to penetrate more than one
European country as a result of that remarkable
preface which Franklin wrote for the issue of 1758.
" The Way to Wealth " was the name of the paper,
and it sought to prove that, with the exercise of
more economy, the inhabitants of the colonies could
easily pay the large taxes imposed upon them as a
result of the French war.

Mr. Saunders set forth his ideas of frugality by
relating the supposed harangue of " Father Abraham," an old man who pointed the moral of his
remarks by numerous quotations from *Poor Richard*,
as, for instance :

> " It would be thought a hard government that should tax its people
> one-tenth part of their time, to be employed in its service, but idle-
> ness taxes many of us much more ; sloth by bringing on diseases, ab-
> solutely shortens life. *Sloth, like rust, consumes faster than labour
> wears, while the used key is always bright,* as poor Richard says.
> *But dost thou love life, then do not squander time, for that is the
> stuff life is made of,* as Poor Richard says. How much more time
> than is necessary do we spend in sleep, forgetting that *The sleeping
> fox catches no poultry,* and that *There will be sleeping enough in the
> grave,* as Poor Richard says."

Of course sentiments inculcating submission to taxation were received with great favour in Europe, and
the speech of " Father Abraham " was translated
into several languages. And yet, the creator of
" Father Abraham " was the man who would secure
the repeal of the Stamp Act imposed upon the American colonies by the mother country.

But we are running on too fast. Let us return to
the time when the *Gazette* was first being issued by

THE ART OF MAKING MONEY PLENTY in every Man's Pocket: by Doctor Franklin.

Messieurs Franklin and Meredith.   Business complications arose, and, as luck would have it, Mr.
Vernon, whose money Franklin had long since made
over to the now vanished Collins, asked for what
was due him.   " I wrote him an ingenuous letter of
acknowledgment," related the offender, " craved his
forbearance a little longer, which he allowed me,
and as soon as I was able, I paid the principal with
interest, and many thanks; so that *erratum* was in
some degree corrected."

But there was a more pressing difficulty.   The
father of Meredith, who should have been the capitalist of the new printing concern, was unable to
advance more than one hundred pounds currency.
Another hundred pounds was needed to pay a merchant; it was not forthcoming.   The prospect of a
lawsuit, in consequence, confronted the partners,
and ruin stared them ominously in the face.

" In this distress two true friends, whose kindness I have never
forgotten, nor ever shall forget while I can remember anything, came
to me separately, unknown to each other, and without any application from me, offering each of them to advance me all the money
that should be necessary to enable me to take the whole business
upon myself, if that should be practicable ; but they did not like my
continuing the partnership with Meredith, who, as they said, was
often seen drunk in the streets, and playing at low games in ale-
houses, much to our discredit."

The two friends were William Coleman and Robert
Grace, and Franklin told them, rightly enough, that
he could not propose a separation while any prospect
remained of the Merediths filling their part of the
agreement.   If this prospect was not realised, then

he should think himself at liberty to accept the proffered generosity.

The bibulous partner soon solved any doubts on the subject by acknowledging that his father was unable to advance more money.

"I see," said the son to Franklin, "this is a business I am not fit for. I was bred a farmer, and it was folly in me to come to town, and put myself, at thirty years of age, an apprentice to learn a new trade. Many of our Welsh people are going to settle in North Carolina where land is cheap. I am inclined to go with them and follow my old employment. You may find friends to assist you. If you will take the debts of the company upon you; return to my father the hundred pounds he has advanced; pay my little personal debts, and give me thirty pounds and a new saddle, I will relinquish the partnership, and leave the whole in your hands."

Franklin must have been greatly pleased at this amicable proposition. He consented to it at once, borrowed the necessary funds from the two friends, and saw Meredith depart for North Carolina.

Life now went on more calmly, and Franklin began to make enough profits by his printing enterprises to provide for the gradual payment of his debt to the beneficent Messrs. Coleman and Grace. He wisely reasoned that it was quite as necessary, in staid, industry-loving Philadelphia, to appear to be a worker as it was to be one, and for the purpose of giving such an impression he sometimes indulged in the spectacular occupation of wheeling a barrow through the streets. Call this exhibition, if you will, a bit of affectation, but remember that the editor of the *Gazette* had his way to carve in the world, and do not blame him if he resorted to a little innocent diplomacy. He was glad, no doubt, that Bradford, the one rival he had to face, was grown rich enough to be careless in his business, and sorry, too, that the latter happened to be post-master. For, under the primitive rules of the colony, the postmaster could forbid the circulation through his mails of any paper but his own—a privilege of which the publisher of the *Mercury* availed himself. So it was only by feeing the post-riders that it was possible to deliver the *Gazette* to its subscribers. There was nothing of the petty tyrant about Frank-lin, and when it should come his turn to be post-master of the town, he would seek to put an end to so absurd a monopoly.

At this period the glazier Godfrey and his family still occupied a portion of the printing-house in which the bachelor publisher lived and worked, and the latter was soon in the meshes of a love-affair. It was one without much romance, for Franklin took too practical a view of matrimony to be classed as a *Romeo*. Runaway matches, or fervent poems to his mistress's eyebrow were not for one who had been brought up in the hard school of adversity. There-fore, when Mrs. Godfrey sought to arrange a mar-riage between him and a young relative of hers, Franklin let it be known that he would expect with the girl a dowry sufficient to pay off the indebted-ness remaining on the printing establishment—say about a hundred pounds. The parents of the young woman asserted that they had not enough money to do anything of the kind. The swain immediately suggested that they might mortgage their house—

4

an advice which met with so little favour that they
soon withdrew their consent to this very cold-
blooded courtship, on the ground that Franklin's
prospects were too uncertain. The lover (?) suspected that the old people were ready to wink at an
elopement, thus leaving them under no obligation
in the way of dowry, but he chose to take them at
their word, and so made no move to see the
daughter.

The affair has about it so little of the ardour and
disinterestedness of youth, that it is pleasant to turn
from it to a scene where real affection shines out
agreeably, if placidly. Deborah Read, otherwise
Mrs. Rogers, was the heroine of the episode. She
had left her husband upon learning that he was
credited, or discredited, with having another wife.
Rogers then ran away to the West Indies, whence
came later the report of his death, and so ended an
ill-starred marriage. But the truant Franklin was
about to return to his first allegiance; one of his
errata was to be corrected. Let him tell the story
himself:

" A friendly correspondence as neighbours and old acquaintances
had continued between me and Mrs. Read's family, who all had a
regard for me from the time of my first lodging in their house. I
was often invited there and consulted in their affairs wherein I was
sometimes of service. I pitied poor Miss Read's unfortunate situation, who was generally dejected, seldom cheerful, and avoided company. I considered my giddiness and inconsistency when in London
as in a great degree the cause of her unhappiness, tho' the mother was
good enough to think the fault more her own than mine, as she had
prevented our marrying before I went thither, and persuaded the
other match in my absence. Our mutual affection was revived, but

there were now great objections to our union. The match was indeed, looked upon as invalid, a preceding wife being said to be living in England ; but this could not easily be proved, because of the distance ; and tho' there was a report of his [Rogers's] death, it was not certain. Then, tho' it should be true, he had left many debts, which his successor might be called upon to pay. We ventured, however, over all these difficulties, and I took her to wife, September 1st, 1730. None of the inconveniences happened that we had apprehended ; she proved a good and faithful helpmate, assisted me much by attending the shop ; we throve together, and have ever mutually endeavoured to make each other happy."

Here, then, is the account of the marriage in Franklin's own words, and it is far better to take it exactly as it stands than to wander off into a discussion as to the validity of the union. The evidence in the matter is circumstantial, rather than direct, but it leads to the conclusion that the ceremony was legal. It was a happy marriage, as all the world knows; it gave to Franklin just that moral poise of which he stood in need, and made of him a good, if not exactly an ardent husband. In years to come he would write tenderly of his wife :

" .   .   . we are grown old together, and if she has any faults I am so used to them that I don't perceive them. As the song says :
  " ' Some faults we have all, and so has my Joan,
      But then they 're exceedingly small ;
    And, now I 'm grown used to them, so like my own,
      I scarcely can see them at all,
    My dear friends,
      I scarcely can see them at all.' " *

The Joan of Franklin's muse seems to have possessed just that practical, domestic vein so essential

* Franklin was quoting from *My Plain Country Joan*, a song written by him for the Junto.

in one who was to be his helpmeet.   Franklin with
an extravagant wife would have been an anomaly.
As he himself puts it :

"We have an English proverb that says, '*He that would thrive,
must ask his wife.*'   It was lucky for me that I had one as much disposed to industry and frugality as myself.   She assisted me cheerfully in my business, folding and stitching pamphlets, tending shop,
purchasing old linen rags for the paper-makers, etc., etc.   We kept
no idle servants, our table was plain and simple, our furniture of the
cheapest.   For instance, my breakfast was a long time bread and
milk (no tea) and I ate it out of a two-penny earthen porringer, with
a pewter spoon."

Domestic economy was not, however, the only
virtue which interested the fertile brain of Franklin ; he also sought to practise what might be termed
moral economy.   In other words, he conceived " the
bold and arduous project of arriving at moral perfection."   The idea was " bold and arduous," without doubt, and it need hardly be added that there
was nothing of the angel about the man.   Although
in many of his attributes he was far beyond the
average of humanity, yet he sometimes slipped and
fell in pursuing the right.   Still he thought much on
the subject, and drew up a set of commandments
which helped to establish in him that wonderful
self-control which, during the troubles of the Revolutionary period, was to be exercised so effectively.
Thirteen virtues were comprised in the list, and they
were duly recorded in a little book where the author's
practice or neglect of each might be registered in
black and white.   Even in matters of the soul was
Franklin methodical.   Originally there were only
twelve virtues in the book, but that of Humility

was added when a plain-spoken Quaker informed the striver after perfection that he was generally thought proud, and in argument overbearing, and rather insolent.

It was about this time (1733) that Franklin made a trip to Boston, and visited his gratified relations. On his return he stopped at Newport, where James Franklin was now living; with him he had a cordial meeting. It is to be supposed that Benjamin the man behaved with more tact than Benjamin the boy had done at the last interview. Later he was to show his magnanimity by educating his brother's son, then a lad of ten years of age. Benjamin himself already had a family. One of his sons, Francis Folger Franklin, was to die, several years later, of small-pox—a victim to the father's prejudice against inoculation.

Thus the editor went on aggressively with the problem of life, taking an interest in every phase of it, printing, studying languages, writing down virtues to be practised, and now and then getting into breezy controversies with his fellow-citizens. One of these controversies arose through the arrival from Ireland of a young Presbyterian minister named Hemphill, who created quite a stir by the brilliancy of his preaching. Among his numerous admirers was soon numbered Franklin. In the sermons of the newcomer he found little of the dogmatic style so common to the clergymen of the time, but a great deal of sound, practical virtue. The unconventional methods of Hemphill stirred up, however, a violent opposition among his more conservative

listeners; he was accused of heterodoxy, and the
excitement among the usually quiet inhabitants of
Philadelphia grew intense. Franklin flew valiantly
to the rescue, raised a strong party in his interest,
and wrote two or three pamphlets in his defence.
" Finding that, tho' an eloquent preacher, he was
but a poor writer, I lent him my pen," says our
Autobiographer, who might have suspected, even
then, that there was something curious in the literary deficiency of a clergyman who could deliver such
well-considered discourses. Knowing as we do the
sturdy spirit of Franklin, it is easy to imagine that
the contest would have resulted in victory for his
protégé had it not been for " an unlucky occur-
rence " which " hurt his cause exceedingly." In
short, Mr. Hemphill was an unblushing plagiarist.
One of his adversaries thought that a sermon which
the reverend gentleman preached with great effect
had a familiar ring; he looked into the matter, and
was delighted to discover that the glowing words
he had heard were published in a British review and
attributed to Dr. James Foster, the London divine.
This settled the career of the stranger in Philadelphia, but Franklin stood by his theological guns,
possibly because he was too nettled to draw out of
a fight which he had taken so much to heart. " I
rather approved his giving us good sermons composed by others, than bad ones of his own manufacture, tho' the latter was the practice of our
common teachers." And yet in that little moral
book of his Franklin had placed " Sincerity " among
the virtues.

When, later on, Whitefield came to Philadelphia
to throw the sombre spell of his religious fervour
and natural eloquence over many of the inhabitants,
Franklin listened with keen, critical attention to the
impassioned words of warning which fell from the
great preacher's lips.   He always tried to keep on
his guard with the reformer, as though half afraid of
being carried away by the flood of oratory, and he
was obdurate enough, when Whitefield returned
from his trip to Georgia, to refuse contributing to the
orphan asylum projected by the evangelist.   Whitefield wished to place the institution in Georgia, while
Franklin wanted it built in Philadelphia, contending
that in a place where material and workmen were
more plentiful it would be far easier to erect the
asylum, and to have transported to the banks of the
Delaware the destitute Southern children whom it
was intended to shelter.   But the " spell-binding "
genius of the visitor was to conquer, and no one
would appreciate the humour of the victory more
than Franklin.

" I happened soon after," writes the latter, " to attend one of his
sermons in the course of which I perceived he intended to finish with
a collection, and I silently resolved he should get nothing from me.
I had in my pocket a handful of copper money, three or four silver
dollars, and five pistoles in gold.   As he proceeded I began to soften,
and concluded to give the coppers.   Another stroke of his oratory
made me ashamed of that, and determined me to give the silver ;
and he finished so admirably that I empty'd my pocket wholly into
the collector's dish, gold and all."

What a scene to have witnessed !   The self-restraint
of the imperturbable Franklin gradually melting before the inspired pleadings of the enthusiast.

The Philadelphia which welcomed Whitefield, and wherein Franklin was already assuming so prominent a position, was a pretty, prosperous town, with a growing commerce and a population that before many years (in about 1744) would swell to the enormous figure of twelve or thirteen thousand souls. Pennsylvania was a thriving province, having for its proprietors the sons of William Penn, with whose interests the people and their Assembly were not always in harmony. Everywhere loyalty to the crown of Great Britain prevailed; there was real affection for the mother-country in the hearts of her American children; everything seemed to point to a continuation of the bonds existing between them. Philadelphia herself was well-to-do, conservative, a little dull, and fond, even then, of good living, and the Quakers still retained an influence which would not be impaired until the enemies of their non-combative theory, with Franklin at their head, should strike a mighty blow. The intellectual life of the city was not exactly brilliant, and conditions were, of necessity, more or less primitive, but men of liberal education could be found.

Franklin himself, by the establishment (1731–32) of the Philadelphia Library, had done a great deal to stir up the mental activity of his townsmen. This institution forms to-day one of the most enduring monuments to his enterprise and sagacity. Until then, a public library was undreamt of in the philosophy of Philadelphians. Good books were hard to obtain unless one went to the trouble of im-

THE PHILADELPHIA LIBRARY.

THE OLD BUILDING ON FIFTH STREET, NOW DEMOLISHED.   FROM THE ENGRAVING BY W. BIRCH & SON.

porting them from England, an expensive and
tedious method, and one seldom employed. The
fact was that the majority of the thrifty citizens
were so much immersed in the carrying on of their
respective trades that they gave little attention,
before the organising of the library, to the demands
of literature. So it remained for Franklin to put the
right kind of reading within their reach. This he
did in a way that was almost accidental.

It appears that the members of the Junto, who
naturally prided themselves on their knowledge of
the liberal arts, had each a few books. When they
gave up a tavern as their place of meeting and
rented a club-room of their own, the precious volumes, at Franklin's suggestion, were placed in the
new quarters, and were borrowed, taken home, and
read. It was a club-circulating library, and the
venture proved so admirable a one that its originator made up his mind to go further and to start a
public subscription library. A plan was accordingly
drawn up, and, after some difficulty, fifty persons,
the most of them young tradesmen, were secured
for the pledging of forty shillings each for the first
purchase of books, and ten shillings per year as
dues.* Reading was not then fashionable, but it
soon became so, and from the organisation of the
Philadelphia Library may be dated that quiet, unostentatious, but none the less pronounced, love of
books so characteristic of the Quaker City. Philadelphia never was, and probably never will be, an

---

* The Philadelphia Library was incorporated in 1742. The first
books for the society arrived from London in October, 1732.

intellectual centre of the Boston type, but it has been for many years a community where the average of general information stands high.

What particularly impresses one at this point is the catholicity, the many-sided nature, of the editor of the *Pennsylvania Gazette*. He publishes a paper, and the founding of a library seems, therefore, a congenial task, but when he rushes—or rather walks sedately—into a far different line of philanthropy and organises a fire company, we hold up our hands in surprise. Yet that was what he did in 1736, after having become impressed with the wretchedly inadequate provision for extinguishing fires. He was determined to have for Philadelphia a regular fire company, on the model of one in Boston, and succeeded so well in his scheme that other organisations of the same kind were not long in being equipped. Many a time must he have run to a fire with his leather buckets, forgetting his business and his books, and working as hard as though he were never to become a Signer of the Declaration of Independence or the petted envoy to France. He will congratulate himself when he comes to write the sketch of his life that since the rise of fire companies Philadelphia " has never lost by fire more than one or two houses at a time," and that " the flames have often been extinguished before the house in which they began *has been half consumed*." What must the fires have resulted in before that fortunate era?*

---

* Another service for which Franklin put Philadelphia in his debt was in suggesting a plan for the reorganisation of the " city watch."

We have not yet traced very far the eventful career of this future hero of the nation, but he has already displayed phases of character and of mental power that stamp him indelibly as one man among millions. Let us glance for an instant at the different guises in which he is revealed to us. Here is the list:

The Craftsman: He has mastered the intricacies of the printer's trade, and there is, perhaps, in all the colonies no better compositor than he, and no one who can set cleaner " copy," make a more efficient foreman, or get out a neater book. He can work a press, bind books, too, keep a stationery store, and could, if circumstances demanded, make soap and candles, turn clerk, cast accounts, or do engraving.

The Publisher: He manages a paper, contributes to it, and performs the multifarious duties of editor, news collector, and head printer.

The Philosopher: He has a knowledge of mankind, a sagacity, and a felicity of expression that place him in the same class with Socrates. More than a century after his death Professor Moses Coit Tyler will draw the following parallel between the two *:

" Besides the plebeian origin of both, and some trace of plebeian manners which clung to both, and the strain of animal coarseness from which neither was ever entirely purified, they both had an amazing insight into human nature in all its grades and phases, they were both indifferent to literary fame, they were both humourists, they both applied their great intellectual gifts in a disciplinary but

* *Literary History of the American Revolution*, vol. ii.   G. P. Putnam's Sons.

genial way to the improvement of their fellow-men, and in dealing
controversially with the opinions of others they both understood and
practised the strategy of coolness, playfulness, and unassuming manner, moderation of statement, the logical parallel, and irony."

The Prose Writer: He has written striking pamphlets, articles for the newspapers, etc., and a number of essays, some of which compare favourably
with the style of Addison.

The Versifier: He is not a poet, but he writes indifferent rhymes.

The Religious Thinker : He has turned from
atheism to deism, and has invented for his observance a moral code, in which the virtues are temperance, silence, order, resolution, frugality, industry,
sincerity, justice, moderation, cleanliness, tranquillity, chastity, and humility.

The Political Economist: He has written a defence
of paper money, and has thereby induced the Assembly of Pennsylvania to defy the orders of the
English Government.

The Sinner: In spite of all his fine resolutions he
has erred like lesser mortals.

The Philanthropist: He supplies Philadelphians
with books, and lessens the damage from fire.

The Diplomat: He has been careful of appearance,
and has an eye to the main chance.

The Reformer: He has the courage of his convic-
tions and can speak out on occasion.

The Saver of Money: He has been penurious.

The Giver of Money: He has been generous.
Vide Collins and Ralph.

The Forgetful Lover: He has jilted Miss Read.

The Faithful Husband: He has married Miss Read.

The Humourist: He can see the lighter side of things.

The Realist: He takes an austere interest in the commonplace affairs of life.

Here we have a set of characteristics some of which might seem strangely at war one with another were it not for the nature of him in whom they are blended so effectively. The printer who is working so energetically with his apprentices in the office of the *Gazette*—that stocky man of medium height, with the gray eyes twinkling shrewdness, kindliness, and humour—is blessed with a vast power of adaptability, and the gift of being many things at once. Above all, and regulating all, is an ambition to succeed. He is solving the problem of existence in his own steady, unimpassioned fashion; he will soon make rapid strides in its solution. We will follow him, and see how the private citizen is already developing into the public man. His ways may not be always the ways of smoothness, and his paths not always those of peace, but there will be length of days, and honour, in store for him.

CHAPTER III

THE SERVANT OF THE PUBLIC

1736-1754

BEFORE describing the public activities of Franklin, which were to continue for half a century or more, let the reader bear in mind that our hero had three qualities destined to prove of essential value in the future. He possessed a mind in which common sense played a more important *rôle* than impracticable enthusiasm; he knew how to make the best of current circumstances while leading up to the accomplishment of great aims; egotist though he was, and despite the assertion of enemies to the contrary, he loved his country better than himself. There have been more brilliant statesmen who have done far less for American progress, simply because they lacked one or all of these virtues. Some of them have had noble conceptions without the worldly wisdom necessary to carry them into effect; some have rebelled at the inevitable, degenerating into political scolds; others have ruined themselves by yielding to the mad longing for personal power and self-aggrandisement. Failure, often even shame, has been the consequence. It is well, therefore, to watch the means employed by Franklin to contribute to the common weal, and to contrast his success with the fall of men either less observing, less stable, or less honest than himself.

His entrance into the arena of public life was made modestly enough in the year 1736, as clerk of the Pennsylvania Assembly. Indeed, he attached little importance to the position beyond the fact that it brought him into closer contact with the legislators, and secured for him a goodly amount of official printing—a business chance which interfered in no wise with his duties, and for which, under the circumstances then prevailing, we cannot really blame him for turning to advantage. The following year he was again chosen clerk, notwithstanding the opposition of one member of the Assembly who favoured a candidate of his own, and who unconsciously advertised the abilities of Franklin by delivering a long speech against him. To win over this opponent, who might put further obstacles in his way, was now the aim of the re-elected officer, and it must be admitted that he went about the task in a mode that bespoke the wisdom of the serpent. To defy the Assemblyman would be worse than foolish; to fawn upon him was out of the question, and not suited to the independent character of the clerk. Franklin sat down and coolly wrote the member, asking the loan of a curious book from his library. The gentleman fell into the good-natured trap, doubtless much flattered by the request, sent the desired volume, and in a few days the borrower returned it with a polite note of thanks. Let us hope that he had read the book. One thing is certain; from that moment the claws of the member were drawn, and he became an intimate friend of his former enemy. A little diplomacy had won the day.

It was now (1737) that Franklin was made postmaster of Philadelphia by ex-Governor Spotswood of Virginia, then Postmaster-General of the colonies. An archaic office, although not a sinecure, the postmastership of even a large town must have been. The mere announcement of the appointment shows that the carrying of the mails had not been elevated to the dignity of a fine art. Far from it, for we read that "the post-office of Philadelphia is now kept at B. Franklin's, in Market street; and that Henry Pratt is appointed Riding Postmaster for all the stages between Philadelphia and Newport in Virginia, who sets out about the beginning of each month, and returns in twenty-four days; by whom gentlemen, merchants, and others may have their letters carefully conveyed, and business faithfully transacted," etc.

Such regular distribution of mails as there happened to be throughout the colonies was attended to by carriers on horseback, and even that system was poor enough. No one had a keener idea of its inadequacy than Franklin, and a time was to come when he would be able to build the foundation for that admirable service which is to-day one of the most creditable departments of the national government.

In 1737 the salary attached to the postmastership was insignificant, even for that era of frugal stipends, but the office was of advantage to Franklin in that it gave him greater facilities for the publishing of the *Gazette*, and imparted to the paper, as it were, an official status that won for it larger circulation and more advertising patronage. In one way, it is pleasant to remember, Franklin refused to imitate Bradford, his predecessor in office—he did not forbid (excepting once at the peremptory orders of Spotswood) the post-riders from carrying the opposition journal, the *Mercury*. This generosity was good policy, too; the *Gazette* thrived wonderfully, and Franklin, who had begun to be a capitalist on a small scale, and to advance money for the establishment of several of his workmen in different colonies, by this time must have ceased to trundle about that ostentatious wheelbarrow.

For ten useful years the ways of Franklin were the ways of peace, and he lived at amity with most men, not forgetting the all-powerful Quakers. But in 1747 he dealt the Quaker policy of non-resistance a blow from which it never fully recovered; he was thus able to influence the trend of public opinion and to infuse into many a Philadelphian a warlike spirit which was to bear striking fruit on the threshold of the Revolution. The warring of France and Spain against Great Britain was the cause of this local earthquake, and a rather indirect cause it might seem were we not to remember that it ex-

5

posed the seaboard of the colonies to the descent of
privateers, with all the cruelty and pillage that such
expeditions brought in their wake.   Massachusetts
had taken the alarm, and gallantly fitted out an
expedition against Louisburg; everywhere " Defence "—defence against warfare of the most despicable type—was the earnest cry.   Philadelphia
was in danger; French and Spanish privateers were
hovering in Delaware Bay.   Yet all was at a stand-
still.   The Pennsylvania Assembly was practically
in the hands of the Quakers, who refused to supply
the money necessary to put the province in the necessary condition of security.   To take up arms, or
actively countenance the taking up of arms, was to
act in opposition to one of their most cherished
beliefs.   The laws of Pennsylvania, furthermore,
sedulously respected their scruples.   Governor
Thomas entreated, but as the non-combative theory
still held the power, he turned his energies to at-
tacking the Spaniards through Cuba.   In short, he
set about organising several companies of volunteers
for the conquest of that island, assuring them that
the Cubans would fly before them, leaving all of
their possessions as booty for the invaders.

Now Franklin, who possessed the rare gift of
knowing when to act and when to remain quiescent,
determined that the time had come for aggressive
opposition to the dangerous conservatism or dogma-
tism of the peace-at-any-price party.   None the less
was he impelled to break up the existing order of
things because of the boldness of the privateers.
One of these vessels had not long before appeared

off Cape May, flying the English colours, and when
a pilot innocently boarded her he was immediately
made prisoner, his boat was seized and manned by
a crew composed, in the main, of Spaniards, who
proceeded up the river, pillaging a plantation, carrying off four negroes, and capturing a ship with a
valuable cargo on it.   It was time to call a halt.
Franklin called it in a characteristic way, by writing a pamphlet which made him many enemies among
the older Quakers, gained over to his views some of
the younger members of the sect, and became the
one topic of conversation in the town.   As for the
party of defence, a numerous and belligerent throng,
they were jubilant.

The pamphlet, which shows us Franklin in his
best form as a patriot of sterling sense, was entitled
Plain Truth, and had as the ostensible author " A
Tradesman of Philadelphia."   It is prefaced by a
quotation from Sallust (*Capta urbe, nihil fit reliqui
victis,* etc, " Should the city be taken, all will be
lost to the conquered "), and starts off with this
well-considered paragraph :

" It is said the wise Italians make this proverbial remark on our
nation, viz., ' The English *feel* but they do not *see.*'   That is, they
are sensible of inconveniences when they are present, but do not take
sufficient care to prevent them ; their natural courage makes them
too little apprehensive of danger, so that they are often surprised by
it, unprovided of the proper means of security.   When it is too late
they are sensible of their imprudence ; after great fires they provide
buckets and engines ; after a pestilence they think of keeping clean
their streets and common sewers ; and when a town has been sacked
by their enemies they provide for its defence, etc.   This kind of
after-wisdom is indeed so common with us as to occasion the vulgar

though very significant saying, *When the steed is stolen you shut the stable door.*"

After this prelude, containing philosophy as apropos to-day as it was a century and a half ago, the writer goes on to expose the dangerous situation of the province from Indians and foreign aggressions alike, to quote Scripture, and to give very strong reasons for the policy of defence.

"The enemy," he continues, "no doubt have been told that the people of Pennsylvania are Quakers, and against all defence from a principle of conscience. This, though true of a part, and that a small part only, of the inhabitants, is commonly said of the whole, and what may make it look probable to strangers is that, in fact, nothing is done by any part of the people towards their defence. But to refuse defending oneself, or one's country, is so unusual a thing among mankind, that possibly they may not believe it till, by experience, they find they can come higher and higher up our river, seize our vessels, land, and plunder our plantations and villages, and retire with their booty unmolested."

Such pungent, hard-headed reasoning made *Plain Truth* the sensation of the year, and elevated the author to the pinnacle of a hero among those who fervently urged the protection of their firesides. The more ultra Quakers might hold up their hands in horror at this temerity, but that frightened not Franklin. The die was cast, the Rubicon crossed; open defiance had been hurled at the *laissez-faire* dogma, and the thing now to do was to act on a hint thrown out in the pamphlet. For the " Tradesman of Philadelphia " had computed that the province contained, exclusive of the peace advocates, sixty thousand fighting men, " acquainted with firearms, many of them hunters and marksmen, hardy and bold." "All we want," he had added, "is order, discipline, and a few cannon." A meeting of citizens was held for the formation of a defence association, a plan for which was drawn up under the auspices of Franklin; many signatures to it were secured, and the movement soon assumed formidable proportions. The provincial Council endorsed the association (Governor Thomas had now returned to England, and Anthony Palmer, President of Council, was acting Governor); there were petitions to government for a ship of war, cannon, arms, and ammunition, and a lottery was devised to obtain three thousand pounds for the erection of a battery in the Delaware, below the city. Bench and pulpit joined in the cry for self-protection. One clergyman preached from the theme, "The Lord is a Man of War." In the early part of December, companies of militia were formed, and to Franklin, perhaps the coolest man among them through all the excitement, was offered the colonelcy of the Philadelphia regiment. He declined the honour, however, but showed his zeal by jogging over to New York with several citizens to persuade Governor Clinton to lend them some cannon for the battery.*

"He at first refused us peremptorily," relates the *Autobiography*, "but at dinner with his council, where there was great drinking of Madeira wine, as the custom of that place then was, he softened by degrees, and said he would lend us six. After a few more bumpers he advanced to ten; and at length he very good-naturedly conceded eighteen."

* This main battery was erected below the Old Swedes' Church. See Scharf and Westcott's *History of Philadelphia*, for some interesting data on the subject.

They were fine pieces of cannon, and were soon mounted on the battery, which Franklin took his turn at guarding, like other members of the association, during the progress of the war abroad.

Governor Palmer and his Council made much of the author of *Plain Truth*, whom they consulted in many things concerning the plans of defence. At his suggestion they proclaimed a public fast whereby to invoke a blessing upon the project. This was an innovation for Pennsylvania, and so Franklin put his Puritan training to advantage by drawing up the proclamation for the fast " in the accustomed stile " of New England. Whether he would be so flattered by the Quakers of the Assembly (which had adjourned in October not to meet again until May, 1748) was quite another question. It was thought that he must surely lose his place as clerk to that body, and on being advised to resign, as a pleasant alternative to having his position ignominiously taken from him, he said with emphasis that he would " never ask, never refuse, nor ever resign an office," adding: " If they will have my office of clerk to dispose of to another, they shall take it from me. I will not, by giving it up, lose my right of some time or other making reprisals on my adversaries." At the next session, strange to say, he was unanimously re-elected clerk, possibly, as he explains, because " they did not care to displace me on account merely of my zeal for the association."

Perhaps when the Assembly came together the dislike which the more strait-laced Quakers felt for Franklin had begun to wear off a trifle. Certainly a combative spirit was not without secret adherents among the younger members of the Society, whose patriotism got the better of their environment. Franklin himself relates an instance of this quiet, but none the less pronounced, defection, and the story is so graphic that it may best be told in his own words:

" It had been proposed that we [*i.e.*, the members of the fire company he had founded] should encourage the scheme for building a battery by laying out the present stock, then about sixty pounds, in tickets of the lottery. By our rules, no money could be disposed of till the next meeting after the proposal. The company consisted of thirty members, of which twenty-two were Quakers, and eight only of other persuasions. We eight punctually attended the meeting; but, tho' we thought that some of the Quakers would join us, we were by no means sure of a majority. Only one Quaker, Mr. James Morris, appeared to oppose the measure. He expressed much sorrow that it had ever been proposed, as he said *Friends* were all against it, and it would create such discord as might break up the company. We told him that we saw no reason for that ; we were the minority, and if *Friends* were against the measure, and outvoted us, we might and should, agreeably to the usage of all societies, submit. When the hour for business arrived it was moved to put the vote ; he allowed we then might do it by the rules ; but, as he could assure us that a number of members intended to be present for the purpose of opposing it, it would be but candid to allow a little time for their appearing.

" While we were disputing this, a waiter came to tell me two gentlemen below desired to speak with me. I went down, and found they were two of our Quaker members. They told me there were eight of them assembled at a tavern just by ; that they were determined to come and vote with us if there should be occasion, which they hoped would not be the case, and desired we would not call for their assistance if we could do without it, as their voting for such a measure might embroil them with their elders and friends. Being thus secure of a majority, I went up, and after a little seeming hesitation, agreed to a delay of another hour. This Mr. Morris allowed to be extreamly fair. Not one of his opposing friends appeared, at which he expressed great surprise ; and at the expiration of the hour, we carry'd the resolution eight to one ; and as, of the twenty-two Quakers, eight were ready to vote with us, and thirteen, by their absence, manifested that they were not inclined to oppose the measure, I afterwards estimated the proportion of Quakers sincerely against defence as one to twenty-one only ; for these were all regular members of that Society and in good reputation among them, and had due notice of what was proposed at that meeting."

This was a bit crafty in our hero, but let it be remembered that the strategy went to benefit a good cause. And no one felt more keenly than he the humours of a situation where a few progressive Quakers found it difficult to make a satisfactory blending of their loyalty and their non-resistance article of faith. For deep down in their hearts was a warm love of country which impelled them to tacitly sanction measures that they could not openly approve.

During all the excitement following the publication of *Plain Talk*, it was a great satisfaction to Franklin to know that James Logan, the one-time agent and friend of William Penn, was openly in favour of the association for defence. He himself had handed to the worthy author of the pamphlet the sum of sixty pounds, to be used in the purchase of lottery tickets in aid of the battery. Like Franklin, the cultivated Logan had a humorous idea of the paradoxical complications frequently arising through belief in the doctrine of non-resistance, and he could cite, by way of illustration, an experience of his own. When he was coming over to Philadelphia in 1699, as Penn's secretary, the good ship

Canterbury, which bore him and his distinguished master, met with an armed vessel that was at first supposed to be an enemy. The captain determined to defend himself, but, knowing the peace policy of the Quakers, he advised Penn and his companions to retire to the seclusion and safety of the cabin—a suggestion adopted by all of the party excepting the independent Logan, who remained on deck, quartered to a gun. The enemy was no enemy at all, but a friendly ship, and when the secretary went below to tell the news, Penn rebuked him severely and publicly for his martial sentiment. The censure stung Logan, who answered, evidently with a good deal of non-Quaker-like heat, " I being thy servant, why did thee not order me to come down ? But thee was willing enough that I should stay and fight the ship when thee thought there was danger." We can imagine that when *Plain Talk* was the one great topic of local conversation Logan related the anecdote to Franklin with much relish.

Meanwhile Mars stalked triumphantly through the City of Brotherly Love. Cannon arrived from England; the newly organised companies were reviewed and drilled. It was requested that, in case of alarm at night, the citizens in sympathy with defence should place lighted candles in the lower windows and doors of their houses, " for the more convenient marching of the militia and well-affected persons who may join them." Privateering was still a dangerous industry, however, and there was general rejoicing when the British sloop-of-war *Otter* came up the Delaware to protect the commerce of

the city.   But the *Otter* met with an accident which
disabled her, and the river offered many terrors to
arriving or departing merchantmen.   On one occasion Captain Lopez, in command of a Spanish brig-
antine, sailed boldly up the Delaware, flying the
English colours, and might have captured a large
vessel anchored at New Castle, had it not been for
the escape of one of his prisoners, an American, who
leaped from the privateer, swam ashore, and put his
compatriots on their guard.   There was firing from
the New Castle battery, and the threatened ship;
firing, too, from Captain Lopez, who displayed his
real colours, and finally sailed gaily down the river
after promising to return with other craft and plunder and burn to his heart's content.   As the enterprising commander expected to include Philadelphia
in his little trip there was much uneasiness; a new
company of artillery was formed, and extra precautions taken.   Surely the Assembly might now be
expected to assist the defenders.   But that provoking body met, did nothing, and adjourned.

Then a fresh alarm was raised.   It was reported
that seven suspicious vessels, one of them carrying
thirty guns, were down in the bay, and it was some
little time before the anxious Philadelphians heard
that the visitors belonged to the English navy.
Then came the great news that the war was at an
end, and that the peace treaty of Aix-la-Chapelle
had been signed (1748).

Philadelphia now settled down to quietude, but
she was not the Philadelphia of old.   Mars had won
a victory within the very gates of his most fervent

enemies, and the dogma of impassiveness was, if by no means dead, maimed by a wound which would never heal. And Franklin had, first by his pen, and then by his acts, done more to bring about this result than any other man in the province. What wonder was it that the public began to claim him more and more, as though he were some willing servant from whom any amount of honest, efficient work might be expected as a matter of right?

Yet Franklin was just comforting himself with the thought that he could now find opportunity to pursue those scientific researches which were destined to contribute so generously to his fame. He had recently taken into partnership his foreman, David Hall, who was to carry on the printing business for him; he was in easy circumstances, and a vista of refined leisure opened up before him.* But there was to be no leisure in his life. No sooner had he determined to be a *savant*, and nothing but a *savant*, than, as he expresses it, the public " laid hold of me for their purposes, every part of our civil government, and almost at the same time, imposing some duty upon me." He was made a justice of the peace, a member of the Common Council, and then an alderman, and elected (1752) to the provincial Assembly.

" This later station," he explains, " was the more agreeable to me,

* Under the terms of partnership the new partner was to pay Franklin a thousand pounds a year for eighteen years, at the expiration of which time Hall should become sole proprietor of the business, no further payments being required. Franklin was to contribute to the *Gazette* and to *Poor Richard's Almanac.*

as I was at length tired of sitting there to hear debates in which, as clerk, I could take no part, and which were often so unentertaining that I was induced to amuse myself with making magic squares or circles, or anything to avoid weariness ; and I conceived my becoming a member would enlarge my power of doing good."

He is candid enough to admit, however, that his ambition was flattered, as well it might be, and he takes pride in recalling that in succeeding years during which he served in the Assembly he never asked an elector for his vote, or signified, either directly or indirectly, " any desire of being chosen." This is a confession worth recommending to a few modern politicians, but we are not to draw any false conclusions from it. Franklin was the soul of honesty in politics, yet he never forgot that he was a business man who was to look out for his own interests, frankly, openly, and without affectation. When he gave up his clerkship in the Assembly, his illegitimate son, William Franklin, got the position. Later on he was to take care of his family in other ways. It must be confessed that there is in this exhibition of thrift something unpleasant, nay, sordid, yet we can never forget that, with all this nepotism, Franklin put the interests of country before his own. If, incidentally, he could benefit those nearest to him, and do it without dishonour, he seized the opportunity. It were better had he been less quick to do so, but such was the man, and we must judge him accordingly, never forgetting that in any account between the nation and himself, he emerged as the creditor rather than as the debtor.

Our Assemblyman soon launched out into a new

rôle, that of an ambassador to the Indians. The visit was a sequel to the contest for American supremacy, which had been going on for many years between England and France. In the then Northwest the French adventurers, explorers, and fur-traders were pushing their way insidiously toward the East, not content with their conquests in Southern territory and the Canadian possessions; a chain of French forts had been established between Quebec and New Orleans, and the valley of the Ohio was threatened. The sovereignty of England in the new continent was being gradually, but none the less surely, imperilled. Thus the attitude of the Indians became more and more important, and it was of the greatest moment that everything should be done to check the growing influence exerted upon so many of them by the daring subjects of Louis XV. It was particularly desirable to make a new treaty with the Ohio Indians, and so it came about that Franklin and Isaac Norris were appointed to represent the Pennsylvania Assembly in treating with these savages at Carlisle. It must have been an odd, picturesque incident, and the author of the *Autobiography* has left a vivid account of it. The Indians wanted fire-water, and the commissioners, who were diplomats rather than temperance disciples, promised them plenty of it when the treaty was concluded. This business was disposed of to the satisfaction of all concerned, the Indians keeping sober for the very simple reason that they had nothing strong to drink.

" They then claimed and received the rum ; this was in the afternoon ; they were near one hundred men, women and children, and were lodged in temporary cabins, built in the form of a square, just without the town.   In the evening, hearing a great noise among them, the commissioners walked out to see what was the matter. We found they had made a great bon-fire in the middle of the square ; they were all drunk, men and women, quarrelling and fighting. Their dark-coloured bodies, half-naked, seen only by the gloomy light of the bon-fire, running after and beating one another with firebrands, accompanied by their horrid yellings, formed a scene the most resembling our ideas of hell that could well be imagined ; there was no appeasing the tumult, and we retired to our lodging. At midnight a number of them came thundering at our door, demanding more rum, of which we took no notice."

The story suggests a chapter from Cooper rather than a page from an autobiography.   But to continue :

" The next day, sensible they had misbehaved in giving us that disturbance, they sent three of their old counsellors to make their apology.   The orator acknowledged the fault, but laid it upon the rum ; and then endeavoured to excuse the rum by saying, ' *The Great Spirit, who made all things, made everything for some use, and whatever use he designed anything for, that use it should always be put to. Now, when he made rum, he said, "Let this be for the Indians to get drunk with," and it must be so.*'

" And, indeed, if it be the design of Providence to extirpate these savages in order to make room for cultivators of the earth, it seems not improbable that rum may be the appointed means. It has already annihilated all the tribes who formerly inhabited the sea-coast."

Were Franklin alive to-day, he would have a great deal more data on which to base his reflections anent liquor and the Indians.   As it was, he never forgot his experience at Carlisle (it was strange that he escaped with his life from the yelling, rum-beseeching redskins who pounded at his door), and subsequently wrote some *Remarks Concerning the Sav-*

ages of North America — a fine, satirical sketch, wherein quiet flings at pale-faced avarice and a slyly humourous exposition of Indian virtues combine to puzzle the reader as to what moral the author really meant to draw.*

Honours were now falling fast upon the wise head of Franklin, the greatest of them up to that period being his appointment (1753), in conjunction with William Hunter, to the postmaster-generalship of the colonies. He took up the duties of the position with his accustomed energy; visited post-offices throughout the country, and instituted a number of reforms. These reforms included an increase in the frequency of the mails, and in the speed of the post-riders. Newspapers were carried at a fair charge, instead of free, as before; postmaster editors were obliged to receive rival publications; unclaimed letters were advertised; the large towns were given a penny post; the postage on letters in general was reduced. The crude state of the postal department, even after the appointment of Franklin, may be inferred from his announcement (1755), that to aid trade, etc., he has arranged for the winter northern mail from Philadelphia to New England, which used to set out but once a fortnight, to start once a week all the year round, " whereby answers may be obtained to letters between Philadelphia and Boston, in three weeks, which used to require six weeks." The celerity of the new order of things must have fairly taken away the breath of staid old Philadelphia.

* This curious pamphlet was not published until 1784. It has puzzled all of Franklin's commentators, dull or wise.

Again we see the unconcealed desire to look out for family interests. William Franklin was made controller of the post-office, and then postmaster of Philadelphia. To the latter position two relatives would, in turn, cheerfully succeed. Here was domestic affection with a vengeance, yet the Post-master-General's solicitude on this score does not blind us to the admirable conduct of his department. If all officials were half as energetic and valuable, a grateful public would not growl at such an exhibition of thoughtfulness.

In the midst of his attention to mails, post-riders, and post-roads, Franklin suddenly loomed up as the originator of a scheme which, though it came to naught, was the prelude, in a certain sense, to the union of the American colonies. The union now projected was directed, not against the mother country, but against the alarming headway which French aggression was making in the British possessions of the Ohio region. Franklin himself had learned, on his visit to Carlisle, that French posts were set up at Erie, Venango, and Waterford, and that the banks of the Monongahela were threatened by the Gallic invaders. Let the onward march of the French continue at this ratio, and it would only become a question of time as to when the English settlers must be driven farther and farther back until the Atlantic Ocean confronted them. There was alarm in the colonies, and alarm, too, in England. Thus it came about that Governor Dinwiddie, of Virginia, sent young George Washington, with a small party, out into the wilderness, for the avowed purpose of inquiring from the commander of the French forces on the Ohio River his reasons for entering the British dominions while " a solid peace subsisted." *

The adventures of the youth are history, and we have not forgotten the hardships of the journey, his conference with friendly Indians, or his arrival at Waterford.   Here stood a well-defended fort, commanded by Saint-Pierre, who threatened to seize every Englishman found in the valley of the Ohio, and who answered, when Washington sought to inquire by what right he held the fort: " I am here by the orders of my general, to which I shall conform with exactness."   On Washington's return to Virginia, early in 1754, the question of resistance to the French became more urgent.   Why should not the colonies unite to repel the enemy ?   That was a query in many mouths, and Governor Glen, of South Carolina, suggested that all the provincial governors should meet in Virginia, there to decide what supplies each colony must grant for the carrying on of the proposed defensive warfare.   Events came rapidly and ominously.   The French were in command of Fort Duquesne, the newly named post captured from the English ; Washington had enjoyed his famous brush with the French, wherein he heard the bullets whistle and found " something charming in the sound " ; the numbers of the enemy increased, and all things pointed to a slow, but none the less certain, diminution of English prestige and

---

* See the interesting account which Bancroft gives of this journey, *History of the United States*, last revision, vol. ii., chap. v.

6

English territory in America. The standard of France might in time float over a whole continent.

It may be imagined that Franklin anxiously watched the progress of affairs, and that no one realised more strongly than he the disadvantage accruing from the disunited condition of the colonies. Before me now is a faded, yellow, but still legible copy of the *Pennsylvania Gazette*, for May 9, 1754, wherein he sounds the note of warning.

" Friday last," he chronicles, " an express arrived here from Major Washington, with advice that Mr. Ward, Ensign of Captain Trent's company, was compelled to surrender his small Fort in the Forks of Monongahela to the French, on the 17th past ; who fell down from Venango with a Fleet of 360 Battoes and Canoes, upwards of 1000 Men, and 18 Pieces of Artillery, which they Planted against the Fort ; and Mr. Ward having but 44 men, and no Cannon to make a proper Defence, was obliged to surrender on summons, capitulating to march out with their Arms, etc., and they had accordingly joined Major Washington, who was advanced with three Companies of the Virginia Forces, as far as the New Store near the Allegheny Mountains, where the men were employed in clearing a Road for the Cannon, which were every Day expected with Col. Fry and the Remainder of the Regiment. . . . The Indian chiefs, however, have dispatched Messages to Pennsylvania and Virginia, desiring that the English would not be discouraged, but send out their Warriors to join them, and drive the French out of the Country before they fortify ; otherwise the Trade will be lost, to their great Grief an eternal separation made between the Indians and their Brethren the English."

This news paragraph, which is quoted because it shows so succinctly the precarious condition in which the colonists on the western border found themselves, goes on to say that, according to rumour, more of the French are coming up the Ohio, and that six hundred French Indians —the invaders knew

how to win savage allies—are about to join them,
" the design being to establish themselves, settle
their Indians, and build Forts just in the Back of
our Settlements in all our Colonies; from which
Forts, as they did from Crown Point, they may
send out their Parties to kill and scalp the Inhabitants and ruin the Frontier Counties." But here
comes the key-note of the whole article :

" The Confidence of the French in this Undertaking seems well
grounded on the present disunited state of the British Colonies, and
the extreme Difficulty of bringing so many different Governments and
Assemblies to agree in any speedy and effectual Measures for our
common Defence and Security ; while our Enemies have the very
great Advantage of being under one Direction, with one Council,
and one Purse."

At the end of the long paragraph is a wood-cut
representing a snake chopped into pieces (each
piece typifying a colony), and beneath it the warning, " Join or Die." A prophetic motto.

The great idea illustrated by this crude wood-cut
had notable enunciation from Franklin when he attended, in the summer of 1754, the convention
which commissioners from the several colonies held
at Albany, by direction of the English Government,
to secure the alliance of the Six Nations, Indians
whose help was of the greatest necessity should an
open rupture arise between Great Britain and France.
It was but natural that the question of a colonial
union should be discussed, and hardly less natural
that the fertile-minded statesman from Pennsylvania
should have a plan of his own to put before the
members. The scheme was elaborately drawn up,

and provided for a general government administered
by a President-General, supported by the crown,
and by a Grand Council to be elected from the assemblies. While the independence of each colony,
so far as related to its internal affairs, was to be maintained, the President-General would be empowered,
with the consent of the Grand Council, to make
treaties with the Indians, conduct Indian wars, levy
taxes for the support of the general government,
and for public defence, and to otherwise exercise
important prerogatives.

The plan had so many virtues that it was finally
adopted by the commissioners, subject, of course,
to the approval of the British Parliament. Never
before had Franklin occupied so commanding a
position before his fellow-colonists ; never before
had his talent for civic law and order been displayed
to such remarkable advantage. Yet the union, as
he outlined it, was not to meet with official favour.
" Its fate," as he himself says, " was singular: the
assemblies did not adopt it, as they all thought
there was too much *prerogative* in it, and in England
it was judged to have too much of the *democratic*."

The chief fault seems to have been that the plan
hinted at too great centralisation of power—or so,
at least, urged its enemies. From the point of view
of its American opponents such a union might
detract from the individual importance of each colony; from the point of view of the English Government the scheme, if logically carried out, was likely
to make the united provinces too self-assertive.
" Reflecting men in England," observes Bancroft,

" dreaded American union as the keystone of independence."

The project, therefore, fell to the ground, but it
remained for Franklin to give a further unconscious
hint of the Revolution by declaring war against the
theory that England might tax the Americans, notwithstanding that they had no representation in
Parliament. This protest came about through the
desire of the home government to substitute for his
plan of union one of its own, " whereby," as he
explained, " the governors of the provinces, with
some members of their respective councils, were to
meet and order the raising of troops, building of
forts, etc., and to draw on the treasury of Great
Britain for the expense, which was afterwards to be
refunded *by an act of Parliament, laying a tax on
America.*" The British idea was divulged to him
by Governor Shirley, when Franklin visited Boston
in the winter of 1754. The latter's objections to it
were immortalised in three noble letters which he
wrote to the Governor. In them he clearly pointed
out that Englishmen possessed, supposedly, an undoubted right not to be taxed but by their own consent, given through their representatives; that the
colonies had no representatives in Parliament; and
that to propose taxing them by Parliament, and to
refuse them the liberty of choosing a representative
Council to meet in the colonies, to consider and
judge of the necessity of any general tax and the
quantum, " shows a suspicion of their loyalty to the
crown, or of their regard for their country, or for
their common-sense and understanding, which they

have not deserved." Here the philosopher had crystallised into logical, sensible form a great principle of right which would in time form the loudest war-cry of rebellious America.

How changing, indeed, is the scene, as we follow the man through that wonderful life of which he made so much! One moment he is calmly setting forth the grandest precepts of patriotism, and in the next we have him chatting gaily over his wine, and getting in a sly little joke about his neighbours, the Quakers, or indulging in a good-natured quarrel with Governor Morris, the new executive of Pennsylvania. The Governor was, inevitably, the creature of the Penns, the proprietors of the province, and it was pretty safe to predict that as his instructions were not altogether in accord with the interests of the Assembly, particularly as the proprietaries insisted on having their own estates exempt from taxation, the relations between him and that body would not be ideal in character. When Franklin first met Morris, who had arrived from England, the latter inquired if he was to expect an uncomfortable administration. " No," said the Philadelphian, " you may, on the contrary, have a very comfortable one, if you will only take care not to enter into any dispute with the Assembly," to which the new Governor pleasantly responded: " How can you advise my avoiding disputes ? You know I love disputing; it is one of my greatest pleasures; however, to show the regard I have for your counsel, I promise you I will, if possible, avoid them." The promise was not kept; Morris and the Assembly

waged bitter warfare, and one of the men appointed
by the legislators to oppose him was Franklin, who
had to draw up many addresses of defiance. The
Governor must have had an abiding affection for his
official enemy, for the two often dined together,
instead, as was to be expected, of passing each other
on the street without a look of recognition.

During these years of political activity, which
would have sufficed to monopolise the time and
energies of almost anyone else, Franklin had been
able to bestir himself in other and very important
directions. He published a short-lived magazine
(1740-41) ; founded the American Philosophical
Society (1743) * ; became instrumental in the opening of an academy which is now considered the
lineal ancestor of the University of Pennsylvania
(1749-50) ; assisted in the establishment of the
Pennsylvania Hospital ; received the degree of
Master of Arts from Harvard and Yale Colleges,
and excited scientific Europe by those wonderful
electrical discoveries, of which mention will be made
in a subsequent chapter.

The magazine episode, which is not hinted at in
the *Autobiography* (probably because it was an unpleasant theme), involved Franklin in a quarrel, and,
unlike most of his plans, resulted in nothing. He
had made up his mind—not so canny a mind in this
instance as usual—that the time was ripe for the
publication of a magazine in the American colonies,
and he went so far as to engage an editor for the

---

* Not in 1744, the date which Franklin incorrectly gives in his
Autobiography.

venture. John Webbe was the fortunate man
selected, and so enterprising and dishonest a gentleman was he that he suddenly came out in the rival
paper, the *Mercury*, with the announcement that he
would start a magazine of his own. It was history
repeating itself ; Webbe was another Keimer.
Franklin, nothing daunted, issued a prospectus for
a *General Magazine and Historical Chronicle for
all the British Plantations in America* (what a title
was that for pomposity!), and announced that in
spite of the perfidy of one to whom he had confided
he would persevere with the scheme as originally
proposed. Then Mr. Webbe assailed Franklin
through the *Mercury ;* Bradford, the printer, was
drawn into the controversy, and finally the charge
was made against our philosopher that as postmaster he prohibited the carrying, by the post-
riders, of the *Gazette's* rival, the aforesaid *Mercury*.
Franklin, thus prodded, defends himself in an
article in the *Gazette* of December 11 (1740).

" The Publick," he observes, solemnly, " has been entertained for
these three weeks past, with angry Papers, written expressly against
me, and published in the *Mercury*. The *two first* I utterly neglected, as believing that both the Facts therein stated and the extraordinary Reasonings upon them, might be safely enough left to
themselves without any Animadversion ; and I have the Satisfaction
to find that the Event has answered my Expectations : But the *last*
my Friends think 't is necessary I should take some Notice of, as it
contains an Accusation that has at least a Shew of Probability, being
printed by a Person to whom it particularly relates, who could not
but know whether it was true or false ; and who, having still some
Reputation to guard, it may be presumed could by no means be prevailed on to publish a Thing as Truth, which was contrary to his own
knowledge."

The writer went on to admit that he had, for upward of a twelvemonth, been obliged to deny the *Mercury* the privilege of the post, by the positive commands of Colonel Spotswood, Postmaster-General of the colonies. He then followed this up by inserting an interesting, if somewhat sensational, letter from Spotswood, in which that functionary wrote Franklin (October 12, 1739), that he had not been able to obtain any account from Bradford, as postmaster at Philadelphia, from midsummer, 1734. This warfare is not agreeable to dwell upon, whether viewed from the standpoint of Bradford, of Webbe, or of Franklin. It might, however, be said, in behalf of Franklin, that the criticism in the *Mercury* had goaded him to the quick, impeaching, as it did, his avowed intention of allowing his rivals' newspapers to circulate through the mails without hindrance. He had, as we have seen, put this generous reform into effect when he became the local postmaster, and it was only countermanded by the angry orders of Colonel Spotswood. Nay, Franklin had even gone so far, after the arrival of the letter, as to allow the *Mercury* to be secretly given to the post-riders, for distribution. Yet the pen-and-ink controversy offers nothing but unpleasantness, nor is it to be wondered at that the respective magazines of Webbe and the postmaster had a short existence. They were stupid publications, even for those formal, ponderous days, and died from the journalistic inanition which comes of public neglect.

The glimpses of Franklin are brighter in other paths of effort. Take him, for instance, when he is

founding that academy which is generally accepted
as the origin of the University of Pennsylvania, despite the assertion, in some quarters, that the great
institution near the Schuylkill dates further back, to
a charity-school project.* Then, it is attractive to
think of him as he busied himself with Dr. Bond, in
working for the new hospital—now an old but progressive hospital—which has done so much, for nearly a century and a half, to relieve sick or maimed
humanity. It has been argued, to be sure, that in
securing a legislative appropriation for the enterprise
Franklin acted with a slyness a trifle too Machiavel-
lian to be approved. Perhaps his enemies are not
without warrant for their criticism, but let the reader
hear the story in his own words, and determine how
far they care to blame his enthusiasm in aiding what
is now one of the greatest hospitals in the world:

" The subscriptions afterwards [*i. e.*, after Franklin had taken
hold of the project] were more free and generous; but, beginning to
flag, I saw they would be insufficient without some assistance from
the Assembly, and therefore proposed to petition for it, which was
done. The country members did not at first relish the project; they
objected that it could only be serviceable to the city, and therefore
the citizens alone should be at the expense of it; and they doubted
whether the citizens themselves generally approved of it. My allega-
tion on the contrary, that it met with such approbation as to leave no
doubt of our being able to raise two thousand pounds by voluntary
donations, they considered as a most extravagant supposition, and
utterly impossible.

"On this I formed my plan, and, asking leave to bring in a bill
for incorporating the contributors according to the prayer of their

* Readers interested in the "pedigree" of the University of Pennsylvania should consult the supplementary chapters written by the
late Dr. Frederick D. Stone for Dr. Wood's history of that institution.

THE PENNSYLVANIA HOSPITAL, PHILADELPHIA.

FROM AN OLD ENGRAVING BY W. BIRCH & SON.

petition, and granting them a blank sum of money, which leave was obtained chiefly. on the consideration that the House could throw the bill out if they did not like it, I drew it so as to make the important clause a conditional one, viz. : 'And be it enacted, by the authority aforesaid, that when the said contributors shall have met and chosen their managers and treasurer, and *shall have raised by their contributions* a capital *stock of . . . value . . . and shall make the same appear to the satisfaction of the speaker of the Assembly for the time being*, that *then* it shall and may be lawful for the said speaker, and he is hereby required, to sign an order on the provincial treasurer for the payment of two thousand pounds, in two yearly payments, to the treasurer of the said hospital, to be applied to the founding, building and finishing of the same.'

"This condition carried the bill through ; for the members who had opposed the grant, and now conceived they might have the credit of being charitable without the expense, agreed to its passage ; and then, in soliciting subscriptions among the people, we urged the conditional promise of the law as an additional motive to give, since every man's donation would be doubled ; thus the clause worked both ways. The subscriptions accordingly soon exceeded the requisite sum, and we claimed and received the public gift, which enabled us to carry the design into execution. . . . I do not remember any of my political manœuvres, the success of which gave me at the time more pleasure, or wherein, after thinking of it, I more easily excused myself for having made some use of cunning."

Cunning it was, without doubt, but many a weary, pain-racked inmate of the hospital has had reason to bless an innocent artifice which produced such a noble result. If the cunning of all public men went no further than this, the book of politics would read like a benign fairy-tale.

CHAPTER IV

THE PHILOSOPHER IN MARTIAL MOOD

1755-1756

HEN General Braddock, brave, blustering, and foolishly confident, came over to Virginia in the winter of 1754-55, with two regiments of English regulars, for the purpose of capturing Fort Duquesne, vanquishing the French invaders, and restoring the ascendency of Great Britain upon the American continent, Franklin became one of his most valuable henchmen and gave him some good advice which, had the officer taken, would have saved the latter from death and disgrace. But Braddock belonged to a stiff-necked generation; he had been sent to put an end forever to French aggression, and he intended to do it in his own way. He knew little about the dangers lurking in the western wilderness, and nothing about Indian warfare, but what mattered that ? Was he not an English soldier, fit to cope with barbarians ? He was, in fine, a martinet, with more than the customary obstinacy of his kind, and he proposed to con-

quer the enemy, Gaul or Indian, on purely scientific
principles, exactly as if he were to deal with an
army of civilised Europe.*

No sooner did Braddock arrive in Virginia, and
begin to prepare his plan of campaign, than Pennsylvania fell under the ban of his displeasure.   There
had been the usual contest between the Governor
and the Assembly, with a reiteration of the right of
the Penns to have their estates exempted from taxation, and, as a result, nothing had ensued but
disagreement and unsatisfactory legislation.   Pennsylvania did, to be sure, borrow £5000 currency, to
be expended under her own direction in defending
the colony, but she had failed to raise a provincial
force to operate, as was desired, under Braddock.
Domestic wrangling rather than a lack of loyalty was
the cause of this tardiness, but the General was too
short-sighted, or too pig-headed, to make any distinction in the matter.   He lost his temper, grew
angry at the slowness of some of the colonies to
come to his help in the way he expected, and acted
throughout with exactly that want of tact to be
looked for in a man of his stupid, burly character.

" You may assure your Assembly," he savagely informs Governor
Morris, " I shall have regard to the different behaviour of the several
colonies, and shall regulate their quarters accordingly, and that I will
repair, by unpleasant methods, what for the character and honour of
the Assemblies I should be much happier to see cheerfully supplied."

Would the General use Pennsylvania as a province

---

*" Desperate in his fortune, brutal in his behaviour, obstinate in
his sentiments," says Walpole, " he was still intrepid and capable."

to be conquered and pillaged, rather than as an ally ?
That was the question which some of her inhabitants
asked themselves, and the fact that Braddock believed the Pennsylvanians to be selling provisions to
the French did not tend to reassure them.* He
went so far as to write home to Lord Halifax that
" the inhabitants of these colonies in general have
shown much negligence for His Majesty's service
and their own interests," and after excepting Virginia from this censure he added:

" I cannot sufficiently express my indignation against the provinces
of Pennsylvania and Maryland, whose interests being alike concerned
in the event of this expedition, and much more so than any other on
this continent, refuse to contribute anything towards the project ; and
what they propose is made upon no other terms than such as are
altogether contrary to the King's prerogatives and to the instructions
he has sent their governors."

Then, in an angry spirit of retaliation, the writer
urges " the necessity of laying a tax upon all His
Majesty's dominions in America."

It cannot be forgotten that Braddock, impatient
and overbearing as he was, had ground for complaint, from the British point of view. Several of

* When the prospect of a war between the two countries (England
and France) was imminent, and the French in Canada were anxious
to buy in a store of provisions, the commercial colonies of New
York, Rhode Island, and Massachusetts hastened to supply them.
Within three months of the first battle, no less than forty English
vessels lay at one time in the harbour of Louisbourg. It is proper
to say that Pennsylvania was not otherwise engaged in this traffic
than in selling flour to the merchants of other colonies, who pursued
it until stopped by the stringent enactments of their own legislatures.
The History of an Expedition against Fort DuQuesne, by Winthrop
Sargent.

the legislatures had, indeed, voted appropriations
for the common defence, but the money was, with
the exception of South Carolina's contribution,
spent under the direction of the several provinces.
There was patriotism, but no unison, and to a man
of the General's temper the situation must have
been exasperating. How different might have been
the state of affairs and the result to the French, had
the English Government shown the courage to
sanction the union of the colonies as proposed by
Franklin!

Here the philosopher looms up again in a meeting
with a man who of all persons resembled him the
least—Braddock himself. Franklin and Braddock
face to face—that is a picturesque contrast which
has always seemed one of the most *bizarre* incidents
of colonial history, and even Fiction, as represented
by the imperishable Thackeray, has sought to im-
mortalise it. Braddock, the beefy example of all
that is dullest in the English nature, and Franklin,
the example of all that is most subtle in the same
nature! Not only greeting each other, too, but
getting congenial into the bargain (trust our Benjamin for that), and having many a pleasant talk with
Major Washington, who was far better suited to
have command of the expedition than was the ill-
fated disciplinarian from Britain.

It was time, indeed, that the great Pennsylvanian
should carry out the request of the Assembly that
he see Braddock, and remove, if possible, the prejudices which the latter had conceived against the
province. That was a hard thing to do, but if the

task was to be attempted not a moment must be lost. St. Clair, Braddock's Quartermaster-General, was already threatening to invade Pennsylvania, where his army would confiscate waggons, horses, and cattle, and burn houses; he announced that if the French defeated them, owing to the delay of the province, he would with his drawn sword march through the country and treat the inhabitants as a " parcel of traitors." Bullying, fire-eating words, but their sound was not comforting.

How was Franklin to accomplish his delicate mission ? To go boldly as an ambassador from the hated province might expose him to insult. Some other method of approach to the English Mogul was necessary. It was decided, therefore, that the envoy should go in the capacity of Postmaster-General, " under the guise of proposing to settle with him the mode of conducting with most celerity and certainty the despatches between him and the governors of the several provinces." It was at Fredericktown, then, that the traveller found Braddock, now fretting and fuming for the return of the parties which had been sent out to collect waggons from the farmers of Maryland and Virginia. Not a very propitious moment in which to approach the martinet, but the thing had to be done, and if we are to judge from results the task of conversion was accomplished with the rarest *finesse*. The General had plenty of oaths, no doubt, for the unpatriotic conduct of Pennsylvania. Why, he asked, had the province refused his army waggons, horses, and food, refused them, too, a road from the camp to her back settlements, and otherwise played the part of a lukewarm, not to say disaffected, colony? What Franklin answered to this torrent of invective we know not in plain, set terms, but we do know that he said enough, during the dinners which he and his son William took with the commanding officer, to remove " all his prejudices." No doubt he placed strong emphasis on that £5000 which the province had authorised for the general cause—to be spent under her own supervision. It must be admitted that there had been little in the conduct of Pennsylvania to impress with favour the arbitrary mind of Braddock, and so much the more, therefore, shines out the persuasive ability of her champion. With a poor case to start with, he yet won over to his view one of the most obstinate men of the age.

Having succeeded in this difficult enterprise the Postmaster-General was about to return to Philadelphia, when the waggon-hunting parties arrived. Braddock was on tiptoe of expectation to know the result. He did not have to wait long; twenty-five waggons, not all of them in serviceable condition, were soon counted. What a " scene " there must have been! " The General and all the officers were surprised, declared the expedition was then at an end, being impossible, and exclaimed against the Ministers for ignorantly landing them in a country destitute of the means of conveying their stores, baggage, etc., not less than one hundred and fifty waggons being necessary." Whereupon Franklin observed that it was a pity the regiments had not been landed in Pennsylvania, as in that country

7

almost every farmer had his own waggon. This seemed as a ray of hope to Braddock, who exclaimed, " Then you, sir, who are a man of interest there, can probably procure them for us; and I beg you will undertake it."

The Postmaster-General, ever business-like, at once asked what terms would be offered the owners of the waggons. It was suggested that he should put on paper the terms he thought necessary. This was done, and after the scheme, as he outlined it, was duly approved, Franklin journeyed back to Pennsylvania, and issued from Lancaster, under date of April 26, 1755, an " advertisement " asking for a hundred and fifty waggons, with four horses to each waggon, and numerous saddle-horses, all for the services of his Majesty's forces. There was to be paid for the use of each waggon, with four good horses and a driver, fifteen shillings per diem, with damages in case of their loss in the service. The advertisement was accompanied by an address " To the inhabitants of the Counties of Lancaster, York, and Cumberland," which was intended to stiffen the patriotic backbone of Pennsylvanians, and to appeal to their sense of fear.

" Friends and Countrymen," Franklin loftily began. " Being occasionally at the camp at Frederic a few days since, I found the general and officers extremely exasperated on account of their not being supplied with horses and carriages which had been expected from this province, as most able to furnish them ; but, through the dissensions between our governor and Assembly, money had not been provided, nor any steps taken for that purpose. It was proposed to send an armed force immediately into these counties, to seize as many of the best carriages and horses as should be wanted, and compel as many persons into the service as would be necessary to drive and take care of them."

After this adroit beginning, wherein the crafty writer hints at what might have happened, he alludes, in apparent innocence, to the inconveniences of such a raid, and then dwells upon the money to be obtained by the inhabitants through the hire of their waggons and horses—to be paid in " silver and gold of the King's money."

" If," he says, " you are really, as I believe you are, good and loyal subjects to his majesty, you may now do a most acceptable service, and make it easy to yourselves; for three or four of such as can not separately spare from the business of their plantations a waggon and four horses and a driver, may do it together, one furnishing the waggon, another one or two horses, and another the driver, and divide the pay proportionably between you ; but if you do not this service to your king and country voluntarily, when such good pay and reasonable terms are offered to you, your loyalty will be strongly suspected. The King's business must be done ; so many brave troops, come so far for your defence, must not stand idle through your backwardness to do what may be reasonably expected from you ; waggons and horses must be had ; violent measures will probably be used, and you will be left to seek for a recompense where you can find it, and your case, perhaps, be little pitied or regarded."

There is almost a tyrannic ring about this proclamation, but the writer thereof had pretty good reason to believe that to play a bit upon the fears of the farmers would help, as much as an appeal to patriotism, to unlock the doors of their barns. And he closes in this laconic but terrifying fashion :

" I have no particular interest in this affair, as, except the satisfaction of endeavouring to do good, I shall have only my labour for my pains. If this method of obtaining the waggons and horses is not

likely to succeed. I am obliged to send word to the general in fourteen days ; and I suppose Sir John St. Clair, the hussar, with a body
of soldiers, will immediately enter the province for the purpose,
which I shall be sorry to hear, because I am very sincerely and truly
your friend and well-wisher.

                                              " B. FRANKLIN."

As it was St. Clair, as before noted, who threatened to treat the Pennsylvanians as " a parcel of
traitors," the bringing in of his name was somewhat
of a master-stroke, albeit a cruel one.   To add to
the strength of his call for help Franklin gave his
personal bond for the performance of the promises
of pay and damages set forth in the advertisement,
and he also loaned, from his own purse, upwards of
two hundred pounds to supplement the seven or
eight hundred pounds given him by Braddock as
advance money.   In two weeks the hundred and
fifty waggons, with two hundred and fifty-nine
carrying horses, were off for the camp, and the delighted General would write home that Franklin's
service was " almost the only instance of address
and fidelity " which he had seen in all the provinces.

There is a colour and vividness in all this Brad-
dock-Franklin episode to which the historian, who
is apt to regard facts more than effect, has never
done justice.   Thackeray, when he came to write
The Virginians, saw how the intimacy of the pair
could be turned to artistic advantage, and he has
left us as attractive a bit of description as ever
graced a novel.   It is fiction, with a few errors, but
for all that the scene brings us closer to reality than
the dry-as-dust data of a hundred biographers.

Braddock is riding in state to visit Madam Esmond, with dragoons in front and Captain Talmadge trotting by the side of the coach.

"Major Danvers, aide-de-camp, sat in the front of the carriage with the little postmaster from Philadelphia, Mr. Franklin, who, printer's boy as he had been, was a wonderful shrewd person, as his Excellency and the gentlemen of his family were fain to acknowledge, having a quantity of the most curious information respecting the colony, and regarding England, too, where Mr. Franklin had been more than once.*   '"T was extraordinary how a person of such humble origin should have acquired such a variety of learning and such a politeness of breeding, too, Mr. Franklin!' his Excellency was pleased to observe, touching his hat graciously to the postmaster.

"The postmaster bowed, said it had been his occasional good-fortune to fall into the company of gentlemen like his Excellency, and that he had taken the advantage of his opportunity to study their honours' manners, and adapt himself to them as far as he might. As for education, he could not boast much of that—his father being but in straightened circumstances, and the advantages small in his native country of New England : but he had done to the utmost of his power, and gathered what he could—he knew nothing like what they had in England.

"Mr. Braddock burst out laughing, and said, 'as for education, there were gentlemen of the army, by George, who did n't know whether they should spell bull with two b's or one.   He had heard the Duke of Marlborough was no special good penman.   He had not the honour of serving under that noble commander—his Grace was before his time—but he thrashed the French soundly, although he was no scholar.'

"Mr. Franklin said he was aware of both those facts.

"'Nor is my Duke [Duke of Cumberland, Braddock's patron] a scholar,' went on Mr. Braddock—'aha, Mr. Postmaster, you have heard that too,—I see, by the wink in your eye.'

"Mr. Franklin instantly withdrew the obnoxious or satirical wink in his eye, and looked into the general's jolly round face with a pair

---

* Thackeray was mistaken in this, as we know ; up to that time Franklin had been in England but once.

of orbs as innocent as a baby's. 'He's no scholar, but he is a match for any French general that ever swallowed the English for *fricassée de craupaud.* He saved the crown for the best of Kings, his royal father, his most gracious Majesty, King George.'

"Off went Mr. Franklin's hat and from his large buckled wig escaped a great halo of powder."

. . . .

"'You shall drink his health to-day, Postmaster. He is the best of masters, the best of friends, the best of sons to his royal old father; the best of gentlemen that ever wore an epaulet.'

"'Epaulets are quite out of my way, sir,' says Mr. Franklin, laughing. 'You know I live in a Quaker City.'

"'Of course they are out of your way, my good friend. Every man to his business. You, and gentlemen of your class, to your books, and welcome. We don't forbid you; we encourage you. We, to fight the enemy and govern the country. Hey, gentlemen? Lord! what roads you have in this colony, and how this confounded coach plunges! Who have we here with the two negro boys in livery? He rides a good gelding.'

"'It is Mr. Washington,' says the aide-de-camp.

"'I would like him for a corporal of the Horse Grenadiers,' said the General. 'He has a good figure on a horse. He knows the country, too, Mr. Franklin.'

"'Yes, indeed.'

"'And is a monstrous genteel young man, considering the opportunities he has had. I should have thought he had the polish of Europe, by George, I should.'

"'He does his best,' says Mr. Franklin, looking innocently at the stout chief, the exemplar of English elegance, who sat swagging from one side to the other of the carriage, his face as scarlet as his coat—swearing at every word; ignorant on every point off parade, except the merits of a bottle and the looks of a woman; not of high birth, yet absurdly proud of his no-ancestry; brave as a bull-dog; savage, lustful, prodigal, generous; gentle in soft moods; easy of love and laughter; dull of wit; utterly unread; believing his country the first in the world, and he as good a gentleman as any in it.''

Thackeray was not an historian (though he did impale the " Four Georges " on the spikes of his satire), yet this glimpse of Braddock and the "little postmaster" brings us nearer to these two worthies than pages of commonplace detail. In several instances the author has gotten away from fact, as when he applies to Franklin the diminutive adjective, but in spirit and general truth of perspective the description is admirable.

Those must have been attractive experiences of camp life for our philosopher. Thoroughly did he enjoy them, and none the less so, probably, because of the important part he played in the scene. Once, at the regimental mess, Colonel Dunbar waxed pathetic over the poverty of the subaltern officers, who could ill afford to purchase in so dear-priced a country the stores needful for their long march through the wilderness. The Postmaster-General was all sympathy, and the next morning he wrote home suggesting that the Assembly should make some appropriate presents to the young men. William Franklin, who was doubtless made much of by the subalterns, and knew their little tastes, drew up a list which his father enclosed in the letter, and in the course of time twenty parcels (each parcel placed on a horse which was intended as a present for one officer) arrived at camp. There were tongues, sugar, cheese, tea, coffee, and much else, not forgetting plenty of Madeira, always regarded as among the "necessities" in those wine-bibbing days when the officer who could not punish a bottle at dinner was looked upon as quite unfit for the service of his most Germanic of Majesties, George II. Franklin was back in Pennsylvania when the provisions reached the army, but he was the recipient of grateful letters, and was further honoured (?) by a request from Braddock to do what he could for the victualling of the forces in Virginia.   To assist in the latter work the Postmaster-General advanced, out of his own pocket, over £1000 sterling, and was fortunate in getting an order for almost the whole of that amount, just before the General's disastrous defeat. The balance due was to remain until the next account—but when the time for settling arrived, Braddock had gone to his own last account, and that was an end to the matter.

It is a tribute to Franklin's sagacity that, civilian though he was, he had given Braddock a piece of advice which, had it been taken, might have turned a disastrous campaign into triumphant victory.   One day the General, in airing before his visitor the plan of campaign, confidently remarked: " After taking Fort Duquesne I am to proceed to Niagara; and, having taken that, to Frontenac, if the season will allow time; and I suppose it will, for Duquesne can hardly detain me above three or four days; and then I see nothing that can obstruct my march to Niagara."

Franklin was not a military man, yet he saw very clearly that there were more difficulties in the way of the English troops than were dreamed of in the arrogant, know-it-all philosophy of Braddock. Having before revolved in his mind the long line the army must make in their march by a very narrow road to be cut for them through the woods and bushes, and recalling the defeat of fifteen hundred

French who had invaded the country of the Iroquois,
he had serious misgivings as to the outcome of the
campaign. And he replied politely to the glowing
prophecies of the General:

" To be sure, sir, if you arrive well before Duquesne, with these
fine troops, so well provided with artillery, that place not yet completely fortified, and as we hear with no very strong garrison, can
probably make but a short resistance. The only danger I apprehend
of obstruction to your march is from ambuscades of Indians, who, by
constant practice, are dexterous in laying and executing them ; and
the slender line, near four miles long, which your army must make,
may expose it to be attacked by surprise in its flanks, and to be cut
like a thread into several pieces, which, from their distance, cannot
come up in time to support each other."

The Englishman smiled good-naturedly at the
sublime ignorance displayed in such a speech. What
could the half-civilised Americans know of the great
art of warfare—that art which the mighty Duke of
Marlborough had raised to such a pinnacle of science? So Braddock answered, half contemptuously:
" These savages, may, indeed, be a formidable
enemy to your raw American militia, but upon the
King's regular and disciplined troops, sir, it is impossible they should make any impression." The
" little postmaster " was modestly " conscious of an
impropriety " in " disputing with a military man in
matters of his profession," and said no more. Little
did he then dream that after the passing of two dec-
ades the " raw American militia " would begin to
open the eyes of British officers who thought as did
the General.

Before the middle of July the bloody battle of the

Monongahela had been fought, and an ambuscade
of French and Indians, of which Braddock had been
so often warned, put an end to a thousand vain-
glorious hopes, and to many a life deserving of a
better death. How the English soldiers, marching
gaily accoutred as though on dress-parade, were
surprised by the enemy when within a short distance
of Fort Duquesne, and led into a veritable trap; how
they were thrown into fatal confusion by the galling
fire which came from the invisible savages planted
behind the trees; and how the action, if action it
could be called, ended in a disastrous rout—the
colonies rang with the appalling description for
many a day. What a scene of slaughter! Not the
regular warfare beloved by Braddock, but an insidious fire from an unseen foe. Officers tried to rally
their men, only to be shot down themselves, while
the General, now that he saw too late the fruits of
his obstinacy and criminal foolishness, stormed and
implored, riding from rank to rank, and trying to
bring order out of chaos.

" In a narrow road twelve feet wide, shut up on either side and
overpent by the primeval forest, were crowded together the panic-
stricken wretches, hastily loading and reloading, and blindly dis-
charging their guns in the air, as though they suspected their
mysterious murderers were sheltered in the boughs above their heads;
while all around, removed from sight, but making day hideous with
their war-hoops and savage cries, lay ensconced a host insatiable for
blood. . . . The regular soldiery, deprived of their immediate
commanders, and terrified at the incessant fall of their comrades,
could not be brought to the charge; while the provincials, better
skilled, sought in vain to cover themselves and to meet the foe upon
equal terms; for to the urgent entreaties of Washington and Sir
Peter Halket [Colonel of the Forty-fourth Regiment, killed in the

battle, with one of his sons] that the men might be permitted to leave the ranks and shelter themselves, the General turned a deaf ear. Wherever he saw a man skulking behind a tree, he flew at once to the spot, and, with curses on his cowardice and blows with the flat of his sword, drove him back into the open road." *

How like Braddock! A blunderer to the last. Nor would he retire from the forest-field until out of his fourteen hundred and sixty men, officers and privates, over four hundred were killed and as many more wounded! Then, " with a mien undaunted as in his proudest hour," he ordered the drums to sound the retreat. The surviving privates, who had behaved with amazing bravery throughout the battle, lost their self-control and fled ignominiously like a flock of sheep. The General, in the meantime, was shot through the lungs and fell from his horse, as his men dashed by him too intent upon their own safety to think of their commander. Braddock, overcome with a sense of his disgrace, wished to die upon the field, but Captain Orme and two American officers bore him tenderly away. He still continued to give his orders, and it was not until the remnant of his army reached the Great Meadows that he breathed his last—heart-broken but brave as of old. Only twice did he refer to the catastrophe, once saying to himself, " Who would have thought it ? " and then, a few minutes before he died, murmuring: " We shall better know how to deal with them another time."

The colonists were thrown into dismay by the rout of Braddock's forces, and visions of further aggres-

* *The History of An Expedition against Fort DuQuesne.*

sion from the French, and cruelty from the Indians, grew more terrible as the possible consequences of the defeat were discussed. Franklin was not surprised, and we can hear him saying to shocked Philadelphia citizens, as he wrote later in the *Autobiography*, that the General was " a brave man, and might probably have made a figure as a good officer in some European war. But he had too much self-confidence, too high an opinion of the validity of regular troops, and too mean a one of both Americans and Indians." The prophet had been vindicated, but both his patriotism and his personal interests prevented him from taking satisfaction in this fresh proof of his sagacity. The affair might, indeed, have proved the financial ruin of Franklin, for there were the waggons and horses which had been abandoned, and for the value of which he had given his personal bond to the owners.

" Their demands," he tells us, " gave me a great deal of trouble, my acquainting them that the money was ready in the paymaster's hands, but that orders for paying it must first be obtained from General Shirley, and my assuring them that I had applied to that general by letter ; but, he, being at a distance, an answer could not soon be received, and they must have patience, all this was not sufficient to satisfy and some began to sue me. General Shirley at length relieved me from this terrible situation by appointing commissioners to examine the claims and ordering payment. They amounted to near twenty thousand pound, which to pay would have ruined me."

But the possibility of succumbing to a series of lawsuits did not prevent the Postmaster-General from doing what he could to restore public confidence, and from advising that Colonel Dunbar, who

led the survivors of Braddock's once stalwart band,
should remain on the defensive until reinforced by
sufficient colonial troops to attempt the capture of
Fort Duquesne. Governor Morris, who was still
fighting with the Assembly of Pennsylvania over
that eternal question of taxing or non-taxing the
Penn estates, agreed with this idea and warmly opposed Dunbar's intention of striking his colours and
marching to Philadelphia. But the ungallant Colonel apparently had seen enough of war; he indulged
in many excuses, and reached the Quaker City toward the end of August. He encamped with his
men on Society Hill, where they remained until
October 1st, and then left for New York and Albany,
deeply grateful for their kindly treatment at the
hands of the inhabitants. Then it was that Franklin wrote to a friend:

"Many more people love me now than ever did before; for, since
I saw you, I have been enabled to do some general services to the
country and to the army, for which both have thanked and praised
me, and say they love me. They say so as you used to do; and if I
were to ask any favours of them, they would, perhaps, as readily refuse
me; so that I find little real advantage in being beloved, but it
pleases my humour."

Governor Morris was not slow to intimate that the
defeat of Braddock was due, in some part, to the
failure of the Pennsylvania legislators to make
the needful provision for the aid of the unfortunate
General. It is recorded that when he gave out the
news of the defeat the Governor was insulted on
the street by indignant and unbelieving citizens who
were to find, only too soon, that he spoke the truth.

The Assembly now offered to appropriate for the King's use the sum of £50,000, but the same old contention between the interests of the selfish Penns and the interests of the colony rendered the legislation abortive. The Assembly stipulated that in the securing of the money all estates, real and personal, were to be taxed, "those of the proprietaries *not* excepted." The Governor, however, insisted that for the word *not* that of *only* should be used, and thereby put a stop to the intended liberality of the Assembly, which refused to yield one jot to the absentee proprietors. "Those who would give up essential liberty," wrote Franklin, bravely and defiantly, "for the sake of a little temporary safety, deserve neither liberty nor safety." He had ever been opposed to the exactions of the Penns, and he did much to keep his companions up to the necessary pitch of firmness. The contest wore on, and with the autumn came terrible Indian disturbances in the western part of the province—nay, nearer home than that—with the horrors of scalping, and the stealing of children. Watson records that the frontiersmen, fearing that the pacific policy of the Quakers had too much influence upon the Assembly, and desiring that the latter should take some measures for their protection, adopted, "to move them to a livelier emotion," a ghastly expedient. It was nothing less than to send on to Philadelphia the bodies of a family murdered by the Indians. "These actually reached Philadelphia in the winter, like frozen venison from their mountains — were paraded through our city, and finally set down be-

fore the legislative hall.'' When the multitude and
their uncanny exhibit reached the State House, the
headquarters of the Assembly, perhaps Franklin
calmly looked out of window at the throng, and
foresaw that help was at hand. The province must
be defended—on that he was resolved—and he had
taken care that the parsimony of the proprietaries and
the absurdity of their demands should be well venti-
lated in England. It was a wise move. The Penns
were frightened into parting with a little of their
money, and sent an order to their Receiver-General
in Pennsylvania to add £5000 to whatever sum
might be given by the Assembly for the defence of
the province.* That body appropriated £60,000,
and by way of proclaiming a temporary truce with
the proprietaries waived (under protest, however)
the immediate question of taxing their estates.

Franklin was always reasonable; he resented as
much as ever the claims of the proprietaries, but
was now ready to leave the question in abeyance
until measures had been taken to protect the province. He was himself appointed one of the commissioners for expending the money, and worked with
all his energy toward the formation of a militia
force. For the latter purpose it was necessary to
have the sanction of the Assembly, and it is at this
point that the statesmanship of the man comes again
to the fore. The Quaker influence in the legislature
was still important, and the passage of a militia bill
was not likely to meet with favour in non-resistance

* With characteristic meanness, however, the Penns provided that
this money was to be obtained from arrears of quit-rents.

circles. So he adroitly drafted a measure which provided for the organisation of volunteer companies of defenders, but expressly stipulated that nothing in the act should have any power to affect in the least " those of the inhabitants of the province who are conscientiously scrupulous of bearing arms, either in their liberties, persons, or estates." Polite mention was made in the preamble of " the people called Quakers, who, though they do not, as the world is now circumstanced, condemn the use of arms in others, yet are principled against bearing arms themselves." It was pointed out that " to make any law to compel them thereto against their consciences, would be not only to violate a fundamental in our constitution, and be a direct breach of our charter of privileges, but would also in effect be to commence persecution." The bill was passed without great difficulty, owing to the Chesterfieldian courtesy which it exhibited toward the opposition, and it is probable that many a Quaker slept more soundly thereafter because of its adoption. It was all very well to refuse to bear arms, but the peace theory—an admirable theory in itself, yet far in advance of the times—could not keep away the tomahawk. The community of Friends, being but human, realised as vividly as did the Episcopalians, or anyone else, the danger from the West.

Not content with helping in other directions, the editor of the *Gazette* wrote a " Dialogue between X, Y, and Z, Concerning the Present State of Affairs in Pennsylvania," wherein the objections against a militia were answered and disposed of by means of

the conversation between the aforesaid Messrs. X,
Y, and Z. Mr. X championed the Assembly bill,
and, after naming its virtues, concluded by grand-
iloquently crying to Messrs. Y and Z:

" O my friends, let us on this occasion cast from us all these little
party views, and consider ourselves as Englishmen and Pennsylvanians. Let us think only of the service of our King, the honour and
safety of our country, and vengeance on its murdering enemies. If
good be done, what imports it by whom it is done ? The glory of
serving and saving others is superior to the advantage of being served
or secured. Let us resolutely and generously unite in our country's
cause, in which to die is the sweetest of all deaths, and may the God
of armies bless our honest endeavours."

There is in this apostrophe a fervour, a convincing
power, and a lofty patriotism difficult to excel. No
wonder that the " Dialogue " had " great effect." *

Now the view shifts as we watch the theatre of
Franklin's activities. He has posed as a legislator,
as a financier, and as a writer, in this work of organising public defence, and next, *mirabile dictu*, he is
to play the *soldier*, and play him well. Colonel
Franklin! The title has an odd sound, but capitally
was it worn by one to whom might be given the
degree of master—not jack—of many trades.

" While the several companies in the city and country were forming, and learning their exercise," he writes, " the Governor [Morris]
prevailed with me to take charge of our Northwestern frontier, which
was infested by the enemy, and provide for the defence of the inhabitants by raising troops and building a line of forts. I undertook this
military business, tho' I did not conceive myself well qualified for it.
He gave me a commission with full powers, and a parcel of blank
commissions for officers, to be given to whom I thought fit."

* Published in the *Gazette* of December 18, 1755.

8

It was time that something was done.   The Moravian village of Gnadenhutten, Northampton County,
had been destroyed by the Indians, who killed the
inhabitants, and the dwellers in that whole section
of the country were in terror.   The new warrior was
not slow in raising men, of whom he secured over
five hundred, nor did he forget to appoint his son
an *aide-de-camp*.   Then they all set out right valiantly to march to Bethlehem, the Moravian strong-
hold, where they arrived after a cold, unpleasant
time of it, but without mishap.   Franklin found the
town in a good condition of defence, for the massacre
at Gnadenhutten had stirred the people to a keen
sense of danger.   The principal buildings were fortified by a stockade; arms and ammunition had been
brought from New York; there were paving-stones
in the houses, for use upon the heads of invading
Indians ; the Moravian brethren had organised a
guard of sentinels.

" It was the beginning of January," says our Colonel, " when we
set out upon this business of building forts.   I sent one detachment
toward the Minisink, with instructions to erect one for the security
of that upper part of the country, and another to the lower part, with
similar instructions ; and I concluded to go myself with the rest of
my force to Gnadenhut, where a fort was thought more immediately
necessary.   The Moravians procured me five waggons for our tools,
stores, baggage, etc.   Just before we left Bethlehem, eleven farmers,
who had been driven from their plantations by the Indians, came to
me requesting a supply of firearms, that they might go back and fetch
off their cattle.   I gave them each a gun with suitable ammunition.
We had not marched many miles before it began to rain, and it continued raining all day ; there were no habitations on the road, to
shelter us, till we arrived near night at the house of a German, where,
and in his barn, we were all huddled together, as wet as water could

make us. It was well we were not attacked in our march, for our arms were of the most ordinary sort, and our men could not keep their gun-locks dry. The Indians are dextrous in contrivances for that purpose, which we had not. They met that day the eleven poor farmers above-mentioned, and killed ten of them. The one who escaped informed, that his and his companions' guns would not go off, the priming being wet with the rain."

This was all dangerous enough, and bodily dis-agreeable, but the commander and his men never flinched. Upon their arrival at the desolate Gnad-enhutten, huts were made out of boards procured from a neighbouring saw-mill; the dead, who " had been half-interred by the country people," were buried more effectually, and a fort of palisades, cut from pine trees, was erected in a week of working days. There were intermediate days when it rained so hard that the volunteers could not do anything. " On the days they worked they were good-natured and cheerful, and, with the consciousness of having done a good day's work, they spent the evening jollily; but on our idle days they were mutinous and quarrelsome, finding fault with their pork, the bread, etc., and in continual ill-humour "—a circum-stance which reminded the Colonel of the sea-captain " whose rule it was to keep his men constantly at work; and, when his mate once told him that they had done everything, and there was nothing further to employ them about, ' Oh,' says he, ' make them scour the anchor.' "

Franklin's presence was now desired at Philadel-phia, where the Assembly was about to meet, with every prospect of further trouble from Governor Morris. As the three frontier forts were finished, and as a New England officer, Colonel Clapham, was willing to take command of Fort Allen, the soldier-philosopher-printer returned home, after commissioning Clapham before the garrison, and introducing him as one who was much more fit than himself for the colonelcy.

The martial spirit was in full swing when Franklin once again saw his adopted city. A large regiment played at soldiering, and no sooner had he put in an appearance than he was asked to be its colonel. This time he accepted, and could do so with a clear conscience, for he had shown the true military instinct upon that risky little journey to Northampton County. No battle had been fought, but there had been work to do, and the Colonel had done it admirably.* What more appropriate, therefore, than to command the Philadelphia volunteers?

"I forget how many companies we had," he says, "but we paraded about twelve hundred well-looking men, with a company of artillery who had been furnished with six brass field-pieces, which they had become so expert in the use of as to fire twelve times in a minute. The first time I reviewed my regiment they accompanied me to my house and would salute me with some rounds fired before my door, which shook down and broke several glasses of my electrical apparatus. And my new honour proved not much less brittle; for all our commissions were soon after broken by a repeal of the law in England."

An officer with an electrical machine—that tells the tale of Franklin's versatility. The tastes of the *savant* set off by the flashing of arms! What won-

* Gnadenhutten, sad to relate, was again destroyed by the Indians in the following November, 1756.

der that he found himself the most popular man in
town, or that he was even asked to attempt the
capturing of Fort Duquesne ?   Many a citizen
would have lost his head as a result of this adulation, and then, by launching forth still further into
the uncertain sea of war, might have lost likewise
his reputation, and his life.   The " little postmaster "
was not of these; he could procure waggons for
an army, give valuable advice to a stubborn general,
build forts, and command a local regiment, but, as
he shrewdly knew, it did not follow that he could
cope with the French in the wilderness.   As it was,
the glamour of militia life, the parade, the fuss and
feathers, must have wearied him a bit, and there
was one occasion when, as he confesses, it decidedly
annoyed him.

He was about to set out for Virginia, on a postal
inspection, and had just mounted his horse, when
up to the house rode the officers of the regiment,
between thirty and forty handsomely uniformed
warriors.   They had arranged to escort their colonel
out of town.   The recipient of this honour was surprised, and a " good deal chagrined " at their
appearance, hating to be put in so spectacular a
position, but there was nothing to be done but
smile and bear it all politely.   More trials were in
store for the modest man.   No sooner had the cavalcade begun to move than the officers drew their
swords and kept them drawn until they had seen
their beloved leader safely out of the city.   Such an
exhibition of ceremony was absurdly pretentious for
provincial Philadelphia, however matter-of-fact it

might appear now, and Franklin must have had hard work to keep his temper. No one, even though he be a philosopher, likes to be made ridiculous.

Of course the incident was commented upon, and, of course, an officious correspondent wrote a full account of it to Thomas Penn, doubtless exaggerating the scene and representing the colonel so unwillingly honoured in the light of a would-be dictator. Whereat Mr. Penn became angry, declaring that neither he, when he visited the province, nor any of his governors had been the recipient of such a military escort—an escort, according to him, only due to princes of the blood royal. Libelled Franklin! He was the last man on earth to exact attentions due a royal duke, for, although he liked the praise and consideration of his fellow-men, he never cared for flummery or ostentation. Nay, the proprietary went so far as to insinuate that the Postmaster-General of the colonies wished to take upon himself the reigns of provincial government, and he even tried, though unsuccessfully, to deprive him of his office. Yet no amount of abuse could dim the lustre of Benjamin Franklin's achievements. He had nobly impersonated his several characters in the drama of colonial life, and not a hundred Thomas Penns could stop his onward progress. What mattered it, after all, if the officers drew their swords and gave to their commander a stately exit? No one in all the provinces deserved it more.

THOMAS PENN.

FROM A PAINTING OWNED BY THE HISTORICAL SOCIETY OF PENNSYLVANIA, AND COPIED BY
M. I. NAYLOR FROM THE PORTRAIT IN POSSESSION OF MAJOR DUGALD STUART.

CHAPTER V

A BATTLE WITH THE PENNS

1756–1762

RANKLIN might soon relinquish his colonelcy, and all the pomps and trappings, such as they were, of a provincial militia, yet none the less was he to shine as an intrepid fighter who would win a glorious victory. This time the warfare would be on constitutional lines, with Richard and Thomas Penn, the proprietaries of Pennsylvania, as the powerful enemy, and with the inevitable question of taxation as the bone of contention. For some years the sordid controversy had agitated the province, frequently paralysing needed legislation, and reaching such a stage that its continuance threatened nothing less than ruin to the colony. While the Assembly was disputing the arrogant assumption of the Penns, who wished practically to make of themselves feudal lords, and while the subservient governors of the latter were trying to uphold the pretension, the public business dragged, and the poor Pennsylvanians stood more and more in danger of Indian invasion and destruction. The situation, which is interesting as we look back at it, in showing the constantly growing spirit of American defiance to unjust exaction, must have been one of the most solid discomfort.

So irksome, indeed, did the state of affairs become to Governor Morris that in 1756 he resigned his office. One of the closing orders of his administration was to forbid Colonel Franklin's regiment from indulging in an artillery salute; whereupon the indignant officers (we know not whether the commander was amongst them) repaired to a tavern, where they drank down their disappointment right royally to the significant sentiment, " The speedy arrival of a new Governor." When the new Governor did arrive, in the person of Captain William Denny, great was the rejoicing, and gallantly was he welcomed by the learned Colonel and his cohort. The regiment was drawn up on Second Street to salute him; there were bonfires, firing of cannon, and ringing of bells. The following day the city authorities gave a handsome dinner in his honour, at which, we need hardly say, the beloved Colonel had an important seat. More than this, the Governor presented to Franklin, before the assembled company, the Copley gold medal awarded him for his scientific researches by the Royal Society, and the new incumbent was pleased to accompany the gift with some remarks highly flattering to the character and attainments of the Postmaster-General of the colonies.

The Captain was, in fine, trying his hand at di-

plomacy; he knew that the recipient of the Copley
medal happened to be not only a *savant* but likewise
the most powerful citizen of Pennsylvania, and he
determined to propitiate him to the utmost.   Perhaps, too, he had heard of the great man's thrifti-
ness, and thought to win him over to the side of the
proprietaries by delicately veiled bribery.   Certain
it is that the Governor watched his chance, and
when the solids of the dinner had been disposed of,
and the guests were settling down to the guzzling
of wine—the thing about the entertainment which
some of them loved the most feelingly—Denny led
the intended victim into an adjoining room.   Here
he ingenuously informed Franklin that he had been
advised by his friends in England to cultivate a
friendship with him " as one who was capable of
giving him the best advice," and of " contributing
most effectually to the making his administration
easy," and the speaker adroitly expressed his readiness to render his new friend every service that might
be in his power.   We can fancy Denny standing
there, suave, conciliatory, watchful of the effect of
his words, while Franklin, with those calm, unread-
able eyes of his, gazes peacefully as a child at the
telltale face of the Governor, who, thinking himself
a paragon of depth, must have been fathomed in a
moment by his more plainly dressed companion.

" He said much to me, also," relates the latter, in the closing
pages of the too quickly ended *Autobiography*, " of the proprietor's *
good disposition towards the province, and of the advantage it might

* Thomas Penn, rather than the other proprietor, Richard, is here
meant.

be to us all, and to me in particular, if the opposition that had been so long continued to his measures was dropt, and harmony restored between him and the people ; in effecting which, it was thought no one could be more serviceable than myself ; and I might depend on adequate acknowledgments and recompenses, etc."

The diners had been quick to perceive the retirement of the Governor and the Colonel, and doubtless there were many whisperings on the subject, with a thousand predictions as to the outcome of so extraordinary an interview. As the guests grew more mellow they became generous, and sent in to the absentees a decanter of choice Madeira, to add life to their deliberations. Denny attacked the gift without delay, and the more wine he drank the larger became his promises and the more fervid his protestations of friendship. Franklin, on the other hand, appears to have left his Excellency free to wrestle with the decanter, and to have kept himself cool and clear-headed. Although he could sip his Madeira as well as the next man, he chose the occasions, and this was not one of them. The Governor had to be answered; his hints at recompense must be repulsed. So the Philadelphian replied, very politely but firmly, that his circumstances, thanks to God, were such as to make proprietary favours unnecessary to him, and that he could not possibly accept of any; that, however, he had no personal enmity against the proprietors, and that, whenever the public measures they proposed should appear to be for the good of the people, " no one should espouse and forward them more zealously " than himself. He was much obliged for the regard

of the Governor, who might rely on his doing all in
his power to make the new administration as easy as
possible, but it was to be hoped that his Excellency
" had not brought with him the same unfortunate
instruction his predecessor had been hampered
with." Whereby the Governor was given to understand that if he came to Pennsylvania to champion
the disputed claims of the proprietary, the fight was
still on.

Of course it was part of Denny's official duty to
insist on these very claims, and it was not long,
therefore, before he became engaged in the customary tilts with the Assembly. His position was un-
enviable in the extreme.

" If he refused to obey the proprietary instructions, he would be
liable to prosecution, while if he refused to obey the mandates of the
Assembly, his salary would be withheld. Proprietary governors thus
had to be indigent or fond of controversy. In fact it had been a
practice of the Assembly to send to the governor favourite measures
for his approbation, and at the same time attach to the bill a resolution appropriating his salary. When the governor refused assent his
salary was of course withheld." *

So the fight began again merrily, and Franklin,
carrying a pen dipped in gall rather than a colonel's
sword, could be seen in the front of the fray. His
personal relations were cordial with Denny, exactly
as they had been with Morris, and many was the conversation which the two men, enemies politically,
had on polite literature and kindred topics. From
the new Governor was it that the Philadelphian

* *History of Proprietary Government in Pennsylvania*, by William
Robert Shepherd, Ph.D.

learned of the success of his whilom friend, James
Ralph, who had fared better in prose than in poeti-
cal writing, and who had secured a pension for services rendered a grateful government.

Finally a crisis came in the civic feud.   Governor
Denny refused to sign a bill granting £60,000 for
the King's use, from an excise tax upon wine and
other spirits.   Some £10,000 of the money was to
be subject to the orders of the Earl of Loudoun,
who had been appointed to the command of the
British forces in North America.   Lord Loudoun
had come to America for the purpose of organising
a permanent army (to carry out what was practically
a plan to place the colonies under military rule), and
one of the purposes of the proposed Assembly
measure was to aid him in properly defending the
province from the still-threatening Indians.   The
bill did not bring up the dangerous point of taxing
the Penn estates, yet, for all that, Denny withheld
assent on the ground that an approval would be
contrary to his " instructions."   This was the last
straw.   The Assembly now resolved to send over to
the home government a remonstrance setting forth
the strained, not to say dangerous, state of affairs,
and the " pernicious consequences to the British interest," and to the inhabitants of Pennsylvania, " if,
contrary to their charters and laws, they were to be
governed by proprietary instructions "—a proceeding to which the legislature was the more moved
from the threat of the Governor to submit the points
of this interminable controversy to the King.

Who so well qualified to carry over the remon-

strance as the subtle yet determined Franklin ?
His name at once suggested itself, and he was asked
to take the uncomfortable voyage to England.   Venerable Isaac Norris, Speaker of the Assembly, was
asked likewise to assist in the mission, but age and
infirmity made him averse to the journey—no child's
play for an old man—and in the end Franklin, after
trying unsuccessfully to induce Norris to go alone,
consented to undertake the patriotic business.   He
was ready to go whenever the Assembly should think
fit to require his service, he said, and probably he
was not half sorry at the opportunity.   Why should
he have been ?

As the unexpected so often happened in the life
of the newly-commissioned agent for the Assembly,
it seems quite natural that interesting things should
develop before he set sail.

" I had agreed with Captain Morris, of the paquet at New York,
for my passage, and my stores were put on board, when Lord Loudoun arrived at Philadelphia, expressly, as he told me, to endeavour
an accommodation between the Governor and Assembly, that his
Majesty's service might not be obstructed by their dissensions.   Accordingly, he desired the Governor and myself to meet him, that he
might hear what was to be said on both sides.   We met and discussed
the business.   In behalf of the Assembly, I urged all the various
arguments that may be found in the public papers of that time, which
were of my writing, and are printed with the minutes of the Assembly ; and the Governor pleaded his instructions ; the bond he had
given to observe them, and his ruin if he disobeyed, yet seemed not
unwilling to hazard himself if Lord Loudoun would advise it.   This
his lordship did not chuse to do, though I once thought I had nearly
prevailed with him to do it ; but finally he rather chose to urge the
compliance of the Assembly ; and he entreated me to use my endeavours with them for that purpose, declaring that he would spare none
of the King's troops for the defence of our frontiers, and that, if we

did not continue to provide for that defence ourselves, they must
remain exposed to the enemy."

It has been complained of Franklin that he was a
"trimmer." He was nothing so craven, but he
knew that by sometimes giving way, in part, to the
exigencies of the moment the concession could be
eventually repaired, and a substantial victory procured. Thus did he reason now, and he induced
the Assembly to draw up another supply bill. This
bill was conformable to the Governor's instructions,
but asserted strenuously that no rights were relin-
quished in the compromise, the exercise of them
being only suspended "through force." Whereupon Captain Denny signed the new measure, and
the noble Earl (who doubtless looked upon Americans as a lot of troublesome, uncouth, quarrelsome
bantams) returned his profuse thanks to Franklin
and took unto himself all the credit for the action
of the legislature. Then the real mediator bethought
him of his packet—and lo! it had sailed away with
all his sea-stores.

There was no remedy but to journey to New
York, there to wait for the departure of the next
vessel. This Franklin accordingly did, early in
April, 1757, in company with his son, who was
to assist him in England. But he was destined to
linger some weary weeks before he could get away
from port. There were packets in the harbour when
father and son reached New York; one of them, it was
reported, would sail in a short time. A "short time"
seemed too vague a date for the precise-minded
Postmaster-General, and he made haste to inquire

of Lord Loudoun (who had returned from Philadelphia before him, and who always arranged the time
of sailing), on exactly what day the packet was to
leave. " I have given out," replied his lordship,
" that she is to sail on Saturday next ; but I may
let you know, *entre nous*, that if you are there by
Monday morning, you will be in time, but do not
delay longer." Imagine the clearance of modern
vessels being regulated in such a *dolce far niente*
fashion. But worse remains to be chronicled. It
was toward the end of June before the impatient
Franklin could leave New York, for the captains of
the packets had orders to wait for Loudoun's letters,
" which were always to be ready to-morrow." What
mattered it if anxious passengers walked the decks
until their feet were sore, and if commerce suffered ?
My lord's letters were never ready, and until they
were, the ships were to remain at anchorage. No
wonder that petty tyrannies like these tended to
disturb the affectionate relations between America
and the mother country.

Very polite was the General of the forces to Franklin, but those letters remained unpenned.

" Going myself one morning to pay my respects," writes the weary
waiter, " I found in his antechamber one Innis, a messenger of
Philadelphia, who had come from thence express with a paquet from
Governor Denny for the General. He delivered to me some letters
from my friends there, which occasioned my enquiring when he was
to return, and where he lodged, that I might send some letters by
him. He told me he was ordered to call to-morrow at nine for
the General's answer to the Governor, and should set off immediately.
I put my letters into his hands the same day. A fortnight after I
met him again in the same place. ' So, you are soon returned,

Innis?' 'Returned! no, I am not gone yet.' 'How so?' 'I have called here by order every morning these two weeks past for his lordship's letter and it is not yet ready.' 'Is it possible, when he is so great a writer? for I see him constantly at his escritoire.' 'Yes,' says Innis, 'but he is like St. George on the signs, *always on horseback and never rides on.*'"

At last the General determined to ride on, and not to stop until he had won a mighty victory against the French. He had planned an expedition to attack Louisburg, and so set sail, with a considerable fleet, on the 20th of June, intending to make a rendezvous at Halifax. The worst of the matter, so far as it concerned the would-be transatlantic travellers, was that the packets were ordered to proceed with the fleet until such time as Lord Loudoun had prepared those tardy letters. The whole history of British rule in the American colonies offers no more exasperating exhibition of stupid selfishness. The passengers, too, were afraid that the ships might slip away at any moment, and for six weeks they remained at Sandy Hook, not daring, as a rule, to go ashore, and walking up and down the decks wondering when the moment of deliverance would arrive. If Franklin kept his temper, as he seems to have done, his was indeed an angelic calmness. When the fleet, with the General and his army on board, actually got off, the unfortunate packets followed obediently in the wake of his Excellency.

"We were out five days before we got a letter with leave to part, and then our ship quitted the fleet and steered for England. The other two packets he still detained, carried them with him to Halifax, where he stayed some time to exercise the men in sham attacks upon sham forts, then altered his mind as to besieging Louisburg, and returned to New York, with all his troops, together with the two paquets above mentioned, and all their passengers!"

It is said that Lord Loudoun decided to abandon the attack on Louisburg upon hearing that there was one more ship in the French fleet than in his own. A fine man to attempt the crushing of French power in America! When Pitt became Prime Minister of England, he was shrewd enough to recall an incompetent soldier from whom he could never get any satisfactory information as to military operations.

The action, or rather the non-action, of Lord Loudoun regarding Franklin's claim for money due on provisions supplied Braddock did not tend to increase the admiration of the Postmaster-General. The accounts for this transaction were presented, examined, and found to be correct, and his lordship promised to issue the necessary order on the paymaster for their settlement. Franklin, who was not likely to forget the matter, called often, but was as often put off with excuses, until the General finally said he had, on better consideration, concluded " not to mix his accounts with those of his predecessors." " When in England," he cheerfully told the creditor, " you have only to exhibit your accounts at the Treasury, and you will be paid immediately." This was truly exasperating, particularly as Franklin had been put to much extra expense by his undesired stay at New York, and he was not slow to intimate to the noble lord the injustice of the latter's decision. He also emphasised the fact that he had charged no commission for advancing the money, whereat Lou-

9

doun exclaimed, scoffingly: " You must not think of persuading us that you are no gainer; we understand better those affairs, and know that everyone concerned in supplying the army finds means, in the doing it, to fill his own pockets." Franklin stoutly denied that he had made a farthing out of the provisions, but His Excellency (who doubtless smuggled his own little percentage out of contractors, and who would have made an ideal political " boss " had he lived to-day) remained unconvinced. And the debt ? It continued to be a debt.

There was always the element of adventure in the career of our hero, nor did it fail him when he crossed the ocean this second time. The ship was chased by privateers, whom she outsailed, and when just at her journey's end, off Falmouth, narrowly escaped destruction. The captain thought that, by making a good run in the night, Falmouth harbour might be reached the next morning.

" We had a watchman placed in the bow to whom they often called, ' *Look well out before there*,' and he as often answered, ' *Ay, ay*,' but perhaps had his eyes shut, and was half-asleep at the time, they sometimes answering, as is said, mechanically ; for he did not see a light just before us, which had been hid by the studding-sails from the man at the helm, and from the rest of the watch, but by an accidental yaw of the ship was discovered, and occasioned a great alarm, we being very near it, the light appearing to me as big as a cart-wheel. It was midnight, and our captain fast asleep ; but Captain Kennedy, jumping upon deck, and seeing the danger, ordered the ship to wear round, all sails standing—an operation dangerous to the masts, but it carried us clear, and we escaped shipwreck, for we were running right upon the rocks on which the light-house was erected."

It was in the latter part of July, 1757, that Frank-

lin and his son reached London.   After a brief stay
with the learned Peter Collinson, at whose house he
met many distinguished men, who called to pay
their *devoirs* to the scientist from the New World,
he obtained comfortable lodgings near the Strand,
set up a carriage, that he might the better support
his dignity as agent for Pennsylvania, and then proceeded to the all-important business of battling with
the Penns.   Old times, however, were not forgotten
in the stress of politics; he was glad to see James
Ralph once again, and found nothing more pleasantly stimulating to his memory than a visit to
Watts's printing-house near Lincoln's Inn Fields,
where he had worked during part of his first London
experience.   The theatrical feature of the return to
the printing-house was the discovery there of his old
press, and his drinking " Success to Printing," in a
gallon of beer shared with two journeymen.   Well
might he toast a trade which had been of such aid
to him, and well, too, might he rejoice at the contrast between the Benjamin of 1757 and the Ben of
the past.

It was suggested to Franklin, by one of his friends
(Dr. Fothergill), that he should defer putting the
complaints of the Pennsylvania legislature before
the Government until a personal interview should be
had with the proprietaries, " who might possibly be
induced by the interposition and persuasion of some
private friends to accommodate matters amicably."
In the meantime Lord Granville, President of the
Council, sent for the agent, received him with great
civility, questioned him as to the state of affairs in

America, and finally burst out with this British assertion:

" You Americans, sir, have wrong ideas of the nature of your constitution ; you contend that the King's instructions to his governors are not laws, and think yourselves at liberty to regard or disregard them at your discretion. But those instructions are not like the pocket instructions given to a minister going abroad, for regulating his conduct in some trifling point of ceremony. They are first drawn up by judges learned in the laws ; they are then considered, debated, and perhaps amended in Council, after which they are signed by the King. They are then, so far as they relate to you, the law of the land, for the King is the *Legislator of the Colonies*."

In other words, Granville would treat the colonies as he might some barbaric, conquered provinces unfit to legislate for themselves. 'T was John Bull in his most short-sighted, least prepossessing mood.

If Franklin felt anger in his heart he was too wise to show any heat; he replied politely, but strongly, and to the purpose.* This idea of government by instruction, he told his lordship, was new doctrine. He had always understood from the charters of the colonies that the laws were to be made by the Assemblies, " to be presented, indeed, to the King for his royal assent, but that being once given the King could not repeal or alter them." And " as the Assemblies could not make permanent laws without his assent, so neither could he make a law for them without theirs." Granville assured Franklin that he was totally mistaken in such a theory, but the American remained firm in his conviction, and felt so uneasy at his lordship's views that he went

* See the brief narrative supplementary to the *Autobiography*, written during the last year of Franklin's life.

home to his lodgings and wrote down the whole conversation. If the principle that the King was the legislator of the colonies should be endorsed at court, what a series of misfortunes must be in store for the provinces!

Then came the meeting with the two proprietors at the house of Thomas Penn, in Spring Garden. The feelings of the brothers as they faced their enemy, without whose opposition they might have found life the pleasanter and Pennsylvanians the more submissive, may be understood by the least imaginative reader. The agent was determined to gain his point, while the Penns, on their side, were equally determined to retain their powers intact and to budge not an inch from the feudal platform of rights upon which they stood. On the surface, however, all was peaceful, with a hypocritical air, on the part of the proprietors, of being willing to do whatever was just in the momentous matter. "The conversation at first consisted of mutual declarations of disposition to reasonable accommodations," reports Franklin, "but I suppose each party had its own ideas of what should be meant by *reasonable*."

When the real questions at issue came to be discussed the veneer of politeness vanished from the features of the Penns; they grew obstinate and arrogant.

"The proprietaries justified their conduct as well as they could and I the Assembly's. We now appeared very wide, and so far from each other in our opinions as to discourage all hope of agreement. However, it was concluded that I should give them the heads of our complaints in writing, and they promised then to consider them.'

The " heads of complaint " which the agent drew up set forth that the Assembly of Pennsylvania, having the right to make laws under its charter, was practically deprived of that power by the " instructions " of the proprietaries; that the Assembly, having the right to raise or withhold supplies, had that right interfered with by the self-same " instructions "; that the proprietary estates should be taxed like other estates in the province; and that these several injustices should be remedied by the proprietors aforesaid. It was waste of time to make out this complaint; the Penns had no intention of heeding it; their one idea was to gain time, shilly-shally, and so end by doing nothing. Thus they put the paper into the hands of their solicitor, Ferdinand John Paris, who managed all their law business, and who wrote the messages, pacific or otherwise, which they were wont to send to the Assembly.

"He was a proud, angry man, and as I had occasionally in the answers of the Assembly treated his papers with some severity, they being really weak in point of argument and haughty in expression, he had conceived a mortal enmity to me, which discovering itself wherever we met, I declined the proprietary's proposal that he and I should discuss the heads of complaint between our two selves [*i. e.*, between Paris and Franklin] and refused treating with anyone but them. They then by his advice put the paper into the hands of the Attorney and Solicitor-General for their opinion and counsel upon it, where it lay unanswered a year wanting eight days, during which time I made frequent demands of an answer from the proprietaries, but without obtaining any other than that they had not yet received the opinion of the Attorney and Solicitor-General. What it was when they did receive it I never learnt, for they did not communicate it to me, but sent a long message to the Assembly drawn and signed by Paris, reciting my paper, complaining of its want of formality, as

a rudeness on my part, and giving a flimsy justification of their conduct, adding that they should be willing to accommodate matters if
the Assembly would send out *some person of candour* to treat with
them for that purpose, intimating thereby that I was not such."

The offender concluded that the alleged rudeness
was, probably, his failure to address the Penns as
" True and Absolute Proprietaries of the Province
of Pennsylvania."

But Franklin has taken us on too rapidly in his
little narrative, and has forgotten to tell us that after
his first skirmish with the two landlords he sank
down with an illness which lasted eight long, weary
weeks.   He describes his colds and fever, however,
in a letter to Mrs. Franklin, and relates how the
doctor cupped him on the back of the head, and
dosed him with so much bark that he " began to
abhor it."   Then came health again, and with it the
determination to fight the Penns to the bitter end.
He tried to obtain an audience with Mr. Pitt, now
Prime Minister, but failed; he began, with his son,
to arrange an " Historical Review " of the long-
standing contest between the governors and the Assembly of Pennsylvania; and he bided his time.
His fame in the magic field of electricity made for
him hosts of friends in England, and as he was no
lover of solitude he was quick to seize the chances
of social relaxation which came, as it were, to his
unpretentious door.   His pleasures were many and
innocent.   He put up an electrical machine at his
lodgings, he dined with the learned, dabbled in
music, heard Handel play, delighted in the acting
of Garrick, studied, wrote, and visited Cambridge

University, where he was made much of by the Chancellor and the lesser dignitaries. A little later he would receive a degree from the University of St. Andrew,* and then Dr. Franklin would pass a few pleasant weeks in Scotland. His was, indeed, one of those happy spirits wherein great capacity for work was blended with an equal capacity for enjoyment. Furthermore, he had the faculty of doing the work and procuring the enjoyment almost at the same moment.

While Franklin was keeping those twinkling eyes of his upon the proprietaries, events unexpectedly favourable to his cause were happening in Pennsylvania. Chief among them was the consent of the now thoroughly tired-out and exasperated Governor Denny to a bill taxing the Penn estates. He was acting in radical defiance of those "instructions," but the man was only human; the warfare carried on by the Assembly had become more bitter; his salary was long in arrears, and his patience, never remarkable in quantity, had become exhausted. When the Penns heard of this surrender they determined to dismiss Denny from his post, and resolved to keep their decision secret until a successor was appointed.† The agent from Pennsylvania was, however, entirely too astute a diplomat to miss so important a piece of news, and no sooner had he learned of the proprietors' intention than he wrote

---

* Before he left England Franklin received the degree of Doctor of Laws from the Universities of Oxford and Edinburgh.

† James Hamilton, who had once before been governor of the province, finally succeeded Denny.

of it to his wife, with a gentle hint that she might
spread the report far and wide.

The action of Governor Denny changed the battle-
ground of the Assembly-Penn contest, while it added
a hundred-fold to the bitterness of the strife.   Personal appeals to the proprietaries were now of no
use; the controversy was to be brought before the
Privy Council, which august body was to decide
whether or not the bill signed by Denny and objected to by his masters should be recommended for
the royal sanction.   This measure granted to his
Majesty the sum of £100,000, and provided for
striking the same in bills of credit, etc., " by a tax
on *all* estates, real and personal."   It goes without
the saying that the Penn brothers, who only loved
Pennsylvania for the money they could make out of
her, looked with jaundiced eyes upon so heretical a
piece of legislation.   They were wise enough to see
the necessity of making of the bill a test case, and
accordingly two lawyers were engaged to represent
them before the Privy Council.   Franklin was not
to be outdone in point of legal precautions; he, too,
employed counsel.   By this time the year 1760 had
more than begun.

Franklin tells the story of the struggle in a few
words, leaving out many of the details and ignoring
the reports of the Lords of Committee, so that to
read what he says one might suppose the Council
had disposed of the matter in a day.   His description is, however, graphic and to the point:

" They [counsel for the proprietors] alleged that the act was intended to load the proprietary estate in order to spare those of the

people, and, that if it were suffered to continue in force, and the proprietaries, who were in odium with the people, left to their mercy in proportioning the taxes, they would inevitably be ruined. We replied that the act had no such intention, and would have no such effect. That the assessors were honest and discreet men under an oath to assess fairly and equitably, and that any advantage each of them might expect in lessening his own tax by augmenting that of the proprietaries was too trifling to induce them to perjure themselves. . . . On this, Lord Mansfield, one of the council, rose, and beckoning me took me into the clerk's chamber, while the lawyers were pleading, and asked me if I was really of opinion that no injury would be done the proprietary estate in the execution of the act. I said, 'Certainly.' 'Then,' says he, 'you can have little objection to enter into an engagement to assure that point.' I answered, 'None at all.' He then called in Paris, and after some discourse, his lordship's proposition was accepted on both sides ; a paper to the purpose was drawn up by the Clerk of the Council, which I signed with Mr. Charles, who was also an Agent of the Province for their ordinary affairs, when Lord Mansfield returned to the Council Chamber, where finally the law was allowed to pass. Some changes were however recommended and we also engaged they should be made by a subsequent law, but the Assembly did not think them necessary."

The narrator does himself one gross injustice in that he gives not an inkling of his own cleverness in winning this great victory over the proprietaries. For it is to be borne in mind that before the Privy Councillors agreed to recommend the bill for the King's approval their Lords of Committee had first submitted a voluminous report reviewing the arguments in the case, and concluding that the measure was " offensive to natural justice, to the laws of England, and to the royal prerogative." Then note the diplomacy of the agent, in whose bright lexicon the word " failure" had no melancholy place. He set about to have the report reconsidered, and undertook that if the bill were approved the Assembly of Pennsylvania should pass an act exempting from assessment the unsurveyed waste lands of the proprietaries and making certain other concessions. Most of these concessions really amounted to nothing, and the Assembly never thought fit to make them (contending, among other things, that the unsurveyed waste lands of the Penns never had been taxed), but they illustrate Franklin's energy in striving to set aside an unfavourable verdict. One might suppose from his own modest account that the initiative in the matter had come from Lord Mansfield, and that the whole point at issue had been settled in a day. As it was, the Lords of Committee made a second report stating that in view of the amendments or concessions proposed it was desirable to leave the act unrepealed. King George II., then on the verge of the grave, appended his royal signature; the arrogance of the Penns received a richly deserved rebuke. Well for the province was it that Franklin had persevered. He had indicated a principle, and, incidentally, prevented the financial panic which must have succeeded a triumph of the proprietaries. The bills for the £100,000 appropriated in the act were already in circulation.

The victory was hailed with delight when news of it reached Philadelphia, where only the upholders of the proprietary interests—not an insignificant clique, by the way—failed to share in the rejoicing. We may take it for granted that Chief-Justice Allen was not one of the gentlemen who joined in the

pæan of praise in honour of the agent from his province, for he was no admirer of the latter, and he
was to write somewhat later (1762), to the Messrs.
Barclay of London: " One would fain hope his
[Franklin's] almost insatiable ambition is pretty near
Satisfied by his parading about England, at the
province's Expense for these five years past, which
now appears in a different Light to our patriots than
formerly, especially, as he has already stayed near
two years longer than they expected."

The abuse of the proprietary party could not
seriously disturb the serenity of the philosopher,
who must have realised that blame from that quarter
was a sort of barometer showing how well or how ill
he had succeeded in battling for the rights of liberty-
loving Pennsylvanians. The higher rose the cries
of the opposition the more clearly were his own
talents emphasised. No amount of vituperation
could prevent his enjoyment of English life, or
abate one jot of the zest with which he observed all
that was going on about him. Nothing had interested him more than the reports, as they came in
glorious succession, of the success of British arms in
his own continent—the abandonment of Fort Duquesne, the surrender of Louisburg, the capture of
Quebec, and finally, the taking, in September, 1760,
of Montreal. Canada had been wrested from the
French, so had possessions in other parts of the
world, and it became a much-debated question as
to whether it would not be better for England to
retain the newly acquired Guadaloupe and give up
Canada! An absurd proposition, yet there actually

BENJAMIN FRANKLIN.

FROM A PAINTING BY CHARLES WILLSON PEALE, OWNED BY THE HISTORICAL SOCIETY
OF PENNSYLVANIA.

rose up a party which advised that preference be given to Guadaloupe. This was too much for Franklin, who hastened to give his views, although not under his own signature, as to the importance of keeping the conquered American territory. As the subject was dear to his heart, the pamphlet had an air of sincerity and a logic that made a deep impression in circles both ministerial and unofficial. Two pamphlets had preceded Franklin's, one of them, by the Earl of Bath, favouring the retention of Canada, and the other, attributed either to William Burke or to Edmund Burke, pleading for Guadaloupe. The next incident in the controversy was a reply to Franklin's paper, wherein the writer said he would address the unknown author, because of all those who had spoken in behalf of Canada, " he is clearly the ablest, the most ingenious, the most dexterous, and the most perfectly acquainted with the *fort* and *faible* of the argument, and we may therefore conclude that he has said everything in the best manner that the cause would bear." The man thus complimented required not the fame of his name to make his reasonings worthy of respect. They were eloquent without a signature.

Verily, the philosopher could no more have ceased to interest himself in public affairs than he could have let that magnificent brain of his lapse into a state of idleness. Thus it was that he watched intently the progress of the French war, and spoke very strongly against the policy of concluding a peace that might prove too advantageous to the enemy. To enforce this view he resorted to an ingenious expedient, by sending to the *London Chronicle* what purported to be an extract from an old quarto volume found by him in a bookstall. The book, he said, bore the date of 1629, and contained discourses addressed to a King of Spain. One of these discourses treated of " The Means of disposing the Enemie to Peace." Franklin asked leave to quote it, as being " so apropos to our present situation (only changing Spain for France) that I think it well worth general attention and observation, as it discovers the arts of our enemies, and may therefore help in some degree to put us on our guard against them." The supposed writer of the book advised the bribing of writers, speakers, and men of learning to recommend a peace dishonourable to their own victorious country, so that the vanquished power might gain, by insidious means, what it could not effect in the field. The inference was, of course, that France was trying by gold to corrupt influential Englishmen to advocate an easy peace, and the alleged " discourse " stirred up more than a flutter of interest, even if it led to nothing tangible. George III., the new King, was strenuously for peace, and even the great Pitt had to bend beneath the autocratic obstinacy of the monarch whose mother had so often said to him: " George, be a King! "

It was this same George whom Franklin, after returning from a trip to Holland and Flanders, saw crowned in regal state. Little did the subject dream that a day was to come when the young sovereign, for whom he cherished such respect and admiration, would be numbered among the greatest of his enemies.

Now, however, there was nothing but love in the American's heart for his King and mother country. When he finally tore himself away from England, and was on the point of sailing for home (August, 1762), Franklin wrote from Portsmouth to his friend Lord Kames:

"I am now waiting here only for a wind to waft me to America, but cannot leave this happy island and my friends in it without extreme regret, though I am going to a country and a people that I love. I am going from the old world to the new; and I fancy I feel like those who are leaving this world for the next: grief at the parting; fear of the passage; hope of the future."

And as if to cement the tie between the returning voyager and the kin he was leaving behind, the English Government appointed his son William, who had become a pronounced favourite abroad, to the vacant governorship of New Jersey. It was an honour which would have for its bitter end the estrangement of father and son, but of such a *finale* there was now no suspicion. The prospect was serene and peaceful. The clouds of revolution had not begun to gather.

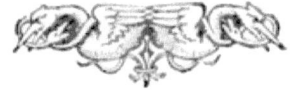

CHAPTER VI

IN THORNY PATHS

1762–1765

IF Franklin, upon reaching home early in November, 1762, nursed the thought that he might now devote himself to a leisurely existence, free of public care, he was destined to have the illusion rudely dispelled. At first, however, all things pointed to a season of peace and quiet for a man who, after valiantly serving his countrymen and attaining the comfortable age of fifty-six, had a right to expect a lull in the storm and stress of life. His return, and the greeting he received, must have warmed a heart so peculiarly susceptible to the admiration of those about him, and have duly compensated for the honours which he had left behind in hospitable England. Mrs. Franklin was of good health, and delighted, in a calm, equable way, to see her lord and master; Sarah, the daughter, had grown into an attractive, accomplished woman, and old friends proved, despite the mutterings of the proprietary party, as hearty and affectionate as ever. Nay, they crowded

into the house of the great doctor, and were not
long in informing him that during his voyage across
the ocean he had once more been elected a member
of the Assembly. When he appeared before his
fellow-legislators, the majority of whom felt the
liveliest gratitude for this successful wrestler with
the stubborn Penns, he must have been hailed with
unstinted enthusiasm. He duly received the thanks
of the Assembly, official and private, and got a still
more practical acknowledgment of services rendered
in a grant of £3000 sterling. The Speaker was
directed to publicly convey the aforesaid thanks to
the agent, and, having done so, there came a " respectful " reply from the recipient, who, addressing
himself to the chair, said that " he was thankful to
the House for the very handsome and generous
allowance they had been pleased to make him," but
that their approbation was, in his estimation, " far
above every other kind of recompense." A very
pretty example of old-fashioned courtesy, yet there
was a welcome place in the philosopher's strong-box
for that trifle of £3000 sterling. His expenses in
England had been considerable; reimbursement was
in order.

By this time William Franklin had gotten back
from London, bringing with him a bride and his
commission as Governor of New Jersey. The greetings between father and son were of an affectionate
character. The former had cherished for the young
man matrimonial hopes in which the present Mrs.
William, a lady from the West Indies, played no
part, but that was an old story now, and the new-

10

comer found her father-in-law all that was affable. A little later the Postmaster-General—for he had not resigned his position—made an official tour of the northern colonies, and after covering sixteen hundred miles right pleasantly, he drove back to Philadelphia, there to recuperate from the jolts and jars of country roads. But there was to be no rest; before many days Franklin would be back again in that public harness which was to enclose him until near the very end. The Indians had begun a bloody warfare along the western frontier of the colonies; murder and the torch played grim pranks with the settlers in the unprotected border counties of Pennsylvania; fear reigned supreme, and so, too, did the spirit of retaliation. To avenge themselves upon the enemy for the destruction of their companions, the burning of their homes, and the taking of unfortunate women and children into captivity, was the first thought of the frontiersmen; to avenge themselves upon a few inoffensive savages, who had learned the peaceful ways of civilisation, was their second and more unnatural thought. The Scotch-Irish settlers of Lancaster County, more particularly the hot-headed " Paxton boys " (who hailed from the township of Paxton or Paxtang), longed for the lives of the poor, harmless Indians of Bethlehem, of Nazareth, or of the manor of Conestoga—quiet, well-behaved little communities by no means so dangerous to the colony as were the Paxton rowdies themselves.

The Indians at Conestoga had dwindled to twenty souls, seven men, five women, and eight children,

now the sad remnant of a once powerful tribe of the
Six Nations.   Every time that a new governor
arrived in the province it was their custom to send
him an address of welcome and fealty; only a few
weeks before (October, 1763) had they tendered
their best wishes to John Penn, the son of Richard
Penn, when that worthy came across the water to
succeed James Hamilton in the gubernatorial chair,
and to thus illustrate the condescension and magnanimity of the long-suffering proprietary.   But
they would soon depart from the jurisdiction of any
earthly governor; a brutal massacre, destined to
mark one of the most disgraceful pages in the history
of Pennsylvania, would annihilate the last of the
Susquehannocks.   The "Paxton boys," who had
vowed their destruction, sallied forth one night,
fifty-seven well-armed and mounted ruffians, and
never stopped riding until they reached Conestoga
at the dawn of day.   Without warning they broke
into the huts of the red men, the one idea being to
give no quarter, and thus to avenge outrages for
which the Susquehannocks were in nowise respon-
sible.   To the Paxtons the only good Indians were
dead Indians—all who lived should be put out of
the world as soon as possible.

"Only three men, two women and a young boy were found at
home, the rest being out among the neighbouring white people [as
Franklin afterward told the painful story]—some to sell the baskets,
brooms and bowls they manufactured, and others on other occasions.
These poor defenceless creatures were immediately fired upon,
stabbed, and hatcheted to death!   The good Shehaes [the old man
of the tribe, who had known William Penn] among the rest, cut to
pieces in his bed.   All of them were scalped and otherwise horribly

mangled. Then their huts were set on fire and most of them burnt down. Then the troop, pleased with their own conduct and bravery, but enraged that any of the poor Indians had escaped the massacre, rode off, and in small parties, by different roads, went home. The universal concern of the neighbouring white people, on hearing of this event, and the lamentations of the younger Indians, when they returned and saw the desolation, and the butchered, half-burnt bodies of their murdered parents and other relations, cannot well be expressed."

The fourteen remaining Indians were taken to Lancaster, where they were placed in the work-house, " a strong building," for their better protection. When the news of the massacre reached Philadelphia (filling Franklin and many of his friends with horror, and being excused by some on the ground that it was a matter of necessity), Governor Penn issued, three days before the pacific feast of Christmas, a ringing, if useless, proclamation. All the officers of the provinces, from the judges down, were ordered to seek out the offenders, so that they might be " proceeded against according to law." But the " Paxton boys " considered themselves above proclamations, just as the modern lynchers seek to rise above the law. They rode to Lancaster, armed as before, " went directly to the work-house, and by violence broke open the door, and entered with the utmost fury in their countenances. When the poor wretches saw they had no protection nigh, nor could possibly escape, and being without the least weapon for defence, they divided into their little families, the children clinging to the parents ";
—again we quote Franklin—" they fell on their knees, protested their innocence, declared their love

to the English, and that in their whole lives they
had never done them injury; and in this posture
they all received the hatchet. Men, women, and
little children were every one inhumanly murdered
in cold blood! The barbarous men who committed
the atrocious fact, in defiance of government, of
all laws human and divine, and to the eternal disgrace of their country and colour, then mounted
their horses, huzzaed in triumph, as if they had
gained a victory, and rode off *unmolested!*" Certainly the cowardly onslaught of the Paxton gang
was a disgrace to what we are pleased to term
civilisation, and it so excited the indignation of
Franklin that when he came to write his *Narrative
of the Late Massacres in Lancaster County*, from
which we have just given extracts, he stigmatised
the episode as one whose "guilt will lie on the whole
land, till justice is done on the murderers." Confiding Susquehannocks! They were unsuspicious
up to the last, and when old Shehaes was told that
some English might come from the frontier to murder him and his family, he replied: "It is impossible; there are Indians, indeed, in the woods who
would kill me and mine, if they could get at us, for
my friendship to the English; but the English will
wrap me in their match-coat, and secure me from all
dangers."

Perhaps in the whole range of the philosopher's
writings there is no finer example than in the before-
mentioned *Narrative* of his power to speak, when
he so desired, with emphasis and picturesqueness of
feeling. His style was not, as a rule, oratorical,

but in this instance indignation carried him far beyond his customary command of the *suaviter in modo*. Referring to the Christian Indians of Bethlehem and Nazareth who had already sought refuge in Philadelphia, only to be sent away from there to New York, and then returned, Franklin exclaimed:

"They have been hurried from place to place for safety, now concealed in corners, then sent out of the province, refused a passage through a neighbouring colony, and returned, not unkindly, perhaps, but disgracefully, on our hands. O Pennsylvania! Once renowned for kindness to strangers, shall the clamours of a few mean niggards about the expense of this public hospitality, an expense that will not cost the noisy wretches sixpence a piece (and what is the expense of the poor maintenance we afford them, compared to the expense they might occasion if in arms against us),—shall so senseless a clamour, I say, force you to turn out of your own doors these unhappy guests, who have offended their own country-folks by their affection for you, who, confiding in your goodness, have put themselves under your protection. Those whom you have disarmed to satisfy groundless suspicions, will you leave them exposed to the armed madmen of their country? Unmanly men! who are not ashamed to come with weapons against the unarmed, to use the sword against women, and the bayonet against young children; and who have already given such bloody proofs of their inhumanity and cruelty."

He ends by saying that "cowards can handle arms, can strike where they are sure to meet with no return, can wound, mangle, and murder," but that it "belongs to brave men to spare and to protect," for, as he quotes the poet,

"Mercy still sways the brave.

The peaceful Indian visitors, in whose behalf Franklin so warmly took up the cudgels, were having a hard time of it in recompense for their

loyalty to the province. They had reached Philadelphia, a frightened band of one hundred and forty,
with the greatest difficulty, for the people along
their route from the Lehigh were intensely hostile
to them, and mob violence was feared. A mob,
indeed, is nearly always brutal and unreasoning,
and to the hot-heads there was no difference between the Indians of peaceful ways and the Indians
of the scalping-knife. The wanderers from the
Lehigh were immediately escorted by their missionaries to the royal barracks in the Northern
Liberties, but not for long could they tarry there.

"A crowd soon gathered : presently it was a mob. Joseph Fox,
the Commissary of the Barracks, hastened to consult the governor,
and late in the afternoon returned with orders to take the Indians to
the buildings on Province Island—the refuge first of the Palatines,
then of the Acadians, now of the Christian Indians. Surrounded by
a menacing crowd, the party drove down Second Street, the missionaries still guarding their flock 'as if from wolves,' and at length
reached boats on the river which took them to the Island." *

This was in November. Then came the massacre
of the Susquehannocks in December, and next a
sensational report that the "Paxton boys" projected a pleasant little jaunt to the Quaker City, in
order to murder the new inhabitants of Province
Island. What was to be done ? Should the refugees
be sent to Nantucket, or even to England ? Finally
it was determined to transport them to New York
—a cowardly expedient. Early one morning, before
the breaking of the dawn, they were smuggled over

* *Memorial History of the City of Philadelphia.* See also Scharf
and Westcott's *History.*

to Philadelphia, and hurried away to the Bristol pike, under the protection of their missionaries and a detachment of Royal Highlanders. Soon, however, they were back again, having been denied admittance to the province of New York; " other troops, a hundred of the Royal Americans, guarded them back, and the simple piety and serene faith of the poor creatures had so reached the soldiers that now, as their waggons came down the street, in the midst of a heavy snowstorm, they were admitted to the Barracks without a word."

Now came a rumour that fifteen hundred men from Lancaster were marching to Philadelphia for the destruction of the Indians. Thereupon the alarmed citizens (or such of them as had no sympathies for " Paxton " principles), and the no less alarmed Governor Penn, looked to Franklin for assistance. The latter had done so much for the city of his adoption that there was a very natural impulse, even among his enemies, to regard him as a tower of strength in time of emergency. A mass-meeting was held at the State House, when the riot act of George I. was read by authority of the Assembly, a new militia association was formed under the auspices of Franklin, and for a time all was frightened bustle and trepidation. The barracks, where the Indians now trembled for their lives, were defended with cannon, a stockade was thrown up, and various other warlike preparations were made. It was ordered that if the alarm bells should sound a warning of the mob's approach all the citizens should rush either to the barracks or to the court-

house. " Business was suspended, shops did not
open, the ferries were dismantled, and couriers
charging back and forth along the streets kept up
the excitement. Even the Quakers forgot their
principles." * Indeed, many of the Friends, young
and old, were so infected with the spirit of the moment that they took up arms. This radical departure from the non-resistance policy made such an
impression that on one occasion, when a well-known
Quaker was seen shouldering a musket, a crowd of
boys followed him along the street with astonished
cries of " Look here! A Quaker with a musket on
his shoulder!"

The excitement and the calling to arms had begun
on a Saturday (February 4, 1764), and by the following Monday the much-feared enemy from the
country of the Paxtons had reached Germantown—
not fifteen hundred strong, as at first reported, but
a hardy party of two hundred frontiersmen, who asserted that they were only the advance-guard of a
formidable gathering. Having gotten thus far on
their march, the would-be avengers heard of the
preparations which had been made to oppose them,
and prudently halted, perhaps to deliberate as to
their future plan of operation. How were they to
be dealt with ? That became the instant topic of
conversation in Philadelphia, and there were some
bellicose citizens who thought that the militia should
promptly attack the invaders. But Governor Penn,
who was leaning more and more on the strong arm
of Franklin, was for treating with them. Accord-

* Scharf and Westcott.

ingly, when Tuesday came, the Postmaster-General and some other citizens repaired to Germantown, met the backwoodsmen, and after listening to their grievance and receiving a " manifesto " setting forth the latter, persuaded them to disband. The next morning a few of the rioters rode into town, failed to identify any of the refugees as murderers, saving an old squaw, and rode away again peacefully. So ended the episode. Throughout it all we see the guiding hand of Franklin, first in putting the city in a condition of defence, and then in throwing aside the mantle of the soldier for that of the diplomatist, by securing a bloodless victory.

" Governor Penn," he relates, anent this excitement, in a letter to Lord Kames, " made my house for some time his headquarters, and did everything by my advice ; so that for about forty-eight hours, I was a very great man ; as I had been once some years before, in a time of public danger. But the fighting face we put on, and the reasonings we used with the insurgents, . . . having turned them back and restored quiet to the city, I became a less man than ever ; for I had, by this transaction, made myself many enemies among the populace ; and the Governor (with whose family our public disputes had long placed me in an unfriendly light, and the services I had lately rendered him not being of the kind that make a man acceptable) thinking it a favourable opportunity, joined the whole weight of the proprietary interest to get me out of the Assembly."

The unfortunate Indians, or such of them as did not die of smallpox, were finally sent back to the Moravians of the Lehigh, but it would be many a long day before the ill-feeling stirred up by the Paxton controversy should die out. For while the Quakers strenuously supported Franklin in his de-

nunciation of the murder of the Susquehannocks, a
strong party had arisen to defend the Paxtons—a
party which soon had for its most imposing adherent
John Penn himself. The Governor had forgotten
his righteous indignation; instead of trying to bring
the slayers of poor Shehaes and his tribe to a tardy
justice, he went so far in the other direction as to
issue a proclamation offering bounties for Indian
scalps. Writers on either side rushed into print with
" poems " and pamphlets, while one might have
supposed, from the tenor of some of the squibs, that
Benjamin Franklin was the most hated man in the
province. The Quakers who had so valiantly and
inconsistently risen to the defence of the city, came
in for their share of lampooning, and one squib thus
made fun of their readiness to use a meeting-house
for the shelter of militia during the short time that
Philadelphia was under arms:

> " Cock up your hats ; look fierce and trim !
>   Nor wear the horizontal brim ;
>   The house of prayer be made a den
>   Not of vile thieves, but arméd men ;
>   Tho' 't is indeed a profanation
>   Which we must expiate with lustration ;
>   But such the present time requires,
>   And such are all the Friends' desires ;
>   Fill bumpers, then, of rum or arrack !
>   We 'll drink success to the new barrack."

But from the Indians the controversy soon drifted
into a discussion of proprietary and anti-proprietary
rights, with Franklin once again siding with the
Quakers (who held the majority in the Assembly),

in their war against the policy of the Penns.   And
now the fight was waxing warm, for the Assembly
had been goaded so far as to contemplate a petition
to the King, praying that Pennsylvania be taken
out of the control of the proprietaries, and that it
be made a royal province, directly under the government of the crown.   It was a bold step to plan,
but one which the conduct of John Penn seemed to
fully justify. The Governor, who had, upon his
arrival, been all conciliation and politeness, now
showed his true colours by vetoing two important
bills.   One was a militia bill (to which he objected
because it did not give him power to appoint all the
officers of the regiment); the other appropriated
money for a campaign against the hostile Indians,
taxing all estates alike, as the legislators were
authorised in doing by the action of the Privy
Council.   These vetoes were exasperating ; the
many grievances against the proprietaries were
forthwith vigorously aired in the Assembly, with
Franklin always in the van of the malcontents.
Finally, the members resolved to adjourn until May
(1764), in order to consult their constituents on the
advisability of drawing up an address to the King,
" praying that he would be graciously pleased to
take the people of this province under his immediate
protection, by completing the agreement heretofore
made with the first proprietary for the sale of the
government to the crown, or otherwise."

No sooner did the Assembly adjourn than a wordy
war of pamphleteering ensued, the respective causes
of the proprietary and the anti-proprietary interests

being debated with warmth, and at times with acrimony. Franklin, ever on the alert, quickly entered into the battle by writing some *Cool Thoughts on the Present Situation of our Public Affairs.* This paper, which he caused to be freely and widely distributed through the city, showed, in a clear, lucid style, the inconveniences of a government under the autocratic yoke of the Penns. We can understand how the adherents of the latter must have hated our " little postmaster " at this period, nor would it be surprising if the " persons of quality " among them indulged in contemptuous flings at his humbleness of birth and his early soap-boiling surroundings. Already was there an aristocratic spirit abroad in Philadelphia, notwithstanding that the city had been settled by colonists in the same class of life as was Josiah Franklin. Indeed, it is by no means improbable that to these members of the " best society," who were trying hard to shake off the familiar atmosphere of the family grocery or of the workshop, the first of all their citizens was a plebeian, and, no doubt, a bit of a demagogue into the bargain.

But what cared Franklin for that ? He was thoroughly independent, financially, socially, and politically, of the Governor's parasites, and was under no necessity to regulate his conduct to suit the timorous people who basked in the sun of official favour. No; he spoke out in ringing tones; nothing could have been more apropos than those *Cool* but emphatic *Thoughts.* Mr. John Penn must have read the pamphlet with feelings of unadulterated anger, and

it is probable that he wished his one-time ally at the
bottom of the Delaware, when he came to a passage
like this:

> " The government, that ought to keep all in order, is itself weak,
> and has scarce authority enough to keep the common peace. Mobs
> assemble and kill (we scarce dare say murder) numbers of innocent
> people in cold blood, who were under the protection of the govern-
> ment. Proclamations are issued to bring the rioters to justice.
> Those proclamations are treated with the utmost indignity and con-
> tempt. Not a magistrate dares wag a finger towards discovering or
> apprehending the delinquents (we must not call them *murderers*)."

And in perusing the conclusion of *Cool Thoughts*
mayhap the Governor was filled with the same un-
christian sentiment:

> " We are chiefly people of three countries. British spirits can no
> longer bear the treatment they have received, nor will they put on the
> chains prepared for them by a fellow-subject. And the Irish and
> Germans have felt too severely the oppressions of hard-hearted land-
> lords and arbitrary princes, to wish to see, in the proprietaries of
> Pennsylvania, both the one and the other united." *

The controversy was not confined, by any means,
to the writing of pamphlets. Public meetings were
held throughout the province, and it may be inferred that the colonists, as a whole, were over-
whelmingly in favour of the address to the King.
When the Assembly re-convened, about the middle
of May, there were found to be over three thousand
signatures to the petition recommending the appeal,
as against less than three hundred signatures up-

* *Cool Thoughts* bore on its face the stamp of Franklin, in thought
and mode of expression, although the paper was ostensibly addressed
to " A Friend in the Country," and signed " A. B."

holding the proprietaries. The momentous subject was discussed at length by the legislature, John Dickinson being the chief speaker in behalf of the present government, and Joseph Galloway, the government's most eloquent opponent. Then the address was put to vote, and adopted by a large majority. Suddenly there came a halt in the proceedings. Isaac Norris, the venerable Speaker of the Assembly, announced that he did not wish to sign an address with which he was out of harmony. He asked for delay, and pleaded illness as a reason for resigning. The upshot of the affair was that Franklin was elected to the speakership, and gladly affixed his name to the document. For the moment the anti-proprietary party was in the ascendent.

Yet there was more work to be done. The election for members of the Assembly would take place in October, and the result of the polling, particularly as it concerned the returns from Philadelphia, might have a very important bearing on the future government of the colony. To defeat Franklin and Galloway now became the aim of the Penn party. Philadelphians girded their loins for the struggle. Once more the contestants hastened into print, and once more the head of the constitutional rebels came in for many a hard dig. Chief-Justice Allen, who now hated the latter more than ever, wrote over to London setting forth that the clamours against the proprietors were " owing to the malice of Franklin and Galloway," adding: " I hope and believe their reign is short, and am persuaded all their efforts for

further mischief will be, in a great measure, prevented
in time to come, whatever way the next elections
are determined, for the people begin to open their
eyes daily, and they would scarce be so hardy as to
attempt the same measures again."

The pamphlets grew more and more scurrilous,
and it may be inferred that the warped Chief Justice
read with pleasure one of them wherein Franklin
was held up to scorn as an immoral and dangerous
politician, and apostrophised in the following polite
terms:

> " Reader, behold this striking Instance of
>   Human Depravity and Ingratitude ;
> An irrefragable Proof
> That neither the Capital Services of *Friends*,
> Nor the attracting Favours of the Fair,
> Can fix the Sincerity of a Man,
> *Devoid of Principles* and
> *Ineffably mean ;*
> Whose Ambition is
>   POWER,
> And whose intention is
>   TYRANNY."

This delicate criticism had been provoked by the
preface which the doctor had written to a speech
against the proprietary government, delivered in the
Assembly by Joseph Galloway, and subsequently
printed for general circulation. This preface is a
lengthy speech in itself, but it reads incisively even
yet, particularly that remarkable memorial, " in the
lapidary style," which the writer suggested as the
proper epitaph for the Messrs. Thomas and Richard
Penn, the non-illustrious sons of the great William :

" Be this a Memorial
Of T—— and R—— P——,
P—— of P——,
Who, with estates immense,
Almost beyond computation,
When their own province,
And the whole British empire,
Were engaged in a bloody and most expensive war,
Begun for the defence of those estates,
Could yet meanly desire
To have those very estates
Totally or partially
Exempted from taxation,
While their fellow-subjects all around them,
Groaned
Under the universal burden.

.   .   .   .

A striking instance
Of human depravity and ingratitude ;
And an irrefragable proof,
That wisdom and goodness
Do not descend with an inheritance ;
But that ineffable meanness
May be connected with unbounded fortune."

Now came the Assembly election with an " old
ticket," headed by Franklin and Galloway, and a
" new ticket," representing the proprietary interests,
in the exciting field.   The Moravians and nearly all
the Quakers supported the " old " ticket ; the
Church of England men and the Dutch Lutherans
were divided in their opinions, and the Dutch Cal-
vinists and the Presbyterians were strongly in favour
of the " new " ticket.   On the first day of October,
at nine o'clock in the morning, the poll was opened,
and from then until nearly midnight there was a
lengthy line of voters, so that at no time could a

11

citizen get from the end of the line to the booth in less than a quarter of an hour.

"About three in the morning, the advocates for the new ticket moved for a close, but (Oh ! the fatal mistake !) the old hands kept it open, as they had a reserve for the aged and lame, which could not come in the crowd, and were called up and brought out in chairs and litters, and some who needed no help, between three and six o'clock, about 200 voters. As both sides took care to have spies all night, the alarm was given to the new ticket men ; horsemen and footmen were immediately dispatched to Germantown and elsewhere, and by nine or ten o'clock they began to pour in, so that after the move for a close, 700 or 800 votes were procured." *

It was three o'clock that afternoon before the polls closed, and it was not until the next day that the votes were counted, and it was found that Galloway and Franklin had been defeated by a very small majority. Yet it is safe to claim that no one heard the result of the election with greater serenity than the Postmaster-General. "Mr. Franklin," we are told, "died like a philosopher," but Mr. Galloway "agonised in death, like a Mortal Deist, who has no Hopes of a Future Existence."

Although Franklin had been ousted, and the anti-proprietary party had been considerably reduced in numbers, that party still maintained a majority in the Assembly, and straightway proceeded to empower their leader to proceed to London, there to put before the King in Council the petition for the change of government. At once there arose a storm of objection from the Penn adherents; a counter-petition was brought into the Assembly, and Mr. Dickinson burst forth before that body in a speech

* Pettit's letter to Joseph Reed.

wherein he asserted that no man in the province was
so much the object of public dislike as Franklin.
After coolly suggesting that Franklin should resign
the proposed special agency, his enemy went on to
say :

" The gentleman proposed has been called here to-day ' a great lu-
minary of the learned world.' I acknowledge his abilities. Far be
it from me to detract from the merit I admire. Let him still shine,
but without wrapping his country in flames. Let him, from a private station, a small sphere, diffuse, as I think he may, a beneficial
light ; but let him not be made to move and blaze like a comet, to
terrify and distress."

When the proprietary's henchmen found that they
could not prevent the triumphant election as agent
of their arch-opposer, they drew up a protest, which
(the Assembly refusing to place it on the minutes)
they proceeded to have printed. This curious paper,
which was signed by ten citizens, among them John
Dickinson, Chief-Justice Allen, and Thomas Willing,
attacked their great adversary in terms more emphatic than truthful or courteous. It was contended :
(1) that Franklin was " the chief author of the measures pursued by the late Assembly, which have
occasioned such uneasiness and *destraction* among
the good people of this province "; (2) that his
" fixed enmity " to the proprietors would preclude
all accommodation of the disputes with them, " even
on just and reasonable terms "; (3) that he was
" very unfavourably thought of by several of His
Majesty's ministers "; (4) that his appointment was
" extremely disagreeable to a very great number of
the most serious and reputable inhabitants of this

province "; (5) that the " unnecessary haste " in making the appointment might subject the Assembly " to the censures and very heavy displeasure of our most gracious Sovereign and his Ministers "; and (6) that " the gentleman proposed has heretofore ventured, contrary to an act of Assembly, to place the public money in the stocks, whereby this province suffered a loss of £6000."

When this protest appeared Franklin was about to sail for England, but in the midst of all his preparations he promptly wrote a reply to the ill-natured charges of Messrs. Dickinson and Company.* No answer could have vindicated more completely the complacent victim of the mud-throwing policy of the proprietary party ; nothing could have been more convincing, manly in tone, and forcible.

" And do those of you, Gentlemen," cried out the slandered agent, in responding to the taunt as to his defeat at the polls, " reproach me with this, who, among near four thousand voters, had scarcely a score more than I had ? It seems, then, that your elections were very near being rejections, and thereby furnishing the same proof in your case that you produce in mine, of your being likewise extremely disagreeable to a very great number of people."

And thus he continues in a vein, sometimes of sarcasm and sometimes of vigorous denial, that must have done more for his cause than could a hundred pamphlets of coarse vituperation.

" Not only my duty to the crown, in carrying the post-office act more duly into execution, was made use of to exasperate the ignorant, as

* *Remarks on a Late Protest against the Appointment of Mr. Franklin as Agent for the Province of Pennsylvania*, dated November 5, 1764.

if I was increasing my own profits by picking their pockets ; but my
very zeal in opposing the murderers, and supporting the authority
of government, and even my humanity with regard to the innocent
Indians under our protection, were mustered among my offences, to
stir up against me those religious bigots, who are of all savages the
most brutish. Add to this the numberless falsehoods propagated as
truths ; and the many perjuries procured among the wretched rabble
brought to swear themselves entitled to a vote; and yet so poor a
superiority obtained at all this expense of honor and conscience !
Can this, Gentlemen, be matter of triumph ?   Enjoy it, then.   Your
exultation, however, was short.   Your artifices did not prevail everywhere ; nor your double tickets and whole boxes of forged votes.   A
great majority of the new-chosen assembly were of the old members,
and remained uncorrupted. They still stood firm for the people, and
will obtain justice from the proprietaries. But what does that avail
to you, who are in the proprietary interests ? "

The after-election cry of " Fraud " is not of modern
origin.

But the most serious of all the charges in the protest was that which accused Franklin of investing
illegally certain public monies entrusted to his care.*

" You might have mentioned," he says in rebuttal, " that the direction of the act to lodge the money in the bank, subject to the drafts
of the trustees of the loan office here, was impracticable ; that the
bank refused to receive it on those terms, it being contrary to their
settled rules to take charge of money subject to the orders of unknown people living in distant countries. You might have mentioned
that the House being informed of this, and having no immediate call
for the money, did themselves adopt the measure of placing it in the
stocks, when they were low ; where it might on a peace produce a
considerable profit and in the meantime accumulate an interest.
.   .   .   and that the loss arose, not from placing the money in
the stocks, but from the imprudent and unnecessary *drawing it out*
at the very time when they were lowest, on some slight uncertain

---

* " The money here meant was a sum granted by Parliament as
an indemnification for part of our expenses in the late war."

rumours of a peace concluded ; that if the Assembly had let it remain another year, instead of losing, they would have gained *six thousand pounds.*

" I am now to take leave (perhaps a last leave) of the country I love, and in which I have spent the greatest part of my life," concluded Franklin. " *Esto perpetuo.* I wish every kind of prosperity to my friends ; and I forgive my enemies."

Five days later the special agent for Pennsylvania was on his way to Chester, there to take ship for England, and with him to that town went three hundred of his fellow-citizens, an admiring cavalcade bearing eloquent testimony to the popularity of this great constitutional fighter among the liberty-loving element of Philadelphia. Another evidence of esteem had been shown in the quickness with which prominent merchants had subscribed £1100 toward his expenses abroad—a sum of money to be repaid by the Assembly, and of which the honoured recipient would only accept a portion. Yet it could not have been altogether a joyful departure. Wife and daughter and all the domestic ties held most dear were, perforce, left at home, and so, too, were enemies who would have only the freer field now that their mighty opponent was gone. The future was one of vast uncertainty. What was to be the outcome ?

" You know I have many enemies," wrote the fond father to the cherished Sarah, as his vessel sailed down the river, " all indeed on the public account, (for I cannot recollect that I have in a private capacity given just cause of offence to any one whatever), yet they are enemies, and very bitter ones ; and you must expect their enmity will extend in some degree to you, so that your slightest indiscretions will be magnified into crimes, in order the more sensibly to wound and afflict me."

SECOND STREET, PHILADELPHIA, SHOWING THE OLD COURTHOUSE ON THE LEFT.

FROM AN ENGRAVING MADE BY W. BIRCH & SON.

And very soon would a blunder, the only great blunder of the statesman's political career, put a weapon into the hands of those enemies.

Strange to say, when Dr. Franklin got to London (December, 1764), the petition to the King was forgotten in the interest attending a much more serious matter. The troubles of the province, great as they undoubtedly were, gave way to an issue of national importance. In short, the English ministry had determined to practically destroy the independence of the colonial assemblies, and to ignore the theory of " no taxation without representation," by imposing a direct stamp-tax upon America. Hitherto the provinces had appropriated money for the King's service, when so desired, by vote of their several legislatures, and had thus been free agents. Now, however, all this was to be changed. The colonies, without representation in Parliament, were, nevertheless, to be forced by Parliament to submit to an arbitary internal tax, so that the aid to the crown would become compulsory in the very worst sense of the word.* The project involved not merely the

* " It is commonly believed," says Professor McMaster, " that this famous tax was the first of its kind known in America. But this is a mistake, for twice had stamp taxes been willingly laid and willingly borne, and, when they expired, as willingly renewed. The first was imposed for one year by Massachusetts in 1755, and reenacted in 1756. The other was passed by New York in December, 1756. It ran for one year, was renewed in 1757 for another year, and created neither discontent nor opposition. Against stamp duties, New York and Massachusetts could therefore make no complaint. It was against stamp duties laid without consent of the colonies that the four London agents protested vigorously on the 2nd of February, 1765."—See *Benjamin Franklin as a Man of Letters.*

using of stamps upon legal documents, newspapers, commercial paper, etc., galling and onerous as that would be in itself; a vital principle was at stake, and Americans saw themselves about to be treated not as free-and-equal citizens, or subjects, of a great empire, but rather as semi-serfs who must do the bidding of the Lords and Commons of Westminster, in whose proceedings they had no voice. For once admit the correctness of the theory on which this stamp act was based, and who was to foretell to what lengths an arrogant Parliament might carry its power ? Furthermore, an elaborate scheme had been suggested by which the colonies were to be brought under more direct and submissive control of the mother country; territorial boundaries would be altered, provincial constitutions remodelled, and popular power abridged. It was no wonder, then, that the intentions of the government as to taxation, which had been broached in the colonies some time before the departure of Franklin, should arouse the most sincere alarm, the gravest misgivings. Nor was it anything but natural that when the matter had been discussed by the Assembly of Pennsylvania in the preceding summer the members heartily condemned the proposed tax, while at the same time officially recording their purpose " to grant aid to the crown, according to their abilities, whenever required of them, *in the usual constitutional manner.*"

No sooner was he in London than the energetic doctor hastened to the aid not only of Pennsylvania, but of the colonies in general, by trying to stem the dangerous current which bid fair to overwhelm the liberties of his country. In company with the other provincial agents he waited upon George Grenville, the Prime Minister, but his arguments, forcible, logical, and temperately expressed as they were, might have been addressed to deaf ears, for any good that they effected. " I have pledged my word for offering the Stamp Bill to the House," said Grenville, " and I cannot forego it; they will hear all objections, and do as they please "; and he remarked politely, but with the spirit of the political tyrant, " you cannot hope to get any good by a controversy with the mother country." In March, therefore, the obnoxious bill was passed as a matter of course; " within doors [Parliament], less resistance was made to the act than to a common turnpike bill."

It was supposed in London that the act, when once made law, would meet with little or no resistance; even Franklin, who usually observed so astutely, and knew so well how to feel the public pulse, fell into this error of judgment. He failed for once to gauge the sentiments of his countrymen. Hard as he had worked against the measure, he deluded himself with the idea that the opposition to it would evaporate, and he seemed disposed to yield to the inevitable. Puzzling inconsistency in one who realised so thoroughly the danger of taxation without representation. Perhaps he was deceived by the optimistic opinions of his English friends.

" The act seemed sure to enforce itself. Unless stamps were used, marriages would be null, notes of hand valueless, ships at sea prizes to the first captors, suits at law impossible, transfers of real estate invalid, inheritances irreclaimable, newspapers suppressed. Of all who acted with Grenville in the government, he never heard one prophecy that the measure would be resisted. 'He did not force the opposition to it, and would have staked his life for obedience.'"

So says Bancroft, who adds, significantly:

"It was held that the power of Parliament, according to the purest Whig principles, was established over the colonies, but, in truth, the Stamp Act was the harbinger of American independence, and the knell of the unreformed House of Commons."

Franklin wrote home to Charles Thomson, in vindication of himself, that he had taken every step in his power to prevent the passage of the bill:

"But the tide was too strong for us. The nation was provoked by American claims of independence, and all parties joined in resolving by this act to settle the point. We might as well have hindered the sun's setting. That we could not do. But since 't is down, my friend, and it may be long before it rises again, let us make as good a night of it as we can. We may still light candles. Frugality and Industry will go a great way towards indemnifying us. Idleness and Pride tax with a heavier hand than kings and parliaments. If we can get rid of the former we may easily bear the latter."

And now Franklin made his great mistake—something which he surely would have set down as an *erratum* had he ever brought the record of the *Autobiography* up to this period. For when Mr. Grenville graciously, if shrewdly, invited the colonial agents to nominate the persons who were to act as stamp officers for America, the agent from Pennsylvania was foolish enough to suggest that John Hughes, an old and tried Philadelphia friend, should be the officer in that city. "You tell me," the Prime

Minister had said, " you are poor, and unable to
bear the tax; others tell me you are able. Now
take the business into your own hands; you will see
how and where it pinches, and will certainly let us
know it, in which case it shall be eased."

The worst that can be said of Franklin in thus
yielding to the suggestion of Grenville is that he
acted with gross unwisdom. Of his good faith in
the matter there can be no possible shadow of doubt,
although his enemies were not slow to assert that
self-interest was the mainspring of the appointment.
The Stamp Act being inevitable, as he must have
reasoned, why not do his friend Hughes a good turn
by allowing him to reap some legitimate benefit
therefrom ? " We none of us, I believe, foresaw or
imagined, that this compliance with the request of
the minister would or could have been called an application of ours, and adduced as a proof of our
approbation of the act we had been opposing."
Thus wrote the agent in explaining, much later, the
position of himself and his colleagues, and he observed: " Otherwise I think few of us would have
named at all; I am sure I should not." *

Yet for all that, the news of Hughes's nomination
excited a storm of indignation in Philadelphia.
There were some persons whose anger against
Franklin led them to the length of declaring that he
had tried to get for himself the position of stamp
distributor. The philosopher began to sink in the
estimation of the town, and some of his warmest

---

* From a letter to the Rev. Dr. Tucker, Dean of Worcester.

friends shook their heads gravely; not that they questioned his integrity, but that for once they were bitterly disappointed in a man who heretofore had appeared to be a pillar of good sense. "How could he have so mistaken the temper of America?" they asked, as they heard from all quarters of the country of the discontent fomented by the passage of the hated bill. Then, in September, came the joyful report that the Grenville ministry had fallen; probably the act would be repealed. The new ministers did not desire repeal, but the unsuspecting Philadelphians rang the church bells, drank loyal toasts, made bonfires, and burned in effigy the unfortunate Hughes. Was this to be the end of Franklin's political usefulness? Bold, indeed, was the citizen who would venture to predict otherwise.

Surely, Hughes must have anathematised the day upon which his patron nominated him for distributor. Drums and bells were muffled in his dishonour; he was expelled from the fire company of which he had been a welcome member; he was treated as a traitor, and made to feel that his life was by no means too secure. The excited Assembly protested vigorously against the stamp tyranny, manfully resolving that "it is the inherent birthright and indubitable privilege of every British subject to be taxed only by his own consent or that of his legal representatives," while a little later a non-importation agreement, which was being circulated throughout indignant America, was signed by the leading merchants of Philadelphia. By this compact it was determined, among other precautions, to order no

English goods during the enforcement of the Stamp
Act, and many were the subscribers to what we
might now term the patriotic boycott. Yes, and
John Dickinson, he who had so valiantly defended
the toryism of the proprietors (how suddenly had
the old controversy sunk into insignificance!) came
out in an address, anonymous but to the purpose,
warning his countrymen of the dangers of the tax.

"Think, oh! think," he says, in urging unflinching obedience to the
non-importation agreement, "of the endless misery you must entail
upon yourselves and your country by touching the pestilential cargoes
that have been sent you. Destruction lurks within them. To receive them is death. It is worse than death; it is SLAVERY!"

Thus did the spirit of defiance take shape until the
enforcement of the tax became a practical impossi-
bility. The public offices were closed; the detested
stamps were burned with ceremony; legal papers
remained undrawn; English manufactures were
tabooed, and home-spun clothes became not only a
sign of protest, but a fad as well.

One ill-advised step had cost Franklin dear. Next
to Hughes he was the most unpopular man in the
province. Not only were his motives assailed (some
of his enemies pretended to believe that he had
secretly favoured the passage of the Stamp Act
from the first), but even his family came in for a
share of abuse. It was feared that Mrs. Franklin
and her daughter might suffer from the violence of
the mob; Governor Franklin wanted them both to
seek a temporary home in New Jersey. The former
lady has left us, in a letter to the husband she would
never see again, a record of her unpleasant ordeal.

" I was for nine days kept in a continual hurry by people to remove, and Sally was persuaded to go to Burlington for safety. Cousin Davenport came and told me that more than twenty people had told him it was his duty to be with me. I said I was pleased to receive civility from anybody. So he staid with me some time; towards night I said he should fetch a gun or two, as we had none. I sent to ask my brother to come and bring his gun also, so we turned one room into a magazine; I ordered some sort of defence upstairs, such as I could manage myself. I said, when I was advised to remove, that I was very sure you had done nothing to hurt anybody, nor had I given any offence to any person at all, nor would I be made uneasy by anybody, nor would I stir or show the least uneasiness, but if any one came to disturb me I would show a proper resentment."

Plucky matron! She was not a woman to set the placid Delaware on fire, but the blood of heroines flowed in her veins.

As it happened, Mrs. Franklin was not molested; so she could dismantle that improvised magazine, dismiss her cousin, and send over to Jersey for the timid Sarah. The hostility toward her lord and master had its most dangerous manifestation in a vast deal of angry condemnation, and in the printing of some scurrilous literature. Perhaps the doctor's enemies hoped that he would resign his offices, come meekly home to Philadelphia, and sink into the semi-obscurity of private life. If they fondly cherished any such idea they were doomed to bitter disappointment. Benjamin Franklin was not the man to be overwhelmed by a transient wave of ill-temper.

CHAPTER VII

WORKING FOR THE COLONIES

1766-1773

AD it remained for Parliament to repeal the Stamp Act for purely sentimental reasons—that is to say, merely from a desire to show a love for the colonies—then might the Americans have awaited deliverance in vain. The new ministry, headed by the Marquis of Rockingham, was at first in no mood for reversing the policy of Grenville and his associates, nor did it expect to treat America otherwise than as a rebellious child who stood in need of a thorough disciplining. But when the refusal of the provincials to buy British goods began to affect the interests of the mother country, causing the home producers to rise up in alarm, and when it became apparent that the tax would be resisted unto the bitter end, a reaction quickly set in, and the government discovered that it was not dealing with a flock of meek, spiritless sheep. What was more, the courageous Pitt, who had been ill when the resolution to impose the tax was taken,

now appeared in the Commons to valiantly defend
the cause of his kin beyond the sea. " We are
told," he said, " that America is obstinate—that
America is almost in open rebellion. Sir, I rejoice
that America has resisted; three millions of people
so dead to all the feelings of liberty as voluntarily
to submit to be slaves would have been fit instru-
ments to make slaves of all the rest."

So forcibly did the expediency of repeal make
itself felt that the ministers soon opposed the efforts
of Grenville to pledge the House to the enforcement
of the measure, nor was it long before Parliament
was employed in hearing testimony, as to the effect
of the tax, from merchants, manufacturers, revenue
officers, and many others. Here was just the opportunity for Franklin, who had been on the alert
to take advantage of the ministerial change of heart
by strenuously preaching repeal, and when he was
asked to appear at the bar of the House, to shed
added light upon the situation, he rose to the occasion in a fashion that displayed in their greatest
brilliance his abilities and mental quickness. For
clearness, conciseness of statement, and the faculty
of making the very most of his case in a compara-
tively short compass, nothing could have surpassed
the famous examination of which he was the imperturbable hero. It matters not that he knew beforehand, through discussion with his friends, the nature
of some of the questions to be put to him; the fact
remains that his answers, several of which were
shrewd replies to unexpected queries from his enemies, show us the man in his finest form as a states-

man keen in observation, impressive in conviction, and powerful in coping with dangerous opposition.

"The dignity of his bearing, his self-possession, the promptness and propriety with which he replied to each interrogatory, the profound knowledge he displayed upon every topic presented to him, his perfect acquaintance with the political condition and internal affairs of his country, the fearlessness with which he defended the late doings of his countrymen, and censured the measures of Parliament, his pointed expressions and characteristic manner ; all these combined to rivet the attention, and excite the astonishment of his audience."

Thus wrote the admiring Sparks, who went even further, however, and fell into the error of stating that the doctor knew not beforehand the nature or the form of any one of the questions.

When asked, " Do you think it right that America should be protected by this country, and pay no part of the expense ? " (a question which the Grenville party designed as a " poser "), Franklin quickly answered : " That is not the case. The colonies raised, clothed, and paid during the last war near twenty-five thousand men, and spent many millions "—and to the further interrogation, " Were you not reimbursed by Parliament ? " he replied : " We were only reimbursed what, in your opinion, we had advanced beyond our proportion, or beyond what might reasonably be expected from us ; and it was a very small part of what we spent. Pennsylvania, in particular, disbursed about £500,000, and the reimbursements, in the whole, did not exceed £60,000."

So the inquisition went on, with Franklin always ready, always having the advantage, until one hundred and seventy-four questions had been answered

12

with inimitable spirit and telling effect. To reproduce
the list would be to transgress the limit of space set
for this memoir, but, ere we leave such a triumphant
episode of our hero's career, let us recall a few of
the most characteristic replies.   For instance:

" Do you not think the people of America would submit to pay the
stamp duty, if it was moderated ? "

" No, never, unless compelled by force of arms."

"What was the temper of America towards Great Britain before
the year 1763 ? "

" The best in the world. . . . They were governed by this
country at the expense only of a little pen, ink, and paper ; they
were led by a thread. They had not only a respect, but an affection
for Great Britain ; for its laws, its customs and manners, and even a
fondness for its fashions, that greatly increased the commerce. Natives of Britain were always treated with particular regard ; to be an
Old-England man was, of itself, a character of some respect, and gave
a kind of rank among us."

" And what is their temper now ? "

" O, very much altered."

" What is your opinion of a further tax, imposed on the same
principle with that of the Stamp Act ? How would the Americans
receive it ? "

" Just as they do this. They would not pay it."

" You say the colonies have always submitted to external taxes,
and object to the right of Parliament only in laying internal taxes ;
how can you show that there is any kind of difference between the
two taxes to the colony on which they may be laid ? "

" I think the difference is very great. An *external* tax is a duty
laid on commodities imported ; that duty is added to the first cost
and other charges on the commodity, and when it is offered to sale,
makes a part of the price. If the people do not like it at that price,
they refuse it ; they are not obliged to pay it. But an *internal* tax
is forced from the people without their consent, if not laid by their
own representatives. The Stamp Act says, we shall have no commerce, make no exchange of property with each other, neither purchase, nor grant, nor recover debts ; we shall neither marry nor
make our wills, unless we pay such and such sums ; and thus it is

intended to extort our money from us, or ruin us by the consequences of refusing to pay it."

"Can anything less than a military force carry the Stamp Act into execution?"

"I do not see how a military force can be applied to that purpose."

"Why may it not?"

"Suppose a military force sent into America, they will find nobody in arms; what are they then to do! They cannot force a man to take stamps who chooses to do without them. They will not find a rebellion; they may indeed make one."

"Supposing the Stamp Act continued and enforced, do you imagine that ill-humour will induce the Americans to give as much for worse manufactures of their own, and use them, preferable to better of ours?"

"Yes, I think so. People will pay as freely to gratify one passion as another, their resentment as their pride."

"If the Stamp Act should be repealed, would it induce the assemblies of America to acknowledge the rights of Parliament to tax them, and would they erase their resolutions?"

"No, never."

"Is there a power on earth that can force them to erase them?"

"No power, how great soever, can force men to change their opinions."

"What used to be the pride of the Americans?"

"To indulge in the fashions and manufactures of Great Britain."

"What is now their pride?"

"To wear their old clothes over again, till they can make new ones."

Nobly had Franklin vindicated himself. In London he was the most talked-of man of the moment, while later on, when the news of his brave defence and of the subsequent repeal of the tax reached his own country, there was much rejoicing, with many a kind word for the upholder of colonial liberties, and some pretty drinking of toasts in his honour. The great man was placed once again upon the pedestal of popularity. For shortly after this ex-

amination came the death of the Stamp Act, much
to the disgust of George III., who had to be content with the passage of a Declaratory Act setting
forth " the right of Parliament to bind the colonies
in all cases whatsoever." Not love for America,
but an appeal to practical issues had won the day, and
in strengthening the force of that argument no one
had done such signal service as Benjamin Franklin.*

In June Franklin wrote to the Assembly asking
for leave to return home the following spring (a request which was practically ignored by his reappoint-
ment as agent); he then set out for a trip on the
Continent, and soon began to wonder how the anti-
proprietaries would fare during the Philadelphia
elections of the coming October. In spite of the
re-established popularity of the philosopher he still
had some bitter enemies in the Quaker city—
enemies who could see neither virtue or honesty in
him—and squibs and lying pamphlets were again
used as a medium for defeating the " old ticket "
party. It was asserted, for instance, that Franklin
had " aimed a poisoned dagger at the breast of his
parent country." In its issue of September 18th
the *Pennsylvania Journal* of the Messrs. Bradford
came out with "An Essay, Towards discovering the
Authors and Promoters of The memorable Stamp
Act," which was ostensibly a letter " from a Gentleman in London, to his friend in Philadelphia." The
writer broadly intimated that the real originator of
the Stamp Act was the agent himself.

---

* The bill for repeal received the King's assent on March 18,
1766.

" He proposed this scheme to General Braddock, and there are persons of good credit in Maryland who heard him deliver his opinion to the General. An opinion which he has cultivated with assiduity, until he found by the issue that it was vain and chimerical. We do not affirm, that he was the very person who proposed the act to G——le ; yet we can even give the strongest proofs of this fact, that the nature of the thing can admit of. The act was doubtless formed and projected under the joint influence of Lord Bute and G——e G——le ; and Dr. F——n's chief interest at court is with Lord Bute. F——n's friends in Philadelphia boasted of his interest with the late ministry ; and when Mr. H——s told Mr. F——n that his want of interest at court was objected as an argument against his appointment as agent, F——n forgot his usual reserve, and swore by his Maker, that it was false, that he had interest with Lord Bute, and asserted that he thought he had also some interest with G——e G——le."

To read on further, and accept the statement of the " Essay " as truth, was to believe that the aforesaid " Dr. F——n " was nothing more or less than a low, unprincipled schemer, from whose machinations America would never be safe unless he reposed at the bottom of the sea. But in this instance calumny was unsuccessful, and the " old " party came in the victors.

" The old ticket forever," wrote Sarah Franklin to Governor Franklin, of New Jersey—who, by the way, was developing into a pronounced Tory official,—" the old ticket forever ! We have it by 34 votes ! ' God bless our worthy and noble agent, and all his family !' were the joyful words we were waked with at two or three o'clock this morning, by the White Oaks."

But events of national import are soon to hurry on so fast that a little thing like a Philadelphia election must sink into insignificance, and the agent from Pennsylvania (who will also in turn become agent

for Georgia, New Jersey, and Massachusetts) will
have much to worry him as new causes for tension
arise ominously between the colonies and the
mother country.

> "To tranquillise America," says Bancroft, "no more was wanting
> than a respect for its rights, and some accommodation to its con-
> firmed habits and opinions. The colonies had, each of them, a
> direction of its own and a character of its own, which required to be
> harmoniously reconciled with the motion impressed upon it by the
> imperial legislature. But this demanded study, self-possession, and
> candour. The parliament of that day, recognising no reciprocity of
> obligations, thought nothing so wrong as thwarting its will."

Such was the temper of a Parliament which, in the
summer of 1767, passed the Townshend bill taxing
the colonies by duties on their imports of paper,
glass, painter's colours, lead, and tea, and encourag-
ing the billeting of royal troops upon the Americans.
Twenty Franklins could not have stemmed this tide
of legislative stupidity, nor could twenty Parliaments have prevented the storm of opposition
which soon arose from beyond the sea. These
taxes, "external" though they were, and the dangerous way wherein the revenue therefrom was to
be appropriated—the direct payment by the crown
of American civil officers and of an American standing army—filled the hearts of all true Americans
with a new dread, a new grievance against the
parent country. As certain Bostonians said:

> "We shall be obliged to maintain in luxury sycophants, court para-
> sites, and hungry dependents, who will be sent over to watch and
> oppress those who support them. . . . The governors will be
> men rewarded for despicable service, hackneyed in deceit and av-

arice ; or some noble scoundrel, who has spent his fortune in every kind of debauchery." *

In fine, if the new policy was to be carried to its natural and logical conclusion, the provincials would be turned into so many puppets, made to dance on strings pulled either at Westminster or—since King George wished to govern—at Windsor Castle. The colonial assemblies might adjourn forever ; free political action on the part of their constituents would become a thing of the past.

No one foresaw more forcibly than did Franklin the perils accruing from the rancour which had now set in against the " rebellious " colonies—a rancour which had for its most illustrious instigator, as the American little realised until much later, the sovereign himself. The King was well-intentioned, but narrow, bigoted, mentally short-sighted, and in his eyes the independent spirit of the provincials, as displayed in their protest against the injustices of Parliament, fell little short of high treason. There were many other eyes, unfortunately, which were blinded in the same way, and try as he did to open them by numerous letters to the London newspapers, the agent from Pennsylvania must have felt that his task was a hard one. So it may have been with a not over-light heart that he crossed the Channel late in the summer of 1767, and visited Paris, accompanied by Sir John Pringle, physician to the virtuous consort of obstinate King George. Yet he had not lost the faculty of enjoying a holiday ; he found his trip a source of diversion, and was not the less

* Bancroft's *History of the United States of America ;* last revision.

pleased, of course, because of the respect with which
he and the worthy Sir John were treated. The
travellers were duly " presented " to the royal
family of France, then at Versailles, and Franklin
writes to a friend that his Majesty, Louis XV.,
" did me too the honour of taking some notice of
me; that is saying enough; for I would not have
you think me so much pleased with this King and
Queen, as to have a whit less regard than I used to
have for ours. No Frenchman shall go beyond me
in thinking my own King and Queen the very best
in the world, and the most amiable." Here was
loyalty with a vengeance. Had the King whom he
eulogised as the " very best in the world " been
endowed with more common sense and political insight, Franklin might have gone on admiring him
unto the end of the chapter.

In the meantime the outcry raised in America
against the imposition of the new taxes, and the
resolution of many of her inhabitants to resort again
to the effective weapon of non-importation, acted as
fuel to the fire already kindled by the British op-
pressors of the colonies. On his return to London,
therefore, Franklin did all that he could, by pen and
in conversation, to place the American side of the
controversy in the proper light. He might have
saved himself the trouble, creditable as was the
effort; English political arrogance had now reached
such a momentum that nothing save the successful
ending of the revolutionary struggle could stop its
course. Then, too, came changes in the ministry,
and he was called upon to exert a diplomatic reserve

between the opposite intentions of Lord Sandwich, the new Postmaster-General, who wished to oust him from his postmaster-generalship of the colonies, and the Duke of Grafton, who wanted the philosopher appointed to some important office directly in contact with the members of the cabinet. " I am told," Franklin writes to his son, " there has been a talk of getting me appointed under-secretary to Lord Hillsborough ; but with little likelihood, as it is a settled point here that I am too much of an American."

Lord Hillsborough was the Secretary of State for America, and it was thought by the friends of the colonies that much good might be accomplished by bringing into his department so distinguished a champion of provincial rights as the doctor. Franklin, on his part, was ready to serve if he could fulfil any useful mission by so doing, but it is evident that he did not look forward to the task with any enthusiasm. As he told Governor Franklin :

" I did not think fit to decline any favour so great a man [as the Duke of Grafton] had expressed an inclination to do me, because at court, if one shows an unwillingness to be obliged, it is often construed as a mark of mental hostility, and one makes an enemy ; yet, so great is my inclination to be at home and at rest, that I shall not be sorry if this business falls through, and I am suffered to retire to my old post ; nor indeed very sorry if they take that from me, too, on account of my zeal for America, in which some of my friends have hinted to me that I have been too open."

The scheme to place the American in the English service did not result in anything. This was fortunate, seeing that the appointment must inevitably have tied his hands, rather than have given him a freer rein. His enemies contented themselves with abusing him in the newspapers, hoping thereby to provoke him to resign his postmaster-generalship of the colonies, but Franklin said, with that calm humour which never failed him : " In this they are not likely to succeed, I being deficient in that Christian virtue of resignation. If they would have my office they must take it."

And now events were marching on across the water, and the doctor could only hope against hope, as the situation grew worse and the bonds between the mother country and her rightly defiant children seemed more and more in danger of being rent asunder. His experience, too, was not always pleasant ; at the beginning of the year 1771 (ten months after the presence of British troops in Boston, kept there to overawe the people, had led to the sad conflict termed the " massacre "), he had a shining illustration of the amenities of party hate. His adversary was Lord Hillsborough, who by reason of his "conceit, wrong-headedness, obstinacy, and passion," was probably the very worst Secretary of State for America that the English Government, or the distressed colonies, could have possessed. No one had a greater contempt for his limited abilities and his narrowness of view than did Franklin. But when the latter was appointed agent for Massachusetts he went, in duty bound, to report the circumstance officially to his lordship, and the reception he there met with must have intensified a hundred-fold his dislike for the Secretary. Franklin

has himself left for posterity a dramatic record of
the interview, and it forms such interesting reading
that we may be pardoned for giving it in full.
Here are the " minutes " :

" Wednesday, 16 January, 1771. I went this morning to wait on
Lord Hillsborough. The porter at first denied his lordship, on
which I left my name and drove off. But before the coach got out
of the square, the coachman heard a call, turned and went back to
the door, when the porter came and said, ' His lordship will see you,
Sir.' I was shown into the levee room, where I found Governor
Bernard, who, I understand, attends there constantly. Several other
gentlemen were there attending, with whom I sat down a few minutes, when Secretary Pownall * came out to us, and said his lordship
desired I would come in. I was pleased with this ready admission
and preference, having sometimes waited three or four hours for my
turn ; and, being pleased, I could more easily put on the open, cheerful countenance that my friends advised me to wear. His lordship
came towards me and said, ' I was dressing in order to go to court ;
but, hearing that you were at the door, who are a man of business, I
determined to see you immediately.' I thanked his lordship and
said that my business at present was not much ; it was only to pay
my respects to his lordship, and to acquaint him with my appointment by the House of Representatives of Massachusetts Bay to be
their agent here, in which station if I could be of any service—(I
was going on to say—' to the public, I should be very happy ; ' but
his lordship, whose countenance changed at my naming that province,
cut me short by saying, with something between a smile and a sneer) :

L. H. I must set you right there, Mr. Franklin ; you are not
agent.

B. F. Why, my lord ?

L. H. You are not appointed.

B. F. I do not understand your lordship ; I have the appointment in my pocket.

L. H. You are mistaken ; I have later and better advices. I
have a letter from Governor Hutchinson ; he would not give his
assent to the bill.

* Secretary to the Board of Trade.

B. F.   There was no bill, my lord ; it was a vote of the House.

L. H.   There was a bill presented to the Governor for the purpose of appointing you and another, one Dr. Lee, I think he is called, to which the Governor refused his assent.

B. F.   I cannot understand this, my lord ; I think there must be some mistake in it. Is your lordship quite sure that you have such a letter ?

L. H.   I will convince you of it directly. (*Rings the bell.*) Mr. Pownall will come in and satisfy you.

B. F.   It is not necessary that I should now detain your lordship from dressing. You are going to court. I will wait on your lordship another time.

L. H.   No, stay ; he will come immediately. (*To the servant.*) Tell Mr. Pownall I want him.

(*Mr. Pownall comes in.*)

L. H.   Have not you at hand Governor Hutchinson's letter, mentioning his refusing his assent to the bill for appointing Dr. Franklin agent ?

SEC. P.   My lord ?

L. H.   Is there not such a letter ?

SEC. P.   No, my lord ; there is a letter relating to some bill for the payment of a salary to Mr. De Berdt, and I think to some other agent, to which the Governor had refused his assent.

L. H.   And is there nothing in the letter to the purpose I mention ?

SEC. P.   No, my lord.

B. F.   I thought it could not well be, my lord, as my letters are by the last ships, and they mention no such thing. Here is the authentic copy of the vote of the House appointing me, in which there is no mention of any act intended. Will your lordship please to look at it ? (*With seeming unwillingness he takes it, but does not look into it.*)

L. H.   An information of this kind is not properly brought to me as Secretary of State. The Board of Trade is the proper place.

B. F.   I will leave the paper then with Mr. Pownall to be——

L. H.   (*Hastily.*) To what end would you leave it with him ?

B. F.   To be entered on the minutes of that Board, as usual.

L. H.   (*Angrily.*) It shall not be entered there. No such paper shall be entered there, while I have anything to do with the business of that Board. The House of Representatives has no right to appoint an agent. We shall take no notice of any agents, but such as are appointed by acts of Assembly, to which the Governor gives his assent. We have had confusion enough already. Here is one agent appointed by the Council, another by the House of Representatives. Which of these is agent for the province? Who are we to hear in provincial affairs? An agent appointed by act of Assembly we can understand. No other will be attended to for the future, I can assure you.

B. F. I cannot conceive, my lord, why the consent of the Governor should be thought necessary to the appointment of an agent for the people. It seems to me that——

L. H. (*With a mixed look of anger and contempt.*) I shall not enter into a dispute with *you*, Sir, upon this subject.

B. F. I beg your lordship's pardon; I do not presume to dispute with your lordship; I would only say, that it seems to me, that every body of men, who cannot appear in person, where business relating to them may be transacted, should have a right to appear by an agent. The concurrence of the Governor does not seem to me necessary. It is the business of the people, that is to be done; he is not one of them; he is himself an agent.

L. H. (*Hastily.*) Whose agent is he?

B. F. The King's.

L. H. No such matter. He is one of the corporation by the province charter. No agent can be appointed but by an act, nor any act pass without his assent. Besides, this proceeding is directly contrary to express instructions.

B. F. I did not know there had been such instructions. I am not concerned in any offence against them, and——

L. H. Yes, your offering such a paper to be entered is an offence against them. (*Folding it up again without having read a word of it.*) No such appointment shall be entered. When I came into the administration of American affairs I found them in great disorder. By *my firmness* they are now something mended; and, while I have the honour to hold the seals, I shall continue the same conduct, the same *firmness*. I think my duty to the master I serve, and to the government of this nation requires it of me. If that conduct is not approved, *they* may take my office from me when they please. I shall make them a bow, and thank them; I shall resign with pleasure. That gentleman knows it (*pointing to Mr. Pownall*), but, while I continue in it, I shall resolutely persevere in the same *firm-*

ness. (Spoken with great warmth, and turning pale in his discourse, as if he was angry at something or somebody besides the agent, and of more consequence to himself.)

B. F. (*Reaching out his hand for the paper, which his lordship returned to him.*) I beg your lordship's pardon for taking up so much of your time. It is, I believe, of no great importance whether the appointment is acknowledged or not, for I have not the least conception that an agent can *at present* be of any use to any of the colonies. I shall therefore give your lordship no further trouble. (*Withdrew.*)"

So ends Franklin's curious recital. "Firmness," even unto the point of idiocy and tyranny, was the remedy which childish statesmen of the Hillsborough cult wished to employ in the curing of colonial discontent. "The Americans," they said in effect, "are a lot of unruly schoolboys; we are their masters, and must whip them into obedience."

Lord Hillsborough, as a man of narrow mind but wide conceit, looked upon the agent's own "firmness" as rank impertinence, and did not hesitate to characterise him, behind his back, as a republican, "a factious, mischievous fellow," and the like. But the doctor stood to his guns, and was rather amused, when he was dining in Dublin some time later with the Lord Lieutenant, to find among the company the Secretary of State for America. His lordship was most civil to the philosopher, and pressed him to visit his country-place in the north of Ireland— an invitation which was gracefully accepted for the twofold reason, perhaps, that the traveller knew the value of reconciliation, and had tasted, too, of the charming hospitality dispensed in the home of an English or an Irish gentleman. Before leaving

Dublin, however, Franklin indulged in a shrewd bit of diplomacy by interviewing the patriots of the Celtic Parliament, whom he found disposed to be very friendly to America. This sentiment he tried to strengthen, " with the expectation," as he says in one of his letters, " that our growing weight might in time be thrown into their scale, and, by joining our interests with theirs a more equitable treatment from this nation might be obtained for them as well as for us."

As for my Lord of Hillsborough, he proved an admirable host, doing everything possible for the comfort and entertainment of Franklin, and discussing American affairs in a spirit of unexpected moderation.   In short, to quote the observing doctor, " he seemed extremely solicitous to impress me, and the colonies through me, with a good opinion of him.   All which I could not but wonder at, knowing that he likes neither them nor me; and I thought it inexplicable but on the supposition, that he apprehended an approaching storm, and was desirous of lessening beforehand the number of enemies he had so imprudently created." *   It seems like a bit of retributive justice that the storm which soon broke over the head of Hillsborough, and brought about his retirement from the ministry, was indirectly stirred up by the agent himself. The latter, who had ever been a great believer in the colonisation of Western America, was interested in a company formed to plant a large settle-

---

* Letter to Thomas Cushing, dated London, January 13, 1772.

ment in Illinois, and in regard to which Hillsborough
persuaded the Lords of Trade to adopt an adverse
report.   Franklin replied in writing to the objections
of the Secretary, who feared that the proposed
colony would become independent of Great Britain;
the Privy Council took up the matter, approved of
the scheme, and Lord Hillsborough forthwith resigned, much to the delight of his fellow-ministers.

"At length we have got rid of Lord Hillsborough, and Lord Dartmouth takes his place, to the great satisfaction of all the friends of
America," writes Franklin to his son, remarking that "all his brother
ministers disliked him extremely, and wished for a fair occasion of
tripping up his heels ; so, seeing that he made a point of defeating
our scheme, they made another of supporting it, on purpose to mor-
tify him, which they knew his pride could not bear." *

The doctor was not vindictive, but he would have
been a little more than human if he had not rejoiced
at the defeat of a minister so dangerous to the fate
of the colonies.   Perhaps, too, he thought of the in-
sulting reception accorded him in trying to thank
his lordship for the civilities extended during that
trip to Ireland.   Four visits did the forgiving Franklin make to the Earl, now returned to London ; each
time he got a curt " Not at home " in reward.   The
last time was on a levee day ; carriages were at

---

* Parton points out that the dislike felt for Lord Hillsborough by
his colleagues does not wholly explain the triumph of Franklin.
" He had induced, it appears, three members of the Privy Council to
become shareholders in the [Illinois] company. So far as the interests of the shareholders were concerned, their triumph was a barren
one, since the formalities requisite to give validity to the grant were
never permitted to be completed. This may have been Hillsborough's work, after all."

Hillsborough's door, and if ever a man was at home the Secretary of State for America was the individual. As was his wont, Franklin drove up in his coach, and the driver, having alighted, was opening the door of the carriage when the porter ran out and insolently rebuked him " for opening the door before he had inquired whether my lord was at home." Then, turning to the visitor, the servant said : " My lord is not at home." The agent for four great American provinces sent away from the house of the Secretary of State for America by an impertinent lackey ! No wonder, with such a brotherly spirit abroad, that the revolution was impending.

Yet Franklin flattered himself that with the accession of Lord Dartmouth affairs were to take a more favourable turn, and he began to hope, in a vague way, that ere many months he might be enabled to close up his official labours as a prelude to returning home. He was now (1772) sixty-six years old, and the comforts of his new house in Philadelphia, and the charm of a quiet old age, eloquently appealed to his taste for a dignified idleness. To be sure, there was much to please him in the whirl of London life. Dining, wining, going to the play, sustaining a voluminous correspondence with friends and relations, watching the ministry, attending to the English business of four colonies, and keeping his pen well inked for the defence of his country— the wonder is how he accomplished so much. His literary services in behalf of America included the publishing of a satirical set of " Rules for Reducing a Great Empire to a Small One,"—a fling at Hills-

13

borough—and of a burlesque " Edict of the King of
Prussia," which created a veritable sensation, and
was for the moment believed, if only by a few
woolly-heads, to be a genuine pronunciamento from
the great Frederick. The King set forth, ostensibly, that as " the first German settlements made
in the island of Britain were by colonies of people
subject to our renowned ducal ancestors, and drawn
from their dominions, under the conduct of Hengist,
Horsa, Hella, Uffa, Cerdicus, Ida, and others ";
and as " the said colonies have flourished under the
protection of our august house for ages past; have
never been emancipated therefrom; and yet have
hitherto yielded little profit to the same ;   and
whereas we ourself have in the last war fought for
and defended the said colonies against the power of
France," etc., it therefore became " just and expedient that a revenue should be raised from the
said colonies in Britain, towards our indemnification ;
and that those who are descendants of our ancient
subjects, and thence still owe us due obedience,
should contribute to the replenishing of our royal
coffers." Thereupon the fictitious King of Prussia
went on to levy heavy customs duties upon British
imports and exports, and to lay iniquitous restric-
tions upon the internal trade and manufactures of
the island.

" And lastly," said the " Edict," " being willing further to favour
our said colonies in Britain, we do hereby also ordain and command,
that all the *thieves*, highway and street robbers, house-breakers, for-
gerers, murderers, s–d–tes, and villains of every denomination, who
have forfeited their lives to the law of Prussia, but whom we, in our
great clemency, do not think fit here to hang, shall be emptied out of

our gaols into the said island of Great Britain, for the better peopling of that country.

" We flatter ourselves that these our royal regulations and commands will be thought *just and reasonable* by our much favoured colonists in England ; the said regulations being copied from their statutes of 10th and 11th William III., C. 10, 5th George II., C. 22, 23d George II., C. 26, 4th George I., C. 11, and from other equitable laws made by their Parliament ; or from instructions given by their princes ; or from resolutions of both Houses, entered into for the good government of their *own colonies in Ireland and America*.

" And all persons in the said Island are hereby cautioned not to oppose in any wise the execution of this our Edict, or any part thereof, such opposition being high treason ; of which all who are suspected shall be transported in fetters from Britain to Prussia, there to be tried and executed according to the Prussian law."

This product of Franklin's imaginative muse was, as need hardly be pointed out, an exquisite satirical paraphrase of the selfish policy pursued by the English Government for many years past toward the colonies, and the copies of the *Public Advertiser*, wherein it was published, in apparent seriousness, sold with unexpected rapidity.   Perhaps the sharpest hit of all was in the editorial note appended to the pretended " Edict "—" All here think the assertion it concludes with, that these regulations are copied from acts of the English Parliament respecting their colonies, a very injurious one ; it being impossible to believe that a people distinguished for their love of liberty, a nation so wise, so liberal in its sentiments, so just and equitable towards its neighbours, should, from mean and injudicious views of petty immediate profit, treat its own children in a manner so arbitrary and tyrannical ! "

At first the authorship of the " Edict " was not

generally attributed to Franklin, although it is
curious that those who knew his peculiar vein of
humour, and his talent for veiling satire under the
guise of matter-of-fact statement, did not at once
suspect him.   Several friends did, indeed, immediately light upon the real writer of the paper, yet
the great world of London, interested as it was in
the publication, proved not so quick.   Lord Mansfield shook his august head, and remarked that the
" Edict " was " very able and very artful indeed,"
but that it would do mischief by giving a bad impression of the measures of government and encour-
aging the colonies " in their contumacy."   Others
averred that it was the " keenest and severest "
piece which had appeared for many a day; a few, as
before indicated, actually fell into the trap, and
thought for the nonce that Frederick contemplated
the conquest of Great Britain.   Meanwhile the
" King of Prussia," otherwise Dr. Franklin, laughed
in his sleeve, and kept silent.   He was one of a
house-party at Lord le Despencer's on the morning
when the post brought down into the country the
number of the *Advertiser* containing the " Edict."
Paul Whitehead, " who runs early through all the
papers, and tells the company what he finds remarkable," came bustling into the breakfast-room
(where were the philosopher, the host, and the rest
of the party), with the paper in his agitated hand.
" Here," cried he, " here 's news for ye! Here 's
the King of Prussia claiming a right to this kingdom! " Everybody looked surprised, including the
astute Franklin. When Whitehead had read two

or three paragraphs of the exciting document one
of the guests roundly abused his Majesty of Prussia
for his impudence. " I dare say," he said, " we
shall hear by next post that he is upon his march
with one hundred thousand men to back this!"
Whereupon Whitehead, shrewder than the rest of
the company, began to realise the situation, and
turning to the author, he exclaimed: " I 'll be
hanged if this is not some of your American jokes
upon us." " The reading went on, and ended with
abundance of laughing, and a general verdict that
it was a fair hit; and the piece was cut out of the
paper and preserved in my lord's collection." *   In
his " Rules for Reducing a Great Empire to a Small
One," the satire is even more trenchant.

" Take special care," he tells all ministers who have the management of extensive dominions, "that the provinces are *never incorporated with the mother country;* that they do not enjoy the same
common rights, the same privileges in commerce ; and that they are
governed by severer laws, all of your enacting, without allowing
them any share in the choice of the legislators."

This and the other rules had about them more sad
truth than burlesque, and served better than a thous-
and pages of commonplace complaint to accentuate
the blundering and pig-headedness of successive
English ministries in their dealings toward America.   Had Franklin done nothing else for the colonies than to write the " Rules " and the " Edict,"
his name would have deserved a place on the scroll
of American patriotism.   No words of his could

* This episode is described by Franklin in a letter to his son
dated October 6, 1773.

avert the inevitable, yet happy the cause which
possessed so acute a champion.

Anxiously did this champion await the mails from
home as they came in slowly and irregularly; eagerly
did he digest the news from Massachusetts—indomitable, defiant Massachusetts.   How had events
shaped themselves in Boston since the fatal March
evening of 1770 when the presence there of British
regiments led to the conflict with the populace, and
the killing and wounding of some citizens ?   In the
following April the duties imposed by the Townshend bill, saving those on tea, were repealed;
whereupon it was agreed that no tea should be imported; then came the constitutional wrangles between the patriots and Governor Hutchinson, that
staunch defender of English so-called prerogative,
and finally the holding of a town meeting (October,
1772) to protest against the dangerous, liberty-
subverting policy whereby the provincial judges now
received their salaries direct from the crown, and
were removable at the pleasure of the King.   From
this gathering dated the formation of the famous
" Committee of Correspondence."   The committee
was organised to state the rights of the colonies, and
the rights of the people of Massachusetts in particular, " as men, as Christians, and as subjects "; it
helped materially to establish communication between the several provinces; and it gave impetus to
the plan of colonial union.*   By the autumn of 1773
the agitation against the importation, by the East

* See " The Revolution Impending," as treated by Mellen Cham-
berlain in vol. vi. of the *Narrative and Critical History of America.*

India Company, of the taxable tea had assumed formidable shape, and on a winter's evening toward the end of the same troubled year occurred that little "tea-party" presided over by the historic Bostonians who, masquerading as Indians, threw into the waters of the harbour eighteen thousand pounds' worth of the fragrant commodity.

By this time Franklin had entered upon one of the most picturesque episodes of his life; and in a few days he was to become the central figure of a little drama which might be taken as a prelude to the far greater drama of the Revolution. For such a scene we will appropriate a new chapter.

CHAPTER VIII

"A MAN OF LETTERS"

1773–1774

 E now come to what may be styled the most sensational incident of Franklin's multi-coloured life—an incident wherein his wondrous calmness and self-possession (qualities all the more striking because invested in a man of positive character and human personality) stand out in noble relief to the meanness and party passion that brought them into play. Many a victim so pursued by calumny might have succumbed to what was nothing more or less than a wave of political spite and littleness; it remained for the hero of our biography to emerge triumphant and find, in the sober judgment of history, as well as in the verdict of his countrymen, a vindication and reward. It is the affair of the Hutchinson letters and the Privy Council ordeal which we are now to briefly narrate.

In the course of an animated conversation with a " gentleman of character and distinction " * (a

---

* So Franklin characterises the mysterious unknown in his *Account of the Transactions Relating to Governor Hutchinson's Letters.*

gentleman whose identity remains a mystery to the
present day), Franklin had complained, not without
a proper resentment, of the sending of British troops
to Boston, and of the general treatment of the
Americans by the home government.   It was a
proof, he said, that England no longer had a paren-
tal regard for her children across the water.   Whereupon the aforesaid " gentleman of character and
distinction " assured the agent, much to the latter's
surprise, that not only the measures he particularly
censured so warmly, but all the other grievances
complained of, took their rise, not from the government, but " were projected, proposed to administration, solicited, and obtained by some of the most
respectable among the Americans themselves, as
necessary measures for the welfare of that country."
This was news to Franklin, who naturally asked for
proofs, if proofs there were, to substantiate so radical an assertion.   A few days later the " gentleman
of character and distinction " called on his friend
and produced a series of thirteen letters, six of which
had been written by Thomas Hutchinson, when
Lieutenant-Governor of Massachusetts (he was now
Governor), and four by Andrew Oliver, now Lieutenant-Governor of that province.   That their addresses were destroyed made little or no matter, for
although it was understood that they were originally
directed to William Whately, a lately deceased
member of Parliament and one-time secretary to
George Grenville, the letters were of a public rather
than a private nature, and had been destined, evidently, for extensive circulation in ministerial quar-

ters. To read them, therefore, was in nowise to infringe on the rights of *bona fide* personal correspondence, and so the American had no scruple in making himself master of their unusual contents.

To say that he was amazed at what he found in them is to express the situation mildly. For the letters were fervid appeals to the English Government to inaugurate in Massachusetts just that policy of foolish oppression which had created such a sea of trouble, and which now threatened to separate forever the parent country and America. Those eyes of Franklin, usually so tranquil, must have glistened with indignation, as he read one epistle after another. " There must be an abridgement of what are called English liberties," is the way in which Hutchinson advises the ministry (under date of January 20, 1769) to repress the independent spirit of the Bostonians, and he adds, grimly: " I doubt whether it is possible to project a system of government in which a colony three thousand miles distant from the parent state shall enjoy all the liberty of the parent state." All that he says, indeed, indicates a desire to coerce Massachusetts into the position of a dependency, ruled by an iron hand stretching from across the Atlantic—a suggestion which unhappily fit in only too well with the ideas of George III. and his satellites in Parliament. Andrew Oliver goes, if anything, even further in illiberal sentiment, although he, like Hutchinson, is a native of the colony which learns to hate him. He harps on the " effectual support " which government needs in Boston; speaks of the patriots as incendiaries (" If there will be no way to take off the original incendiaries, they will continue to instill their poison into the minds of the people, through the vehicle of the *Boston Gazette*"); suggests the formation of an Order of Patricians, and otherwise seems anxious to stamp out popular rule in the province, and to substitute therefor a half-military, half-aristocratic administration.   Another contributor to the famous set of letters is Charles Paxton, Commissioner of Customs at Boston, who writes in June, 1768, under the influence of a great fright due to an outburst of popular indignation, " Unless we have immediately two or three regiments, 't is the opinion of all the friends of Government that Boston will be in open rebellion."

Franklin looked upon the writing of such letters as outrageous, yet he felt that if the Americans could be brought to believe that the repressive measures taken in Boston were due rather to hints from that place than to English initiative, the animosity toward Britain might be lessened materially.

" Though astonished," he relates, " I could not but confess myself convinced, and I was ready, as he [the before-mentioned 'gentleman of character and distinction '] desired, to convince my countrymen ; for I saw, I felt indeed by its effect upon myself, the tendency it must have towards a reconciliation, which for the common good I earnestly wished ; it appeared, moreover, my duty to give my constituents intelligence of such importance to their affairs ; but there was some difficulty, as this gentleman would not permit copies to be taken of the letters ; and, if that could have been done, the authenticity of those copies might have been doubted and disputed.   My simple account of them, as papers I had seen, would have been still less certain ; I therefore wished to have the use of the originals for that purpose, which I at length obtained, on these express conditions : that they should not be printed ; that no copies should be taken of them ; that they should be shown only to a few of the leading people of the government ; and that they should be carefully returned."

The letters were quickly on their way to the Committee of Correspondence of the Massachusetts Assembly. When they arrived, and were handed about among the chosen few, the contempt already felt for Governor Hutchinson—a man, by the way, whose abilities were worthy of a more patriotic cause—increased a hundred-fold. As soon as the Assembly met, in the summer of 1773, the temper of the legislature was forcibly shown by the passing of a long series of resolutions aimed against the authors of the correspondence, and by the adoption of a petition to the King asking for the removal from office of Hutchinson and his Lieutenant-Governor, the crawling Oliver.*   In due time the petition reached Franklin, who sent it off post-haste to Lord Dartmouth, with a brief diplomatic note of explanation, wherein he assured his lordship that there existed in Massachusetts a sincere disposition to be on good terms with England. The Assembly, he said, had declared their desire " only to be put into the situation they were in before the Stamp Act. *They aim at no novelties.*" There was significance in the sentence last quoted, and the agent did well to put

---

* To the upholders of the English " prerogative " such action on the part of the Assembly must have seemed nothing short of sacrilege. How the Tory bosom of burly Dr. Johnson must have filled with rage when he read of it !—the same Johnson who once said of the Americans : " They are a race of convicts, and ought to be thankful for anything we allow them short of hanging."

it in italics.   He might be trusted for never missing
a point, even if that point—to be paradoxical—was
nothing more than an italic line.   Several days later
came a pretty reply from the noble Earl.   He would
place the petition before the King the next time he
should be admitted to the royal presence, and he
wrote, right genially :

> " I cannot help expressing to you the pleasure it gives me to hear,
> that a sincere disposition prevails in the people of that province
> [Massachusetts] to be on good terms with the mother country, and
> my earnest hope that the time is at no great distance when every
> ground of uneasiness will cease, and the most perfect tranquillity
> and happiness be restored to the breasts of that people."

It was late in the summer of 1773 when this polite
correspondence passed between Franklin and the
Secretary of State for America, and one might have
been warranted in supposing that something would
be done to relieve the province of Massachusetts of
its hated chief magistrate.   A peaceful solution of
all the difficulties might be read, presumably, in the
political horoscope.   In reality, however, the horoscope had nothing so propitious to promise; neither
the King nor the ministry as a whole had any desire to punish such staunch defenders of royal claims
as Hutchinson and his coadjutor; it would not be
long ere the atmosphere of the colonial office would
become surcharged with all manner of dangerous
currents.   Franklin would find the court party crying out against him as an incendiary, and he must
write later that " the very action upon which I
valued myself, as it appeared to me a means of
lessening our differences. I was unlucky enough to

find charged upon me, as a wicked attempt to increase them." Well might he add, " Strange perversion!"

The first muttering of the impending storm came in the shape of a duel. Thomas Whately, a banker, and the brother and executor of William Whately, the Englishman to whom the letters of Hutchinson *et al* were ostensibly addressed, intimated that John Temple, a one-time colonial lieutenant-governor, had stolen the documents. Temple vigorously denied the accusation; the scandal worked its way into the newspapers, and as the all-important letters had by this time mysteriously appeared in print on both sides of the water, the matter furnished food for gossip to many a staid old Londoner. The banker did not directly charge Temple with the theft, but his public statement was enough to make an innocent man burn with anger. Mr. Temple, he explained, had been allowed to go over the correspondence of the deceased Whately, for the purpose of taking certain letters to which he was legitimately entitled, and had thus enjoyed free access to the whole mass of writing which made up the literary remains, as it were, of the dead Grenvillian.

"I made no scruple to lay before him, and occasionally during his visit to leave with him, several parcels of letters from my late brother's correspondents in America, in the exact state in which they had come into my possession ; some regularly sorted, and some promiscuously tied together ; and some of them were from Mr. Temple himself and his brother, and from Governor Hutchinson, Mr. Oliver, and others ; and, during the intervals that I was in the room with Mr. Temple, we did together cast our eyes on one or two letters of Governor Hutchinson, and I believe one or two other correspondents of my late brother."

To this impeachment, the more contemptible because so indirect, and yet so calculated to prejudice
the town, Temple replied by pointing out, very
justly, that Thomas Whately had no knowledge
that the compromising letters were in William
Whately's possession at the time of the latter's
death. No one could have read this verbal war
with keener interest than did Franklin —he who knew
who had procured the letters, and who guarded the
secret so admirably that such it will, in all likelihood, ever remain. He kept silence, however, for,
as he tells us, he thought the altercation would end,
" as other newspaper controversies usually do, when
the parties and the public should be tired of them."
—" I had not the gift of prophecy; I could not foresee that the gentlemen would fight."

But fight the two gentlemen did, very early on a
cold December morning. Arthur Lee, who was
then in England studying law, and holding the position of " substitute " for Franklin as agent for the
Massachusetts Assembly, has left us a record of the
encounter, in which he himself was interested.

" Mr. Temple determined to send Mr. Whately a challenge. Mr.
Izard * bore it, and offered to be his second. Mr. Whately accepted
the meeting, but refused to have a second. Four o'clock, in the
ring at Hyde Park, was the appointment. Mr. Izard and myself
went to the park in his carriage to attend the issue. On our way to
the ring our attention was drawn to another quarter, by the report of
pistols. Thither we went and met Mr. Whately coming from the
field of action, having received a slight wound in the breast and one
on the shoulder a little behind; both with a sword. He made no
charge to us of unfair play on the part of his antagonist. Mr. Izard

* Ralph Izard, of South Carolina.

offered his carriage to carry him home, which he accepted, and Mr.
Izard accompanied him.   I went in quest of Mr. Temple, and we
walked together to Mr. Izard's house.   He informed me that some
persons being at the ring Mr. Whately and he agreed to go to a different part.   Mr. Whately had a sword but no pistols.   He lent him one
of his, they fired without effect, and then appealed to the sword ; at
which he found his antagonist so little skilled that his life was at his
mercy ; that he wounded him slightly in order to make him beg his
pardon.   A whisper, however, was soon circulated that Mr. Temple
had attempted to stab his opponent when down.   To corroborate
which, a declaration from Mr. Whately supported by the affidavits
of an alehouse-keeper and some stable-boy were published, affirming
that when Mr. Whately fell on his face the other stabbed him
behind."*

Thomas Whately was, in fact, a mean, despicable
specimen of humanity, as we shall see anon in his
treatment of Franklin.

Lee continues :

" As this business was in fact political and concerned America, I
wrote a justification of Mr. Temple, in which I stated that Mr.
Whately had accused him on mere suspicion ; that he refused to have
seconds ; came without pistols ; made no charge against Mr. Temple
when we met him, warm from the encounter, and most likely to
have exclaimed against such treatment ; neither did those who had
parted the combatants and were with him, say a word of it.   That
the slight wound on the shoulder, which gave countenance to this
malignant charge, might well have happened from Mr. Temple
being in the act of thrusting when his opponent fell, and by that
means unintentionally touching him on the shoulder."

It may be imagined that when affairs were left in
this unsatisfactory shape, and a second duel was
spoken of, Dr. Franklin should think it high time to
pour oil upon the troubled waters.   He held the
key to the mystery of the letters, and though he

---

* *Life of Arthur Lee, LL.D.*, by Richard Henry Lee.

could not reveal the identity of the " gentleman of character and distinction," he must at least vindicate the ill-used Temple. Accordingly, on Christmas Day, an appropriate time for a kind action, he wrote to the *Public Advertiser* declaring that he alone was the person who obtained and transmitted to Boston the letters in question.

" Mr. W.," he explained, " could not communicate them, because they were never in his possession ; and for the same reason they could never be taken from him by Mr. T. They were not of the nature of *private* letters between friends. They were written by public officers to persons in public stations, on public affairs, and intended to procure public measures ; they were therefore handed to other public persons, who might be influenced by them to produce these measures. Their tendency was to incense the mother-country against her colonies, and, by the steps recommended, to widen the breach ; which they effected. The chief caution expressed with regard to privacy was, to keep their contents from the colony agents, who, the writers apprehended, might return them, or copies of them, to America. The apprehension was, it seems, well founded ; for the first agent who laid his hands on them thought it his duty to transmit them to his constituents."

To which communication the writer manfully signed himself, " B. Franklin, Agent for the House of Representatives of Massachusetts Bay."

The agent had thus spoken for himself, as well as for Temple, but little good would the justification do him so far as those in power were concerned. The temper of the King and government was now for stern dealing with America; there were to be no concessions, and no punishment of Hutchinson and Oliver; on the contrary, the provincials at large were to be regarded as a lot of traitors, with the pestifer-

14

ous Franklin (whose transmission to Boston of the Hutchinson letters was considered an unforgivable crime) as the chief conspirator. And as he was in London, an easy prey to official abuse and ill-usage, why not let him suffer *in propria persona* for the sins of his countrymen, as well as for those upon his own head ? We shall see how the cabal against him and his was prosecuted.

On a Saturday in January, 1774, Franklin received word that the Privy Council would meet on the Tuesday following, to consider the petition of the Massachusetts Assembly *in re* the removal of Hutchinson and Oliver. It was a short notice, in all conscience, and the doctor at once bestirred himself. Should he employ other counsel than Mr. Bollan ? (agent for the Council of Massachusetts) was the question, and he proceeded to ask that gentleman. Mr. Bollan thought it not advisable to employ other counsel. " He had sometimes done it in colony cases, and found lawyers of little service. Those who are eminent, and hope to rise in their profession, are unwilling to offend the court; and *its disposition on this occasion was well known.*" He would undertake to support the petition himself, in his capacity as agent for the Council. So far, so good. But late on Monday afternoon Franklin heard, to his great surprise, that Israel Mauduit, agent for the Governor and Lieutenant-Governor of Massachusetts, had obtained leave to bring counsel to the Cockpit the next morning, to defend his clients before their lordships. Of course it was too late, by this time, to do anything in the way of engaging

distinguished lawyers in behalf of the petition, and
so Tuesday found Franklin on hand with no one but
Bollan to assist him.

The first thing the lords of the Privy Council did
was to refuse recognition to Bollan, on the plea that
as he did not represent the Assembly of Massachusetts he had no right to speak upon a petition presented from that body.   It may have been good law
to decide against him, but to raise the point was un-
generous, and none the less so because it left Franklin to bear the full brunt of defending the appeal to
the King.   However, Bollan was duly extinguished,
while the doctor manfully prepared for a battle
which, as he must have suspected, would prove a
losing one for the colony—a battle wherein his
chief antagonist was the unprincipled Wedderburn,
Solicitor-General for the government, who was
present to represent Mauduit, to discountenance the
cause of the petitioners, and to espouse the treachery
of Hutchinson and Oliver.   It was only with difficulty, owing to the opposition of Wedderburn, that
the Assembly's agent could induce the court to accept as evidence authenticated copies of the famous
letters, but, having at last accomplished this, he informed their lordships that he was surprised that
counsel should have been employed against the
petition ; that he apprehended this matter " was
rather a question of civil or political prudence,
whether on the state of the fact that the governors
had lost all trust and confidence with the people,
and become universally obnoxious, it would be for
the interest of his Majesty's service to continue

them in those stations in that province "; that he conceived this " to be a question of which their lord-ships were already perfect judges, and should receive no assistance in it from the arguments of counsel "; but, that if counsel were to be heard on the other side, he must request leave to bring someone to represent the Assembly.

Whereupon Mr. Mauduit was asked if he would waive the leave he had to appear by counsel, so that their lordships might proceed immediately to con-sider the petition. The fact was, that the Privy Council, having made up its mind beforehand, was probably anxious to go on with the sitting, and to make its report. But Mauduit was not to be shunted off in this wise. " I know well Dr. Frank-lin's abilities," he shrewdly informed the court, " and wish to put the defence of my friends on a parity with the attack; he will not therefore wonder that I choose to appear before your lordships with the assistance of counsel." It was finally agreed, therefore, that the hearing should be adjourned until the 29th of January. The implacable Wedderburn, who saw in the case a glorious opportunity to bask in the sunshine of royal and governmental favour, announced that he would reserve to himself the right of asking at that time how the Assembly came into possession of the letters, through what hands and by what means they were procured.

" Certainly," replied Lord Chief-Justice De Grey with austerity, " and to whom directed; for the perfect understanding of the pas-sages may depend on that and other such circumstances. We can receive no charge against a man founded on letters directed to nobody, and perhaps received by nobody. The laws of this country have no such practice."

Then, as he was quietly putting up his papers, Franklin was asked by the Lord President whether he intended to answer such questions. " In that, I shall take counsel," was the prudent reply.*

Franklin began at once to get ready for the struggle by asking the advice of the great Mr. Dunning, a barrister of remarkable abilities, but with a voice, presence, and delivery singularly unprepossessing. Must he answer the most important question threatened by Wedderburn — the question as to who originally put the Hutchinson letters into the hands of the agent ? No, said Dunning; the agent could not be forced so to do. The American breathed more easily. He did not expect to meet with any success in behalf of the petition, but no stone should be left unturned whereby he could place the cause of Massachusetts in the proper light, even if that light were not to penetrate the wilfully closed eyes of obsequious courtiers. Soon Arthur Lee came up from Bath to help his chief; Mr. Dunning and John Lee, another able lawyer, were engaged to appear before the Council; a line of policy was mapped out. The doctor also kept well informed as to the rumours that were floating about, and had many reasons to think that he was in the worst possible odour with the ministry and the friends of royalty. It was even hinted that there was a design to arrest him, to seize his papers, and to pack him off to Newgate,

* See Franklin's letter to Thomas Cushing, of Boston, under date of February 15, 1774.

there to meditate, no doubt, on his audacity and ingratitude. He was to be deprived of his post-master-generalship; the petition was to be scornfully rejected; the Assembly of Massachusetts would be censured, and the Governor would be picked out for well-deserved honours. Such were the reports.

While Franklin was calmly listening to this ominous gossip, and making ready his brief, Thomas Whately suddenly clapped upon his back a disagreeable Chancery suit. The basis of action was ludicrous enough, it being falsely contended that the doctor had caused the Hutchinson-Oliver correspondence to be printed; that he had disposed of great numbers of the copies thereof; and that he should therefore be compelled to render an account for the profits of the aforesaid printing to the injured plaintiff, as administrator of the estate of the late William Whately. The suit was the result of political animus rather than of personal spite, but viewed in any light it bore ample testimony to the meanness of the living Whately, who was under deep obligation to Franklin. The philosopher had helped him to reclaim some valuable lands in Pennsylvania, purchased years before by Whately's grandfather. Here was an exhibition of the grandson's gratitude. Franklin drew up the necessary defence to the suit (a suit which came to naught, it is pleasant to add), and he was soon able to trace the motive of this attack upon him to its proper source. For he writes:

"It was about this time become evident, that all thoughts of reconciliation with the colony of the Massachusetts Bay, by attention to their petitions, and a redress of their grievances, was laid aside ; that severity was resolved ; and that the decrying and vilifying the people of that country, and me their agent, among the rest, was quite a court measure. It was the *ton* with all the ministerial folks to abuse them and me, in every company and in every newspaper . . . but the attack from Mr. Whately was, I own, a surprise to me ; under the above-mentioned circumstances of obligation, and without the slightest provocation, I could not have imagined any man base enough to commence, *of his own* motion, such a vexatious suit against me. But a little accidental information served to throw some light upon the business. An acquaintance * calling on me, after having been at the Treasury, showed me what he styled *a pretty thing*, for a friend of his ; it was an order for one hundred and fifty pounds, payable to Dr. Samuel Johnson, said to be one half of his yearly pension, and drawn by the secretary of the Treasury on this same Mr. Whately. I then considered him as a banker to the Treasury for the pension money, and thence as having an interested connexion with the administration, that might induce him to *act by direction* of others in harassing me with this suit ; which gave me if possible a *still meaner* opinion of him, than if he had done it of his own accord."

As the time approached for the adjourned hearing before the Privy Council, it began to be pretty well understood that something highly entertaining, if not actually startling, was to take place. England was to have her innings against America, and it was playfully whispered among the inner governmental circles that the fiery Wedderburn had a pretty rod in pickle for that troublesome, rebellious Dr. Franklin. There were worthy gentlemen, therefore, who looked forward to the coming examination as they might have anticipated a comedy at Drury Lane ; all thought of statecraft or patriotism was sunk in the idea that the Lords of the Council were preparing an amusing production of spectacular adjuncts,

* William Strahan, M. P., the King's printer.

with the Solicitor-General as the leading actor—call
him comedian, hero, heavy villain, or what not—in
the curious performance.   Nor is it strange, therefore, that when the ardently expected morning
arrived the Cockpit was crowded with a throng
anxious to witness the real business of the day,
which would be the impaling of Franklin rather than
the respectful consideration of a respectful petition.
That day proved one of the least creditable in the
long history of a nation to which one is accustomed
to look for great things, not for littleness.

When the examination began the room presented
a brilliant spectacle, with its array of handsomely
dressed Privy Councillors, who were seated at a long
table, and who had for a background all the tip-
toeing spectators fortunate enough to penetrate the
not over-large apartment.   Dr. Franklin, the intended victim, stood near the fireplace, gazing
stoically upon his enemies.   He was clad in a full-
dress suit of spotted Manchester velvet (that historic
suit which he was to don again on a more propitious
occasion), and his head was adorned by an old-
fashioned, flowing wig.   There he remained throughout the ordeal, "conspicuously erect," without
betraying a telltale movement in any part of his
body.   "The muscles of his face had been previously composed, so as to afford a placid, tranquil
expression of countenance."   The man was waiting
to play his part—one of immobility and seeming
indifference to the taunts of prejudice.

After the preliminaries of the hearing had been disposed of (the petition being read, and the copies of

the letters admitted as evidence), it was remarked
that Wedderburn asked none of the threatened questions.   He was reserving his ammunition for more
interesting game.   In the meanwhile, the counsel
for the Assembly, Messrs. Dunning and John Lee,
spoke of the discontent of the Bostonians, " and acquitted themselves," as Franklin narrates, " very
handsomely ; only Mr. Dunning, having a disorder
on his lungs that weakened his voice exceedingly,
was not so perfectly heard as one could have
wished."   That defect, however, made no manner
of difference ; their lordships had come to hear the
Solicitor-General, not counsel for the " defence."
And the Solicitor-General had primed himself to
please their lordships.

Wedderburn, upon rising to address them,
launched into a glowing eulogy of Governor Hutchinson, whom he painted in the colours of a suffering hero, oppressed by turbulent, unfeeling men.
But praise of Hutchinson was merely the prelude to
his harangue ; he soon branched off into the most
outrageous abuse of Franklin, " who stood there
the butt of his invective ribaldry for near an hour,
not a single lord adverting to the impropriety and
indecency of treating a public messenger in so
ignominious a manner."

" How these letters came into the possession of anyone but the right
owners," Wedderburn went on, " is a mystery for Dr. Franklin to
explain.   They who know the affectionate regard which the Whatelys
had for each other, and the tender concern they felt for the honour of
their brother's memory, as well as their own, can witness the distress
which this occasioned.   My lords, the late Mr. Whately was most
scrupulously cautious about his letters.   We lived for many years in

the strictest intimacy [which may have been true, for Wedderburn loved to cultivate men in the confidence of ministry], and in all those years I never saw a single letter written to him. These letters, I believe [he believed nothing of the sort], were in his custody at his death ; and I as firmly believe that without fraud they could not have been got out of the custody of the person whose hands they fell into. His brothers little wanted this additional aggravation to the loss of him. The letters, I say, could not have come to Dr. Franklin by fair means. The writers did not give them to him ; nor yet the deceased correspondent, who from our intimacy would otherwise have told me of it. Nothing, then, will acquit Dr. Franklin of the charge of obtaining them by fraudulent or corrupt means, for the most malignant purposes, unless he stole them from the person who stole them. This argument is irrefragable. I hope, my lords, you will mark and brand the man, for the honour of this country, of Europe, and of mankind. Private correspondence has hitherto been held sacred in times of the greatest party rage, not only in politics but religion. He has forfeited all the respect of societies and of men. Into what companies will he hereafter go with an unembarrassed face, or the honest intrepidity of virtue? Men will watch him with a jealous eye ; they will hide their papers from him, and lock up their escritoires. He will henceforth esteem it a libel to be called *a man of letters ; Homo Trium literarum !*"

In classic Latin Wedderburn had stigmatised Franklin as a thief—*Fur*—" a man of three letters." Then he continued :

"Your lordships know the train of mischiefs which followed. Wherein had my late worthy friend or his family offended Dr. Franklin, that he should first do so great an injury to the memory of the dead brother, by secreting and sending away his letters ; and then, conscious of what he had done, should keep himself concealed, till he had nearly, very nearly, occasioned the murder of the other. After the mischiefs of this concealment had been left for five months to have their full operation, at length comes out a letter, which it is impossible to read without horror (*sic*), expressive of the coolest and most deliberate malevolence. My lords, what poetic fiction only had penned for the breast of a cruel African, Dr. Franklin has realised and transcribed from his own.   His, too, is the language of a *Zanga* : *

> " ' Know then 't was ——— I.
> *I* forged the letter, —*I* disposed the picture,
> *I* hated, *I* despised, and *I* destroy.' "

This was the language to which the venerable agent was obliged to listen in philosophical silence. Not a feature of his face moved; not a muscle quivered in angry response to the insults heaped upon him.   As the speech grew more vindictive, the audience watched the American even more intently than before, but his countenance might have been of wood for all the feeling to be traced upon it. Never had he been so sublimely superior to the " slings and arrows of outrageous fortune."

What made the ordeal the greater was that the Privy Councillors, the very Councillors who should have represented the dignity and the majesty of the crown, encouraged the taunts of Wedderburn by loud laughter and applause.   Surely there was something " rotten in Denmark," or in English politics, when men of distinction could lend themselves so openly to such an exhibition.   At the sallies of Wedderburn's sarcastic wit, says Dr. Priestley, " all the members of the Council, the President himself (Lord Gower) not excepted, frequently laughed outright.   No person belonging to the Council behaved with decent gravity except Lord North, who, coming late, took his stand behind the chair opposite to me." †   Doubtless the

---

* Wedderburn was quoting from Dr. Young's *Revenge*.

†" Not one of their lordships," Franklin writes to Thomas Cush-

appreciation of flings like the following was particularly keen on the part of their lordships:

"A foreign ambassador, when residing here, just before the breaking out of a war, or upon particular occasions, may bribe a villain to steal or betray any state papers ; he is under the command of another state, and is not amenable to the laws of the country where he resides ; and the secure exemption from punishment may induce a laxer morality. But Dr. Franklin, whatever he may teach the people of Boston, while he is *here*, at least, is a subject, and if a subject injure a subject, he is answerable to the law. And the Court of Chancery will not much attend to his new self-created importance.

"The letters from Boston for two years past have intimated that Dr. Franklin was aiming at Mr. Hutchinson's government. It was not easy before this to give credit to such surmises. But nothing surely but a too eager attention to an ambition of this sort, could have betrayed a wise man into such conduct as we have now seen. Whether these surmises are true or not, your lordships are much the best judges. If they should be true, I hope that Mr. Hutchinson will not meet with the less countenance from your lordships for his *rival's* being his accuser. Nor will your lordships, I trust, from what you have heard, advise the having Mr. Hutchinson displaced, in order to make room for Dr. Franklin as a successor.

"On the part of Mr. Hutchinson and Mr. Oliver, I am instructed to assure your lordships," Wedderburn hypocritically concluded, "that they feel no spark of resentment, even at the individuals who have done them this injustice. Their private letters breathe nothing but moderation. They are convinced that the people, though misled, are innocent. If the conduct of a few should provoke a just indig-

ing, "checked and recalled the orator to the business before them, but, on the contrary, a very few excepted, they seemed to enjoy highly the entertainment, and frequently burst out in loud applauses. This part of his speech was thought so good that they have since printed it, in order to defame me everywhere, and particularly to destroy my reputation on your side of the water ; but the grosser parts of the abuse are omitted, appearing, I suppose, in their own eyes, too foul to be seen on paper, so that the speech, compared to what it was, is now perfectly decent."

nation, they would be the most forward, and, I trust, the most effi-
cacious solicitors to avert its effects, and to excuse the men.   They
love the soil, the constitution, the people of New England ; they
look with reverence to this country, and with affection to that.   For
the sake of the people they wish some faults corrected, anarchy abol-
ished, and government re-established.   But these salutary ends they
wish to promote by the gentlest means, and the abridging of no
liberties which a people can possibly use to its own advantage.   A
restraint from self-destruction is the only restraint they desire to be
imposed upon New England."

This is not all of the speech, but it is enough to
indicate the nature of the attack.   Delivered, as it
was, with much rhetorical emphasis, and with an
assumed air of indignant sincerity, it fell delightfully
upon the jaded ears of the Privy Councillors, and
made of the Solicitor-General a momentary hero.
Not, of course, to all the listeners was he a hero,
and his malevolent eloquence so fired the heart of
Dr. Priestley with a virtuous contempt that the good
gentleman refused to speak to Wedderburn at the
close of the so-called examination.   As for the
formal action of the Privy Council, it was embodied
in a cut-and-dried report advising his Majesty that
the petition of the Massachusetts Assembly was
founded upon resolutions " formed upon false and
erroneous allegations," being " groundless, vexatious, and scandalous; and calculated only for the
seditious purposes of keeping up a spirit of clamour
and discontent in the said province."   Franklin
came in for the inevitable censure (*Mr.* Franklin
the report styled him), and the King was finally told
that nothing had been laid before the Councillors
" which does or can, in their opinion, in any man-

ner, or in any degree, impeach the honour, integrity,
or conduct of the said Governor or Lieutenant-Governor; and their lordships are humbly of opinion,
that the said petition ought to be dismissed." Accordingly, and with great pleasure, George III. was
pleased to take the advice of his faithful Council,
and did so order that the said petition be dismissed
as groundless, vexatious, scandalous, etc., etc. The
Revolution was on the way.

The day after the Privy Council farce, Dr. Priestley went to breakfast with Franklin, at the latter's
lodgings in Craven Street. The philosopher was
serene, as usual, and remarked, anent the outrageous tirade of Wedderburn: " I have never before
been so sensible of the power of a good conscience;
for, if I had not considered the thing for which I
have been so much insulted as one of the best actions of my life, and what I should certainly do
again in the same circumstances, I should not have
supported it." Nor did the insult end with the
entertainment of the Cockpit. Within twenty-four
hours Franklin received formal notice that his
Majesty's Postmaster-General " found it necessary " to dismiss him from his office of Postmaster-
General in North America.

" The expression," as the deposed official wrote to Thomas Cushing,
" was well chosen, for in truth they were *under a necessity* of doing
it; it was not their own inclination; they had no fault to find with
my conduct in the office; they knew my merit in it, and that, if it
was now an office of value, it had become such chiefly through my
care and good management."

The persecution of the great American had now

been accomplished to the satisfaction of King
George and his ministerial henchmen; the stiff-
necked provincials were rebuked in the person of
their distinguished representative.   But the gentlemen of government forgot that in loading Franklin
with abuse they had increased a hundred-fold his influence with his own countrymen.   To make a man
a martyr is to make him likewise a power.

CHAPTER IX

1774-1776

AD " B. Franklin, agent," as he modestly described himself, packed up his trunks during the spring of 1774, and sailed away from the country whose public servants had used him so ill, he would have found himself, on reaching home, the most popular man in America. His treatment by Wedderburn, the hatred shown him by the court party, and the loss of his postmaster-generalship, served only to endear the philosopher to those who guarded so anxiously the threatened liberties of their native land. What more natural, therefore, than to return to his own shores, and there reap the reward of his Titanic, if unsuccessful labours, by playing the hero and enjoying the approbation and applause of the colonies? The prospect would have held out temptations to a statesman of the selfish, vainglorious kind. But Franklin was cast in a different mould: although he had his share of vanity, as he was free to confess, egotism could

not run away with his head or heart. His usefulness as a colonial agent was gone completely, now
that the Privy Council had insulted both him and
those he represented; yet for all that, he reasoned,
he might aid America by staying in London and
working indirectly rather than officially. Despite
the clamours of government, to whom the question
of provincial rights had become as the red rag to the
proverbial bull, many Englishmen took a fair-minded
view of the situation, and among them were certain
members of Parliament with an influence and kindly
disposition which seemed worth the cultivation.
There, for instance, was that shining champion of
America, Lord Chatham (the one-time Mr. Pitt),
whose moral support might mean volumes, even
though he happened to be in opposition to the ministry. Thus it came to pass that Franklin, still
hopeful as a schoolboy, determined to stick to his
colours, and to try the effect of a little quiet diplomacy. It was about this time that he devised the
famous emblematic picture representing the future
condition of Great Britain, should she persist in her
oppression of the colonies. The design was reproduced on copper-plate, struck off on cards, and
printed, too, with an " explanation " and " moral "
attached.

" Great Britain," said the explanation, " is supposed to have been
placed upon the globe ; but the colonies (that is, her limbs), being
severed from her, she is seen lifting her eyes and mangled stumps to
Heaven ; her shield, which she is unable to wield, lies useless by her
side ; her lance has pierced New England ; the laurel branch has fallen from the hand of Pennsylvania ; the English oak has lost its head,
and stands a bare trunk, with a few withered branches ; briers and

15

thorns are on the ground beneath it ; the British ships have brooms at their topmastheads, denoting their being on sale ; and Britannia herself is seen sliding off the world (no longer able to hold its balance) her fragments overspread with the label, DATE OBOLUM BELISARIO."

On one thing, however, the agent was determined ; he would attend no more the levees of any of the ministers. Some proper show of resentment, both for personal and national reasons, was plainly necessary. " I made no justification of myself from the charges brought against me," he afterward explained to his son, in detailing this period of his public service; " I made no return of the injury by abusing my adversaries; but held a cool, sullen silence, reserving myself to some future opportunity." And now and then he had the satisfaction of hearing that the " reasonable part of the administration " were ashamed of the way in which they had treated him. Perhaps, too, the " reasonable part of the administration " had enough common sense to view with alarm the spirit of revenge displayed toward the colonies by the " unreasonable part " of their official family. For we must not forget that in the spring of 1774 Lord North brought into Parliament, and had passed, that vindictive bill closing the port of Boston until such time as " order " was restored and indemnification made for the tea so merrily pitched into the water. Two other oppressive measures, more sweeping in scope and no less iniquitous, were likewise enacted ; furthermore, General Gage arrived in Boston to relieve the despised Hutchinson (who went to England to confer with the Government); and by midsummer vessels

GREAT BRITAIN TRUNCATED.

AFTER THE EMBLEMATICAL DESIGN PREPARED BY FRANKLIN AND ENGRAVED FOR HIM ON COPPERPLATE.

loaded with British troops were sailing into the harbour. The real contest was about to begin. Already were preparations being made throughout the excited provinces for the Continental Congress to be held at Philadelphia in the coming September.

Each idiotic act of the ministry only increased the desire of the discountenanced agent to do what he could, in the byways rather than in the highways of politics, to avert the gathering storm. A coalition ministry, more favourably disposed toward the colonies, was now the hope of the Parliamentary minority, and to assist, however indirectly, in the formation of such a cabinet became his dearest wish. Numerous were the interviews he had with the " reasonable " members of both Houses, whom he besought and conjured " not to suffer, by their little misunderstandings, so glorious a fabric as the present British empire to be demolished by these blunderers "—for, in spite of all that had gone before, Franklin still desired an honourable union between the mother country and her far-away plantations.* It was in the heat of all this eloquent appeal to the English conscience that Lord Chatham, from whom, once upon a time, he could not get an audience, asked to see the distinguished American and was pleased to treat him with an " abundance of civility." The reader with an imagination cannot but envy the witnesses of a meeting in which the great English statesman expressed a

* The reader is referred to *An Account of Negotiations in London for Effecting a Reconciliation between Great Britain and the American Colonies*, written by Franklin for his son.

love for his brethren across the Atlantic, and the
hope that they would " continue firm and united in
defending by all peaceable and legal means their
constitutional rights."

If Franklin, on his part, did not contrast the past
inaccessibility of the noble Earl with the new conditions, he must have been less human than biographers fondly suppose. Perhaps the doctor
deferred any such triumphant comparison until
later. Be that as it may, he assured Lord Chatham
that he lamented the impending ruin of a magnificent empire, and " hoped that if his lordship, with
the other great and wise men of the British nation,
would unite and exert themselves, it might yet be
rescued out of the mangling hands of the present
set of blundering ministers." His lordship was
pleased with this exposition of the case—that the
ministers were blunderers who should know better
than the resourceful, far-seeing Pitt ?—but he spoke
of the proposed coalition cabinet as something
rather to be desired than expected. Then there
was the opinion prevailing in England that America
aimed at complete independence—" what of that ? "
he asked. The ready Franklin was quick with a comforting answer. He had more than once travelled
almost from one end of the American continent to
the other, and " kept a great variety of company,
eating, drinking, and conversing with them freely,"
but never had he heard " in any conversation, from
any person, drunk or sober, the least expression of
a wish for a separation, or hint that such a thing
would be advantageous to America." Lord Chat-

ham felt reassured, and did not fail to say how glad
he was to learn from the good doctor's lips that
" independence " was not an issue, and he conde-
scendingly intimated a desire to see his new friend
" as often as might be." The visitor, who was
charmed with the politeness and liberal sentiments
of the great Englishman, murmured how sensible
he was of such an honour, and of the advantages he
should reap from his lordship's instructive conversation, and so bowed himself out. Before another
year had ended the first blood of the Revolution
flowed at Lexington and Concord; in less than two
years from the date of the Chatham-Franklin interview American independence had become a fact,
with the philosopher as one of its most devoted sup-
porters. *Tempora mutantur !*

But who so bold as to foretell, on that August
day of 1774, when these two patriots met for the
first time, that America would ere long become a
sovereign nation and a power unto herself ? The
situation then seemed as inscrutable as a complicated game of chess—a game, in this instance, whose
happy solution was materially prevented by the
presence on the board of a troublesome King. And
it was through chess-playing, curiously enough, that
a few Englishmen sought to engage Franklin in a
scheme to effect the reconciliation between the two
countries, and to use him as a well-rewarded negoti-
ator who should bring every influence to bear in
putting his fellow-Americans in a more amiable
frame of mind. It was a colossal scheme, which
had for its beginning an invitation to take part in a

friendly little game with the Honourable Mistress Howe, a sister of the Admiral Lord Howe, who was later to figure in the Revolutionary struggle. Mistress Howe, Franklin was told, desired to meet him, for she fancied she could beat him at his once favourite chess. Although the doctor was out of practice, he gallantly sent word that he would wait upon the lady when she should think fit. He was a democrat and, when he so willed, a terrible stoic, but to resist the attention of an attractive member of the aristocracy was not in his nature. Amid all his troubles he could never despise the *éclat* of a London drawing-room, nor forget that the more he went out among " people of quality " the more did he increase his own influence and power to benefit the country of his birth.

So to the house of the Honourable Mistress Howe he repaired one day, accompanied by a member of the Royal Society, and played a few games with the fair hostess, whom he found of such " sensible conversation and pleasing behaviour " that he was easily induced to arrange for another trial of skill. He was a susceptible old gentleman was our hero. Thus far, so he says, he had no suspicion that the kings and knights and pawns were but a pretext. Nor did he see any connection between chess and politics when David Barclay, M.P., hinted to him, just at this time, at the " great merit that person would have who could contrive some means of preventing so terrible a calamity " as civil war between England and America. No one might effect more in that direction than Franklin himself, said Mr.

CARPENTERS' HALL, PHILADELPHIA.
WHEREIN MET THE FIRST CONTINENTAL CONGRESS, 1774.

Barclay, particularly as it was understood that the
ministry would be very glad to emerge from their
embarrassments on any terms, " only saving the
honour and dignity of government." The doctor
was dubious, but promised to consider the matter;
he ended by being drawn into a conference with Dr.
Fothergill, at whose request he wrote out a plan by
which, he thought, a reconciliation might possibly
be brought about. This plan suggested as a concession to Great Britain that the tea thrown into
Boston harbour should be paid for by Massachusetts
(a proposition which caused Samuel Adams to cry
out: " Franklin may be a good philosopher, but he
is a bungling politician "), but it exacted from the
mother country the repeal of the tea-duty and of all
acts restraining manufactures in the colonies, and
provided, in a general way, for the granting of a
liberal but judicious autonomy to the people of
America.

It was in the afternoon preceding the evening on
which Franklin had his interview with Dr. Fothergill and David Barclay that he enjoyed—remarkable
coincidence—his second chess party with the Honourable and highly entertaining Mistress Howe.
After a pleasant experience with the chessmen, the
two players drifted into a little chat, first on a
mathematical problem, and then on the disposition
of the new Parliament. Here we begin to see the
fine diplomatic hand of the woman. " And what
is to be done with this dispute between Great Britain
and the colonies ? " she asked, doubtless with all the
innocence appertaining to femininity; " I hope we

are not to have a civil war ? "   " Why, they should
kiss and be friends," responded the philosopher;
" what can they do better ?   Quarrelling can be of
service to neither, but is ruin to both."   Then Mistress Howe grew more intimate.   " I have often
said," she sighed, " that I wished government would
employ you to settle the dispute for them; I am
sure nobody could do it so well.   Do not you think
that the thing is practicable ?"   " Undoubtedly,
madame," answered Franklin, " if the parties are
disposed to reconciliation; for the two countries
have really no clashing interests to differ about.   It
is rather a matter of punctilio, which two or three
reasonable people might settle in half an hour.   I
thank you for the good opinion you are pleased to
express of me; but the ministers will never think of
employing me in that good work; they choose rather
to abuse me."   " Aye," said Mistress Howe, with
a pretty indignation, let us suppose, in her sympa-
thetic voice, " they have behaved shamefully to
you.   And indeed some of them are now ashamed
of it themselves."   So the talk ended.   " I looked
upon this as accidental conversation; thought no
more of it," relates Franklin.   We must take his
word for this statement of his unusual want of per-
ception, yet are we to be blamed if, deep down in
our consciousness, there lurks the thought that the
doctor was not *quite* so ingenuous as he would lead
us to believe ?   His was a difficult path to tread; any
attempt that he could make to bring on a reconciliation must be done in an unofficial way, without
authority of the Continental Congress now as-

sembled in Philadelphia. What more natural, therefore, than that he should proceed with caution, and simulate the virtue of childish innocence, though he had it not ?

No sooner had Franklin's plan of accommodation (which he called " Hints for Conversation upon the Subject of Terms that might probably produce a Durable Union between Britain and the Colonies ") been properly formulated than it mysteriously reached members of the ministry. Then arrived the petition addressed to his Majesty by the Continental Congress—a waste of good brains and paper, as it proved—and finally, on the evening of Christmas Day (1774), there was another little game with the obliging Mistress Howe. The moment that he entered her house the lady informed Franklin that her brother, Lord Howe, wished to meet him. The doctor said he would be glad to have that honour. As his lordship was near by, the sister soon had the pleasure of introducing to each other the two men whose last meeting in this world would be of a rather different nature from their first one. After the passing of the inevitable compliments, made obligatory by an ornate eighteenth-century etiquette, Lord Howe showed his hand by offering, practically, to serve as an intermediary between a stiff-necked ministry and him whose pardon that ministry had not the manliness to ask. He set forth his regard for America, and, to quote Franklin, " hoped his zeal for the public welfare would, with me, excuse the impertinence of a mere stranger, who could have otherwise no reason to expect, or right to request, me to open my mind to him on these topics; but he did conceive that, if I would indulge him with my ideas of the means proper to bring about a reconciliation, it might be of some use; that perhaps I might not be willing myself to have any *direct* communication with this ministry on this occasion; that I might likewise not care to have it known that I had any *indirect* communication with them, till I could be well assured of their good dispositions; that, being himself upon no ill terms with them, he thought it not impossible that he might by conveying my sentiments to them, and theirs to me, be a means of bringing on a good understanding, without committing either them, or me, if his negotiation should not succeed; and that I might rely on his keeping perfectly secret everything I should wish to remain so.''

Here was a glowing temptation. The fact that Franklin yielded to it only throws his patriotism into the stronger light. He had no authority to negotiate any treaty of compromise, and as meddling might bring censure it would be easier to leave Congress to deal with the vexed problem. But the doctor kept to himself his fears of criticism, if he had any; he promised Lord Howe to draw up some more proposals for a reconciliation, and entered, with all the alacrity of a conspirator in grand opera, into a little ruse whereby he was to continue his chess-playing with Mistress Howe, and thus have opportunity to meet her brother without attracting attention. Thereby the well-intended little plot developed. The agent sketched out a second plan, which Mistress Howe copied and privately sent to his lordship; this new paper and the " Hints " were handed about in ministerial circles, and enough mystery was made of the whole business to suggest that a treasonable, rather than a highly creditable, correspondence was in progress. There is something so refreshing about a secret.

Nor was the cultivation of Lord Chatham forgotten by the American diplomat, who called on that nobleman after the petition from Congress had arrived, and was delighted to hear him describe the gathering in Philadelphia as " the most honourable assembly of statesmen since those of the ancient Greeks and Romans, in the most virtuous times." A little later, on the 19th of January, Lord Chatham sent word to Franklin, by Lord Stanhope, that on the following day he was to make a motion, in the House of Lords, concerning America, and that he greatly desired his friend should hear it.

" The next morning," says Franklin, " his lordship (Stanhope) let me know by another card, that, if I attended at two o'clock in the lobby, Lord Chatham would be there about that time, and would himself introduce me. I attended, and met him there accordingly. On my mentioning to him what Lord Stanhope had written to me, he said : ' Certainly, and I shall do it with the more pleasure, as I am sure your being present at this day's debate will be of more service to America than mine ' ; and so taking me by the arm was leading me along the passage to the door that enters near the throne, when one of the door-keepers followed, and acquainted him that, by the order, none were to be carried in at that door but the eldest sons or brothers of peers ; on which he limped back with me to the door near the bar, where were standing a number of gentlemen, waiting for the peers who were to introduce them, and some peers waiting for friends they expected to introduce ; among whom he delivered me to the door-keepers, saying aloud, ' This is Dr. Franklin, whom I

would have admitted into the House,' when they readily opened the
door for me accordingly."

The honour of Lord Chatham's intimacy pleased
Franklin not a little, and when the peer called upon
him in Craven Street, on a certain Sunday, and left
his carriage standing at the door so long that the
people coming from church grew curious, the agent
was elated. As he confesses: " Such a visit from
so great a man, and so important a business, flattered not a little my vanity; and the honour of it
gave me the more pleasure, as it happened on the
very day twelve months that the ministry had taken
so much pains to disgrace me before the Privy
Council."   In fact, his lordship had a little plan of
his own for the happy settlement of the American
situation, and he came to show it to the would-be
peace-maker.   When, in the course of a few days,
Chatham presented the paper to Parliament, Franklin was on hand to hear the debate in the Upper
House.   Here he had the honour of an insult from
my Lord Sandwich, who arose and moved that the
plan be rejected " with the contempt it deserved."
He could never believe, the speaker protested, that
it was the work of a British peer, and, turning
toward the agent, he said, " he fancied he had in
his eye the person who drew it up, one of the bitter-
est and most mischievous enemies this country has
ever known." Immediately many of the lords
looked toward the seemingly unconscious enemy,
who kept his features immovable. The insult was
compensated for by the compliment which it drew
from Lord Chatham, who rebuked the tirade of

THE EARL OF CHATHAM.

FROM AN OIL PAINTING IN THE POSSESSION OF THE HISTORICAL SOCIETY OF

Lord Sandwich, and declared that the gentleman so
injuriously alluded to was one whom " all Europe
held in high estimation for his knowledge and wisdom,"—one who was an honour " not to the English nation alone, but to human nature." Again
the philosopher remained impassive, although he
kept up a fierce thinking, and wondered how it was
that these hereditary legislators dared to claim sovereignty over three millions of sensible Americans,
" since they appeared to have scarce discretion
enough to govern a herd of swine." " Hereditary
legislators!" he said to himself, contemptuously.
" There would be more propriety, because less hazard of mischief, in having (as in some university of
Germany) hereditary professors of mathematics!"
The one-time loyalty of the sage was fast turning
into something not so reverent.

How the several " plans " to ward off the Revolution failed, how the feelings of ministry settled
down into a sort of blind rage against the colonies,
and how Franklin grew so angry as almost to lose
control of that well-ordered temper of his, are matters of history. The chess-playing ceased after a
while, pleasant as it had proved, although before
the agreeable games came to an end Lord Howe
had asked whether, in case he were sent to America
as a commissioner for settling the differences, the
doctor would go with him. He accompanied the
request with the promise of a substantial bribe.
" That the ministry may have an opportunity of
showing their good disposition towards yourself,
will you give me leave, Mr. Franklin, to procure for

you previously some mark of it; suppose the payment here of the arrears of your salary, as agent for New England, which I understand they have stopped for some time past?" The scheme was simple enough; the well-known business frugality of the agent was to be tempted; for a few hundred pounds he was to sell himself to the purposes of the English Government, and to plead with his fellow-Americans, at so much per head, to take whatever terms might be offered.

' My lord," replied Franklin, " I shall deem it a great honour to be in any shape joined with your lordship in so good a work ; but, if you hope service from any influence I may be supposed to have, drop all thoughts of procuring me any previous favours from ministers ; my accepting them would destroy the very influence you propose to make use of : they would be considered as so many bribes to betray the interest of my country ; but only let me see the propositions, and, if I approve of them, I shall not hesitate a moment, but will hold myself ready to accompany your lordship at an hour's warning."

This project fell to the ground, like all the rest, and Franklin prepared to return to Philadelphia. It would be a sad home-coming, for he had lately received news that his " dear child," the worthy Deborah Franklin, was no more. The wife who had watched so faithfully the unfolding and the development of his public life, and who had guarded so zealously his personal interests, from the time that she helped to tend the little store on Market Street, had left him before the climax to his own work had been reached.* It was a hard blow for an

* Mrs. Franklin died of paralysis on the 19th of December, 1774. " Her death," wrote Governor Franklin to his father, " was no more

old man to bear, but he had the spirit of a Socrates. He never forgot, through all the trying time prior to his sailing from England, to keep before him the needs of the colonies. Even the danger of a public insult, like the one offered by Lord Sandwich, could not frighten him away from Parliament. Once, when he attended a session of the House of Lords, and heard his countrymen abused as the lowest of mankind, he returned in a heated mood to his lodgings, and drew up a memorial for presentation to Lord Dartmouth. It was a rather fiery exposition of the wrongs of Massachusetts: fortunate it proved that he listened to some sage advice, and never sent the paper to the Secretary. Had he done so, he might have been promptly arrested.

When the exile reached Philadelphia, early in May, he was welcomed not only by his daughter Sarah (now Mrs. Bache) and her family, but by all Philadelphia as well. There were hundreds of fervent greetings, while the most distinguished mark of honour and esteem was shown in the action of the Pennsylvania Assembly, which proceeded, upon the day after Franklin's return, to elect him a delegate to the Second Continental Congress. There was work to be done; the actions of Lexington and Concord and the tyranny of General Gage had

---

than might be reasonably expected after the paralytic stroke she received some time ago, which greatly affected her memory and understanding. She told me when I took leave of her on my removal to Amboy, that she never expected to see you unless you returned this winter, for that she was sure she should not live till next summer."

changed the spirit of the scene; the spectre of war stalked grimly through the land. The country was rising to defend its liberties, perhaps its very existence; it wanted but several days to the assembling of the colonial representatives who were to direct the national resistance and elect George Washington commander-in-chief of the army. Franklin had scarcely a minute to recuperate from the tiresome voyage; once more he put on the armour of energy, and no one in all excited Philadelphia was more ready to assist than he, despite the fact that he was nearly seventy years old. Perhaps it would be more appropriate to say that he was nearly seventy years young.

" His mind never grew old; and his body, at this time, was not perceptibly impaired. Writers of the period describe him as having grown portly, and he himself frequently alludes, in jocular exaggeration, to his great bulk. He had now discarded the cumbersome wig of his early portraits, and wore his own hair, thin and gray, without powder or pigtail. His head being remarkably large and massive, the increased size of his body was thought to have given proportion as well as dignity to his frame. His face was ruddy, and indicated vigorous health. His countenance expressed serenity, firmness, benevolence; and easily assumed a certain look of comic shrewdness, as if waiting to see whether his companions had ' taken' a joke."*

It was as a hard, effective worker and counsellor, rather than as an orator or a man of showy brilliancy, that Franklin now shone forth in the important proceedings of Congress.

" My time was never more fully employed," he writes to the good Dr. Priestley. " In the morning, at six, I am at the Committee of Safety, appointed by the Assembly to put the province in a state of

* Parton's *Life and Times of Benjamin Franklin.*

defence ; which committee holds till near nine, when I am at the Congress, and that sits till after four in the afternoon. Both these bodies proceed with the greatest unanimity, and their meetings are well attended. It will scarce be credited in Britain, that men can be as diligent with us from zeal for the public good, as with you for thousands per annum. Such is the difference between uncorrupted new states and corrupted old ones."

It was only two days before the date of this letter that he had written those famous lines to his friend William Strahan :

" You are a member of Parliament, and one of that majority which has doomed my country to destruction. You have begun to burn our towns, and murder our people. Look upon your hands, they are stained with the blood of your relations ! You and I were long friends ; you are now my enemy, and I am yours."

Meanwhile Franklin was doing something more than indulging in outbursts of patriotism. He served on a number of important committees, occasionally relieving the tedium of their meetings by an apt witticism which tickled the members' sense of humour, and in addition to all his other burdens he had thrust upon him, not unwillingly, perhaps, the new office of Postmaster-General under direction of Congress. Matters of finance, war, the mails, Indian negotiations, statesmanship, *et cætera*—there was no subject on which he could not give much needed counsel. He even found time to outline a plan for the permanent union of all the British colonies, among which he actually included Ireland, maybe as a theatrical, if useless, bit of defiance to his Majesty of England. Then, after the adjournment of Congress, the doctor paid a visit to his son, Governor Franklin, of New Jersey, whose own son, William Temple Franklin, had been with the philosopher in London. It would come to pass that as the weeks went on a complete estrangement was to take place between Dr. Franklin and the Governor, who would go over heart and soul to the cause of the British, and that William Temple Franklin would remain with his grandfather rather than with his Tory parent. For it was not long ere the Governor, in his enthusiasm for the royal interests, got himself into bad odour with the patriots, and finally into prison.*

With the re-assembling of Congress in September came more work for Franklin. So little did his friends scruple to pack duties upon his brave old shoulders, that the members of the Pennsylvania Assembly elected him to a seat among them, and the Continental delegates chose him as one of a committee of three to discuss with General Washington, at Cambridge, as to the best means of sup-

---

* There was so much of the talented and agreeable in Governor Franklin's nature that one must regret that he did not join the ranks of the patriots, wherein he might have served the country well, made his own name something to be pleasantly remembered, and have saved his father many a regretful thought. But William Franklin was a greater Tory than the average Englishman—more loyal than the King—and as a result of his pernicious activity in behalf of the royalists he had to spend many weary months in a Connecticut jail. " The people of the Jerseys," says a contemporary notice, " on account of his abilities, connections, principles, and address, viewed him as a mischievous and dangerous enemy in that province, and consequently thought it expedient to remove him, under a strong guard, to Connecticut."

porting and regulating the American army. Not
heeding the inconveniences of the journey to Massachusetts, the stout-hearted citizen set out manfully
with his two colleagues on the committee, Benjamin
Harrison and Thomas Lynch, after having written
the day before to Dr. Priestley that America was
as determined and unanimous as ever.

"Britain, at the expense of three millions, has killed one hundred
and fifty Yankees this campaign, which is twenty thousand pounds a
head; and at Bunker's Hill she gained a mile of ground, half of
which she lost again by our taking post on Ploughed Hill. During
the same time sixty thousand children have been born in America,"
from which it was easy to calculate, added the writer, "the time
and expense necessary to kill us all, and conquer our whole territory."

No sooner had they arrived at Cambridge than the
three delegates entered with Washington into the
business of formulating plans for the maintenance
of the army, the raising of new regiments, and the
revising of the articles of war. We are warranted
in supposing that Franklin had many a talk with
the commander-in-chief about the interesting days
when the two of them, neither so famous or so full
of responsibility as at present, used to meet in the
camp of poor, half-forgotten Braddock. Times had
changed since then; France was no longer the common enemy; the redcoats were become the targets
for American bullets.

When Franklin got back to Philadelphia he may
have deluded himself with the idea that he was to
engage in no more cross-country expeditions. False
hope! When April of the memorable '76 had come,

and the spirit for independence was setting in throughout the distraught colonies—when the English Government was treating her American children more and more as rebels, fit only for ignominious subjection—the philosopher was on the waters of the fair Hudson, treading the deck of a sloop destined for Albany. He went with Samuel Chase and Charles Carroll, of Carrollton, to aid, if possible, in forming a union between the colonies and Canada, and to hold a conference, at Montreal, with the then heroic Benedict Arnold. In company of these three commissioners appointed by Congress was Father John Carroll, afterward Archbishop of Baltimore, who was expected to influence the Roman Catholic clergymen of the North in the interests of the American cause. The boat sailed up the river, not without a storm to diversify the trip; at Albany the commissioners left their perilous craft, and thence came jolting rides over country roads, and uncomfortable experiences with bateaux, oxen, and calèches, until tired out and shaken up, the party reached Montreal.

Here General Arnold paid his distinguished visitors every attention, but the information he gave them as to the disposition of Canada toward the Continental cause must have filled them with disgust. American financial credit, American arms, and, in short, all things American, so far as the term applied to the colonies southward, were at a humiliating discount among the Canadians.

" Not the most trifling service can be procured," as the commissioners straightway wrote to Congress, " without an assurance of instant pay in silver or gold.   The express we sent from St. Johns, to inform the General of our arrival there, and to request carriages for La Prairie, was stopped at the ferry, till a friend passing changed a dollar bill for him, into silver ; and we are obliged to that friend for his engagement to pay the calashes, or they would not have come for us."

Congress was looked upon in the North as an irre- sponsible, insolvent, rebellious body, and the posi- tion of the commissioners proved irksome in the extreme, pestered as they were " with demands, great and small, that they could not answer," in a place where their enemies predominated, where the garrison was weak, and where the approach of a British force would have turned the negative hostil- ity into one of a positive sort.   When news came of the arrival, at Quebec, of a British fleet laden with troops, and of its defeat of the poor little American army, the commissioners wisely gave up the fight. Canada was lost.   Franklin promptly set out on his homeward journey, taking with him Father Carroll, an undaunted hopefulness for the colonies, and some symptoms of the gout.   He must have taken back, likewise, a grimly humourous view of Canadian prudence and ignorance, and, indeed, he was heard to say that if another mission to the North were to be undertaken it should consist of schoolmasters.

Franklin arrived home in time to assist in the irre- sistible movement for throwing off all allegiance to the British crown: he had the privilege of affixing his signature to the imperishable Declaration of In- dependence which transformed a series of vassal colonies into an embryonic nation.   It was a privilege which promised as much of danger as of honour, for should British arms finally triumph over American resistance, each signer of the parchment had before him the prospect of a gallows and a halter furnished through the generosity of his Most Gracious and Obstinate Majesty, George III., Defender of the Faith, Defender of British Prejudice, and Defender, likewise, of Obsolete Prerogative. But the die was cast, and no one realised more the necessity for the great step, or placed his name more cheerfully on what might come to be a roll of treason, or a death-warrant, than did Benjamin Franklin. More than that, he was one of the committee of five, with Thomas Jefferson at its head, which Congress appointed to draft the Declaration. He had nothing to do with the shaping of the document, beyond making a few verbal suggestions. Jefferson wrote the draft of the Declaration; he then submitted it in turn to Franklin and John Adams, and finally to the whole committee.

From the committee the paper was sent to Congress, where it ran the gauntlet of a pretty free criticism before its slight amendment and final adoption. While listening to the debate, and writhing under the fire of questions and remarks to which the Declaration gave rise, Jefferson was partly consoled for his ordeal by a bit of humour from the lips of Franklin, next to whom he sat.

"I have made it a rule," whispered the philosopher to the Virginian, "whenever in my power, to avoid becoming the draftsman of papers to be reviewed by a public body. I took my lesson from an incident which I will relate to you. When I was a journeyman printer, one of my companions, an apprenticed hatter, having served out his time, was about to open shop for himself. His first concern was to have a handsome sign-board with a proper inscription. He composed it in these words: *John Thompson, Hatter, makes and sells Hats for ready Money*, with a figure of a hat subjoined. But he thought he would submit it to his friends for their amendments. The first he showed it to thought the word *hatter* tautologous, because followed by the words *makes hats*, which showed he was a hatter. It was struck out. The next observed that the word *makes* might as well be omitted, because his customers would not care who made the hats; if good and to their mind they would buy, by whomsoever made. He struck it out. A third said he thought the words *for ready money* were useless, as it was not the custom of the place to sell on credit. Everyone who purchased expected to pay. They were parted with, and the inscription now stood, *John Thompson, sells hats*. 'Sells hats,' says his next friend; 'why nobody will expect you to give them away. What, then, is the use of that word?' It was stricken out, and *hats* followed, the rather as there was one painted on the board. So his inscription was ultimately reduced to *John Thompson*, with the figure of a hat subjoined."

Fortunately for the nation, and for the temper of Thomas Jefferson, the Declaration was treated with more respect than John Thompson's dwindling sign.

Throughout all the trials of this critical period of American history, so fraught with uncertainty and even gloom, the venerable doctor preserved his sense of fun. It came out now and then as refreshing as a glimpse of golden sunshine on a dark day. When John Hancock remarked solemnly, just prior to the signing of the Declaration, " We must be unanimous; there must be no pulling different ways; we must all hang together," it was the quick-witted Pennsylvanian who replied: " Yes, we must indeed all hang together, or, most assuredly, we shall all hang separately."

Four days after the " Fourth " Franklin was

elected a delegate to the Convention chosen to form a republican government for the Commonwealth of Pennsylvania—a Convention which made him its President and gave him the largest number of votes received by any of the nine representatives whom it sent to Congress. The old Assembly had ceased to exist; Pennsylvania was indeed a sovereign state, and the days of the proprietaries were no more. The not over-exuberant sum of £130,000 sterling would recompense the Penns for the loss of their estates, and close forever the accounts between them and their unappreciative " subjects."

Thus the activities of Franklin seemed to increase rather than diminish; he had tasks which might well have taxed the powers of a man but half his age. Never did he flinch, however, and he managed to divide his time in such a fashion as to produce the best results. Frequently he was at the Convention; again he could be found attending the sittings of Congress; at all times was he looked up to as a man of commanding intelligence, quick of expedient, sound of advice, and leonine of heart in love for the new confederation. Soon did the patriot have a chance to exercise anew his diplomatic talents in an interview with his old friend Lord Howe, who had come over to America to command the British naval forces operating against New York. The Admiral and his brother, Sir William Howe (who was to command the army), arrived in a dual capacity, being sent either to wage an aggressive campaign, or, if possible, to act as commissioners in restoring peace between Great Britain and the colonies. Lord

Howe had a sincere desire to effect reconciliation, but as his only remedy was the promising of pardons to submissive and repentant colonists, with a vague hint of future good-will on the part of the crown and Parliament, the prospects of a settlement were neither great nor alluring. " Get down on your knees and beg our forgiveness, and we may forget all your wickedness," was practically the message sent by King George and his ministers.*

As such a promise was little more than an impertinence it may be imagined that the Americans did not respond to the invitation of the commissioners with the hoped-for alacrity. However, after the battle of Long Island had been fought, and Lord Howe had made overtures for a conference with some members of Congress, " as private gentlemen," Dr. Franklin, John Adams, and Edward Rutledge were appointed a committee to see the Admiral and learn from him " whether he has any authority to treat with persons authorised by Congress for that purpose on behalf of America, and what that authority is, and to hear such propositions as he shall think fit to make respecting the same." Howe had already written to Franklin in terms of the greatest cordiality. The reply of the philosopher expressed the belief that when his lordship found it impossible

---

* The commissioners were authorised " to declare any province, colony, county, district, or town, to be at peace with His Majesty ; that due consideration should be had to the meritorious services of any who should aid or assist in restoring the public tranquillity ; that their dutiful representations should be received, pardons granted, and suitable encouragement to such as would promote the measures of legal government and peace."

to secure " reconciliation," the latter would " relinquish so odious a command, and return to a more
honourable private station."

The committee were two days in getting from
Philadelphia to Amboy.   The conference took
place on Staten Island, in an old stone house, one
room of which had been " made romantically elegant " by decorations of moss, and branches of
trees.   The three Congressmen were received by
Lord Howe with every show of civility and regard;
there was liberal entertainment of the gastronomic
kind, and no end of presenting-of-arms from the
soldiers.   When the wine and the more solid cheer
were disposed of, my Lord Howe opened the conference by setting forth his desire for peace, and his
love for the colonies.   " I feel for America as for a
brother, and if America should fall, I should feel and
lament it like the loss of a brother," said the Admiral.

" My lord," quickly put in Dr. Franklin, with a
pleasant, smiling bow, and a *naïve* air, " we will use
our utmost endeavours to save your lordship that
mortification."   Whereupon his lordship remarked,
" I suppose you will endeavour to give us employment in Europe," and then went on to harp upon
the fact that he was receiving the committee in a
private capacity rather than as the representative of
an illegal Congress.

DR. FRANKLIN. Your lordship may consider us in any view
you think proper. We, on our part, are at liberty to consider ourselves in our real character. But there is, really, no necessity on
this occasion to distinguish between members of Congress and individuals. The conversation may be held as among friends.

MR. ADAMS.   Your lordship may consider me in what light you please.   Indeed, I should be willing to consider myself for a few moments in any character which would be agreeable to your lordship except that of a British subject.

LORD HOWE.   Mr. Adams is a decided character.

MR. RUTLEDGE.   I think, with Dr. Franklin, that the **conversation** may be as among friends.

A little more conversation disclosed how meagre were the powers of the commissioners from his Majesty—powers which Lord Howe said were " to restore peace and grant pardons, to attend to complaints and representations, and to confer upon the means of a reunion upon terms honourable and advantageous to the colonies and to Great Britain." He was told very plainly that the Americans would never come again under the English Government; that the Declaration of Independence had settled the matter, and that " they would not, even if the Congress should desire it, return to the King's government."   The conference ended thus:

LORD HOWE.   If such are your sentiments, gentlemen, I can only lament that it is not in my power to bring about the accommodation I wish.   I have not authority, nor do I ever expect to have, to treat with the colonies as states independent of the crown of Great Britain.   I am sorry, gentlemen, that you have had the trouble of coming so far to so little purpose.   If the colonies will not give up the system of independency, it is impossible for me to enter into any negotiation

DR. FRANKLIN.   It would take as much time for us to refer to and get answers from our constituents, as it would the royal commissioners to get fresh instructions from home, which, I suppose, might be about three months.

LORD HOWE.   It is in vain to think of my receiving instructions to treat upon that ground.

DR. FRANKLIN. Well, my lord, as America is to expect nothing but upon unconditional submission——

LORD HOWE (*interrupting*). No, Dr. Franklin. Great Britain does not require unconditional submission. I think that what I have already said proves the contrary, and I desire, gentlemen, that you will not go away with such an idea.

DR. FRANKLIN. As your lordship has no proposition to make to us, give me leave to ask whether, if *we* should make propositions to Great Britain (not that I know, or am authorised to say we shall), you would receive and transmit them?

LORD HOWE. I do not know that I could avoid receiving any papers that should be put into my hands, though I am doubtful of the propriety of transmitting them home. Still, I do not say that I would decline doing so.

Having succeeded in accomplishing nothing, unless it were to verify the absurdity of his Majesty's proposals for submission, the committee returned to Philadelphia and reported the result, or non-result, of the interview. Here the matter ended. The Revolution went on.

CHAPTER X

THE MISSION TO FRANCE

1776–1778

OW must come another shifting of the scenes, and a radical one, in a narrative which has already been as full of contrast, perforce, as the changing colours of a kaleidoscope. Old-fashioned Philadelphia, with its galaxy of delegates, who eventually will be driven from the town by the advance of the British forces, must give way to the far different atmosphere of Paris—the Paris of Louis XVI. and Marie Antoinette, of Voltaire and De Beaumarchais, of tinsel and gaiety, oppression and poverty—the Paris under which is smouldering the fire of a coming revolution. It is here, at the French capital, that we discover this very Beaumarchais working for the freedom of America, and it is here, too, that some of the most famous days of Franklin's closing years will be spent.

To speak of these two men in the same breath would seem nothing short of paradoxical were it not that, for the nonce, Fate found them labouring, each

in his own peculiar way, for the same great cause.
For Beaumarchais, the brilliant, the adventurous,
the unstable, saw in the struggles of the colonists
just enough of the romantic to appeal to his chame-
leon-like, volatile disposition. The man who had
begun life as an obscure but clever watchmaker, and
who had finally penetrated into the sacred circle of
the French court, there to enjoy the intimacy of the
poor King Louis and to receive kind words and
glances from Marie Antoinette, knew so much of
the dash and picturesqueness of existence that the
dangers, the uncertainties, of American defiance exerted for him an undoubted fascination. That he
looked upon England as the natural foe of France
made his sympathy all the keener, nor was he slow
to point out to his sovereign the benefits to be de-
rived, selfish and sentimental, from any aid furnished
the insurgents across the ocean. It was an idea which
had occurred to other Frenchmen, but it had not
always the benefit of so eloquent an advocate, or of
one so near the ear of government, as the Sieur de
Beaumarchais.

The ex-watchmaker took flying trips to London,
to find out how war and politics were going; he
drew up a memorial to the King, which he entitled
" Peace or War," and he employed all his plausibility
to convince his Majesty and the Count de Vergennes, Minister for Foreign Affairs, that the time
had come for weakening England by strengthening
the hand of her rebellious provinces. It was the only
way to preserve France from British aggression, he
told the King, for " if England triumphs, they will

Attest Cha Thomson Secy.

To
Our Great, faithful and beloved Friend and Ally Louis the Sixteenth, King of France, and Navarre

FRANKLIN'S CREDENTIALS AS MINISTER TO FRANCE.

Great faithful and beloved Friend and Ally,

The Principles of Equality and Reciprocity on which you have entered into Treaties with us, give you an additional Security for that good Faith with which we shall observe them from motives of Honor and of Affection to Your Majesty. The distinguished part you have taken in the support of the Liberties and Independence of these States cannot but inspire them with the most ardent wishes for the Interest and the Glory of France. We have nominated Benjamin Franklin Esquire to reside at your Court, in quality of our Minister Plenipotentiary, that he may give you more particular assurances of the grateful Sentiments which you have excited in us and in each of the United States. We beseech you to give entire Credit to every thing which he shall deliver on our Part, especially when he shall assure you of the Permanency of our Friendship, and we pray God that he will keep Your Majesty our great, faithful and beloved Friend and Ally in his most holy Protection.

Done at Philadelphia the twenty first day of October 1778.

By the Congress of the United States of North America your good Friends and Allies

_____
President

Attest Cha Thomson secy.

To our Great, faithful and beloved Friend and Ally Louis the Sixteenth King of France and Navarre.

seek to make up the cost necessary for such a struggle by seizing our West India sugar islands," while " if America conquers the English will try to make up the loss of some of her American colonies by acquiring all of ours." He further informed the monarch that Arthur Lee (who had succeeded to Franklin's agency in London, where he was now stationed as a sort of private emissary for Congress) " offers a secret treaty of commerce in exchange for secret help," finally concluding that " we can preserve peace only by giving aid to the Americans; two or three millions may save us our sugar islands, worth three hundred."

At last Beaumarchais won the day. He was to be the medium of assisting the Americans, but the aid should be given stealthily, and in a peculiar manner. So much the more attractive became the scheme to this iridescent individual; to let him carry it out in a mysterious fashion was to please his sense of the theatrical. In fine, it was agreed, after hesitation and discussion, that a commercial house should be established in Paris with a capital of two millions of francs (contributed in equal parts by France and Spain), for the purpose of sending to the colonies the supplies needed in the maintenance of the war. Ostensibly the business was to be a private enterprise, and De Vergennes made this a *sine qua non* with Beaumarchais, who was to be the head of the new house.

"The operation," said the Count, " must have essentially in the eyes of the English Government, and even in the eyes of the Americans, the aspect of an individual speculation, to which we are strangers. That it may be so in appearance, it must be so to a certain extent in reality. We will give you secretly a million. We will endeavour to persuade the court of Spain to unite in giving you another. With these two millions you shall found a great commercial establishment, and at your own risk and peril you shall furnish to America arms and everything else necessary to sustain war. Our arsenals will deliver to you arms and munitions, but you shall pay for them. You will not demand money of the Americans, for they have none; but you can ask return in their staple products."

The project was hailed with delight by the spirited Beaumarchais; it promised more intrigue than the plot of his recently produced comedy, *The Barber of Seville*. In August of 1776 a new firm, bearing the grandiloquent name of " Roderique Hortalez et Cie," put up its sign at the old Hotel de Hollande, and it need hardly be added that the senior partner who installed himself in the building was *not* a Señor Hortalez. There was " no such person " as Señor Hortalez; the head of the establishment was a poetic and uncommercial gentleman, who thus found himself, as he had often done before, in a very interesting situation.*

Where was the less romantic Franklin during this little court conspiracy ? To answer that question we must go back for a second to Philadelphia, where some time before (November 29, 1775), the doctor had been placed on a committee of Congress, from whose labours may be traced the course of events that led up to the great French alliance. As this committee was authorised to carry on a secret correspondence " with friends in Great Britain, Ireland,

---

* See Parton ; also *Franklin in France*, by Edward E. Hale and Edward E. Hale, Jr.

and other parts of the world," and to find out, by
the employment of confidential agents, what assistance America might expect from foreign powers, it
is self-evident that no better man could have been
chosen to head it than the astute ex-agent of London.   The delicacy of the task appealed to him; he
was soon sending despatches to Europe, one of
which was addressed to his Parisian friend and admirer, Dr. Dubourg.   Then came a bit of diplomacy
of the kind that would have gladdened the heart of
the far-away Beaumarchais.   The committee chose
Silas Deane, of Connecticut, to make a quiet trip
to Paris, in the guise of an inoffensive American
merchant, and to find out how much of practical
friendship and support the colonies might expect
from the government of Louis XVI.   So Deane
stole away one day in April (1776), loaded with letters, cautions from Franklin, and some invisible ink
wherewith he was to write his reports.   The innocu-
ous name of " Timothy Jones " would be affixed to
such of his letters as might meet the public eye, and
it was understood that he should go so far in his in-
cognito as to buy a cargo or so of goods, in the hope
of drawing wool over the eyes of the curious by
giving to his character of merchant the semblance
of reality.   The wool was not very thick, as it came
to pass; Mr. Deane was soon able to emerge into
the light of day and to pursue his labours with a
trifle less circumspection.   The new condition of
things might not be as thrilling as the story of a
future " revolutionary novel," but it would have
compensations.

17

In September, when the American cause seemed in anything but a brilliant shape from the military point of view, and when the necessity of aid from France was becoming more and more apparent, Franklin received an interesting letter from the friendly Dr. Dubourg. The Frenchman, as he informed his " dear master," had bestirred himself valiantly in behalf of Congress and the colonies.

" Knowing that the United States had pressing need of a certain kind of men, and a certain kind of provisions," he wrote, " I have exerted myself to procure both the one and the other for her. I have knocked (if I may so express myself) at every door for that end ; I have talked vaguely to some, enigmatically to others ; I have half confided to many and as little as possible have I wholly confided in anyone whatever, except the King's ministers and a nephew, of whom I am thoroughly satisfied, and whom I have drawn from his own province on purpose to second me in everything. I have had the satisfaction of being well received in every quarter, and of seeing that no one demands other assurances than my own word to treat with me upon affairs of the greatest consequence, and concerning which I freely acknowledge to have received neither full power, nor even the least commission or instruction, by word of mouth any more than by letter. Ministers to whom I have never made my court have given me the most flattering marks of confidence from my first interview ; have talked to me without winding or mystery ; have discussed with me the weightiest matters ; and have deliberated with me the plans to be pursued, and the means to accomplish them. Private individuals, merchants, military men, and others, have attended without scruple to take from me conditional arrangements, promising to execute them when it shall be required, though I had declared to them, on my part, that I could not warrant anything at all positively."

Nothing could show better than this how the wind of French favour was blowing towards America.

" I have been six (and three times more in the latter part of June) different times to Versailles within a month," continued the savant.

" to see not only the ministers, but everyone who approaches them
or continues near them, and to sound or get sounded the dispositions
of everyone ; for it must not be thought that they are all equally
well-intentioned ; however, I wanted to draw some advantage from
all. And, in fact, though I had rather praise some than others, yet
there is not one of whom I could complain without ingratitude."

Dubourg then went on to state what he had been
able to accomplish in a practical way. He had obtained from the royal arsenals, in a mysterious,
roundabout manner, some fifteen thousand muskets,
and he could have secured brass cannon after the
same method were it not " for the circumstance of
their bearing the King's arms and cipher, which
made them too discoverable." He had obtained
long furloughs for French officers of artillery, who
might come over to America, and he had been useful in other directions of a warlike nature. His
attachment to Franklin, explained the enthusiastic
Dubourg, answered sufficiently for his devotion to
the aims of Congress. " I would die contented,"
he said, " could I see my country and yours intimately united ; and could I contribute towards it,
I should be at the summit of my wishes."

This letter, the first definite news which had come
from Paris relative to the kindly disposition of the
French ministry—acted on Congress as a pleasant
stimulant and had for its immediate result the appointment of Franklin, Jefferson, and Silas Deane
as envoys to the court of King Louis. Jefferson
was obliged to decline service in France, owing to
the illness of his wife, and Arthur Lee, whose jealousy and pettiness of spirit were to give the philosopher many a weary quarter of an hour, had the

honour of being elected in the place of the greater
Virginian.   Lee was then in London.   As for our
doctor, he never for an instant shirked the responsibility of the mission, or pleaded, as he might well
have done, the weight of his seventy years.   " I am
old and good for nothing," he said to Dr. Rush,
" but as the store-keepers say of their remnants of
cloth, I am but a fag end, and you may have me for
what you please."   There was, of course, a little
affectation of modesty in such a speech.   Had
Franklin suspected for an instant that he was so
much of a " fag end " as to be of no more use to
his country he would have been too wise—too proud,
indeed—to venture once again upon an uncomfortable ocean.   He knew that there was yet in him a
deal of the old-time energy.

After having shown the practical quality of his
patriotism by loaning the sorely pressed Congress
the substantial sum of nearly four thousand pounds,
and gladdened by the secret intelligence that France
proposed to send over to America a liberal quantity
of arms and ammunition ere the beginning of the
next campaign, Dr. Franklin sailed from Marcus
Hook in the *Reprisal*, a swift sloop-of-war.   Heaven
alone knew when or how he would return, for the
outlook for America was far from radiant ; New
York was in the power of the British ; there seemed
only too much reason to fear that the Revolution
might end in ignominious collapse.   The envoy was
accompanied by two grandsons, William Temple
Franklin and Benjamin Franklin Bache, lads who
must have found the exciting voyage (enlivened by

the inevitable pursuit of the sloop by English cruis-
ers and by the *Reprisal's* capture of two prizes) quite
in harmony with the adventurous ideals of unthinking youth. To the grandfather, the attentions of
the enemy could not have appeared so attractive;
yet he kept up a characteristic serenity, made some
experiments to throw new light on the presence of
the Gulf Stream, and arrived at Quiberon Bay, on
the 29th of November, so fatigued by the experience
that he could scarcely stand. He had reached the
cordial atmosphere of France not a whit too soon.
Silas Deane, whose abilities were not of a kind to
move mountains, and Arthur Lee were sadly in
need of the third member of the American legation.

To Deane, indeed, the path of diplomacy had
latterly been strewn with thorns; few primroses
were to be found growing along its devious, uncertain way. Upon his arrival at Versailles he had
secured a non-official interview with M. de Vergennes (the American was then playing the opera-
bouffe *rôle* of conspirator, or merchant, and deceiving
no one), and was assured by the minister that France
would indirectly aid the sending of war supplies to
the colonies, but that for the present she could do
nothing openly. To prevent a rupture with England it would be necessary to act under the rose, or
to pursue what we might irreverently term a purely
winking policy. Next, the fantastic Beaumarchais
appeared on the scene; the new firm of Roderique
Hortalez and Company established an *entente cor-
diale* with the envoy; the comedy-writing Frenchman and the commonplace Connecticut lawyer

became bosom friends; ere long merchandise and warlike stores were awaiting shipment to America. The pretended Hortalez revelled in the situation, cultivated an air of comic mystery, and acted his part with much light-and-airy bravado, but his masquerade was soon discovered, even by Lord Stormont, the indignant British Ambassador. The purposes of the new firm, though not its aid from government, were apparent.

" From a Frenchman that I was," Beaumarchais relates, " I became an American merchant, a politician, and a writer. I imparted my warmth to honest but timid minds, and formed a society under a name unknown. I gathered together merchandise and warlike stores in all our ports, always under fictitious names. Your agent [Deane] was to have provided vessels to transport them to America ; but not one could he find ; and it was still I who, with double zeal and labour, succeeded in procuring them for him at Marseilles, Nantes, and Havre, paying out of my own pocket two thirds of the freight in advance, and finding security for the remainder. The most severe orders everywhere thwarted my operations. What I could not accomplish in the open day, was executed in the night. If government caused my vessels to be unloaded in one port, I sent them secretly to re-load at a distance in the roads. Were they stopped under their proper names, I changed them immediately, or made pretended sales, and put them anew under fictitious commissions. Were obligations in writing exacted from my captains to go nowhere but to the West India Islands, powerful gratifications on my part made them yield again to my wishes. Were they sent to prison on their return, for disobedience, I then doubled their gratifications to keep their zeal from cooling, and consoled them with gold for the rigour of our government. Voyages, messengers, agents, presents, rewards—no expense was spared. One time, by reason of an unexpected counter-order, which stopped the departure of one of my vessels, I hurried by land to Havre twenty-one pieces of cannon, which, if they had come from Paris by water, would have retarded us ten days."

From this it will be seen that the French Govern-

P. A. CARON DE BEAUMARCHAIS.

ment often had to oppose, for political reasons, and at the behest of Lord Stormont, the very man it desired to help. Indeed, it was not until after many delays and hindrances that Beaumarchais could get his stores to the Americans.

The story reads like a romance, and the matter-of-fact Silas Deane must have rubbed his amazed eyes more than once and wondered if he were not in a dream. There were times, however, when stern reality rather than visions confronted the American. He too often found himself without money or credit, unless Beaumarchais came to his rescue; the prospects for an open alliance with France began to grow ominously dim; the British Ambassador lodged loud complaints with Vergennes, and all things pointed towards failure. And where was Arthur Lee? Trying to sow dissensions and sulking because Beaumarchais had made of Deane so intimate a friend. The fictitious Hortalez had shifted his connection, personal and commercial, from Lee to Deane, and thereby put the former gentleman in a temper from which he never recovered.

Meanwhile the doctor has travelled from his ship to Nantes, where he becomes the lion of the day, and from which place he writes to John Hancock, the President of Congress:

" In thirty days after we left the Capes of Delaware, we came to an anchor in Quiberon Bay. I remained on board four days, expecting a change of wind proper to carry the ship into the river Loire ; but the wind seemed fixed in an opposite quarter. I landed at Aury, and with some difficulty got hither, the road not being well supplied with means of conveyance. . . . Our friends in France have been a good deal dejected with the *Gazette* accounts of advantages obtained against us by the British troops. I have helped them here to recover their spirits a little, by assuring them, that we still face the enemy, and were under no apprehension of their armies being able to complete their junction. I understand that Mr. Lee has lately been at Paris, and Mr. Deane is still there, and that an underhand supply is obtained from the government of two hundred brass field-pieces, thirty thousand firelocks, and some other military stores, which are now shipping for America, and will be convoyed by a ship of war. The court of England (M. Penet tells me, from whom I have the above intelligence) had the folly to demand Mr. Deane to be delivered up, but were refused. Our voyage, though not long, was rough, and I feel myself weakened by it; but I now recover strength daily, and in a few days shall be able to undertake the journey to Paris. I have not yet taken any public character, thinking it prudent first to know whether the court is ready and willing to receive ministers publicly from the Congress; that we may neither embarrass it on the one hand, nor subject ourselves to the hazard of a disgraceful refusal on the other."

The letter is purposely cheerful in tone, yet it would be interesting did we know just what thoughts were revolving, as Franklin wrote, in that fur-becapped head of his. Did he think the Revolution was to end in triumph or in a hanging-party ?[*]

Friendly as was France to the cause of the colonies, the newly arrived envoy might well stop to inquire as to the intentions of the court and ministers. He came as the representative of a country over which Great Britain still claimed sovereignty, and to receive him publicly might bring upon the government of Louis XVI. a series of undesired com-

---

[*] In a letter written about a month later to Mrs. Hewson, Franklin says, in a jocose strain: " Figure to yourself an old man, with grey hair appearing under a martin fur cap, among the powdered heads of Paris. It is this odd figure that salutes you, with handfulls of blessings on you and your dear little ones."

plications with their neighbours across the Channel. So afraid, indeed, of the influence and ability of the doctor was Lord Stormont that he threatened to leave Paris if the " chief of the American rebels " entered the city—a threat which he failed to keep. M. de Vergennes evaded the situation, or perhaps it is more correct to say that he sat upon the diplomatic fence. He wished to give a sort of vague, unofficial recognition to the American and to keep, at the same time, a surface peace with the British Embassy. More than that he could not do; an alliance with, or an open recognition of, America was out of the question; her star had risen, as it seemed, only to be soon extinguished. So Vergennes contented himself with assuring Lord Stormont that a courier had been sent to meet Franklin and forbid his coming to the capital; but he added that if, by a mischance, the doctor should reach Paris without encountering the messenger, the government would not like to send him away, " because of the scandalous scene this would present to all France, should we respect neither the laws of nations nor of hospitalities." With that my Lord Stormont had to be content.

Of course the courier never put in an appearance. Franklin was posting from Nantes as rapidly as roads and the rather shaken state of his health permitted, and getting on his way a taste of the cuisine provided by provincial inns. In one of these hostelries, says Dame Tradition, he heard that Gibbon, he of the *Decline and Fall of the Roman Empire*, happened to be a fellow-guest, so he politely sent

his compliments to the historian, with the request
for his agreeable company on that evening.   Mr.
Gibbon, we are told, declined to meet a man who
had revolted against his King, much as he admired
the private character of Franklin—a snub to which
the latter gentleman responded by writing to the
Englishman that " though Mr. Gibbon's principles
had compelled him to do without the pleasure of his
conversation, Dr. Franklin had still such a respect
for the character of Mr. Gibbon as a gentleman and
historian that when, in the course of his writing the
history of the *decline and fall* of empires, the *decline
and fall* of the British Empire should come to be
his subject, as he expected it soon would, Dr.
Franklin would be happy to furnish him with ample
materials which were in his possession."

The philosopher arrived in Paris just before Christmas.   It is no exaggeration to say that from the
moment he put his foot in the gay city he became a
public idol.   He did not as yet excite any enthusiasm in court circles (that was forbidden by the
exigencies of politics and by the spying policy of the
British Ambassador), but in general society, in the
domain of science, philosophy, and literature, and
with the populace, the great " Insurgent " became
the hero of the hour.   So great was his versatility,
so varied had been his labours, that he was discussed
in the wine-shops as well as in the *salons;* he was
written about, too, in an almost fulsome vein, and
thrice welcomed for his wit, learning, devotion to
liberty, and possibly for his perennial success.   The
Parisians, then, as now, loved the *éclat* of prosper-

FRANKLIN FOUND BY DIOGENES.

FROM AN OLD FRENCH ENGRAVING

ity. They loved oddity, too, and to them Franklin
was a new experience, a refreshing contrast to the
ordinary mould of humanity. Not that he lacked
polish or *savoir faire;* but he came as a breath of
bracing air from a new country, and brought with
him that belief in democratic ideals which was fast
coming into fashion among the cognoscenti of Paris.
As a novelty for a novelty-seeking people he was a
shining mark.

When Franklin retired in a short time to the
suburb of Passy, where he established himself in a
state befitting his position, and discarded just
enough of the much-vaunted American simplicity
to put on a properly luxurious front before the eyes
of France, admiration and adulation followed him
with unrelenting steps. Men and women paid him
their homage, and hung upon his words as something to be treasured and repeated for the benefit of
posterity. His portrait became the vogue; his sayings were quoted eagerly *; and his appearance at
the theatre was the signal for applause.

"His name was familiar to government and people, to Kings,
courtiers, nobility, clergy, and philosophers, as well as plebeians, to
such a degree that there was scarcely a peasant or a citizen, a *valet
de chambre*, coachman or footman, a lady's chambermaid or a scul-
lion in a kitchen, who was not familiar with it, and who did not consider him a friend to human kind. When they spoke of him they
seemed to think he was to restore the golden age." †

* When Franklin was asked as to the truth of an assertion made
by Lord Stormont he answered, " No, sir, it is not a truth, it is a
Stormont "—a saying which went the rounds of all Paris, and made
of " a Stormont " the polite synonym for a lie.

† John Adams.

There was much that proved delightful in all this
enthusiasm, but like the proverbial cup that cheers
without intoxicating it did not destroy the equi-
librium of its recipient.   Franklin revelled, after a
calm fashion, in the society and entertainment of
congenial hosts, but he never forgot that he had
come abroad on a mission of the most serious import.   Hardly had he been a week in Paris before
he was paying a very quiet visit to the Count de
Vergennes, in company with Messrs. Lee and
Deane, and receiving from that minister assurances
of profound esteem, and a hint that France would
be glad to help America in any way short of breaking the existing relations with Great Britain.   Louis
XVI. could not recognise at present the new republic, but there came promise of a secret loan to
Congress of two million francs.   For the rest Franklin could only work and watch without ceasing,
arrange with Mr. Deane to keep up the latter's activities with the romantic Beaumarchais, and behave
as diplomatically as possible to the ardent French
officers who came to the doctor sighing for commissions and future glory in the American army.   Thus
events slowly dragged along.   The Marquis de Lafayette went off to win military laurels in the new
world; Arthur Lee tried to visit the court of Spain
to sound the tocsin of an alliance, but was given to
understand that his presence in Madrid would become an embarrassment; and off across the Atlantic
the campaign was leading on—the fates only knew
where.   The good philosopher had need for all his
wisdom and patience; he put on a merry exterior

when he dined with the dear duchesses and com-
tesses and all the rest of the smart set; he wrote
some articles to keep up the public interest in the
uncertain affairs of the colonies, and doubtless had
many a hard word to say in private of the bovine-
headedness of the storming Stormont.   For be it remembered that in reply to two letters sent by the
envoys to the British Ambassador, concerning the
exchange of some American seamen confined at
Portsmouth, his lordship wrote: " The King's Embassador receives no application from rebels, unless
they come to implore His Majesty's mercy."   This
letter, which bore neither date nor signature, was
returned by the envoys with the following laconic
remark: " In answer to a letter which concerns some
of the most material interests of humanity, and of
the two nations, Great Britain and the United
States of America, now at war, we received the in-
closed indecent paper, as coming from your lordship,
which we return, for your lordship's more mature
consideration."   The " little postmaster " had a
hand in shaping that document.

Next our malevolent friend Arthur Lee looms up
like some honest *Iago*.   He has returned from Berlin, after an unsuccessful attempt to secure for his
country a Prussian alliance, and is in a bad humour
which grows none the less as he perceives the continued adulation bestowed upon his venerable colleague.   He finds fault with Beaumarchais, despises
Deane, cultivates a veiled contempt for the doctor,
and sets himself about to be as disagreeable as possible at a time when harmony in the legation is the

thing of things to be preserved. He writes home accusing Deane of dishonesty and Franklin of inability and senility, and while frequently dining at the table of the latter is doing all he can to undermine him with the members of Congress. If he can get his two fellow-envoys removed to less important courts than that of Versailles, and contrive to remain where he now is as an independent plenipotentiary, so much the better. In the meantime he goes on sounding discords and thinking only of self-interest, while the fate of his country is hanging in the balance and the heart of Franklin, brave as it is, beats with a nervousness born of hope deferred. Nor are we to forget that it was this marplot who prevented Congress from reimbursing the house of " Hortalez," by representing that Beaumarchais and Deane were seeking to line their private purses. Of the internal dissensions to which the conduct of Lee gave rise in the Franklin household we need not speak; the picture, save for one majestic figure in the foreground, would hardly prove alluring. Throughout all the unpleasantness Franklin retained his dignity, and old as he then was, he yet lived long enough to triumph over the spleen of a man whose wild ambition outran principle or talent.

The doctor kept, too, the nimbleness of wit that made him a veritable joy to the frequenters of the *salons*. He was always ready with an answer, and in eagerness to hear his *bon mots* the Parisians were as so many Boswells to a Dr. Johnson. Once, when playing chess with the old Duchess of Bourbon, the wary republican took a king which had been put into prize. " Ah," cried the Duchess, " we do not take kings so!" " We do in America," said the doctor. On another occasion he upset, by an unexpected method, a pet theory of the Abbé Raynal. A party in which Frenchmen and Americans were equally represented was dining one day at Passy with the philosopher, when the Abbé began to wax eloquent upon the degeneracy of animals, including man, on the American continent. " Come," spoke up the host, " let us try this question by the fact before us. We are here one half Americans and one half French, and it happens that the Americans have placed themselves on one side of the table, and our French friends are on the other. Let both parties rise, and we will see on which side nature has degenerated." The Abbé was " a mere shrimp "; the other Frenchmen were all small of stature, and the American guests happened to be men of height. The experiment, while it proved nothing, made a good story to tell at Monsieur Raynal's expense.

As the autumn of 1777 wore on the prospects for the poor colonies, so far as the envoys had means of judging, were getting darker and darker. General Burgoyne might have won a brilliant victory in America, for all that they knew to the contrary, and despite the expectation of further financial help from the King, American affairs were not proceeding over well in France. Then, to make matters worse, came the news that General Howe was in Philadelphia; the outlook was as black as night. But Franklin hid his fears, as was his wont, and when an Englishman said to him, exultingly, " Well, doctor, Howe has

taken Philadelphia," he replied: " I beg your pardon, sir, Philadelphia has taken Howe."   Soon this
continued pluck was to have a fitting reward.   In
the beginning of December there came to Passy a
courier who bore jubilant despatches.   Franklin lost
for a second his usual imperturbability.   " Sir," he
demanded, ere there was time to open the letters,
" is Philadelphia taken ?"   " Yes," cried the
courier, " but I have greater news than that; General Burgoyne and his whole army are prisoners of
war!"

The glorious news found its way through Europe
with amazing rapidity.   Wherever England had an
enemy there was rejoicing.   The people of Paris
seemed as elated as if they had won the victory
themselves, and the exultation of the French ministry, prudently expressed as it was, formed a refreshing contrast to the gloom of tenacious George III.,
who declared, says the legend, that he would sell
Hanover and all his private estates before he should
desert " the cause of his loyal American subjects
who had suffered so much for him."   The time for
an active foreign policy had arrived; it was not long
before M. de Vergennes was sending congratulatory
messages to Passy, and actually inviting the envoys
to revive the propositions, which they had heretofore made in vain, for an alliance with King Louis.
Dr. Franklin quickly responded to the suggestion
by writing out the necessary memorial.   On the
16th of December, M. Gerard, Secretary of the
Council of State, announced to the expectant household at Passy that the King had decided, after care-

ful deliberation, to recognise the independence of
the Americans, and to make with them " a treaty of
commerce, and a second treaty for an eventual treaty
of alliance." The compact was, however, to be
kept a profound secret for the present, and it was
not until the 6th of February that the happy envoys
had the honour of placing their names on the treaties
which were to add inspiration to America and establish war between Great Britain and his Most Christian Majesty of France. For Franklin the moment
was triumphant, and he showed his satisfaction and
the clearness of his memory in a curiously effective
way. When he signed the papers, it was observed
that he wore the famous suit of Manchester velvet
wherein he was clad on the day of the Privy Council
outrage.*

A more resplendent date, suggesting the glitter
of court costume, the charm of gorgeously appar-
elled femininity, and the pomp of royalty, is the

---

* In commerce each party [to the treaties] was to be placed on the
footing of the most favoured nation. The King of France promised
his good offices with the princes and powers of Barbary. As to the
fisheries, each party reserved to itself the exclusive possession of its
own. . . . The absolute and unlimited independence of the
United States was described as the essential end of the defensive alliance ; and the two parties mutually engaged not to lay down their
arms until it should be assured by the treaties terminating the war.
Moreover, the United States guaranteed to France the possessions
then held by France in America, as well as those which it might ac-
quire by a future treaty of peace ; and, in like manner, the King of
France guaranteed to the United States their present possessions and
acquisitions during the war from the dominions of Great Britain in
North America. A separate and secret act reserved to the King of
Spain the power of acceding to the treaties.—BANCROFT.

18

20th of March, 1778. It is a red-letter day for
America. The envoys are to be received in state at
Versailles; the treaties will be officially acknowledged. My Lord Stormont, who has, of course,
known for some time of the existence of the alliance,
finds his usefulness in the French capital at an end;
all subterfuge is thrown to the winds, and France
emerges into the field as an open abettor of America.
Before midsummer Count d'Estang will arrive with
his friendly fleet at the mouth of the Delaware
River, and from then until the little episode of Yorktown the helping hand of the Gaul will be stretched
out in full sight of the British ministers.

On this 20th of March, then, Franklin put on
an unostentatious black suit, with white silk stockings and silver buckles, discarded the necessary wig
(it is said that the one ordered for the occasion was
too small for his head, and was thrown away by the
disgusted hair-dresser), and in company with the
other two envoys — who paled into insignificance
whenever they appeared with their senior — proceeded in state to Versailles. The three gentlemen,
together with William Lee and Ralph Izard, the unreceived American ministers to Berlin and Tuscany,
respectively, were duly presented to Louis XVI.,
who would have taken a more heartfelt interest in
the ceremonial had it not gone against the royal
grain to smile upon republicanism. He had yielded
for reasons of state, but he could not forget that in
aiding the Americans he was likewise aiding enemies
of a royal authority akin to his own. Perhaps, even
then, he had a vague premonition that this would

not be his only experience with the relentless march
of Revolution.

Yet the King was polite enough.   In addressing
the envoys he was graciously pleased to say that he
wished Congress to be assured of his friendship, and
that he was highly satisfied with the conduct of the
plenipotentiaries during their residence in his kingdom.   The ceremony was witnessed by a brilliant
gathering ; there was much enthusiasm, and the
affair ended with an elaborate dinner given by M.
de Vergennes.   Throughout it all Franklin, and
only Franklin, had been the real attraction ; his was
the leading part ; his was the honour.   Arthur Lee
must have eaten out his heart in impotent jealousy
at the popularity of the man who went to court
with as much confidence and aplomb as if he had
not, in his dressing, violated the awesome rules of
royal etiquette.

In the evening, after the presentation to the King,
the envoys had the honour of watching members of
the reigning family play at cards for very high
stakes.   Louis d'ors were scattered in profusion over
a large table at which sat, among others, the still
lovely Marie Antoinette.   The Queen had a generous, if unthinking, sympathy for the American
rebels.   When she saw the doctor enter she asked
him to stand near her ; spoke to him often in the
most civil terms, and flashed upon the white-haired
diplomat many a smile that must have gone straight
to his youthful heart.   *Poor Richard* was indeed the
fashion.   The taste for reckless gambling hardly appealed to the preacher of frugality, yet we may be

sure that he comported himself with the dignity of
a courtier.   Wigless he might be—but not witless;
the apostle of the new *régime* had that within him
which appeared passing pleasant in the eyes of the
fairest member of a dying despotism.   It was, in fine,
the ability of Franklin to appear agreeable to all sorts
and conditions of humanity, without being under
the necessity of changing his manners or of divest-
ing himself of an interesting personality.   He had
long been master of the useful art of self-possession,
to which he combined a delicacy of tact and a quickness of apprehension that allowed him to feel at
home either in a printer's office or in a king's dress-
ing-room.   There is nothing paradoxical in the
thought of the philosopher hovering near the chair
of Marie Antoinette, nor is it hard to understand
how he could number among his admirers two such
opposite personages as the Queen of France and the
aged Voltaire.   Voltaire embraced the doctor to
the joy of the French Academicians of Science;
ladies of the court crowned him with a wreath of
flowers.

With a little lessening of the old vigour, with a
longing for a richly deserved ease, was it strange
that the envoy found this burning of popular incense very fragrant and innocently seductive ?   Who
had a greater right than he to so pretty a reward ?
To be sure, John Adams, when he arrived in Paris
to replace Silas Deane, was a trifle shocked at the
worship bestowed upon the idol, and perhaps shook
his patriotic head over what he might consider the
demoralisation of a gouty old man who should be

MARIE ANTOINETTE.

back on the banks of the Delaware, there preparing his last will and testament.

> "He loves his ease," the New Englander writes to Samuel Adams, "hates to offend, and seldom gives any opinion till obliged to do it. . . . There are so many private families, ladies and gentlemen, that he visits so often, and they are so fond of him, that he cannot well avoid it,—and so much intercourse with Academicians, that all these things together keep his mind in a constant state of dissipation."

All of which might be true, yet there is about this pen-sketch more of acerbity than charity.

Amid all this "constant state of dissipation," America—stronger America now, full of life and fight, and hope—was still Franklin's leading thought. Not only of the America of his own time did he muse; his fancy sometimes carried him away to the country as it would be after he had paid the rapidly maturing debt of nature.

> "I must soon quit this scene," he writes to General Washington, "but you may live to see our country flourish, as it will amazingly and rapidly after the war is over; like a field of young Indian corn which long fair weather and sunshine has enfeebled and discoloured, and which in that weak state, by a thunder gust of violent wind, hail, and rain, seemed to be threatened with absolute destruction; yet the storm being past, it recovers fresh verdure, shoots up with double vigour, and delights the eye, not of its owner only, but of every observing traveller."

Franklin prophesied, as he builded, better than he knew.

CHAPTER XI

PLAY AND POLITICS

1777–1783

O read over the correspondence which punctuated Franklin's life in France is to regret that a volume rather than several short paragraphs cannot be devoted to the lighter phase of the philosopher's exile, wherein we see him acting the gallant to clever women, and settling down, ere he should leave the earthly scene forever, to warm his cheery old heart and gouty limbs in the sunshine of enjoyment. Here again appears the versatility of the man. One day he is writing upon subjects the most abstruse or the most grave, and at another time he is gaily describing a fantastic dream for the edification of the blue-stocking widow of the great Helvetius. "Mortified at the barbarous resolution pronounced by you so positively yesterday evening, that you would remain single the rest of your life, as a compliment due to the memory of your husband, I retired to my chamber. Throwing myself upon my bed, I dreamt that I was dead, and was

transported to the Elysian Fields." Then follows
the dream, which is described with a grace and airy
humour more suggestive, let us say, of a Beaumarchais than of the usually matter-of-fact Franklin.

Another day he resuscitates, for the benefit of his
friend Monsieur l'Abbé de la Roche, a " little drinking song which I wrote forty years ago," wherein
are to be found allusions to Venus, Lucifer, and the
joys of " friends and a bottle." It is quite in the
style of (although more grammatically expressed
than) the inevitable ditty rattled off, to the accompaniment of clinking tin cups, by a sad-eyed chorus
in comic operetta. Then he has another attack of
gallantry, and tells his dear Madame Helvetius that
statesmen, philosophers, historians, poets, and men
of learning of all sorts are drawn around her " as
straws about a fine piece of amber." Yet he is the
correspondent who can write, almost in the same
breath : " When a religion is good, I conceive that
it will support itself ; and when it cannot support
itself, and God does not take care to support it, so
that its professors are obliged to call for the help of
the civil power, it is a sign, I apprehend, of its being
a bad one." * The *parsifleur* and the thinker upon
religion, all in one! What pleasure he gets from the
pen ; how the using it so frequently keeps him fresh
and young, besides leaving many an agreeable literary tid-bit for posterity!

When he has the gout he finds distraction from
the pain by composing a little dialogue between
himself and his tormentor, which incidentally gives

* From a letter to Richard Price.

us a glimpse of his mode of life at seductive Passy.

" You would not only torment my body to death," says the doctor to Madam Gout, "but ruin my good name; you reproach me as a glutton and a tippler; now all the world, that knows me, will allow that I am neither the one nor the other."

GOUT. The world may think as it pleases; it is always very complaisant to itself, and sometimes to its friends; but I very well know that the quantity of meat and drink proper for a man who takes a reasonable degree of exercise, would be too much for another, who never takes any.

FRANKLIN. I take—eh—oh! as much exercise—eh! (*here a twinge of pain seizes him*) as I can, Madam Gout. You know my sedentary state, and on that account it would seem, Madam Gout, as if you might spare me a little, seeing it is not altogether my own fault.

GOUT. Not a jot; your rhetoric and your politeness are thrown away; your apology avails nothing. If your situation in life is a sedentary one, your amusements, your recreations, at least, should be active. You ought to walk or ride; or, if the weather prevents that, play at billiards. But let us examine your course of life. While the mornings are long, and you have leisure to go abroad, what do you do? Why, instead of gaining an appetite for breakfast, by salutary exercise, you amuse yourself with books, pamphlets, or newspapers, which commonly are not worth the reading. Yet you eat an inordinate breakfast, four dishes of tea, with cream, and one or two buttered toasts, with slices of hung beef, which I fancy are not things the most easily digested. Immediately afterward you sit down to write at your desk, or converse with persons who apply to you on business. Thus the time passes till one, without any kind of bodily exercise. But all this I could pardon, in regard, as you say, to your sedentary condition. But what is your practice after dinner? Walking in the beautiful gardens of those friends, with whom you have dined, would be the choice of men of sense; yours is to be fixed down to chess,* where you are found engaged for two or three hours.

---

* " Dr. Franklin was so immoderately fond of chess, that one evening at Passy, he sat at that amusement from six in the afternoon till sunrise."—WILLIAM TEMPLE FRANKLIN,

The doctor had diagnosed his own case in this bit
of pleasantry born of pain, but he never did very
much in the way of reforming the sedentary ways.
The routine of his French life was too attractive; his
venerable legs had grown too lazy; it was far easier
to play chess, or to entertain at his own table, or
drive to the no longer youthful Veuve Helvetius or
to the amiable Madame Brillon—" a lady of most
respectable character and pleasing conversation."
At the Brillons the septuagenarian found a second
home, where he was accustomed to spend at least
two evenings every week.   Madame Brillon, he
writes, " has among other elegant accomplishments,
that of an excellent musician; and, with her daughter, who sings prettily, and some friends who play,
she kindly entertains me and my grandson with little
concerts, a cup of tea, and a game of chess.   I call
this my *Opera*, for I rarely go to the Opera at Paris."
This is quite an idyllic portrait of the lady in whose
honour he composed several of his famous *Bagatelles*,
including *The Ephemera* and the *Story of the Whistle*.
The latter was elevated years ago to the dignity of a
classic.   Who does not recall the familiar cases of the
unfortunates who paid too much for their whistles ?

The philosopher not only wrote much while at
Passy, but he unwittingly inspired several of his
neighbours to try their own literary powers by composing verses in his praise.   On one memorable occasion he was made the victim—perhaps not a very
bored one—of a *fête champêtre* and a poem, thrust
upon him by the admiring Countess d'Houdetot, at
her château in the valley of Montmorency.   The

assembled guests, all members of the Houdetot
family, did not even wait for the doctor's arrival,
but walked out about half a mile to meet his carriage. The Countess helped him to alight, and
broke out with a rhapsodic verse setting forth the
homage due a man who had made his fellow-citizens
so happy ("Au mortel qui forma des citoyens
heureux"). When the château was reached, dinner served, and the first glass of wine offered, the
company continued the poetic infliction by singing
in chorus another instalment wherein the guest of
honour was referred to intimately as "Benjamin."
Then the Countess sang a verse which politely set
forth that virtue herself, in order to be adored, had
assumed the form of Franklin; others drank to the
philosopher and recited each a stanza of the epic,
and finally, when dinner was ended, the Countess
led the doctor to the gardens of Sanoy. Here,
seated in Arcadian state under an arbour, he was
presented with a Virginia locust tree, "which, at
the request of the company, he planted with his
own hands." To make the ceremony the more impressive the Countess burst forth with another piece
of the inevitable poem (afterwards inscribed upon a
marble pillar near the locust tree), and ere the guest
could tear himself regretfully away, at eventide, the
good lady followed him to the door of his carriage,
speaking a little epilogue, also of her own composition:

> "Législateur d'un monde, et bienfaiteur des deux,
> L'homme dans tous les temps te devra ses hommages ;
> Et je m'acquitte dans ces lieux
> De la dette de tous les ages,"

All of which is very pretty without doubt, but we
must not forget, amid all this atmosphere of pane-
gyric and private pleasures, to recall briefly the
political life of Franklin from the time that the
French alliance was avowed in so open and brilliant
a form.   Not the least interesting phase of his experience proved to be the attempt of several members of Parliament to find out from him whether
there was any possibility of reconciliation with
America.   To one of these Englishmen, David
Hartley, the envoy wrote that famous letter in reply
to the curious remark, that the alliance between
France and America was " the great stumbling-
block in the way of making peace."   It is a letter
which shows us how the once ardent admiration for
George III., the " very best " of kings, had gone
the way of vain illusions.

"We know," says Franklin, "that your King hates Whigs and
Presbyterians; that he thirsts for our blood, of which he has already
drunk large draughts [obstinate, and worse, the King surely was,
but to paint him as a melodramatic yearner after blood is hardly just
on the doctor's part] ; that weak and unprincipled ministers are ready
to execute the wickedest of his orders, and his venal Parliament
equally ready to vote them just.   Not the smallest appearance of a
reason can be imagined, capable of inducing us to think of relinquish-
ing a solid alliance with one of the most amiable, as well as most
powerful princes of Europe, for the expectation of unknown terms of
peace, to be afterwards offered to us by *such a government :* a government, that has already shamefully broken all the compacts it ever
made with us.   This is worse than advising us to drop the substance
for the shadow.   The dog, after he found his mistake, might possibly have recovered his mutton ; but we could never hope to be trusted
again by France, or indeed by any other nation under heaven.   We
know the worst you can do to us, if you have your wish, is, to confiscate our estates and take our lives, to rob and murder us ; and this

you have seen we are ready to hazard, rather than come again under your detested government."

The writer had no desire to fasten any of this criticism upon the peace-loving Hartley, and he adds:

"You must observe, my dear friend, that I am a little warm. Excuse me. It is over. Only let me counsel you not to think of being sent hither on so fruitless an errand, as that of making such a proposition. It puts me in mind of the comic farce entitled, *God-send; or, The Wreckers*. You may have forgotten it; but I will endeavour to amuse you by recollecting a little of it."

This is the "comic farce," as Franklin gives it for Hartley's edification:

SCENE.—MOUNT'S BAY.

(A ship riding at anchor in a great storm. A lee shore full of rocks, and lined with people, furnished with axes and carriages to cut up wrecks, knock the sailors on the head, and carry off the plunder; according to custom.)

FIRST WRECKER.   This ship rides it out longer than I expected; she must have good ground tackle.

SECOND WRECKER.   We had better send off a boat to her, and persuade her to take a pilot, who can afterward run her ashore, where we can best come at her.

THIRD WRECKER.   I doubt whether the boat can live in this sea; but if there are any brave fellows willing to hazard themselves for the good of the public, and a double share, let them say "Ay."

SEVERAL WRECKERS.   I, I, I, I.   *(The boat goes off, and comes under the ship's stern.)*

SPOKESMAN.   So ho, the ship, a hoa!

CAPTAIN.   Hulloa.

SP.   Would you have a pilot?

CAPT.   No, no!

SP.   It blows hard, and you are in danger.

CAPT. I know it.

SP. Will you buy a better cable? We have one in the boat here.

CAPT. What do you ask for it?

SP. Cut that you have, and then we'll talk about the price of this.

CAPT. I shall do no such foolish thing. I have lived in your parish formerly, and know the heads of ye too well to trust ye; keep off from my cable there; I see you have a mind to cut it yourselves. If you go any nearer to it, I'll fire into you and sink you.

SP. It is a rotten French cable, and will part of itself in half an hour. Where will you be then, Captain? You had better take our offer.

CAPT. You offer nothing, you rogues, but treachery and mischief. My cable is good and strong, and will hold long enough to baulk all your projects.

SP. You talk unkindly, Captain, to people who come here only for your good.

CAPT. I know you come for all our *goods*, but, by God's help, you shall have none of them: you shall not serve us as you did the Indiamen.

SP. Come, my lads, let's be gone. This fellow is not so great a fool as we took him to be.

In comparing the English ministry to a party of wreckers Franklin may have been unnecessarily severe; yet he was justified in growing indignant when a sane Englishman suggested a breaking of the French treaties, and a return to the uncertain mercies and condescensions of George III. and his Parliament. This was not the only chance the envoy had for plain writing upon the subject of impossible reconciliations. Once a paper addressed to him was thrown into a window of the legation; upon examination it proved to be a letter signed " Charles de Weissenstein," dated from Brussels, June 16 (1778), and containing a fantastic plan for settling the war,* with suggestions for pensioning off the leading patriots, and for the creating of American peers. The paper was taken with much seriousness. Franklin, who believed that it had been inspired by King George, wrote an answer which was expected to bring the blood tingling into the royal ears. As it happened, the answer never was sent to "Weissenstein," but it has been preserved for us in the great mass of Frankliniana, and we cannot easily forget this unmistakable dig at the political morals of his Britannic Majesty:

"I now indeed recollect my being informed, long since, when in England, that a certain very great personage, then young, studied much a certain book, called *Arcana Imperii*. I had the book and read it. There are sensible and good things in it, but some bad ones; for, if I remember rightly, a particular King is applauded for his politically exciting a rebellion among his subjects, at a time when they had not strength to support it, that he might, in subduing them, take away their privileges, which were troublesome to him; and a question is formally stated and discussed, *Whether a prince, who, to appease a revolt, makes promises of indemnity to the revolters, is obliged to fulfil those promises.* Honest and good men would say, Ay; but this politician says, as you say, No."

And again the writer says, in pointed terms:

"This offer to corrupt us, sir, is with me your credential, and convinces me that you are not a private volunteer in your application. It bears the stamp of British court character. It is even the signature of your King."

---

* In case his Majesty, or his successors, should ever create American peers (so wrote the unknown peacemaker), then Franklin, Washington, John Adams, Hancock, and others, "shall be among the first created, if they choose it; *Mr.* Washington to have immediately a brevet of Lieutenant-General, and all the honours and precedence incident thereto, but not to assume or bear any command without a special warrant, or letter of service, for that purpose, from the King."

"Weissenstein," the inscrutable, had advised
Franklin that the reply must be given to a stranger
who would be found on a certain Monday in the
Cathedral of Notre Dame, and who was to wear a
rose in his hat by way of identification. The tryst
was not kept; the letter was held back in deference
to the wishes of the French Government. John
Adams (who was now duly established in the legation as the successor to Silas Deane) relates that
the day after the one appointed for the meeting M.
de Vergennes sent a police report, stating that at
the hour and place suggested by the mysterious correspondent "a gentleman appeared, and finding
nobody, wandered about the church, gazing at the
statues and pictures, and other curiosities of that
magnificent cathedral, never losing sight, however,
of the spot appointed, and often returning to it,
looking earnestly about, at times, as if he expected
somebody. His person, stature, figure, air, com-
plexion, dress, and everything about him were ac-
curately and minutely described. He remained two
hours in the church, and then went out, was followed through every street, and all his motions
watched to the hotel where he lodged." "We
were told," continues Adams, "the day he arrived
there, the name he assumed, which was Colonel
Fitz—something—an Irish name that I have forgotten—the place he came from, and time he set off to
return. . . . Whether the design was to seduce
us Commissioners, or whether it was thought that
we should send the project to Congress, and that
they might be tempted by it, or that disputes might

be excited among the people, I know not.   In either
case it was very weak and absurd, and betrayed a
gross ignorance of the genius of the American
people.''

The idea of the King of Great Britain seeking to
get up a clandestine correspondence with his one-
time admirer—if that idea be not idle fancy—and
the presence in Notre Dame of a secret emissary to
accomplish that purpose, supply quite the flavour of
romance.   We see here and there other flashes of
the picturesque as we pursue the path of Franklin
—see him hobnobbing with Beaumarchais, his anti-
thesis, or sending a courier to London to confer
with members of Opposition in Parliament,* or ex-
tending aid and friendship to that prince of dashing
privateers, Captain Paul Jones.   It was Jones who
gave to one of the vessels in his prize-taking fleet
the name of the *Bon Homme Richard*, because he
had secured this fourteen-year-old ship from the
French Government by acting upon *Poor Richard's*
maxim: " If you would have your business done,
come yourself; if not, send.''   He had gone to
Versailles, after much weary waiting, and obtained
by his presence what any amount of correspondence
had failed to accomplish.   It was to Paul Jones
whom Franklin wrote, when the commander was
preparing for a descent upon the English coast, that

* Jonathan Loring Austin, the courier who brought to the envoys
at Passy the news of Burgoyne's surrender.   During his dangerous
stay in England he was domesticated in the family of Lord Shelburne, and was actually introduced to the young Prince of Wales
(later George IV.) when that prince was in company with Mr. Fox.

BENJAMIN FRANKLIN IN 1779.

FROM AN OIL PAINTING IN THE POSSESSION OF THE HISTORICAL SOCIETY OF PENNSYLVANIA.

" although the English have wantonly burned many
defenceless towns in America, you are not to follow
this example, unless when a reasonable ransom is
refused; in which case your own generous feelings
as well as this instruction will induce you to give
timely notice of your intention, that sick and ancient persons, women and children, may be first
removed." It was Jones who replied, like a seasoned courtier: " The letter I had the honour to
receive from you to-day would make a coward
brave."

Perhaps the most blessed personal incident for
Franklin, was the departure from France of Arthur
Lee. In company with the suspicious Ralph Izard,
the unreceived minister to Tuscany, Lee had done
all he could to undermine the reputation of his
chief. Fortunately that reputation was too great to
be affected in any permanent way, but the tension
of the situation became extremely disagreeable as
the eyes of the senior were gradually opened to the
treachery about him. The pitiful wrangling is best
described by what he told John Adams, on the
latter's arrival from America, namely, that Lee was
" a man of an anxious, uneasy temper, which made
it disagreeable to do business with him; that he
seemed to be one of those men, of whom he had
known many in his day, who went on through life
quarrelling with one person or another, till they
commonly ended with the loss of their reason."
Ralph Izard, he further informed Mr. Adams, " was
joined in close friendship with Mr. Lee; that Mr.
Izard was a man of violent and ungoverned pas-

sions; that each of these had a number of Americans about him, who were always exciting disputes, and propagating stories that made the service very disagreeable." Mr. Izard, indeed, did not hesitate to write home to Congress that Franklin was guided by principles neither of virtue nor of honour, while Arthur Lee professed to have quite as low an opinion of the philosopher. Again, it was through the nasty charges made by Lee that Silas Deane fell into bad odour with the Continental legislators. Deane was accused of acting dishonestly in the business of his French mission, and as the indirect outcome of the lies told about him, he was to die poor, and estranged from his native land.

However distressing all this plotting and scheming proved, relief finally came in the shape of the Marquis de Lafayette, who drove to see Franklin one day in February, 1779, bringing with him from America the commission of Congress appointing the doctor sole plenipotentiary to France. The three commissioners had agreed that the interests of America would be best served by the maintaining of only one envoy, but it would be going many lengths too far to add that two of them were united in hoping that Franklin would be the fortunate man. Franklin was the fortunate man, however; and it is with pleasure, and good-bye assurances of contempt, that Mr. Izard (now recalled to America) and Mr. Lee make their exits from our narrative. To follow them further would serve no useful purpose, although it is worth the noting that ere Lee gave up the fight his friends in Congress made a desperate but unsuccessful effort to secure the recall of Franklin, and to put the Virginian in his place. It was high time that the unrest at the legation should be succeeded by a more peaceful environment. The sole plenipotentiary had his hands full in dealing, at long range, with the financial problems besetting Congress, and coaxing loans from the French Government—a line of diplomacy wherein his skill is shown from the fact that he secured in this wise, from 1777 to 1782, some 26,000,000 francs.

Although we have thus bid farewell to Messrs. Lee and Izard we must renew our acquaintance with another of the Passy household, the sturdy John Adams, under rather unpleasant conditions. For after going home to America for a brief visit Mr. Adams returns to France in the February of 1780, armed with powers to arrange a peace with England, at some future day, and is soon involved in a controversy with the Count de Vergennes. Perhaps the American forgot how necessary it was to act with tact towards a minister who had shown himself so friendly to the colonies; perhaps he wrote more than was consonant with a diplomatic reserve, but view the affair as we will, according to our personal bias, it is certain that the two men fell out, and that Vergennes thought Adams deficient in the necessary gratitude, or politeness, for the good offices of France. The matter came to an open rupture when the New Englander wrote to the minister that he doubted the usefulness of the fleet which had sailed for America under De Rochambeau. At this De Vergennes notified Adams that

he would no longer correspond with him—" Mr.
Franklin being the sole person who has letters of
credence to the King from the United States "—and
the Count even went so far as to ask Franklin to
submit his reply to Congress.

The doctor found himself in a delicate predica-
ment. He had no desire to do anything to the
prejudice of John Adams, yet he knew far better
than did that impolitic gentleman the necessity for
keeping on the fairest terms with the minister.
America—money-wanting America—was in no condition to dispense with so valued an ally as France.
So he took the bull by the horns and wrote to the
President of Congress a frank letter in which he set
forth the circumstance of the quarrel.

" It is true," he said, " that Mr. Adams's proper business is elsewhere ; but the time not being come for that business, and having
nothing else here wherewith to employ himself, he seems to have
endeavoured to supply what he may suppose my negotiation defective
in. He thinks, as he tells me himself, that America has been too
free in expressions of gratitude to France ; for that she is more
obliged to us than we to her ; and that we should show spirit in our
applications. I apprehend that he mistakes his ground, and that this
court is to be treated with decency and delicacy. The King, a young
and virtuous prince, has, I am persuaded, a pleasure in reflecting on
the generous benevolence of the action in assisting an oppressed
people, and proposes it as a part of the glory of his reign. I think it
right to increase this pleasure by our thankful acknowledgments, and
that such an expression of gratitude is not only our duty, but our
interest. A different conduct seems to me what is not only improper
and unbecoming, but what may be hurtful to us. Mr. Adams, on
the other hand, who, at the same time, means our welfare and interest as much as I, or any man, can do, seems to think a little apparent
stoutness, and a greater air of independence and boldness in our demands, will procure us more ample assistance. It is for Congress to

judge and regulate their affairs accordingly. . . . It is my intention, while I stay here, to procure what advantages I can for our
country, by endeavouring to please this court; and I wish I could
prevent anything being said by any of our countrymen here, that may
have a contrary effect, and increase an opinion lately showing itself in
Paris, that we seek a difference, and with a view of reconciling ourselves to England. Some of them have of late been very indiscreet in
their conversations."

Fortunately for all and everything concerned, the
indiscretions of Mr. Adams had no sequel, beyond
the inevitable discussion of the matter by Congress.
That he came very near to becoming an uninten-
tional mischief-maker cannot be doubted. He had
arrived in Paris much impressed with the idea of
trying to open immediate negotiations for a peace
with England; M. de Vergennes thought, or pretended to think, that the time had not come for com-
municating with the British Government; and from
this difference of opinion the American had foolishly
drifted into a quarrel. But to dwell upon this episode would be ungracious; to pick flaws in so valiant
a champion of America as honest John Adams is
not our mission.

Rather let us carry on our chronicle to the final
achievements of Franklin in that diplomatic sphere
for which it might be said that nature specially had
intended him, were it not that he seemed equally at
home in other lines of usefulness. Now the Revolution has reached its climax; Lord Cornwallis has
surrendered at Yorktown (October 17, 1781); the
philosopher is to use his powers in the direction of
reconciliation. An as opponent to England he has
proved a veritable giant; as a peace-maker, in a *rôle*

well suited to the mellowness and charity of old age, he will be hardly less successful.

In the spring of 1781 the doctor had asked permission of Congress to retire from the French mission, but instead of relieving him that body merely put another task upon the envoy by appointing him joint commissioner, with John Jay and John Adams, to settle terms of peace. Later, when Lord North and his colleagues give way to a Whig ministry, informal negotiations are already in progress, and Franklin is writing to Lord Shelburne, of the new cabinet, expressing his hope for a general peace, " which I am sure your lordship, with all good men, desires, which I wish to see before I die, and to which I shall, with infinite pleasure, contribute everything in my power." This friendly note was unofficial, but it brought a response from Shelburne, and also an agent of his lordship's in the person of Richard Oswald, a merchant who was to find out the views of Franklin and to talk over the whole question of amity between France, America, and Great Britain. There were conferences between the agent, the envoy, and the Count de Vergennes, and once, after returning from Versailles, Oswald intimated that if in any proposed settlement France should make humiliating demands of England, " the spirit of the nation would be roused, unanimity would prevail, and resources would not be wanting." As Franklin relates:

" He [Oswald] said, there was no want of money in the nation; that the chief difficulty lay in the finding out new taxes to raise it; and, perhaps, that difficulty might be avoided by shutting up the

THE AMERICAN PEACE COMMISSION.

AFTER AN UNFINISHED PAINTING BY BENJAMIN WEST.

FROM THE PHOTOGRAPH IN THE MUSEUM OF FINE ARTS, BOSTON.

Exchequer, stopping the payment of the interest to the public funds, and applying that money to the support of the war. I made no reply to this ; for I did not desire to discourage their stopping payment, which I considered as cutting the throat of the public credit, and a means of adding fresh exasperation against them with the neighbouring nations. Such menaces were besides an encouragement with me, remembering the adage that *they who threaten are afraid.*"

Franklin, in his intercourse with Oswald, displayed his usual tact and caution, and quite won over that emissary to his own way of thinking. He went further than this, however, by boldly suggesting the cession of Canada to the United States, in a paper called "Notes for Conversation," which, after a proper show of diffidence, he allowed the agent to convey to Lord Shelburne. It was a suggestion, of course, which could not be seriously considered, but nothing was lost, as the astute American must have realised, in putting his own case on an ambitious level.

To attempt to describe all that went before the peace—the vast amount of correspondence, the interviews, the fluctuations of the British ministry, the scheming of the Count de Vergennes, the manœuvring of Messrs. Franklin, Jay, and Adams—would be to get entangled in a maze of data to which only a lengthy story could do justice. To delve into the details is to become absorbed in something that reads like a diplomatic novel; and the chronicler who does so is sorely tempted to quote therefrom far beyond the limits of space assigned to him. The provocation is great, and in one instance must it be yielded to, in describing a little contretemps. The humour of it was not lost sight of by Franklin, who wrote an account of the incident on the day it happened:

"The Count du Nord, who is son of the Empress of Russia, arriving at Paris, ordered, it seems, cards of visit to be sent to all the foreign ministers. One of them, on which was written, ' *Le Comte du Nord et le Prince Bariatinski,*' was brought to me. It was on Monday evening last. Being at court the next day I inquired of an old minister, my friend, what was the etiquette, and whether the Count received visits. The answer was, ' *Non ; on se fait écrire ; voila tout.*' This is done by passing the door, and ordering your name to be written on the porter's book. Accordingly, on Wednesday I passed the house of Prince Bariatinski, Ambassador of Russia, where the Count lodged, and left my name on the list of each. I thought no more of the matter ; but this day, May the 24th, comes the servant who brought the card, in great affliction, saying he was like to be ruined by his mistake in bringing the cards here, and wishing to obtain from me some paper, of I know not what kind, for I did not see him.

"In the afternoon came my friend, M. Le Roy, who is also a friend of the Prince's, telling me how much he, the Prince, was concerned at the accident, that both himself and the Count had great personal regard for me and my character, but that, our independence not yet being acknowledged by the court of Russia, it was impossible for him to permit himself to make me a visit as minister. I told M. Le Roy it was not my custom to seek such honours, though I was very sensible of them when conferred upon me ; that I should not have voluntarily intruded a visit, and that in this case, I had only done what I was informed the etiquette required of me ; but if it would be attended with any inconvenience to Prince Bariatinski, whom I much esteemed and respected, I thought the remedy was easy ; he had only to erase my name out of his books of visits received, and I would burn their card."

As a comment upon this amusing piece of redtapeism, Franklin says:

"All the northern princes are not ashamed of a little civility committed towards an American. The King of Denmark, travelling in

England under an assumed name, sent me a card, expressing in strong terms his esteem for me, and inviting me to dinner with him at St. James's. And the Ambassador from the King of Sweden lately asked me, whether I had powers to make a treaty of commerce with their kingdom, for, he said, his master was desirous of such a treaty with the United States, had directed him to ask me the question, and had charged him to tell me, that it would flatter him greatly to make it with a person whose character he so much esteemed, etc. Such compliments might make me a little proud, if we Americans were not naturally as much so already as the porter, who, being told he had with his burden jostled the great Czar, Peter, then in London, walking the street, ' *Poh!* ' says he, ' we are all Czars here.' " *

Had the philosopher found nothing more disagreeable than the vagueness of his position before the diplomatic world he would have considered himself a fortunate man. But it so happened that ere the signing of the preliminary articles of peace he was brought into a passive opposition to Messrs. Jay and Adams. Mr. Jay had a very positive and well-grounded suspicion that the Count de Vergennes was seeking to restrict the territory of the United States west of the Alleghanies, and to play into the hands of Spain at the expense of America ; Mr. Adams supported his colleague in this belief, and the doctor, very naturally, if not, perhaps, so sagaciously as we might expect, continued to show faith in the disinterestedness of the French ministry. Mr. Jay was anxious to negotiate directly with Great Britain, without the co-operation of France, and contrary to the wish of Congress that the ministry of Louis XVI. should be allowed to work in harmony with the commissioners. The situation

* From the *Journal of the Negotiations for Peace with Great Britain.*

might have become more than embarrassing, but the doctor yielded the point; the preliminary treaty of peace was negotiated directly with Great Britain; Franklin was left to make apologies to the disgusted Vergennes, and to prevent the rising of discord between France and the United States. Nothing better tested the sterling patriotism of Franklin than the wisdom of this concession. He would have treated France as an honoured ally, not as an object of suspicion, yet he realised the danger of delay, and rather than bring about a series of complications, he gracefully said " Yes " to Messrs. Jay and Adams, rendered noble assistance in drawing up the treaty which recognised the independence of his country, and sank in love of that country all personal feeling or predilection. That he was too charitable in his estimate of Gallic diplomacy lessens not one whit the merit of this acquiescence, or the value of his services in the conferences preceding the settlement.

The preliminary treaty between Great Britain and the United States (under the terms of which the sovereignty of the latter nation was conceded, the British troops within her territory ordered to be withdrawn, boundaries agreed upon, etc.) was signed on the 30th of November, 1782. It seemed now as if the cup of the "little postmaster's" felicity had been filled to the brim. Surely, Father Time had dealt leniently in allowing an erstwhile subject of Queen Anne to live under the rule of three succeeding sovereigns, and finally to assist, as one of its most honoured founders, in the erection of a colos-

sal republic. But there was no chance to indulge
in sentiment and " spread-eagleism." Mr. Jay,
Mr. Adams, and Henry Laurens, who was also
acting as a peace commissioner, still left to their old
colleague the duty of pacifying the Count de Vergennes. This difficult task he skilfully accomplished,
after the exhibition of the expected hauteur on the
part of the minister, and we find the envoy writing
to the latter that " nothing has been agreed in the
preliminaries contrary to the interests of France, and
no peace is to take place between us and England,
till you have concluded yours. Your observation
is, however, apparently just, that, in not consulting
you before they were signed, we have been guilty
of neglecting a point of *bienséance*. But, as this
was not from want of respect for the King, whom
we all love and honour, we hope it will be excused,
and that the great work, which has hitherto been
so happily conducted, is so nearly brought to perfection, and is so glorious to his reign, will not be
ruined by a single indiscretion of ours." " And
certainly," said the veteran, " the whole edifice
sinks to the ground immediately if you refuse on
that account to give us any further assistance."
The letter was a masterly combination of an apology and a request for money. It succeeded in both
directions; M. de Vergennes was finally appeased,
and the French Government loaned to the United
States another sum of 6,000,000 francs—results
which testified very plainly to the soothing talents
of Franklin, and to the honour, even veneration,
wherein he was held. Well might Jefferson say,

when asked, some time later, if he had come to France to replace the doctor: " No one can replace him, sir; I am only his successor."

In the following January the preliminaries of a general peace between Great Britain, France, and Spain were signed at Versailles, Franklin being one of the joyful spectators of the scene; the beginning of September witnessed the sealing of the definitive treaty between England and the United States. The Revolution was, indeed, a thing of the past, and the envoy who had done so much to bring it to a successful issue began to long for Philadelphia, where he might " enjoy the little left him of the evening of life in repose, and in the sweet society of his friends and family." He had obtained of glory more than enough. " Could I have hoped at such an age, to have enjoyed such happiness ? " he cried to his friend, the Duc de la Rochefoucauld.

CHAPTER XII

E have had, of necessity, so much to do with the public activities of Franklin, and have so often left placid Philadelphia to follow the fortunes of our hero in the old world, that the glimpses of his home life must seem few and far between. We may be pardoned, therefore, in exercising the prerogative of the historian by turning back, before farewells are said, to look for a moment at the philosopher as he appears in his own house. That is a view in which the average " great man " does not always figure to advantage, but with Franklin the more we peer into his establishment on Market Street the more distinct becomes his kindliness of heart and domesticity of disposition.

One of the best pictures that we get of him in this beneficent light is furnished in the diary of Daniel Fisher,* a gentleman who came up to Phila-

* Extracts from this diary, contributed by Mrs. Conway Robinson Howard, may be found in the *Pennsylvania Magazine of History and Biography*, vol. xvii., No. 3.

delphia from Williamsburg, Virginia, in the May of 1755, in the hopes of winning fortune in the Quaker City. Mr. Fisher was armed with a letter of introduction to Chief-Justice Allen, a dignitary upon whom he made haste to call after he had quartered himself at the " Indian King " tavern, " kept by one Mr. John Biddle, a very civil, courteous Quaker." Mr. Allen, as ill-luck had it, could or would do nothing for the Virginian, notwithstanding the presentation of the note from the Honourable Mr. Nelson. The Chief Justice expressed his warm regard for the writer, but regretted that it was not in his power to help the visitor.

"He advised me," says Fisher, "to look about myself, and if I found anyone inclined to employ me in any shape, on my applying to him, he would inform them of the character Mr. Nelson had given me. This, I own, was a reception I was not prepared for ; yet mortified and confounded as I was I begged he would reflect I was an utter stranger in the place, to which I observed he was sensible. I had travelled merely at the instance and advice of the Honble. Mr. Nelson. That I was now so destitute of acquaintance, that I did not know where, nor to whom to apply for a private lodging, for want of which advantage, I shall be obliged, both horse and myself, at a large expense, to continue at a public inn. But this instead of exciting in him any feeling of my distress or anxiety only increased his impatience to get rid of me, keeping me standing, and moving divers times towards the door, as if he apprehended that I did not know the way. However, at the third or fourth motion, I took the hint, walking out of the room into the passage, he very civilly keeping me company to the street door ; but before we parted, I entreated to know whether I might have the liberty of waiting on him again, when he had considered my case, and I might have the happiness of finding him more at leisure. As to that, he said, he might generally be spoke with about nine in the morning."

Fisher returned in a melancholy mood to his inn.

It seemed as if the Chief Justice had no idea of helping him, and repeated visits confirmed the correctness of this gloomy theory.

" Thus circumstanced," continues the stranger, " in a kind of despair it entered my romantic head to communicate my unhappy condition to Mr. Franklin, a gentleman in good esteem here and well
known to the Philosophical World. I without reserve laid the whole
of my affairs before him, requesting his aid, if such a thing might be
without inconvenience to himself. This in writing I sent to him
June 4th, early in the morning. The same day I received a note by
a servant under a wafer in these words :

" ' Mr. Franklin's compliments to Mr. Fisher and desires the
favour of his Company to drink Tea at 5 o'clock this afternoon.'

" I went at the time, and in my imagination met with a humane,
kind reception. He expressed concern for my afflictions and promised to assist me into some business provided it was in his power. In
returning from Mr. Franklin's, a silversmith in the neighbourhood
of Mr. Franklin, seeing me come out of that gentleman's house,
spoke to me as I was passing his door and invited me to sit down."

The name of the silversmith was Soumien; the
result of the meeting was that in a few hours Mr.
Fisher had installed himself as a lodger in the
Soumien household, and was " very well pleased "
to observe that the family " seemed to be acquainted
with Mr. Franklin's." So cordial, indeed, was the
acquaintance that the very next afternoon Mrs.
Franklin paid the Soumiens a visit, of which the
diarist makes this curious entry :

" As I was coming down from my chamber this afternoon a gentlewoman was sitting on one of the lowest stairs, which were but
narrow, and there not being room enough to pass, she arose up and
threw herself upon the floor and sat there. Mr. Soumien and his
wife greatly entreated her to arise and take a chair, but in vain ; she
would keep her seat, and kept it, I think, the longer for their en-

treaty. This gentlewoman, whom, though I had seen before, I did not know, appeared to be Mrs. Franklin. She assumed the airs of extraordinary freedom and great humility, lamented heavily the misfortunes of those who are unhappily infected with a too tender or benevolent disposition, said she believed all the world claimed a privilege of troubling her Pappy (so she usually calls Mr. Franklin) with their calamities and distress, giving us a general history of many such wretches and their impertinent applications to him."

It is evident that Mr. Fisher was not over-much impressed with Deborah Franklin, among whose many virtues could be found neither polish nor breeding of the Vere de Vere type. Perhaps she, on her part, looked upon Fisher as an impecunious Virginian who was giving her " Pappy " entirely too much trouble. But we quote again from the diary:

" Thursday, the 12th (June).—This morning about nine Mr. Franklin sent for me to copy a pretty long letter from General Braddock, acknowledging the care of the Pennsylvanians in sending provisions, etc., to the forces, Mr. Franklin in particular, and complaining of the neglect of the governments of Virginia and Maryland especially, in speaking of which two colonies, he says: They had promised everything and had performed nothing ; and of the Pennsylvanians, he said : They had promised nothing and had performed everything. . . . When I had finished several hasty copies for which the post then waited, he desired I would breakfast with him the next morning and he would then give me more work.

" June 13 and 14.—I was closely employed on several copies of a manuscript treatise entitled, ' Observations Concerning the Increase of Mankind, Peopling of Countrys, Etc.'

" From June 16 to July 10: employed generally in writing or sorting of papers at the printing office. I should observe that on St. John the Baptist Day (June 24), there was the greatest procession of Free Masons to the church and their Lodge, in Second Street, that was ever seen in America. *No less than 160* being in the procession in gloves, aprons, etc., attended by a band of music. Mr. Allin, the Grand Master, honouring them with his company, as did the Deputy Grand Master, Mr. Benjamin Franklin and his son, Mr. William Franklin, who walked as the next Chief Officer. A sword bearer with a naked sword drawn headed the procession. They dined together elegantly, as it is said at their hall upon Turtle, etc. [Poor Fisher ! The thought of turtle—Turtle with a capital T as he spells it—must have gone to his hungry soul.]

"Friday, July 18.—This afternoon about three o'clock we were terribly alarmed by an express by way of Maryland from Colonel Innis, dated at Mill's Creek or Fort Cumberland, July 11, giving an account that the forces under General Braddock were entirely defeated by the French. . . . Having as yet made no settled agreement with Mr. Franklin, I was not certain that he had any real occasion for my services, having several days together nothing for me to do."

At this juncture Mr. Fisher met one Captain Coultas, a "person of sense and character," and learned that in case the said captain was selected Sheriff of Philadelphia, he (Fisher) might expect employment. The diary continues:

"Extremely pleased with the humanely rational generosity of this sensible man, I immediately flew to my friend, Mr. Franklin, with the news, that he might participate in my satisfaction, but was somewhat surprised that he did not consider what I had done in the same view with myself. He allowed Captain Coultas was a very worthy man, and would sincerely perform everything I was encouraged to expect or hope for, but could not apprehend that anything he could do for me would be worthy my acceptance ; that he had himself thought of several ways of serving me, and has rejected them only because he esteemed them too mean. Particularly, he said, he could immediately put me into the Academy, in the capacity of English School Master, a place of £60 a year, with some other advantages, but refrained mentioning it to me in hopes of having it soon in his power of doing better for me. I assured him with the utmost gratitude, the employ did not appear in so mean a light to me ; and the only reason I had for declining the favour, was the diffidence of my ability in doing justice to his recommendations, a thing which he said, he was not in the least apprehension of. However, presuming
20

it gave him no offence, I craved his leave to decline the kind offer, and he declared himself very well satisfied. Having informed him that I should prefer serving him as a clerk provided he had any occasion for me, on Monday morning, July 28th, I received the following letter from him :

"'Monday morning, July 28.—Sir—Till our new building is finished, which I hope will be in two or three weeks, I have no room to accommodate a clerk. But it is my intention to have one, though my business is so small that I cannot afford to give more than I have always given, Viz. Diet at my own Table, with Lodging and Washing and £25 per Annum. I could never think this worth offering to you but if you think fit to accept it, till something better shall fall in the way, you shall be very welcome to &c. B. Franklin.'

"'P. S.—It may commence from the time you first began to write for me, in which case I discharge your Board, etc., at Mr. Soumien's, or from the present time, and then I pay you for the writing done, or if you chuse it, I will get you into the charity school, as I mentioned before.'"

This was gracious and benevolent treatment of a man who had come to Franklin without the slightest claim upon his generosity, barring despair and a "romantic head." Mr. Fisher tells us that he quickly accepted the tendered clerkship, and then describes a peculiar condition of affairs in the Franklin household anent the status therein of Mr. William Franklin, the future Governor of New Jersey :

"Mr. Soumien had often informed me of great uneasiness and dissatisfaction in Mr. Franklin's family in a manner no way pleasing to me and which in truth I was unwilling to credit, but as Mrs. Franklin and I, of late, began to be friendly and sociable, I discerned too great grounds for Mr. Soumien's reflections, arising solely from turbulence and jealousy and pride of her disposition. She suspecting Mr. Franklin for having too great an esteem for his son in prejudice of herself and daughter, a young woman of about 12 or 13 years of age, for whom it was visible Mr. Franklin had no less esteem than for his son. Young Mr. Franklin, I have often seen pass to and from his father's apartment upon business (for he does not eat, drink, or sleep in the house), without least compliment between Mr. Franklin and him or any sort of notice taken of each other, till one day I was sitting with her in the passage when the young gentleman came by, she exclaimed to me (he not hearing) :

" 'Mr. Fisher, there goes the greatest Villain upon Earth.'

" This greatly confounded and perplexed me, but did not hinder her from pursuing her invectives in the foulest terms I ever heard from a gentlewoman. What to say or do I could not tell, till luckily a neighbour of her acquaintance coming in I made my escape. I ever after industriously avoided being alone with her and she appeared no less cunning in seeking opportunities of beginning the subject again, in so much that I foresaw a very unpromising situation. The respect due this young man, which his father always paid him and which I was determined he should receive from me, would not, I perceived clearly, be endured by a woman of her violent spirit, and I began to wish my engagement had been with Captain Coultas."

Evidently Mr. Fisher was not a philosopher. Fortunately for his peace of mind he now received news which seemed to promise him a more prosperous career should he return to Virginia.

" The uncertainty of my situation, my apprehensions of Mrs. Franklin's turbulent temper, together with reflecting upon what might be the consequence of General Braddock's defeat, brought me to a resolution of seeing my family and Mr. Walthoe at Williamsburg before I came to any certain determination of a settlement; yet I showed Mr. Franklin my letter, and craved his opinion, who very readily came into mine, assuring me that he would wait a considerable space for the result of our conferences before he supplied himself with a clerk or the school with a master. So I fixed upon Sunday the 10th for setting out on my journey to Williamsburg. Being not determined which road I should take (there being several) Mr. Franklin said if I went the Upper he would get me to take an order for a small matter of money on Mr. Mercer in Virginia, with whom he had had no settlement for nine years, upon which I told him I did not regard a few miles of riding to serve him and he might depend upon my making Mr. Mercer's in my way. He gave me also six pistoles, asking if that was sufficient for the trouble he had given me. I told him it was. The evening (Saturday) before I set out, I was with him till after 11 o'clock, when he pressed me to accept ten guineas more, which I refused, and I said that in case of accident from my horse failing or any other misfortune I had a gold watch in my pocket which would give me some credit. It was very near twelve when we parted with mutual good wishes."

At five the next morning Fisher set out for Williamsburg, leaving behind him the pretty lanes of Philadelphia and the hospitality of its chief citizen.

Here was a diary written for private rather than public use, and the impressions which it records are frank and unconstrained. How much the more pleasant, therefore, is the insight it gives us into the helpfulness of Franklin! If the portrait of Deborah be uncomplimentary, it is not to be forgotten, nevertheless, that as time wore on the relations between the good lady and her step-son became far more cordial. When she died she was at peace with William Franklin, and he, in turn, had not neglected to pay her all necessary respect and attention. The " turbulent temper " had softened with the years. It was better that Mrs. Franklin did not live to see the son turn Tory. She might have returned to her earlier way of thinking.

Barring the little frictions inevitable in almost any household, there must have been much to charm in the home life of the doctor and his wife. Throughout all the views thereof it is curious to see how essentially domestic was the philosopher in his tastes, and how different he appeared from a certain type of public man who is never so bored as when removed from the eyes of the world, or of the town.

Had Franklin spent all his years in Philadelphia, in the enjoyment of a moderate income and enough leisure to read and pursue his scientific investigations, he would have been quite as happy as the better-known Franklin—colonial agent in London, Signer of the Declaration of Independence, Envoy to France, President of Pennsylvania, *et cetera, et cetera*. There was nothing about the house too small for his observation; there was no petty detail in which he could not take an interest. Even the quality of food, the shape of a coffee-cup, or the decoration of a room, not to speak of such important things as the education of his daughter or the dresses of his wife, were of consequence to the man who helped to lead national thought, oppose a national enemy, and establish a republic. His was a mind of wondrous receptivity.

So great, indeed, was this love of home and home-gods that no amount of foreign distraction could deprive him of it. He might go to England on affairs of state, but the house in Philadelphia was never forgotten.

"I send you by Captain Budden," we find him writing from London to Mrs. Franklin, "a large case, and a small box. In the large case is another small box, containing some English china ; viz. melons and leaves for a desert of fruit and cream, or the like ; a bowl remarkable for the neatness of the figures, made at Bow, near this city ; some coffee cups of the same ; a Worcester bowl, ordinary. To show the difference of workmanship there is something from all the china works in England ; and one old true china bason mended, of an odd colour. The same box contains four silver salt ladles, newest, but ugliest, fashion ; a little instrument to core apples ; another to make little turnips out of great ones. . . . Also seven yards of printed cotton, blue ground, to make you a gown. I bought it by candle-light, and liked it there, but not so well afterwards. If you do not fancy it, send it as a present from me to Sister Jenny. There is a better gown for you, of flowered tissue, sixteen yards, of Mrs. Stevenson's fancy, cost nine guineas ; and I think it a great beauty. There was no more of the sort, or you should have had enough for a *négligée* or suit."

It is evident that buried in Franklin's heart was the feeling that perhaps, in the matter of choosing gowns, he was, after all, quite as hopeless as any other specimen of benighted man, and that the taste of his landlady, Mrs. Stevenson, could be relied upon more successfully. What joy the "large case" must have given the family in Philadelphia! The doctor goes on, in his letter, to enumerate with a minuteness almost feminine the various articles the box contained—snuffers, music for Sally, two sets of books, and much else that will surely bring forth enthusiasm. And he says:

"Sally's last letter to her brother is the best wrote that of late I have seen of hers. I only wish she was a little more careful of her spelling. I hope she continues to love going to church, and would have her read over and over again the *Whole Duty of Man* and the *Lady's Library*. Look at the figures on the china bowl and coffee cups, with your spectacles on ; they will bear examining. I have made your compliments to Mrs. Stevenson. She is indeed very obliging, takes great care of my health, and is very diligent when I am any way indisposed ; but yet I have a thousand times wished you with me, and my little Sally with her ready hands and feet to do, and go, and come, and get what I wanted. There is a great difference in sickness between being nursed with that tender attention, which proceeds from sincere love ; and——"

How the pretty comparison was to end must be left to the imagination, for the conclusion of the letter is long since lost. There is enough of the comparison to show that in his love of home Franklin strove valiantly to atone for those *errata* of an irregular youth.*

When the beloved Sally was engaged to Richard Bache (whom she married in October, 1767), the father, then on another visit to England, wrote to Mrs. Franklin a characteristic epistle wherein paternal solicitude and domestic economy have amusing combination.   He must leave it to his wife's judgment, he says, to act " as shall seem best " in the proposed match.

"If you think it a suitable one, I suppose the sooner it is completed the better.   In that case I would advise, that you do not make an expensive feasting wedding, but conduct everything with frugality and economy, which our circumstances now require to be observed in all our expenses.   For, since my partnership with Mr. Hall is expired, a great source of our income is cut off ; and, if I should lose the post-office, which, among many changes here, is far from being unlikely, we should be reduced to our rents and interest of money for a subsistence, which will by no means afford the chargeable housekeeping and entertainments we have been used to.   For my own part, I live here as frugally as possible not to be destitute of the comforts of life, making no dinners for anybody and contenting myself with a single dish when I dine at home ; and yet such is the dearness of living here in every article, that my expenses amaze me."

Then the prudent Franklin goes on to assure Deborah that Mr. Bache must not expect too much from his parents-in-law.

"I hope his expectations are not great of any fortune to be had with our daughter before our death.   I can only say, that, if he proves a good husband to her and a good son to me, he shall find me as good a father as I can be ; but at present, I suppose you would

* This letter was written February 19, 1758.

agree with me, that we cannot do more than fit her out handsomely in clothes and furniture, not exceeding in the whole five hundred pounds of value. For the rest, they must depend, as you and I did, on their own industry and care, as what remains in our hands will be barely sufficient for our support, and not enough for them when it comes to be divided at our decease."

For Sarah the doctor always had the greatest fondness; no rush of public business, no absence from America, could abate a jot of his affection. Yet he could find fault with her, as with others, and it is quaint enough to see him chiding her, in a letter from France, for a seemingly extravagant order which she had sent abroad:

"When I began to read your account of the high prices of goods, 'a pair of gloves seven dollars, a yard of common gauze twenty-four dollars and that it now required a fortune to maintain a family in a very plain way' [Mrs. Bache had been quoting Philadelphia revolutionary prices to her dear papa], I expected you would conclude by telling me that everybody, as well as yourself, was grown frugal and industrious; and I could scarce believe my eyes in reading forward, that 'there never was so much pleasure and dressing going on'; and that you yourself wanted black pins and feathers from France, to appear, I suppose, in the mode! . . . The war, indeed, may in some degree raise the prices of goods, and the high taxes which are necessary to support the war, may make our frugality necessary; and, as I am always preaching that doctrine, I cannot in conscience or in decency encourage the contrary by my example, in furnishing my children with foolish modes and luxuries. I therefore send all the articles you desire, that are useful and necessary, and omit the rest."

Such fatherly caution must have been a blow to poor Mrs. Bache. Even the sternest example of unornamental man will admit, that she who expects a consignment of feathers and other trifles from Paris, and receives only "useful and necessary" things, is pretty sure to view the world through darkened glasses for at least twenty-four unpleasant hours. And who so stoic, even though she be the daughter of a philosopher, as to read with equanimity a succeeding clause in this letter ? " If you wear your cambric ruffles as I do, and take care not to mend the holes, they will come in time to be lace ; and feathers, my dear girl, may be had in America from every cock's tail." This was unkind unto the verge of sarcasm.

" How could my dear papa give me so severe a reprimand," Mrs. Bache wrote back to her father, " for wishing a little finery. He would not, I am sure, if he knew how much I have felt it. Last winter (in consequence of the surrender of General Burgoyne), was a season of triumph to the Whigs, and they spent it gaily ; you would not have had me, I am sure, stay away from the Embassador's or Gerard's entertainments, nor when I was invited to spend a day with General Washington and his lady ; and you would have been the last person, I am sure, to have wished to see me dressed with singularity. Though I never loved dress so much as to wish to be particularly fine, yet I never will go out when I cannot appear so as to do credit to my family and husband. The Assembly we went to, as Mr. Bache was particularly chosen to regulate them ; the subscription was fifteen pounds ; but to a subscription ball of which there were numbers, we never went to one, though always asked. I can assure my dear papa that industry in this house is by no means laid aside ; but as to spinning linnen, we cannot think of that till we have got that wove which we spun three years ago."

If Franklin could resist this bit of feminine argument, he was less susceptible to family affection than we are warranted in thinking. No one knew better than he—his simplicity nevertheless and notwithstanding—the value which the world attached to appearances. He was neither ostentatious nor a

seeker after social position, but he was quite willing
that his family should take a prominent part in the
life about them, and that Mrs. Bache should make
a pretty figure at an " Assembly," which was then,
as now, the gathering-ground of Philadelphia's
" Four Hundred."

But behold, after starting out to trace the home
ties of our hero, we have wandered off with him as
far away as France. That, perhaps, is pardonable.
If we retrace our steps and look into the Market
Street house, in the old days of his editorial energy,
Franklin may often be found absorbed in those
electrical researches which contributed so magnifi-
cently to his fame. It was during a visit to Boston,
in 1746, that this still unexplored department of
science was first brought to his attention, through
some experiments imperfectly performed by Dr.
Spence. The whole subject presented a new field
to Franklin, and the tests, poor as they were, filled
him with pleasure and ideas.

" Soon after my return to Philadelphia," as he tells us in the *Autobiography*, " our library company received from Mr. P. Collinson,
Fellow of the Royal Society of London, a present of a glass tube,
with some account of the use of it in making such experiments. I
eagerly seized the opportunity of repeating what I had seen at Boston ; and, by much practice, acquired great readiness in performing
those, also, which we had an account of from England, adding a
number of new ones. I say much practice, for my house was con-
tinually full, for some time, with people who came to see these new
wonders."

This rush of the curious promised to be incon-
venient, and Franklin, ever fertile of expedient, bethought himself of a remedy.

FRANKLIN'S ELECTRICAL MACHINE.
OWNED BY THE FRANKLIN INSTITUTE, PHILADELPHIA

" To divide a little this incumbrance among my friends, I caused
a number of similar tubes to be blown at our glass-house, with which
they furnished themselves, so that we had at length several perform-
ers.   Among these, the principal was Mr. Kinnersley, an ingenious
neighbour, who, being out of business, I encouraged to undertake
showing the experiments for money, and drew up for him two lectures, in which the experiments were ranged in such order, and accompanied with such explanations in such method, as that the
foregoing should assist in comprehending the following.   He procured an elegant apparatus for the purpose, in which all the little
machines that I had roughly made for myself were nicely formed by
instrument makers.   His lectures were well attended, and gave great
satisfaction ; and after some time he went thro' the colonies, exhibit-
ing them in every capital town, and picked up some money."

Philadelphia, it seems, almost lost her sedate
head in astonishment at the mysterious manifesta-
tions.

Franklin wrote to Mr. Collinson the accounts of
these experiments, but the Royal Society, before
which the letters were read, did not even deem them
worth printing in its transactions.   As for one paper,
in which the Philadelphian had the temerity to suggest " the sameness of lightning with electricity "—
well, so " absurd " a theory was actually laughed at
by the English scientists!   A copy of the papers
was, however, translated into French and printed
in Paris with surprising results.

" The publication offended the Abbé Nollet, preceptor in natural
philosophy to the royal family and an able experimenter, who had
formed and published a theory of electricity, which then had the
general vogue.   He could not at first believe that such a work came
from America, and said it must have been fabricated by his enemies
at Paris, to decry his system.   Afterwards, having been assured that
there really existed such a person as Franklin at Philadelphia, which
he had doubted, he wrote and published a volume of Letters, chiefly

addressed to me, defending his theory, and denying the verity of my experiments, and of the positions deduced from them."

The doctor did not answer the Abbé—" and the event gave me no cause to repent my silence; for my friend, M. le Roy, of the Royal Academy of Sciences, took up my cause and refuted him; my book was translated into the Italian, German, and Latin languages; and the doctrine it contained was by degrees universally adopted by the philosophers of Europe, in preference to that of the Abbé; so that he lived to see himself the last of his sect, except Monsieur B—— of Paris, his *élève* and immediate disciple."

" What gave my book the more sudden and general celebrity," continues the pleased scientist, " was the success of one of its proposed experiments, made by Messrs. Dalibard and De Lor at Marly, for drawing lightning from the clouds. This engaged the public attention everywhere. M. de Lor, who had an apparatus for experimental philosophy, and lectured in that branch of science, undertook to repeat what he called the *Philadelphia Experiments*; and, after they were performed before the King and court, all the curious of Paris flocked to see them."

And the writer modestly adds:

" I will not swell this narrative with an account of that capital experiment, nor of the infinite pleasure I received in the success of a similar one I made soon after with a kite at Philadelphia, as both are to be found in the histories of electricity."

This experiment of the kite, by which Franklin gave practical illustration to his discovery of the identity of lightning with the electric fluid, must be as familiar to the average schoolboy as is the multi-

plication table.   The episode has been as much immortalised as the story of the George Washington
hatchet, and has the advantage, unlike the latter
classic, of being absolute fact.   Yet when Franklin,
accompanied by his son, went out into the field—a
field which now forms one of the busiest and noisiest
districts of Philadelphia—and took with him the
silken kite, the famous key, and the Leyden jar, he
was doing something more than furnishing an anecdote for children or literature for primers.   It was
posterity at large that was to thank him; when he
brought down the electric message from the clouds
he vindicated a mighty thought, and incidentally
put in his debt all the coming generations.

It was in 1752 that the kite played its important
part, but before that Franklin had astonished the
philosophical world by a wonderful treatise which
he styled laboriously, " Opinions and Conjectures
concerning the Properties and Effects of the electrical Matter, and the Means of preserving Buildings,
ships, etc., from Lightning, arising from Experiments
and Observations made at Philadelphia, 1749."   In
this paper he suggested the famous plan of placing
on a high tower or steeple a sort of sentry-box,
" big enough to contain a man and an electric
stand," and from the middle of which stand an iron
rod, pointed very sharp at the end, was to pass out
through the door.   Here was the doctor's idea of
drawing off the fluid through the power of points,
by the lightning-rod, for he asks in the same article
whether the knowledge of this power may not be of
use to mankind " in preserving houses, churches,

ships, etc., from the stroke of lightning, by directing us to fix, on the highest parts of those edifices,
upright rods of iron made sharp as a needle, and
gilt to prevent rusting, and from the foot of those
rods, a wire down the outside of the building into
the ground, or down round the shrouds of a ship,
and down her side till it reaches the water." No
wonder that the purveyor of lightning-rods had
cause to bless Franklin.

As the Philadelphian worked away at his beloved
experiments, giving and receiving shocks, meeting
more than once with a dangerous accident, using
the new knowledge as a spur to his inventive genius,
and elaborating his hypotheses and conclusions, he
waited patiently for recognition in conservative
England. It came at last, although not soon
enough to take away from France the credit of
having first made widely known the most daring
scientist of the age.

"Dr. Wright, an English physician, when at Paris"—we quote
from the *Autobiography*—" wrote to a friend, who was of the Royal
Society, an account of the high esteem my experiments were in among
the learned abroad, and of their wonder that my writings had been so
little noticed in England. The Society, on this, resumed the consideration of the letters that had been read to them, and the celebrated
Dr. Watson drew up a summary account of them, and of all I had
afterwards sent to England on the subject, which he accompanied
with some praise of the writer. This summary was then printed in
their transactions; and some members of the Society in London, particularly the very ingenious Mr. Canton, having verified the experiment of procuring lightning from the clouds by a pointed rod, and
acquainting them with the success, they soon made me more than
amends for the slight with which they had before treated me. Without my having made any application for that honour, they chose me
a member, and voted that I should be excused the customary pay-

ments, which would have amounted to twenty-five guineas ; and ever since have given me their transactions gratis."

In 1753 Franklin had won the Copley gold medal, and in making the award the Earl of Macclesfield, then President of the Royal Society, was pleased to say some flattering things of the *savant* of the backwoods, and to graciously remark that " though some others might have begun to entertain suspicions of an analogy between the effects of lightning and electricity, yet he took Mr. Franklin to be the first, who, among other curious discoveries, undertook to show from experiments that the former owed its origin entirely to the latter." * It was recognition like this which put the seal of English approval upon the philosopher's researches, and aided indirectly, by establishing his fame, to increase his political influence and sphere of patriotic usefulness. When he went to England to fight the Penns he was something more than " B. Franklin, agent "—he was a man whose name, written in letters of electric fire, could never die.

Nor does it appear strange, when we take into consideration the character of Franklin, that these electrical studies formed but a part of his contributions to the domain of science and invention. His fund of ingenuity and diversity of theme were phenomenal. Navigation, the building of ships, the consumption of smoke, the paving and cleaning of streets, ventilation, agriculture, the temperature of the Gulf Stream, the origin of storms, and the treat-

---

* In April, 1756, Franklin was further honoured by the Royal Society, which elected him one of its Fellows.

ment of colds—upon all these subjects, not to speak
of others, his mind found an occupation for which
succeeding generations of his countrymen have been,
or should have been, deeply grateful.   He made the
Armonica,* he brought his genius into the region of
fire and chimneys, and he invented the " Franklin
stove."   Of the latter device he published a description—" An Account of the new-invented Pennsylvania Fireplaces," etc.   A cleanly printed copy of
the pamphlet is now before me, and a reading of it
shows in how thoroughly practical a manner the
creator of this stove went into the business of dis-
crediting the old-fashioned and more picturesque
fireplace, or " strong drawing chimneys," of the
day.   The eye falls at random on his quotation of a
Spanish proverb:

---

* In London he saw for the first time an instrument consisting of
musical glasses, upon which tunes were played by passing a wet finger
around their brims.   He was charmed with the sweetness of its tones ;
but the instrument itself seemed to him an imperfect contrivance,
occupying much space and limited in the number of its tones.   The
glasses were arranged on a table, and tuned by putting water into
them till they gave the notes required.   After many trials he succeeded in constructing an instrument of a different form, more com-
modious, and more extended in the compass of its notes.   His glasses
were made in the shape of a hemisphere, with an open neck or socket
in the middle, for the purpose of being fixed, on an iron spindle.
They were then arranged one after another, on this spindle, the
largest at one end and gradually diminishing in size to the smallest
at the other end.   The tones depended on the size of the glasses.
The spindle, with its series of glasses, was fixed horizontally in a
case, and turned by a wheel attached to its larger end, upon the principle of a common spinning-wheel.   The performer sat in front of the
instrument, and the tones were brought out by applying a wet finger
to the exterior surface of the glasses as they turned round.—SPARKS.

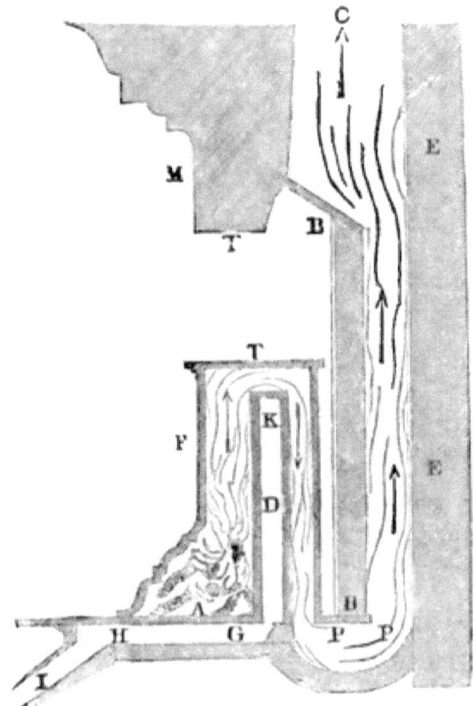

THE PENNSYLVANIA FIRE-PLACE.

Profile of Franklin's invention, showing (M) mantlepiece, (C) funnel, (B) false
back, (E) true back, (T) top of fire-place, (F) front, (A) fire, (D)
air box, (K) hole in side plate, (I, H, G) fresh-air
hollow, (P) passage under false back.

> " If the wind blows on you through a hole,
> Make your will, and take care of your soul"

—a gloomy couplet, of which Franklin hastens to observe:

> " Women particularly, from this cause, as they sit much in the house, get colds in the head, rheums, and defluctions, which fall into their jaws and gums, and have destroyed early many a fine set of teeth in these northern colonies. Great and bright fires do also very much contribute to damage the eyes, dry and shrivel the skin, and bring on early the appearances of old age."

That was a threat calculated to make every feminine reader of the " Account " a ready convert to the " Franklin stove." Diplomatic inventor!

This stove was a free-will offering to the public; there was no fortune in it for Franklin. Governor Thomas offered to give him a patent upon the device, but the temptation was resisted upon the principle that, " as we enjoy great advantages from the inventions of others, we should be glad of an opportunity to serve others by inventions of ours; and this we should do freely and generously "—a very worthy motive now more honoured in the breach than in the observance. The inventor would, indeed, have proved a poor client for a patent lawyer, for he says:

> " An ironmonger in London, however, assuming a good deal of my pamphlet, and working it up into his own, and making some small changes in the machine, which rather hurt its operation, got a patent for it there, and made, as I was told, a little fortune by it. And this is not the only instance of patents taken out for my inventions by others, tho' not always with the same success, which I never contested, as having no desire of profiting by patents myself, and hating disputes."

21

Such was Franklin, with the comprehensiveness of a Galileo and the practical qualities, let us say, of an Edison. Soaring one moment in the clouds of theory, and snatching a grand truth from the thunderstorm; the next moment teaching the Americans how to warm themselves. In both moods he succeeded; he became the greatest utilitarian of the age. " Whether in directing the construction of chimneys or of constitutions, lecturing on the saving of candles or on the economy of national revenues, he was still intent on the same end, the question always being how to obtain the most of solid tangible advantage by the plainest and easiest means." * To prove useful became to him a business.

In Franklin's writings we see the same great idea; he wrote for a purpose. If we except a very few of his contributions, there is always a motive, and a practical one, lurking beneath the surface, and it is for this reason that the pen was to him a means rather than an end. With the furbelows of literature he bothered himself but little, although he could be graceful and Addisonian enough when he chose; to pose as an author or man of letters was far from his thoughts. Thus his style is generally clear, lucid, direct, rather than elegant; the reader gets at once at the writer's idea without becoming distracted by beauty of metaphor, by originality of expression, or by the thousand and one things which distinguish the professional book-maker from the lay writer. It is none the less true that some of Franklin's papers bid fair to survive as long as there

* John Foster

is an English literature; that many of them afford
as much interest to-day as they did a century ago or
more, and that they have already outlived the
achievements of numberless ambitious authors whose
fame has sunk into the limbo of oblivion.   When
the philosopher wrote he had something to say, and
he said it in good, well-chosen English; he never
soared above the public intelligence; he knew just
when to be witty and when grave; and he was able
to get from his readers the greatest possible attention with a minimum of effort on their part.   That,
in brief, is the secret of Franklin's success in the
empire of letters.   Essayists, reformers, and statesmen who wish to hold the popular ear should study
his methods.

An attempt has been made in this volume, by per-
tinent quotations, to give a glimpse of the doctor's
style and scope of subject, but to obtain a compre-
hensive knowledge of the latter it is necessary to
spend some hours in a judicious perusal of his collected works.   The task always repays those who
undertake it; they find it an entertainment, and instead of leaving the pages with the sense of having
delved into old-fashioned pomposity, they come
away refreshed and amused.   Let the novice read
every line of the imperishable *Autobiography*, glide
almost haphazard through the great mass of correspondence, and then take two or three of the *Busybody* papers, the *Necessary Hints to those that would
be Rich*, the *Way to Wealth*, the *Dialogue between
X, Y and Z, Cool Thoughts*, the *Examination before
the House of Commons*, the *Rules for Reducing a*

Great Empire to a Small One, and the *Bagatelles*. Having done this he has acquired a delightful, if not exactly a profound, impression of Franklin's writings, and if he does not soon return to the occupation, with a thirst for more letters and more essays, it will be his fault or misfortune rather than that of the doctor.   Franklin wrote for the comprehension of all men; they who run may read him, and need not tarry by the way to organise societies wherewith to ferret out his meanings.

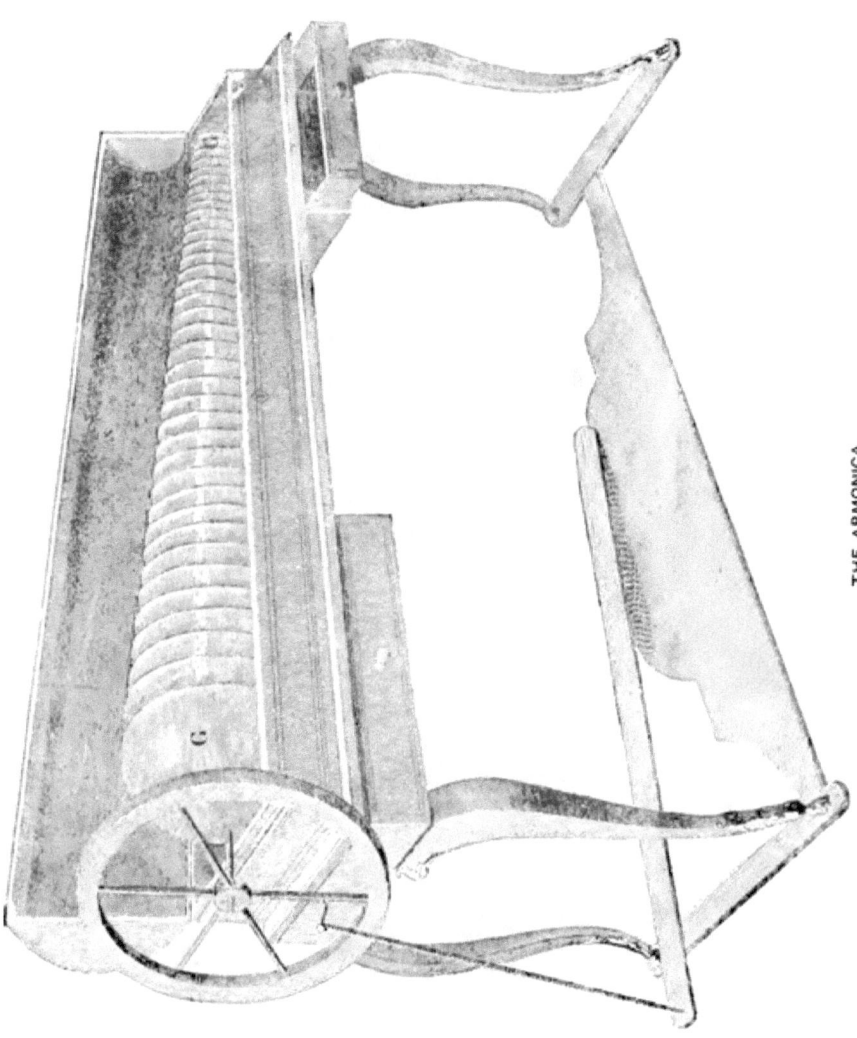

THE ARMONICA.

INSTRUMENT DESIGNED BY FRANKLIN AS AN IMPROVEMENT UPON THE MUSICAL GLASSES.

CHAPTER XIII

FINAL DAYS

1784-1790

AVING done such yeoman's service in the establishment of peace, Franklin's thoughts turned again towards the home wherein he might await, in semi-comfort of body and complete tranquillity of mind, the approach of that Grim Visitor who had so considerately allowed him to exceed the three score and ten of existence. He felt tired and feeble. But Congress still refused to recall the envoy, and his stay in France assumed such a length that he began to fear that he would not have left enough of health to make the tossing journey to America. Still, life at Passy was very charming; friends increased as the months glided on, and the atmosphere breathed good-will and reconciliation. "It is a sweet word," the philosopher had said of that self-same reconciliation. Possibly the truism came home to him when William Franklin, ex-American and at present in London as a *protégé* of the British Government, wrote to his

father, in the summer of 1784, with dutiful tenders
of affection. The doctor never forgot the political
apostasy of his son,* but he was ready to forgive;
and so he replied that he would be glad to revive
the old ties.

"It will be very agreeable to me; indeed, nothing has ever hurt
me so much, and affected me with such keen sensations, as to find
myself deserted in my old age by my only son; and not only deserted,
but to find him taking up arms against me in a cause, wherein my
good fame, fortune, and life were all at stake. You conceived, you
say, that your duty to your King and regard for your country required
this. I ought not to blame you for differing in sentiment with me in
public affairs. We are men, all subject to errors. Our opinions are
not in our own power; they are formed and governed much by circumstances that are often as inexplicable as they are irresistible.
Your situation was such that few would have censured your remaining
neuter, though there are natural duties which precede political ones,
and cannot be extinguished by them. This is a disagreeable subject.
I drop it; and we will endeavour, as you propose, mutually to forget
what has happened relating to it, as well as we can. I send your son

---

* Franklin showed, in the following clause of his will, that he did
not indulge in the luxury of forgetfulness. "To my son, *William
Franklin*, late Governor of the Jerseys, I give and devise all the lands
I hold or have a right to, in the Province of Nova Scotia, to hold to
him, his heirs and assigns forever. I also give to him all my books and
papers, which he has in his possession, and all debts standing against
him on my account books, willing that no payment for, nor restitution
of, the same be required of him by my executors. The part he acted
against me in the late war, which is of public notoriety, will account
for my leaving him no more of an estate he endeavoured to deprive
me of." William Franklin was rewarded for his Toryism by a pension from the British Government. He spent the latter part of his
life in England, and lived to be eighty-two years old. The son,
William Temple Franklin, went to England after the death of Benjamin Franklin; he subsequently edited, and poorly, the works of the
latter (he tampered with the wording of the *Autobiography*), and died
at Paris in 1823.

[William Temple Franklin] over to pay his duty to you. You will find him much improved."

In the same letter Franklin says:

"I did intend returning this year; but the Congress, instead of giving me leave to do so, have sent me another commission, which will keep me here at least a year longer, and perhaps I may then be too old and feeble to bear the voyage. I am here among a people that love and respect me, a most amiable nation to live with; and perhaps I may conclude to die among them; for my friends in America are dying off, one after another, and I have been so long abroad that I should now be almost a stranger in my own country."

For all this talk as to dying in France, Franklin really wished to die at home. Thrice had he asked Congress for permission to return, yet it was not until March, 1785, that the long-desired consent was reluctantly given, and that Thomas Jefferson was appointed to succeed him. Jefferson had been in France for some months, to assist in making commercial treaties with the European governments, and it remained for the doctor, ere his departure, to conclude a compact with Prussia which Washington considered to be the most liberal treaty ever agreed upon between independent nations. Early in May the retiring minister wrote to his friend, the Count de Vergennes, explaining that his ill-health would not permit him to go to Versailles for farewell, setting forth his appreciation of the goodness of his Majesty and the favours of De Vergennes, and praying that " God may shower down his blessings on the King, the Queen, their children, and all the royal family to the latest generations." Little did the writer, he who had seen so much of the sunshine of France and so little of its gathering clouds, imagine that the path of Louis XVI. and Marie Antoinette led to the guillotine. But those tragedies had not come as yet; the King could still dispense graciousness. He sent to the republican a portrait of the royal features, set with over four hundred diamonds, while M. de Vergennes wrote a pretty letter of good-bye. The passing of the philosopher seemed a national incident; Passy, inconstant Paris, even France, regretted his going; friends pressed him to remain; Madame Helvetius, and the worthy Brillon, no doubt shed tears.

It was hard to leave such homage, but Philadelphia triumphed. On the 12th of July, 1785, Franklin set out for Havre in a comfortable litter belonging to the Queen, and " carried by two very large mules." With him went his two grandsons. At Nantes the Cardinal de la Rochefoucauld sent word that the travellers must visit his château at Gaillon, playfully adding that he would take no excuse; for, being all-powerful in his archbishopric, his Eminence would stop them *nolens volens*, and not permit any escape. The invitation was not to be resisted; the Cardinal did the honours in a fashion worthy of his rank. Then came more attentions (among them the visit of a deputation from the Academy of Rouen) until Havre was reached on the 18th of the month. Here were further civilities, and four days later the gratified American sailed for England, never to set eyes again upon the country which had loved him so well. At Southampton he was welcomed by a party including William Franklin (with whom he had a formal reconciliation), and his staunch friend, the good Bishop of St. Asaph.

"The Bishop and family lodging in the same inn, the Star," Franklin writes, in a diary of the journey, "we all breakfast and dine together. I went at noon to bathe in Martin's salt-water hot-bath, and floating on my back, fell asleep, and slept near an hour by my watch, without sinking or turning! A thing I never did before, and should hardly have thought possible. Water is the easiest bed that can be."

If the diarist was not recording this incident in a Pickwickian sense he acquitted himself, for a feeble old man, with remarkable aquatic vigour.

The middle of September found the wanderer home again, hardly more shaky in his legs than he had been when he sailed from England, and with a mind still so bright that he had written three pamphlets during the voyage.

"With the flood in the morning"—he jots down this entry as the ship comes up the familiar Delaware—" came a light breeze, which brought us above Gloucester Point, in full view of dear Philadelphia! when we again cast anchor, to wait for the health officer, who, having made his visit and finding no sickness, gave us leave to land. My son-in-law came with a boat for us; we landed at Market street wharf, where we were received by a crowd of people with huzzas, and accompanied with acclamations quite to my door. Found my family well. God be praised and thanked for all His mercies!"

Did Franklin contrast this last river-entry into Philadelphia with the first? If he did, he may have smiled at the turn which the wheel of fortune had made, and possibly reflected that he himself had much to do with the revolution thereof. Nothing could have exceeded in enthusiastic sincer-

ity the reception given him upon this return. The
citizens flocked to pay their respects; societies
waited upon him, and the Assembly drew up an
address wherein it was said, with more truth than is
usually to be found in such official flattery, that the
philosopher's services would be " recorded in the
pages of history " to his " immortal honour."
Then General Washington wrote a letter of welcome:

> " Amid the public congratulations on your safe return to America,
> after a long absence and the many eminent services you have ren-
> dered it, for which as a benefitted person I feel the obligation, permit
> an individual to join the public voice in expressing a sense of them ;
> and to assure you, that, as no one entertains more respect for your
> character, so no one can salute you with more sincerity or with greater
> pleasure, than I do on the occasion."

How Washingtonian this was, and how it must
have pleased the recipient!

Franklin might luxuriate in the attentions of his
daughter and grandchildren, but a part of his time
must again be given to the public. His election to
the Council was followed by a far more ambitious ele-
vation to the Presidency of Pennsylvania, a position
in which he served the State effectively, exerted an
influence at once imposing and benign, and laboured
without personal profit, indirect or pecuniary. Yet
the doctor's energies as head of a great Commonwealth were trifling compared to his usefulness as a
member of the memorable Convention which met in
Philadelphia (May, 1787) to frame a constitution
for the better union of the loosely jointed States of
America. Here his ripened wisdom and knowledge

SHIP PLANKING.

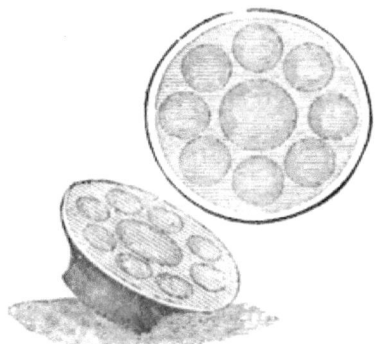

SOUP DISHES FOR SHIPBOARD.

THE RIGGING OF A SHALLOP.

MARITIME OBSERVATIONS

AFTER DESIGNS OF NAUTICAL IMPROVEMENTS SUGGESTED BY FRANKLIN.

of affairs played a leading, if unostentatious part in bringing the nation under a federal system which has now withstood the wear and tear of over a century.

The period from the surrender of Lord Cornwallis to the holding of the Convention was one of the most critical in our history. Although the Revolution had succeeded, there was no cohesion between the several States; the country was in a condition of unrest born of internal weakness; opinions as to method of government were divided, and the outlook grew gloomy and then gloomier.

" The want of power in the central government, arising from the defects of the old confederation, was becoming more and more apparent, and the evils arising from this want of power were pressing severely on every side. While the war lasted the external pressure held the government together ; but on the return of peace its dissolution had become imminent. . . . It had, in fact, no power to regulate commerce or collect a revenue. This made it incapable of executing treaties, fulfilling its foreign engagements, or causing itself to be respected by foreign nations. While at home, its weakness was disgusting the public creditors and raising a clamour of discontent and dissatisfaction on every side. An alarming crisis was rapidly approaching." *

Thoughtful Americans clearly saw the threatening danger.

" Our affairs," as John Jay wrote to Washington in the summer of 1786, " seem to lead to some crisis, some revolution—something that I cannot foresee or conjecture. I am uneasy and apprehensive, more so than during the war. *Then* we had a fixed object, and though the means and time of obtaining it were often problematical, yet I did firmly believe that justice was with us. The case is now altered ; we are going and doing wrong, and therefore I look forward to evils and calamities, but without being able to guess at the instrument, nature, or measure of them."

* *The Life and Times of Washington*, by J. F. Schroeder, D.D.

In his reply Washington was no less apprehensive.

" Things cannot go on in the same train forever," he said, with calm sagacity. " It is much to be feared, as you observe, that the better kind of people, being disgusted with these circumstances, will have their minds prepared for any revolution whatever. We are apt to run from one extreme into another. To anticipate and prevent disastrous contingencies, would be the part of wisdom and patriotism. What astonishing changes a few years are capable of producing! I am told that even respectable characters speak of a monarchical form of government without horror. From thinking proceeds speaking : thence to acting is often but a single step. But how irrevocable and tremendous! what a triumph for our enemies to verify their predictions! What a triumph for the advocates of despotism, to find that we are incapable of governing ourselves, and that systems founded on the basis of equal liberty are merely ideal and fallacious! "

Was the glory of the Revolution to be tarnished by anarchy, or would a despotism far greater than the overthrown British rule fasten its clutches upon the land ? The question was hard to answer, and none the less so when the band of rebels under Daniel Shay frightened the law-preserving people of Massachusetts, by demands which we should now term populistic.

The insurrection came to an end, and when the delegates from all the States (Rhode Island alone excepted) assembled in Philadelphia on that May morning of 1787, the eyes of a waiting nation were upon them. The results of the four months' deliberations, with the difficulties in the way of draughting the constitution, are matters of familiar history.* Throughout the sessions the helping hand and pru-

---

* One party in the Convention was anxious to enlarge, another to abridge, the authority delegated to the general government. This

dent common sense of Franklin exerted an influence
destined to leave an imperishable impress. Indeed,
Mr. Bigelow has said that to Franklin, perhaps more
than to any other man, " the present constitution
of the United States owes most of those features
which have given it durability, and have made it the
ideal by which all other systems of government are
tested by Americans." The instrument, as adopted,
was not, of course, just what Franklin would have
made it had his opinion been followed in all things.
He was in favour of making the Presidential term
seven years, the incumbent being debarred from a
second term, and he was Utopian enough to urge
that the executive should receive no salary.

"I think," said he, " I see inconveniences in the appointment of
salaries ; I see none in refusing them, but, on the contrary, great
advantages. Sir, there are two passions which have a powerful influence on the affairs of men. These are *ambition* and *avarice* ; the
love of power and the love of money. Separately, each of these has
great force in prompting men to action ; but, when united in view of
the same object, they have in many minds the most violent effects.
Place before the eyes of such men a post of *honour*, that shall at the
same time be a place of *profit*, and they will move heaven and earth
to obtain it." And what kind of men, asked the doctor, will strive
for the Presidency, " through all the bustle of cabal, the heat of contention, the infinite mutual abuse of parties, tearing to pieces the
best of characters ?" " It will not be the wise and moderate, the
lovers of peace and good order, the men fitted for the trust. It will
be the bold and the violent, the men of strong passions and indefat-
igable activity in their selfish pursuits. These will thrust themselves
into your government and be your rulers."

was the first germ of parties in the United States ; not that materials
were wanting, for the dissensions of the Revolution had left behind
some bitterness of spirit, and feelings that only awaited an opportunity for their disclosure.—JOHN HOWARD HINTON.

That the delegate failed to carry his point is, perhaps, just as well, for a non-salaried Presidency
would have become an office only adapted to
wealthy incumbents.

But it was in settling the vexed problem as to the
basis of representation between the large and small
States of the Union that Franklin put the Convention, and the nation, under an eternal obligation.
The question threatened to imperil the success of
the deliberations, for while the more populous States
desired representation according to their importance
and extent, the lesser ones were jealous of any
system tending to diminish their own power. At
this point Franklin proposed that the session should
be opened each day with prayer, so as to secure the
assistance of Providence in bringing order out of
chaos, and a constitution out of disagreement.
" The small progress we have made, after four or
five weeks' close attendance and continual reasonings
with each other, our different sentiments on almost
every question, and several of the last producing
as many Noes as Ayes, is, methinks, a melancholy
proof of the imperfection of the human understanding." Thus he addressed Washington, who presided
over the Convention, and to remedy this uncertainty he suggested a daily prayer for inspiration.
The motion was rejected. Later on Franklin came
forward with another remedy—a compromise, of
which it has been said that it saved the Union. His
first contention had been for a single legislative
body, but now he proposed, as a concession intended to destroy the jealousies and fears of the

various States, that there should be two Houses, with equal representation of States in the Senate, and with representation according to population in the lower House.   The bitterly contested issue was solved, and the fruits of that compromise are seen in our government as it is constituted to-day.   At the age of eighty-one the philosopher had given one of the most enduring proofs of his powers of state-craft; he had shown anew that nobly could he serve his exacting master, the Public.

Franklin did not flatter himself that the constitution, as finally agreed upon, was a perfect affair, but he believed, prophetically enough, that it would serve its great purpose.

"I doubt," said he, "whether any other Convention we can obtain, may be able to make a better constitution; for, when you assemble a number of men, to have the advantage of their joint wisdom, you inevitably assemble with these men all their prejudices, their passions, their errors of opinion, their local interests, and their selfish views.   From such an assembly," he asks, "can a perfect production be expected?"

He confesses, in his speech at the close of the Convention, that he is astonished to find the constitution so near perfection as it is—" and I think it will astonish our enemies, who are waiting with confidence to hear that our counsels are confounded like those of the builders of Babel, and that our States are on the point of separation, only to meet hereafter for the purpose of cutting one another's throats.   Thus, I consent, sir, to this constitution, because I expect no better, and because I am not sure that it is not the best.   The opinions I have

had of its errors I sacrifice to the public good."
It was the singular good fortune of Franklin that
having signed the constitution he likewise lived long
enough to see its ratification, and to witness the
election of Washington as first President of the
nation which the two of them had helped so valiantly
to create.

The doctor's end was not far away; infirmities
were increasing, and a serious internal trouble
began to undermine his once rugged constitution.
Yet he took the same keen enjoyment in life as of
old, and found in correspondence the familiar
pleasure. Letters on all conceivable subjects illu-
mine these final years with a brilliance more akin to
the noonday sun than to the twilight of genius.
Would that he had finished the *Autobiography* while
the hand remained to guide the ready pen. He
writes to his friend, M. Le Veillard (February,
1788), that he would have gone on with the mem-
oirs " if I could well have avoided accepting the
chair of President [of Pennsylvania] for this third
and last year; to which I was again elected by the
unanimous voice of the Council and General Assembly in November. If I live to see this year ex-
pire, I may enjoy some leisure, which I promise
you to employ in the work you do me the honour
to urge so earnestly." The *Autobiography* was continued, but death found the narrative provokingly
incomplete. It must not, however, be forgotten
that in keeping up his correspondence until the very
last the veteran was finishing an autobiography less
connected, yet hardly less interesting, than a more

formal record. There are pretty little touches in
these sunset letters, as when, for instance, Franklin
tells Madame Lavoisier:

" I have a long time been disabled from writing to my dear friend,
by a severe fit of the gout, or I should sooner have returned my
thanks for her very kind present of the portrait, which she has herself done me the honour to make of me. It is allowed by those,
who have seen it, to have great merit as a picture in every respect ;
but what particularly endears it to me is the hand that drew it. Our
English enemies, when they were in possession of this city and my
house [one of the enemies thus accused, probably wrongly, was
André], made a prisoner of my portrait, and carried it off with them,
leaving that of its companion, my wife, by itself, a kind of widow.
You have replaced the husband, and the lady seems to smile as well
pleased. It is true, as you observe, that I enjoy here everything a
reasonable mind can desire, a sufficiency of income, a comfortable
habitation of my own building, having all the conveniences I could
imagine ; a dutiful and affectionate daughter to nurse and take care
of me, a number of promising grandchildren, some old friends still
remaining to converse with, and more respect, distinction, and public
honours than I can possibly merit. These are the blessings of God,
and depend on His continued goodness ; yet all do not make me forget Paris, and the nine years' happiness I enjoyed there, in the sweet
society of a people whose conversation is instructive, whose manners
are highly pleasing, and who, above all the nations of the world,
have, in the greatest perfection, the art of making themselves beloved by strangers. And now, even in my sleep, I find, that the
scenes of all my pleasant dreams are laid in that city, or in its neighbourhood."

Another letter of a far different kind is addressed
to the President of Congress, and prays that Franklin's accounts with the government may be audited
and settled.

" It is now more than three years that those accounts have been
before that honourable body," he explains, " and, to this day, no

22

notice of any such objection [as to the accuracy of these accounts] has been communicated to me. But reports have, for some time past, been circulated here, and propagated in the newspapers, that I am greatly indebted to the United States for large sums, that had been put into my hands, and that I avoid a settlement. This, together with the little time one of my age may expect to live, makes it necessary for me to request earnestly, which I hereby do, that the Congress would be pleased, without further delay, to examine those accounts, and if they find therein any article or articles, which they do not understand or approve, that they would cause me to be acquainted with the same," etc.

It is almost needless to add that the newspaper reports were untrue, and that if there happened to be any question as to balance due, the doctor was the creditor and not the debtor. But Congress, no longer as noble a body as in the days of '76, did not take the trouble to grant his request.

Of the rancour of the press, from which, as we have just seen, even he was not altogether exempt, Franklin had something trenchant to say in a satire which he published in the September of 1789, after he had retired from public life and was fast nearing the end of all earthly controversy. "An Account of the Supremest Court of Judicature in Pennsylvania, viz. the Court of the Press" was the suggestive title of the brochure, and in it the writer asserted that the aforesaid court had been established in favour " of about one citizen in five hundred, who, by education or practice in scribbling, has acquired a tolerable style as to grammar and construction, so as to bear printing, or who is possessed of a press and a few types. This five-hundredth part of the citizens have the privilege of accusing and abusing

the other four hundred and ninety-nine parts at
their pleasure; or they may hire out their pens and
press to others for that purpose." The support of
such an institution, it was contended cynically, was
" founded in the depravity of such minds, as have
not been mended by religion, nor improved by good
education :

>   " ' There is a lust in man no charm can tame,
>   Of loudly publishing his neighbour's shame.'

" Hence :

>   " ' On eagle's wings immortal scandals fly,
>   While virtuous actions are but born and die.'
>   —DRYDEN.

" Whoever feels pain in hearing a good character of his neighbour,
will feel a pleasure in the reverse. And of those who, despairing
to rise into distinction by their virtues, are happy if others can be
depressed to a level with themselves, there are a number sufficient in
every great town to maintain one of these courts by their subscription. A shrewd observer once said, that, in walking the streets in a
slippery morning, one might see where the good-natured people
lived by the ashes thrown on the ice before their doors ; probably he
would have formed a different conjecture of the temper of those
whom he might find engaged in such a subscription."

Journalism of to-day does not, as a whole, justify
this estimate of a past condition, although even now
there are a few newspapers which do not put ashes
in front of their doors. Franklin ends his critique
by asking how the abuse of libel is to have checks
placed upon it.

" Hitherto there are none," he says. " But since so much has
been written and published on the Federal Constitution, and the necessity of checks in all other parts of good government has been so

clearly and learnedly explained, I find myself so far enlightened as to suspect some check may be proper in this part also ; but I have been at a loss to imagine any that may not be construed an infringement of the sacred *liberty of the press.* At length, however, I think I have found one that, instead of diminishing general liberty, shall augment it ; which is, by restoring to the people a species of liberty, of which they have been deprived by our laws, I mean the *liberty of the cudgel.* In the rude state of society prior to the existence of laws, if one man gave another ill language, the affronted person would return it by a box on the ear, and, if repeated, by a good drubbing ; and this without offending against any law. But now the right of making such returns is denied, and they are punished as breaches of the peace ; while the right of abusing seems to remain in full force, the laws made against it being rendered ineffectual by the *liberty of the press.* My proposal then is, to leave the liberty of the press untouched, to be exercised in its full extent, force and vigour ; but to permit the *liberty of the cudgel* to go with it *par passu.* Thus, my fellow-citizens, if an impudent writer attacks your reputation, dearer to you perhaps than your life, and puts his name to the charge, you may go to him as openly and break his head. If he conceals himself behind the printer, and you can nevertheless discover who he is, you may in like manner way-lay him in the night, attack him behind, and give him a good drubbing. . . . If, however, it should be thought that proposal of mine may disturb the public peace, I would then humbly recommend to our legislators to take up the consideration of both liberties, that of the *press,* and that of the *cudgel,* and by an explicit law mark their extent and limits ; and, at the same time that they secure the person of a citizen from *assaults,* they would likewise provide for the security of his reputation."

This was a pretty virile protest for an octogenarian, to whom life, through the inroads of disease, was now become a physical burden. Franklin passed much of his time in bed, and he wrote to Washington that " for my own personal ease I should have died two years ago; but, though those years have been spent in excruciating pain, I am pleased that I have lived them, since they have

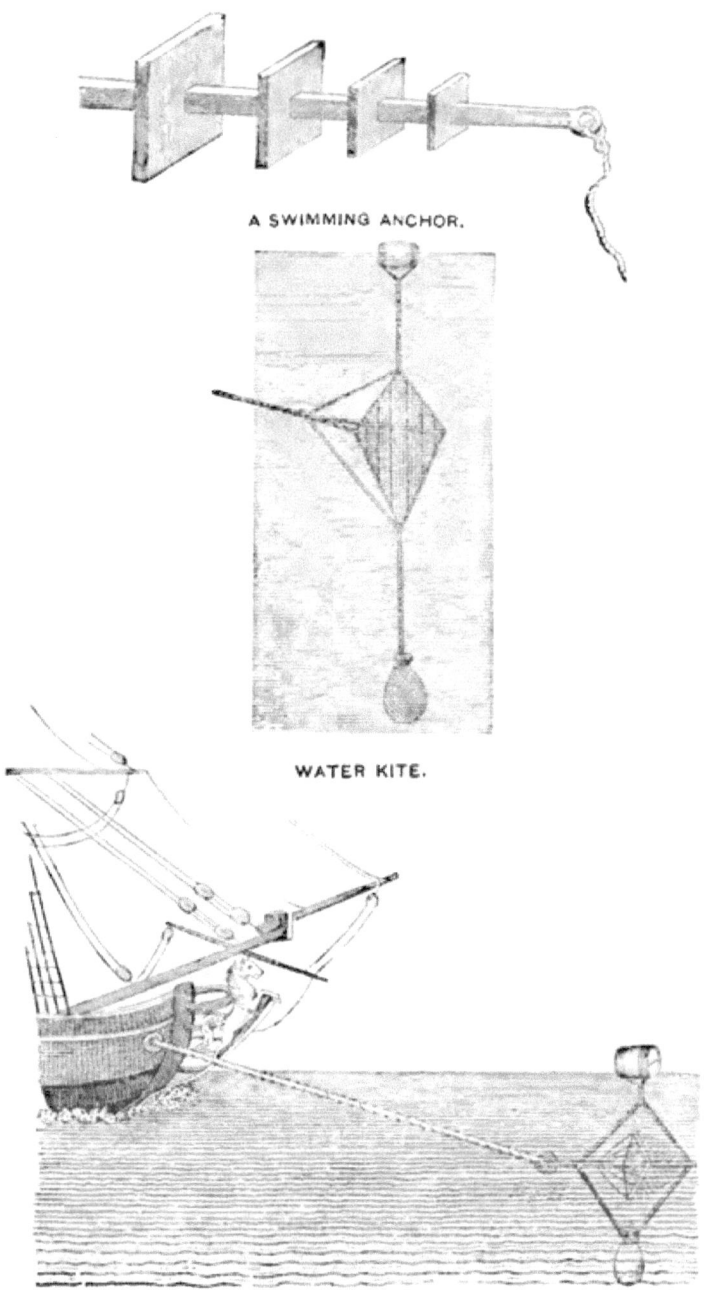

A SWIMMING ANCHOR.

WATER KITE.

WATER UMBRELLA.

MARITIME OBSERVATIONS.

AFTER DESIGNS OF NAUTICAL IMPROVEMENTS SUGGESTED BY FRANKLIN.

brought me to see our present situation." Ill as he
was, his interest in America and in humanity at large
never flagged; less than a month before his death
the philosopher issued a parody directed against the
slave trade, and practically in support of the aims
of the Pennsylvania Society for Promoting the
Abolition of Slavery, of which he was the President. He was often a prey to the most intense
suffering—so much so, indeed, that strong sedatives
were given him—but at other times he read, talked
with members of the household or with visitors,
and in every instance, as his physician related, " displayed not only that readiness and disposition of
doing good, which was the distinguishing characteristic of his life, but the fullest and clearest possession
of his uncommon mental abilities; and not infre-
quently indulged himself in those *jeux d'esprit* and
entertaining anecdotes which were the delight of all
who heard him." Early in April of 1790, the condition of the patient was complicated by a fever;
this finally left him, and the family were beginning
to hope for at least a rally when respiration became
difficult, a stupor ensued, and during the evening
of the seventeenth of the month Benjamin Franklin
was peacefully released from the world wherein he
had played so earnest and glowing a part. A great
light had gone out; there was darkness in Philadelphia that night.

The funeral of Franklin was in harmony with the
reputation that he left behind him. There was
dignified ceremonial rather than ostentation, and
sincere sorrow instead of expressions of perfunctory

sympathy.   His body was laid beside that of his
wife in Christ Church burying-ground, and over
twenty thousand citizens took part in the procession which marched to Fifth and Arch Streets to
the accompaniment of tolling bells and the firing of
minute guns.*   Eloquent tributes to the virtues of
the deceased came from all quarters, and in Congress it was resolved unanimously that the members
should wear a badge of mourning for one month,
" as a mark of due veneration to the memory of a
citizen whose native genius was not more an orna-
ment to human nature than his various exertions of

---

* The tomb of Franklin and his wife bears but this inscription ·

BENJAMIN }
AND   } FRANKLIN
DEBORAH }
1790.

The simplicity of the wording was in accord with the instructions
contained in Franklin's will. Nothing was said therein about the
fanciful epitaph which he wrote for himself when twenty-three years
old, to wit :

THE BODY
OF
BENJAMIN FRANKLIN
PRINTER

(Like the cover of an old book
   Its contents torn out
And stript of its lettering and gilding)
   Lies here, food for worms.
But the work shall not be lost
   For it will (as he believed) appear once more
In a new and more elegant edition
   Revised and corrected
      by
    The Author.

it have been precious to science, to freedom, and to
his country." In France the respect and affection
for the memory of the dead philosopher had striking
illustration.

" Franklin is dead !" said Mirabeau solemnly, as he addressed the
National Assembly. "The genius which gave freedom to America,
and scattered torrents of light upon Europe, is returned to the bosom
of the Divinity. The sage, whom two worlds claim ; the man, disputed by the history of the sciences and the history of empires, holds,
most undoubtedly, an elevated rank among the human species."

Upon the motion of Mirabeau the Assembly wore
mourning for three days ; its President wrote a
letter of condolence to Congress ; eulogies were
spoken ; the Paris Commune marked the event in a
fitting way, and the printers of the capital held a
meeting at which, in the presence of a great assem-
blage, they did honour to the departed member of
their craft. A little later one of the streets of Passy
was named after the beloved Franklin. It seemed
as if the tide of homage would never turn.*

---

* Franklin's fortune was valued, before his death, as worth at least
$150,000—a large sum for those days. In his will he provided lib-
erally for Mrs. Bache and her husband, made lesser bequests to various other members of his family, remembered several of his old
friends by presents of personal effects, and left, besides other lega-
cies, a fund of £2000 sterling to be used, primarily, in assisting
" young married artificers " of Boston and Philadelphia, who desired
to borrow small sums at interest—a very charitable idea, which did not,
however, prove as popular with the " artificers " as the testator expected. One of Franklin's private bequests was to Washington :
" My fine crab tree walking stick, with a gold head curiously wrought
in the form of the cap of liberty, I give to my friend, and the friend
of mankind, *General Washington*. If it were a sceptre he has
merited it ; and would become it."

Thus to a life of singular completeness came a well-rounded, appropriate ending. As it was Franklin's privilege to bring to a successful issue so many of the projects, great and small, for which he laboured, so was it his fortune to die in the incense-burning atmosphere that rises from the ministering love of kindred and the admiration of the world. He lived to see America take her place among the nations of the earth, to see the realisation of his fondest hopes, and then, ere age had dimmed that brilliant mind or caused him to lag superfluous on the scene, friendly death arrived at the nick of time.

The best estimate of the philosopher's genius is to be found in the simple record of his achievements, and in the indelible mark which they have left behind as a noble heritage to posterity. These achievements speak more eloquently than a hundred orations or pages of adjectives. Franklin had his weaknesses and his *errata*, but he was of heroic mould, for all that, and everyone, save professors of a cheap cynicism, can forget the failings of the man in recalling his magnificent usefulness, the natural gifts which he employed in the finest spirit of altruism, and the patriotic heart that guided the mighty head. Lofty, yet practical, in statesmanship, brilliant in science, luminous in writing, fearless in love of country, humane in disposition, genial in intercourse with his fellows, helpful in all things, and colossal in the power to compass his ends —such was he upon whose like we are not to look again. For there can be but one Franklin. There have been, as there will be again, greater statesmen, deeper thinkers, and more dazzling personalities than he, yet in versatility of talent, catholicity of intellect, and variety of accomplishment he stands without a peer. As his " single breast contained the spirit of his nation," so, likewise, did it contain the spirit of a hundred different interests. The world at large has cause to thank him, while to Americans he will always be the typical patriot. That is not the patriot of the pyrotechnic kind, who poses as a stage hero, nor the politician whose heart is in his purse; it is the patriot who has been essential to his country, and whose honesty of purpose should be studied within the halls of every legislature in the land.   Such was Benjamin Franklin.

INDEX

www.ingramcontent.com/pod-product-compliance
Lightning Source LLC
Chambersburg PA
CBHW030823110726
47900CB00006B/1726